MAN OF THE YEAR

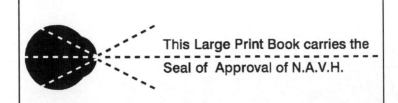

This Large Print Book carries the
Seal of Approval of N.A.V.H.

MAN OF THE YEAR

CAROLINE LOUISE WALKER

THORNDIKE PRESS
A part of Gale, a Cengage Company

Farmington Hills, Mich • San Francisco • New York • Waterville, Maine
Meriden, Conn • Mason, Ohio • Chicago

GALE
A Cengage Company

LIBRARY OF CONGRESS CIP DATA ON FILE.
CATALOGUING IN PUBLICATION FOR THIS BOOK
IS AVAILABLE FROM THE LIBRARY OF CONGRESS

ISBN-13: 978-1-4328-6767-6 (hardcover alk. paper)

Published in 2019 by arrangement with Gallery Books, an imprint of Simon & Schuster, Inc.

Printed in Mexico
1 2 3 4 5 6 7 23 22 21 20 19

For Beverly Bennett Walker and
Douglas Walker, the best I know.
Thank you for showing me how.

We cannot tear out a single page of our life, but we can throw the whole book in the fire.

— George Sand

1.

Our omniscient observer flaps her hand at us. "Closer," she demands. "Squeeze in. There you go."

Contrary to the assumption held by photographers around the world, wearing black and avoiding conversation does not render one invisible at parties. She needn't shout and wave her arms as though we're children.

"Pretend you like each other." She laughs at her own tired joke.

She fancies herself a fly on the wall, both an artist and an illusionist, zooming around like a goth banshee in this pop-up ballroom in a fancy tent, capturing moments so that we may objectify ourselves later. We'll sort through pages of proofs to find the images that best represent us — which is to say, represent us most handsomely. She stands on chairs for better angles. She drags my family outside so we can pose in better light.

I wrap my arm around Elizabeth's shoulder and pull her into my armpit.

"I can't feel my cheeks," she mutters without breaking her smile.

"Missed your calling," I whisper.

"Oh yeah? What's that?"

"Ventriloquist," I say, and she goes *ha-ha* without moving her lips.

The photographer wags her finger. "Give me just one more minute, Dr. Hart, and you can talk all you want."

Jonah groans. "Can we take the picture, please?" He's being rude, but it's what we're all feeling. There are hands to shake and an open bar to drain. We've been held hostage long enough.

"Cool it, Son," I say. "Let the girl do her job."

Another flick of the hand, another test shot, then showtime. "Beautiful family," she declares: unsolicited approval. "Just great. Okay, now everyone — say, *'Forhe'sajolly-goodfellow!'* "

We laugh despite ourselves, and the flash pops, and my beautiful family is digitally captured in a state of joy and intimacy.

"Christmas card," Elizabeth says. She drops her head and massages her temples. "If that turns out, we should make it our Christmas card."

"We'll see." It's only June, and besides, it

feels vulgar to send Season's Greetings with an image taken solely in honor of me.

Jonah is already halfway to our table when Elizabeth shouts, "Come back here." To the photographer, she says, "Wait."

I take my wife gently by the elbow. "Do you have Stockholm syndrome? We're free to go. Let's go."

She's looking past me, nervously assessing someone or something over my shoulder. "Don't you think we ought to take one with Nick?"

"With Nick? No. Let's go."

"Look at him, Bobby." I follow her gaze to the brooding young man leaning against the reception table, waiting for Jonah. My eyes linger on a giant poster of my face — pupils large as thumbprints, smile as big as a dinner plate — bearing the caption *Dr. Robert Hart: Sag Harbor Citizen of the Year.*

"Yeah," I concede, "he's photogenic. Doesn't mean he should be in our picture."

"Not what I meant. You don't think it's cruel to make him watch us take family photos when he doesn't have any family at all?"

"We hardly know the kid."

"He's not a stranger, Bobby."

"You know what I mean."

"He's important to Jonah," Elizabeth says.

11

"That's what matters. I want him to feel comfortable and not resentful."

Resentful of what? Our happy family? I'm not concerned with Nick Carpenter's resentments, but I do care about my son, and Lizzie's right, of course. Nick has been good for him. Jonah was a grade-A loner those first two years in the dorms, but now he has a roommate who's also a friend, which means he must have a social life, which means maybe he'll stop threatening to drop out of college every time the going gets rough, and maybe he'll figure out what he wants to do with this privileged life of his.

Jonah joins our huddle. "What's up?"

"Lizzie thinks Nick should be in a picture."

Disregarding the stage of our current debate, Jonah waves his friend over. So that settles that. Without taking his hands out of the pockets of his rented tuxedo, Nick pushes his body off the table and saunters toward us. He should have shaved for tonight. He should have combed his hair at least, but something tells me this messy look is intentional. Is that the style? And moreover: When did I get old enough to start thinking, *Kids these days* . . . ?

"One more," Elizabeth tells the photographer, who has been fidgeting with straps and tripods during our family meeting, while awaiting our verdict. To Nick, Lizzie smiles and says, "Get in here."

And so, once more we squeeze together, pretending to like one another, and this time when the flash pops, we say, *Cheese.*

Raymond is ready for me when I meet him at the bar. He hands me one of the gin and tonics in his hands and clinks my glass with his. "Nice speech you gave up there, Sergio de Berniac."

"Cyrano," I say. We drink.

"What?"

"Cyrano de Bergerac."

"Okay, Yale-boy," he mocks.

"Hey, I'm not the only Yalie in the house tonight, dickhead."

Scanning a crowd of stand-up citizens in black tie, he says, "Clearly not. I'm about to go into septic shock from all the bullshit in the air."

"Cute." I down the rest of my drink and toast the bartender with my empty glass. "Two more?" He nods and goes about making our watered-down cocktails.

"I'm not kidding," Raymond tells me. "That speech was something else. Got a tear in my eye, no lie."

13

"Sure it wasn't from all the bullshit in the air?"

"Fuck you."

"You're biased."

"That's true, but it was still touching. You're sort of a big deal around here, huh?"

I roll my eyes.

"Hey, enjoy it while it lasts," he says. "Once you reach the pinnacle, there's nowhere to go but down."

"I'm having second thoughts about inviting you."

He laughs. "In all seriousness, I'm proud of you, man. This is great."

"Thanks." I choke down the compliment. "It was cool of you to come. You really didn't have to."

"Hey, my oldest friend gets knighted, and you think I'd miss it?"

"Knighted. Yeah, right. Sir Man of the Year right here."

"Sir Citizen, actually."

"Whatever."

"Exactly. Fuck these guys. They don't even know."

"No they don't," I say, and we clink glasses and drink again.

Raymond Harrison: my only friend from the South Shore who stayed true long after I left town. Ray gets me, and he forgives

14

me, because even though he's stayed loyal to West Babylon and claims he'd never leave for a million bucks, we both know his conviction is born of fear. As long as he shields himself from what he's missing, he won't miss it. So he visits me in Sag Harbor sometimes, and we talk about the old days and how Long Island has changed. He'll tell me about some new bar that just opened, or about his new supervisor or apprentice, and we'll debate whether renovations at the Coliseum were worth the Islanders' troubles, and how the Jets still can't seem to pull it off, but how the Mets might surprise us — until they don't. When we run out of things to hash and rehash, we'll talk about our families. He'll ask too many questions, wanting to know if his troubles are normal. Then he'll go home to his normal and I'll go home to mine, and we'll each do our best to forget about the other normal: the one he'll never have, the one I left behind. Six months later, we'll do it again.

On the far end of the dance floor, a twelve-piece band begins playing "Lady in Red." Given as how the only woman wearing a red evening gown tonight is my wife, de facto lady of honor, I take this as my cue to showcase romance for public approval.

"I ought to go," I tell Ray. A city council-man with an untied bow tie is asking my wife to dance. She's looking around, pre-sumably for me, presumably for a rescue from wandering hands and whiskey breath. The pervert takes her by the waist. "Duty calls."

"Yeah, I really feel for you, man." Ray smirks. "I swear, if she was anybody's wife but yours . . ."

"Gross."

"I said *if*. Give me a break. But believe me when I say there's not a man in this room who wouldn't if he could."

"I get it. You want to bang my wife."

He laughs out loud. "No, Bobby. Every-one wants to bang your wife."

I slap him on the back. "Class act as always, Raymond. Class act."

"Hey, I'm just looking out for you. Like I said, shit gets real at the top. You've got a position to defend." This cracks him up.

"Thanks for the support. Now, if you'll excuse me, I'd better get to the front lines."

His laughter lingers even as I turn my back and walk away. It takes everything in me not to throw a middle finger in the air, but there are cameras here, and we both know his fuckery is an expression of endear-ment. Ray still sees himself as a big dog teasing the runt of the litter, which may be as close to brotherly love as I'm liable to get in this lifetime, so I'll take it. Let him laugh. We both know this runt is doing just fine.

The dance floor is clear except for a few couples on the periphery still hugging in circles or cycling through their stock sequences of dips and spins — and Elizabeth, of course. All eyes are on my Elizabeth, a slip of fire, red satin fluttering at her feet. In this moment, she is not just desirable. She is desired. And she is mine. Is there anything more seductive than knowing I'm the one they all wish they could be? The political perv has been replaced by Nick Carpenter — all of what, twenty? He rests his fingers on my wife's lower back. Lizzie twirls under his other hand and lets him spin her toward his chest, where he catches her body and twists with it. They laugh. Guests form a crescent moon around them.

"Excuse me," I mumble, pushing my way through a crowd that's nearly an audience. "Coming through." I say it loud enough to amuse the guests, as though I'm Bogie going after Bacall. People applaud when I cross the shiny parquet floor, tap this kid (who should have shaved) on the shoulder, and say, "May I cut in?"

To his credit, Nick understands that it

isn't a question. He bows and takes his hands off my wife, and he is young and bashful after all. Good on him to take the moment by the balls, but now his moment is over. I grab Elizabeth's waist and let the room explode with cheers and whistles. As if I'd fired the gun that says go, couples flood the floor for one last slow dance before driving home drunk to pay baby-sitters on time, or to gossip about who did what when, who looked different and why, how the food was, how the band was, who should be nominated next year, and who should win. Every man will elect himself, and tonight, when they watch their own wives crawl into bed, they'll wonder if Elizabeth Hart sleeps in stained T-shirts and cotton briefs too, but I'll be the only one who knows unequivocally that no, she does not.

"I see Ray's here," Elizabeth acknowledges. She smiles, as if this pleases her. Anyone watching us now would think we're talking about someone she likes. "Did you two have a nice chat?"

"He is and we did," I say. "It was good of him to come."

"So good. Any lewd comments worth reporting, or is the night still young?"

"Nothing to report," I lie. "He's on his

18

best behavior." Raymond is still leaning against the bar, sipping gin and watching us dance. Elizabeth and I nod in his direction. He raises his glass. *Here, here.* "See? Perfect gentleman."

"A regular Prince Charming." She kisses me on the mouth. Somewhere behind me, a camera flash flares.

"He liked your speech," I tell her as she twirls out, then back, settling into the nook where my neck and shoulder meet.

"Your speech," she corrects.

"Said it nearly made him cry."

"Gauche *and* sensitive, is he? What a special man."

"He said the part about my wife being my rock gave him a hard-on."

She slides her cheek away from mine and gives me that look, and she knows what she's doing with her little smile, those sleepy eyes. "You liked that, did you?"

With one strong hand on her back and another at her waist, I pull her body closer, pressing her hips into mine. "Yes. I did." I delight in her act of discovery.

"Wow," she says. "Everyone's hot for my speech tonight, huh?"

"My speech," I whisper.

She brings her lips to my ear and whispers

back, "Song's almost over. You'd better put that thing away."

2.

The evening ended peacefully enough. Guests echoed their congratulations. Ray disappeared without saying good-bye. I spoke to a reporter from the local paper who asked for additional remarks now that the event was over. I reiterated gratitude and humility and great happiness. My erection went unnoticed.

Luna Parks forced centerpieces on us. "Take them, please," she insisted. "What am I going to do with twenty dozen rotting roses?"

"Enjoy them," Elizabeth answered. "Toss petals in a hot bath and relax. You must be exhausted."

"I feel a little high, to be honest. We made a killing in the silent auction and still sold tickets at the door. Ten steps closer to cutting that ribbon on the Children's Wing." She tapped a perfectly manicured fingernail on my lapel. Pink polish with white at the ends. "Seems you bring out the generous in us, Mr. Sag."

"Hey, I just showed up. The credit is all yours."

She shook her head violently. "I'm the decorations chair, honey. I don't do the committee any fiscal favors, believe me."

"Well," Elizabeth said, "everything looked beautiful. Money well spent."

Luna pinched Lizzie's arm — the sort of childish act of affection that leaves a mark — and said, "No shit."

Through gritted teeth, Elizabeth asked, "How's Graham?"

Luna shook her head. "You know, he's hanging in there. Our doctors say that some people do bounce back from a stroke like his, and you'd better believe that's what Graham intends to do. He spends more time with his speech therapist these days than with me." She looked directly at Elizabeth and whispered loudly, "Should I be worried?"

This cracked Luna up, so Elizabeth and I laughed too, but I didn't say, *That's the least of your worries, lady.* In my estimation, anyone who would legally change her name to that of a Coney Island amusement park — yes, even for marriage; even if Parks isn't Park, I don't care — is a special kind of crazy ripe for worries. Society at large should be worried, frankly. She didn't even hyphenate.

Elizabeth forced a sleepy smile and said, "Let us know if there's anything we can do."

"You can take some of these damn arrangements off my hands. They're going in the trash if you refuse."

We refused, but she insisted, so we waited for Luna to get her car, and we waited for her to find the perfect parking spot, and we helped load decorations into the back of her Expedition; and when we'd finished, we let her drive us to my car just so we could undo half of what we'd just done, transferring arrangements we didn't want in the first place, tiling the trunk of my Audi with glass cubes full of marbles and white flowers. Now what am I supposed to do with ten dozen rotting roses?

"The vases are from the florist, nothing special," Luna told us. "Keep them. Please. Or if you want to rinse them out and drop them off whenever, that's fine too. Whatever works. Or I'm happy to pick them up. You know I'm dying to see your house. I heard you might spruce up that Palladian window? Maybe even restore your widow's walk so you can join the architecture tour one of these summers?"

23

I forced a smile and withheld my great fantasy: to bulldoze the same classic, high-maintenance features she's dying to see, the ones I have no intention of restoring, now or ever.

"Anyway," Luna said, "if you do bring those vases over, make sure to call first. Just try not to call before ten. Or after eight. Graham's sleep is so wonky these days. That's freesia, you know. Smell it." When we did not obey quickly enough, Luna reached into my trunk and lifted an arrangement, holding it up to our faces. Elizabeth inhaled and smiled. I couldn't smell a thing. "Isn't that something? Just impossible to replicate. Reminds me of Cape Town. Have you been? Oh, you just have to go." Luna held the flowers to her own nose, closed her eyes, and inhaled hard before putting them back in my trunk. "You know, actually, I probably would reuse the vases if you don't want them. Only if you don't want them, obviously."

"Of course," Elizabeth said.

Luna yawned, patted her open mouth and said, "Excuse me," feigning embarrassment as though we'd witnessed an intimate body function, when clearly, she relished flaunting her fatigue, so honorably earned. "I guess maybe I am exhausted after all. What do you bet I crash hard tomorrow?" She pointed at us and gave a stern order: "Now, don't you dare call the house before ten."

We all laughed, like the Parkses' schedule was an absolute riot, and said our good-byes as Luna blew kisses. As soon as Luna was out of earshot, Elizabeth mouthed, "She hates me."

"That's ridiculous." I opened her door.

She made sure every inch of red satin was tucked into the car before looking back up at me and saying, "It's not."

It's not.

Luna Parks does, in fact, hate my wife. So do half the women who smiled at her tonight. They hate her for the same reason their husbands love her, which is that they all know what Elizabeth is capable of. She's capable of adultery. I'm their proof. They know I'm capable of the same, of course. We'd both been married. We'd both cheated. What sets us apart is that we fell in love. We made it work. We were the rare exception to the rule, as evidenced by this marriage — ten years in October — far outlasting our previous marriages. My secretary, Simone, tells me that ten is the diamond anniversary, but Elizabeth insists that it's aluminum. Pliability, she tells me, is the reference. Strong but flexible. That's all well and good, but

I'll be damned if I give her Reynolds Wrap come autumn, so Simone is helping me find the perfect earrings. We're zeroing in. None of that matters to our neighbors, though. Time and commitment can't rewrite our origin story. Diamonds or tin, these Sag women remember, and they still hold a grudge, and they still hold their husbands close, because — I'm no fool — their horny husbands remember too.

Leaving the Yacht Club tonight, I'd felt content. We all did, despite having been detained by Luna Parks for half an hour. Elizabeth unbuckled her shoes. The boys unwound in the backseat, loosening their ties and laughing about who knows what. Jonah interrogated Elizabeth about food in our fridge.

"Do we have stuff for nachos?"

"I think so," she said.

"Quesadillas?"

"Sure."

"Margaritas?"

"Jonah."

"Dessert?"

The marina is only ten minutes from home, but we detoured for ice cream. When the ice cream shop was closed, Elizabeth sent Jonah and Nick into the supermarket for four pints of Ben & Jerry's and four

26

plastic spoons. We ate right there in the car because we couldn't be bothered to put on shoes and step outside. We couldn't wait. I opened the sunroof. We looked for stars. I spilled Phish Food on my tuxedo shirt, destroying it completely and not caring one bit. Elizabeth ate her mint chip from a spoon turned upside down, like she does. She looked so beautiful staring up at the moon — her bare feet propped on the dash, her gold toenail polish reflecting fluorescent light — sucking her spoon like a lollipop. It was a moment worthy of intrusive photographers lurking over my shoulder. It was a moment I would like to have captured.

Things got melty. We came home. Jonah and I went upstairs to change out of our formalwear, but Elizabeth insisted upon first bringing fresh towels to the guesthouse. As for Nick, he was doing whatever it is he does. Brooding. Thinking deep thoughts. Accepting fresh towels from my wife.

I assumed we would all end the night the same way it began: a family toast without fanfare — a toast to me for my once-in-a-lifetime honor. Was my expectation self-indulgent? Of course. Absolutely. But just for one night out of thousands and thousands in my life, that was sort of the point, wasn't it? Usually I'm showing up for other

27

people's indulgent parties, or doing nice things for them, or taking care of them, even though that's my job. I shouldn't have needed to make a special request for it to end in peace. It should have been a sleepy coda. Eventless. Pleasant. I don't believe that's asking too much. I don't believe in too much of a good thing, or in cups running over — or rather, that overflow is dangerous — but Elizabeth must, because she hacked a leak into my nice evening, and now we're up here arguing in coarse whispers behind a closed door.

"You're acting crazy," she tells me.

"It was a perfectly reasonable reaction," I reply.

"It's insane."

"Insane? Sort of a hysterical choice of words, don't you think?"

She huffs and abandons me to brush her teeth.

I'm not acting crazy. Maybe I misunderstood, but my initial assessment was fair and reasonable. What I saw is what seemed crazy. I'd gone out to the guesthouse to find her. Plain and simple. I'd been waiting forever for our cozy debrief. Fifteen minutes at least, maybe more. Plenty of time to deliver the laundry. And yes, I opened the door without knocking, because the guesthouse is my property, but she didn't need to jump when I caught her leaning close to Nick, whispering numbers and watching him enter them into his phone. She yelped when she saw me. She shouted my name.

"Bobby!" She'd laughed. "You scared me."

"What's there to be afraid of?" I'd asked.

She told me Nick somehow never got the alarm code to the house, so she was making sure he had it. In case of an emergency. Well, he never got the code because no one ever gave it to him, mystery solved. But fine. It makes sense now. No big deal.

On the other side of the wall, Elizabeth spits toothpaste and begins to gargle. I throw my tuxedo shirt into the garbage and do my best to hang the rest, cummerbund and all, while shaping my argument. When she comes back into the bedroom and crosses her arms tightly against her chest, I state my case: "All I'm saying is, you don't have to be so defensive."

"Excuse me?"

"If it's not a big deal, then why are you making it a big deal?"

"It's not any sort of deal," she says. "I'm just sorry to see you so insecure."

Well, there it is. She has a knack. She knows my loudest nerves and how to strike them with ease and elegance. I want to drop it, honestly I do, but wanting and doing are at odds tonight. I end up saying, "I could ask the same of you."

"Oh really?"

"Yeah. Seeking attention and validation from a college kid? C'mon, Elizabeth. It's too soon for a midlife crisis."

She doesn't flinch. We're locked in a silent standoff. Four, five seconds at least. I win when she opens her mouth. "Why don't you take the couch tonight."

I roll my eyes. "Because I don't want to sleep on the couch. You're being absurd."

"Just for tonight," she says. "I love you. I am so proud of you. I really am, but I am not having a midlife crisis, and I am not doing this tonight." She doesn't even look mad, just tired.

"You're drunk," I tell her.

"I'm really not."

"He's not some Dickens character, you know. He's not Oliver Twist or whatever."

She thrusts sheets against my chest. "Good night, Bobby."

"This is stupid, Elizabeth. All I was saying is that if you're going to start handing out our personal security codes, maybe you want to run it by me first. That's all."

She shrugs, spiting me by not reacting, and because yes, I want her to engage — is that so bad? — I aim for guilt. "This was my night. Is it really that hard to just give me one night?"

Elizabeth switches off her lamp, burrows under blankets, and curls up with her back turned to me. "Good night, Robert."

She gives me nothing. I take my leave.

How did this happen? An hour ago, I was Man of the Year, and now I'm persona non grata, standing in the hallway hugging goose down in the dark, wondering if Elizabeth has lost her mind — or if she's right. Am I being unreasonable? There really is nothing wrong with the boy, but there's nothing wrong with communicating, either. She should have asked me before handing out the code. She should have delivered the laundry and returned to my side for one last toast.

I carry my pillows, flat sheet, and silk fleece blanket down to my office and make up the couch. It's a daybed, technically: nice for naps and domestic disputes. Had I known this piece of furniture would turn on me, I'd have left it on the floor at Restoration Hardware. I'm all worked up now, though, and hardly tired, so I head to the wet bar in the living room to fix myself a drink. Chivas and soda. Through a wall of windows, I watch the blurry silhouettes of my son and his friend, masked behind curtains and yellow light in the guesthouse across the yard. I step outside. Muffled music radiates from this little after-hours the boys have going.

Bob Marley. *Legend.*

The half-moon is electric tonight, and the air is warm, so I close the door and take a seat in a reclining pool chair. I wonder if I'm imagining the smell of pot coming from the guesthouse — if it's my paternal projection born of experience, because I was once twenty, too — and decide that yes, I'm probably imagining it, and no, it isn't my business anyway.

"Three Little Birds" begins, and I relax. Across the yard and behind a door, my son and his friend laugh. Why would I hesitate to let Nick feel at home here? What kind of father would give Elizabeth's hospitality a second thought? It's true: Nick isn't a stranger. He's been coming around all year. Last summer, he and Jonah would go to the beach to watch girls, then come back to my house to eat all my food. He didn't bother me then, nor does he bother me now, I just never got a feel for the boy. He never sent thank-you notes acknowledging our generosity. He never brought a houseplant or a box of pastries. Of course, I never expected thank-you notes from Jonah's high school friends, who were far less gracious or considerate — splattering the kitchen with queso and Mountain Dew, blasting *Call of Duty* after midnight, sneaking girls over to skinny-dip in our pool when Jonah was asleep but I wasn't — so maybe I should cut the kid some slack.

Besides, Elizabeth's assessment is dead-on. It's been good for Jonah to have a friend, any friend. My son is making smart choices. He came home this summer to save money and take extra classes, for crying out loud — composition or something like it at Stony Brook, where Elizabeth teaches — and he's staying with me, for once. Jonah's not a screwup. He's just hard to read, despite being my own flesh and blood, because even though he's half me, Vanessa shifted his balance when she got custody. Primary custody. Adultery is good ammo, after all. She hated me, and she hated Elizabeth even more. She hates us both a little less now, though. And Jonah is a little less complicated these days. He has someone to hang out and listen to music with like a normal college kid. I should encourage this normalcy.

The boys change records, shifting from reggae to funk. A cool breeze reminds me that I'm only wearing boxer shorts. Goose bumps travel across my arms and legs. I down the last of my drink and feel sleep calling, but before I can answer, the guesthouse door opens. A blast of volume disrupts the night's calm. Great. The neighbors will call our HOA to complain in the morning.

"Night, man," Jonah says, and Nick replies with something I can't hear beneath a rush of bass and horns. Then the door closes, muffling the music once again, and Jonah is shuffling through the grass with his head down. Even from my perch at the deep end of the pool, I smell pot as he passes the shallow end. He never looks up. He doesn't see his old man sitting in the dark in his underwear, holding an empty highball glass, watching. He just goes inside and, mercifully, forgets to lock the door behind him, so I'll be able to get back inside without making a scene. Lucky me.

A George Clinton track ends. Earth, Wind & Fire begins. Through glass, I watch Jonah climb the stairs and disappear on the landing, and I allow a minute for him to brush his teeth and take a leak, then I head inside too.

JONAH

I brush my teeth, take a leak, and roll into bed. So that wasn't a total disaster: the party, the small talk. I warned Nick that this night would fall somewhere between corny and mortifying, but the music wasn't half bad, and those teriyaki skewers were legit; plus, Dad barely acknowledged me in his speech, which is a major upgrade from what I'd expected, which was that he'd embarrass the shit out of me, so that's cool.

My stupid headphones are downstairs, way too far at the moment, so I stomach silence and check my phone to make sure Kayla didn't text.

She didn't. I mean, why would she? Except maybe she's waiting for me to text her. But it's two in the morning and what am I going to say? *What's up?* That's dumb.

So whatever. I'll wait.

I don't even have to close my eyes to

picture the way her hair sort of lit up in the sun.

I don't even know why she'd text me, anyway.

God, I'd kill for a teriyaki stick right now.

My phone buzzes and my gut reaction is, *Maybe it's Kayla,* which basically feels like my guts have been electrocuted, but then I look and it's just Nick and I'm weirdly bummed — weird only because I didn't explicitly ask her to text me *(did I?)* — and I have to remind myself to stop being an idiot.

Nick's text: *"Nothing tmrw, right?"*

I text back: *"Nada. You're off the hook from here on out."* No more family parties, family photos, family commitments for a family that's not his. We get a few days to chill before he has to peace out.

He sends a thumbs-up.

I plug my phone into its charger and roll onto my stomach to get some sleep. I'm not going to obsess about this girl tonight. *I'm not even going to think about her,* I promise myself, which basically guarantees she's all I'll think about. It's so stupid. I hardly know her. I'd never even talked to her until — what was it? Four days ago? Five? It was the day Nick got here, which was Tuesday, so I guess five days ago now? Practically nothing.

I mean, I knew *about* her, obviously. Everyone knows what happened between Kayla Scott and J.R. Voss. Plus, we went to high school together and everything, but she was a sophomore when I was a senior — not that age matters to her, considering what happened with Mr. Voss.

On the day Nick got here, when we pulled into the parking lot by the beach and saw those guys shit-talking Kayla, I was shocked but not surprised to hear them calling her a cocktease and jailbait and a slut, but the really disturbing part was how Kayla was with her little sister. I mean, come on. That's a little off-sides. The two of them were holding hands and had their heads down, just trying to cross the road, but those douche bags were blocking the exit and making stupid-ass porn sounds like a bunch of crazy cavemen. Nick doesn't know anyone here, so he had nothing to lose by shouting at them, "Yo, what's your problem?"

They were high-school brats — maybe even Kayla's classmates, now that I think about it — trying to act all tough, so then they came for us, like, "Who the fuck are you?" Behind them, Kayla gave me and

Nick a nod like *thanks* and bolted across the road with her sister while I shouted at the punks, "Yeah, what's your fucking problem?"

The douche bags were all talk, though. They got in their fancy cars and peeled out of there, blasting shitty music from expensive speakers.

Nick was like, "Do you know that girl?"

And I was like, "Not really," and told him all about Kayla and how she used to babysit for the Voss kids but then tried to blackmail Mr. Voss by saying he'd molested her or whatever, but so then Mr. Voss called her bluff and was like, *Prove it,* and all of a sudden she was like, *Oops, my bad. That never happened.*

"Did it happen?" Nick asked me.

"Dude, look at her," I said. Kayla was all the way down near the water by then, but even from a distance it was obvious she's all woman, not some helpless little girl.

"I don't even know what that means," Nick said, "but that dude sounds shady."

Nick didn't grow up here, so he wouldn't understand, but J.R. Voss is like a pillar of our community or whatever. I mean, he's not perfect. I even said to Nick, "They probably fucked and she thought he was going to leave his wife, and when he didn't, she went psycho. Who knows. But, I mean, she basically ruined his life. She practically called him a child molester."

And Nick was like, "I don't know, man. If the whole point was to get revenge, why would she ruin her own life too?"

For real, though, I'd never thought about it like that. I'd only ever thought of it how Dad does, which is that the whole thing is a total disgrace. So I was like, "Good point. It's all gossip anyway. Who knows what really happened."

"Who knows," Nick said.

Later on, Kayla came up to us when her sister was playing near the water and said, "Thanks for before."

Nick was like, "Don't thank us for being decent. Those guys are dicks. Sorry you have to deal with people like that," which kind of annoyed me, because come on, dude. Laying it on a little thick. Except obviously he was right. I felt bad for Kayla then.

She introduced herself and we did the same, and she nodded toward her sister and said, "I usually bring her out in the morning when it's empty. Lesson learned, I guess. Anyway, nice to meet you guys." And she left.

I wasn't surprised when Nick said later

on, "Wanna hit up the beach again tomorrow? A little earlier, maybe?"

I didn't tell him I was thinking the same thing.

So I guess it was, like, nine when we got there the next day. Nick went for a run and I was reading alone when I sensed someone walking toward me. I didn't want to seem too eager, though, or like a stalker, so I pretended not to notice until she was standing over me saying, "Hey."

I made a show of pulling my earbuds out of my ears and acting like I hadn't heard her before when I went, "Huh?"

She said, "Hey," again.

I nodded.

"Where's your friend?"

I jerked my head toward the far end of the beach. "Down there somewhere. Jogging."

"Ambitious," she said, and she sat down next to me without asking.

"You just graduated, right?" (I wanted to kill myself for admitting I knew who she was.)

"Yeah, finally," she said. "I can't wait to get the hell out of here."

"Tell me about it."

She laughed. "Didn't you just get back for the summer?" (So, hey, she knows me too.)

40

"Yeah," I said, "but I get it. You going to school far away or something?"

"No." Her red hair fell in her face and kind of glowed from the sunlight. "I'm taking a year off. A gap year, as they say in Australia." She said that last part in a really bad Aussie accent, which made us both laugh. "My grandma gave me an around-the-world ticket for graduation. She's sort of my savior."

"Damn," I said. "That's cool."

"Yeah, well." Her attention trailed off somewhere mysterious. "I kind of fucked up getting my college applications together this year."

"Oh." Not so mysterious after all, then. I guess there wouldn't have been much time for essays and SATs during all that drama with Mr. Voss.

"Yeah," she said, like she was reading my mind. "I bet you've been overseas lots."

"Couple times," I told her, but I didn't say that both times were London. "You?"

"I went to Paris with French class last year. It was cool. I've been to Canada, too, if you count that."

I don't really, but I nodded. Nick's dad was from Canada. I tell Kayla, "That's funny, because they speak French in some parts of Canada, too."

41

"Yeah, I know," she said. She didn't say it mean, but I still wanted to tell her she didn't have to be a bitch about it. I don't know why. I've never talked to a girl that way in my life.

"You going to Crowley's party next weekend?" Kayla asked.

Ugh. Sam Crowley's the kind of guy who's always looking around to make sure people are laughing at whatever lame story he's telling — and then he'll tell the same story later just so he can include the part about how everyone laughed so hard when he told it before. He's the worst. "I don't know," I told Kayla. "Kind of doubt it. Have to finish writing a paper."

"Summer school?"

"Yeah. Lit and Comp. What about you?"

"Summer school?"

"No, Crowley's. Are you going?"

"I was thinking about it," she said.

I kind of wish she hadn't told me that. Kayla's the type of girl who calls movies "films" and isn't embarrassed to tell you she plays piano for fun, but is embarrassed about how pretty she is, because she's pretty without even trying. I don't know why she gives a crap about who goes to Sam's thing or whether she should go. The saddest part of parties like that is when girls like Kayla start doing keg stands or when they puke on the kitchen floor and everyone freaks.

"Anyway," Kayla said, "you should go. It'll be fun."

I nodded and told her, "I'll think about it." But seriously, we had nothing to say to each other after that. It wasn't awkward, though, which was cool. Awkward silences don't bother me anymore, anyway. They used to back when I thought I was the one who didn't know how to talk to people, but I don't think that now. Nick helped me realize I'd just been talking to the wrong people my whole life.

Like, I used to think my sense of humor was dumb. I'd crack a joke at lunch and everyone would still be staring at me like, "Wait, was that the punch line?" I thought I was legitimately stupid, too, because I'd ask questions in class and the teacher would be like, "Okaaay. Anyone else?" Eventually I stopped raising my hand and being funny out loud.

Sometimes it was almost like I was speaking another language, like whenever I tried to find common ground with Dad — asking medical questions maybe, like, *Why do I get charley horses at night but not so much in the daytime?* — except instead of answering me he'd be all sarcastic, like, *I don't know, Son.*

Maybe it's related to your psychedelic urine, because I asked him one time why my pee turns neon when I take vitamins, which is an excellent question, actually, but he acted like I was a hypochondriac or trying to be special. Maybe if he'd have just answered like a normal dad, I'd have been interested enough in his area of expertise to want to be a doctor too.

On the flipside, if it wasn't for Nick, maybe I'd still feel guilty for *not* wanting to be a doctor. It might have taken me a whole lot longer to figure out that some things just aren't my things — same as how some people just aren't my people.

Looking back, it's crazy to think I almost had a nervous breakdown over having to live with Nick. The whole reason I applied for the solo dorms early was because I had zero interest in rooming with a stranger. But then I got that letter saying I'd been assigned a double anyway. The head of residence didn't give two shits when I called to appeal. He said people are often "pleasantly surprised." I seriously wanted to punch him in the nuts for that, but he wasn't wrong, because honestly, I probably never would have even talked to Nick if they hadn't forced us to live in that shoebox for two semesters, and we definitely wouldn't have rented our house last year. Now it seems like I lucked out with the only other normal person in our entire class, and now I feel kind of bad about spazzing on the head of residence.

This one time, I told Nick he was the weirdest person I'd ever met. I wasn't a dick about it. I was just like, "Dude. You're so weird." And he was like, "So?" And I was like, "My point *exactly.*" I'd never met anyone before who gives zero fucks about being cool, or about being a certain type of person other than himself. There I was trying to be the premed kid, like it was my whole identity or whatever, but hating myself for hating it so much, and Nick was like, "Do it if you want to. Don't do it if you don't." Turns out it really was that simple. Why had it always seemed so much more complicated before?

If anyone else had pulled that life-is-too-short-to-*blah-blah-blah* crap, I'd have told them to shove it, but Nick's been through some shit. He knows better than anyone how short life can be. I mean, life *is* too short to bust my ass for a job I hate, or to worry about what guys like Sam Crowley think about me, or to miss out on getting to know people like Kayla, who's supposed to be radioactive but, as it turns out, is pretty cool and pretty much wants to get to know me too.

After we'd talked for a while at the beach that day, Kayla stood up, zipped her hoodie, tightened the drawstring around her face and said, "Maybe I'll see you this weekend," and I guess I was thinking that *life's-too-short* crap when I said, "Do you want to take my number?" She didn't answer right away, so I said, "In case Crowley's thing changes. It's supposed to rain next week."

So we exchanged information and she said, "Tell Nick I said hi. See you guys around."

I nodded. "For sure."

She smiled at me. "See you, Jonah."

I guess I forgot to tell Nick, but only because I figured we'd see her soon anyway. I had this dumb idea she might be at Dad's party tonight, which I now realize was legit stupid, because the Vosses practically bank-roll those shindigs. See, that right there is another thing I'd never thought about: the people and places Kayla has to avoid because of him.

Through my floor, I can hear Dad coughing. He almost had his perfect night, but then he went and picked a fight with Elizabeth. Now he's sleeping in the office instead of in bed with his wife. He thinks I'm an idiot who doesn't notice that stuff, but I can hear when he pulls out the hideaway, or coughs, or stubs his toe and curses. He thinks I'm clueless, but I don't take it personally anymore, because I get it now: he just isn't my people.

3.

"Robert." Her voice is barely a whisper. She strokes my head and I crack my eyes. Nautical twilight paints the walls soft violet. "The boys will be up soon."

Elizabeth is standing over me, half asleep and wrapped in a robe, and although she didn't bring me a cup of coffee to start my day, I smell a pot brewing in the kitchen. She hands me the boxer shorts I'd dropped at the end of the couch last night. I put them on without saying a word. She doesn't ask how I slept, but she does help me carry bedding so we won't have to answer Jonah's questions if he sees pillows in my office. We tiptoe through the living room and up the stairs, and with every step, the drama of last night loses power and relevance. It was stupid. We were tired. We hang a right and close our bedroom door behind us.

"I'm sorry," she says. "I should have talked it over with you first."

"What's done is done," I tell her. "It's not a big deal anyway."

"I know. Are you mad?"

"Not really. Are you?"

"I don't think so," she says. Heaven knows she shouldn't be.

I say, "We were both surprised. No big deal."

"I just want to do what's right for Jonah." She props a pillow against the headboard and gets back in bed, sitting upright with her knees drawn to her chest and a blanket wrapped around her feet. "What do you think of him?"

"Of Jonah?" What a strange question.

"No, of Nick."

I scratch my belly and answer to the best of my ability. "I don't think much of him."

"Really?"

"I don't think badly of him. I just don't think about him. I haven't given him much thought, period. How's that?"

"Hm." She drapes her forearms around her shins and stares at the ceiling fan.

The sun has cleared the horizon, and the safe in-betweenness of dawn is behind us. I'm not much for reliving fights in broad daylight. What's done is done. It's not yet five thirty, and it's Sunday, and Elizabeth's robe is falling open above the sash tied in a bow at her waist, so I move toward the bed and stand over her, just as she stood over me minutes ago, and I wrap my fingers around one loose end of satin and I pull, undoing the knot. She lets go of her legs, so I slide them toward the foot of the bed until she is laid out long in front of me. Her eyes are closed, and her skin is warm and velvet soft when I slip my fingers under silk and press my palm against her ribs. I bring my mouth to her body. With one finger, I strip off my boxers before climbing on top of my wife, and I spit in my hand out of habit, but there was no need. She is ready for me. I find her warmest place, and we find our rhythm, and we follow it, chase it with tremendous heat. Her eyes are still closed, but mine are open, so I get to watch the surprise broadcast on her face when, for only the third time in over a decade of sleeping together, she climaxes from penetration alone.

She feels incredible, beyond, so I come too, and only when the mad rush has passed do I take note of another thing I can count on one hand: simultaneous orgasms — and this time I'm certain she's not faking.

When we are entirely finished, when the aftershocks clear our systems completely, I collapse on top of her body. Dead weight.

We lay like this until I guess I fall asleep, because she nudges my back the way she does when I start snoring. So I kiss her forehead and her stomach, and I head to the bathroom to take a long shower. It's an excellent shower. When I get out, a cup of coffee (cream, no sugar) is by the sink. I hadn't even felt a draft when the door must have opened and closed.

I expect Elizabeth to have fallen back asleep, or maybe to be reading in bed while waiting for the bathroom, but she's not here, and even after I've dressed and made the bed, she hasn't returned. I hear her voice, though, on my way downstairs. She's speaking in a soft, low whisper to someone else speaking just as soft and low.

"Robert," Elizabeth says when she sees me. She's sitting on the countertop by the sink, holding a mug of coffee between her knees. "Did you know we have a master angler in the house?" She's not wearing a bra.

"I did not," I say.

She tells Nick, "Show him the Northern Pike." Elizabeth hates fishing. She wouldn't know a pike from a guppy. I bet the only reason Nick showed her pictures was to get her to lean close to him with her shirt draped low.

"You're up early, Nick," I say.

He tilts his head. "Old habits from military school."

"Ah, that's right. I forgot. Military school. That must have been interesting."

"I guess. It's all I knew."

"Robert fishes," Elizabeth says. "He used to, anyway. He's hardly gone out on the boat at all this year." She says it to Nick, but she says it at me.

"We had a late spring." It occurs to me that Elizabeth hasn't taken a shower yet. I move close to her and breathe her in.

"Well, we're having a beautiful summer now," she argues.

Nick looks at me like it's my serve on the tennis court. Most people would pretend to be doing anything other than hanging on their hosts' every loaded word, but Nick is shamelessly entertained. Strange one, this kid.

"The shower is all yours," I tell Elizabeth. "Sorry I took so long."

"Oh, I'm fine," she says.

"Are you sure, Lizzie?" My encrypted glance, coded by ten years of partnership and silent messages in crowded rooms, says, *No you're not.* Below that: *No really, darling. You smell like sex.* She doesn't read it, though, because she's busy refilling her mug

52

with black coffee, no sugar.

"Yes, Robert. I'm sure." She laughs. "Nick, show him that pike."

It's a forty-four-and-a-quarter-inch Northern, a beauty by any standard. He'd gone all the way up to Ontario to catch it. He's telling me the story, but I'm only half listening, because I'm preoccupied by the shirtless figure in the photo — sweaty and tan, classic Ray-Bans, white teeth. So fucking young. What kind of guy shows shirtless photos of himself to another man's wife in another man's house?

"Anyway," Nick is saying, "it was a special trip. Nobody around for miles. Peaceful like you wouldn't believe."

"You like the water?" I ask.

"Love it."

"You didn't grow up near water, though."

"No." He slips his phone into his back pocket. "Grew up in Ohio. We had some lakes nearby, but nothing special." He nods toward the windows facing the yard, the harbor, the sea. "This is exotic to me."

I'm struck with a sudden urge to assess this Nick Carpenter, to size him up. He's been Jonah's sidekick for a couple of years — long enough for me to have formed a clear opinion, and yet I have none, which must be why he bugs me. I'm a data guy. I should get acquainted with this person who shares early morning coffees, privileges, and conveniences with my family, who brags about the size of his pike to my wife as she leans in close with no bra and no clue what she's doing to the boy. So I say, "Maybe you'd like to hitch a ride to a different beach one of these mornings? Change things up. I can drop you off on my way to work."

"Sure," Nick says. "That'd be great."

"Maybe you'd like to go fishing." Two heads snap up to gauge my sincerity.

"Yeah," Nick finally says. "That would be cool."

"We should go today." I smile at Elizabeth, who seems puzzled even though she was the one who practically suggested it. "How about it?"

Nick pats his pockets and glances left to right, as though needing to check a calendar or consult an assistant before making plans. Of course, he doesn't have an assistant or plans, because he's our houseguest, and his only friend here is asleep upstairs.

"Sure," he finally says. "If Jonah's up for it, I'm in."

"Great. Know anything about boats?"

"A little." He scratches his head and rubs the back of his neck, glancing upstairs toward Jonah's closed door. "Are you sure this is convenient?"

"Hey," I say, looking at Elizabeth, "why not? We're having a beautiful summer."

Elizabeth shakes off her bewilderment and tells Nick, "You've seen how it's been around here. That party last night was exhausting. Take the boat out. Relax." To me, she says, "A day off will be good for you. It'll be good for everyone. God knows you've earned it, Robert."

"You're telling me," I say.

"Besides, I have a million papers to grade and could use the peace and quiet."

"Fair enough. We'll roll out when Jonah gets up."

Nick stuffs his hands in his pockets, lifts his shoulders and gives me this cowboy nod, saying, "I'm going to go clean up and I'll be back to help out. Thanks so much, Dr. Hart."

"Not at all." When he steps outside, I turn to Elizabeth and say, "Take a shower."

Jonah sleeps and sleeps. If I hadn't known him his entire life, I might suspect anemia or hypothyroid, but I do know him, and he's just lazy. Maybe *he's* the one who should have gone to military school. Maybe we made the kid soft.

I wake him up at eight o'clock to tell him

the plan, taking a second to look around a room that's only ever been his part-time home at best. To my surprise, the floor is moderately clean. No dirty plates of moldy food in sight, no jizz-filled socks. Maybe he is growing up. Maybe there's hope for him after all.

"We're leaving for the marina at nine," I say.

He moans and mumbles, "Sounds good," before rolling over, still buried in covers. "Give me fifteen minutes."

I leave the door open so he'll be vulnerable to downstairs chatter and the smell of bacon while I buy and print fishing licenses, my treat. Fifteen minutes later, he still hasn't appeared, so I go back and nudge again, and he whines, "I'm up. I said, *I'm up.*"

Back in the kitchen, I bemoan my son's bad manners, making sure Nick knows my parenting isn't to blame, and Elizabeth comes to my rescue, saying, "Why don't you and Nick head to the dock and get the boat ready. I'll blast Carly Simon and send Jonah over when he gets his ass in gear."

There it is. She has my back. Her whole demeanor has brightened, and I feel bad for being annoyed with her before. She's so damn good most of the time, and Nick's perviness isn't her fault. She's taken a shower. She's wearing a bra. Maybe she does see Oliver or Pip, but maybe that's not so dreadful, because if Nick represents an opportunity to flex repressed maternal instincts, I should support the exercise. Heaven knows she didn't get the chance with Jonah. Elizabeth missed the first half of his life. She's never seen her DNA imprinted on an infant. I would have had another child if she'd wanted one — hell, I'd have had two — but it was her decision to send me off to get snipped. She was the one who made that call.

"I'm not willing to trade my autonomy for a seven-million-dollar pet," she used to say. Remarkably, she'd say it with zero emotion, let alone grief. I'd argue she lost her autonomy the day she married me, technically, and that Jonah is not a pet, but she'd hold her ground, saying only, "You know what I mean."

I guess I do.

Vanessa had wanted a baby so badly, and although we were both young — far too young to have started a family — conceiving didn't come easy. It wasn't as simple as shooting sperm through her cervix, but we were never ones to shy away from challenges. A baby stopped being the goal. Mak-

57

ing a baby was all we could see. We didn't do the grueling things our neighbors are doing today, but Vanessa did endure a few rounds of Clomid after getting her fallopian tubes flushed. Determination usurped ambivalence. True achievers, we wanted success.

We got Jonah. He was extraordinary. He was darling, of course, but he would cry and cry and nothing would soothe him in that first month. We were certain it was colic or some gastrointestinal problem, but the pediatrician said, "No, he's just a baby."

Babies cry, we learned. Babies, much like puppies, keep owners up all night; they vomit and defecate when it's inconvenient and urinate where we're expected to clean it up. In no time, they want chew toys. They break Limoges boxes and shred magazines. They want attention, and when they don't get it, they whine. They beg for indigestible treats, but we are supposed to feed them very particular foods at regular intervals, *or else,* because that's our job, *don't fuck it up.* They need vaccines, socialization, discipline, and fresh air, and so we work our asses off to give them all these things and more: education, vacations, culture, comfort. We love them with every atom of ourselves because we have to — because if we allow for even the slightest possibility that we don't know why we did this, our whole reason for being would collapse. So we tell other parents the same thing they tell us, which is that we wouldn't trade it for the world. We tell ourselves this because we don't have a choice, because there's no trade on the table.

Tutors, training, lessons, braces, a new car, a new computer, the latest software, the latest trend, seven thousand lunches, seven thousand dinners, fifty-odd pairs of shoes, countless tanks of gas, lift tickets, Christmas presents, birthday parties, warmth, and water. We give commands — *Sit, Stay* — and teach them tricks: multiplication tables, long division, grammar, manners, how to be liked, how to get accepted, how to get ahead in the real world. Before the real world, though, there's college. Assuming he manages to make it out in four years, Jonah's undergrad will run me a quarter of a million dollars, and because I've worked tirelessly to make all this money to pay for all his stuff, we won't qualify for desirable scholarships or grants.

The hope, I guess — the expectation, even — is that he will grow up to find something he enjoys doing, and that he'll do it long enough to find it deeply unsatisfying. His patents won't get approved. His book won't fly off the shelves. Awards won't make him immortal. The grand dreams that carried him from A to B to wherever he is will suddenly look like cardboard cut-outs, so he'll light them on fire. His great plans will turn to ash. He'll wonder what the point is, what the hell he's doing here — and then, maybe, if he's lucky, he'll meet someone whose life has lost meaning too, and they'll fall in love, and for reasons they can't explain, they'll decide that making a baby is the most profound thing they can do — or the most creative, or the most spiritual, depending upon where they are in their lives. They'll decide that the most basic fact of life is actually a miracle, and that their miracle is special, and that this uniqueness will give their lives purpose, finally — and then the work begins. Cue a parade of necessary distractions: vaccines, socialization, discipline, fresh air. Cue the consolation. We see ourselves in little creatures, in our seven-million-dollar pets, and we find comfort in believing we will live forever through them, all the while knowing that when death closes in — because who are we kidding, death always finds us — we can call upon our investments to provide comfort and care.

And if we've made mistakes? If we've

pushed too hard or haven't pushed hard enough, if a new virus breaks out, if new hard drugs make the rounds, or if it turns out Jonah's mood swings are bigger than ordinary angst — if he blows his brains out, or blows the library up, or blows the dean and someone sees and takes pictures that get plastered on the internet — then what? If he drives off a cliff late at night and dies — or doesn't die, but ends up with locked-in syndrome — then what? Will it all have been worth it then?

Of course it would.

There's no dollar value on the value of a son. No grief could be so big that it could swallow my love for my boy. No good night's sleep could diminish the joy of fatherhood, which isn't easy and isn't always fun but is my greatest achievement by far. Heaven knows I wouldn't trade it for the world.

Elizabeth, though — her scales are balanced differently. She'll take the good night's sleep. She's impulsive in a self-preservative way. She'd rather spend her money on a vacation than diapers or dorms. She values serenity. Aside from the drama of our early days, she's lived a life aimed toward comfort, not complication, and love is nothing if not complicated. I was her

61

glitch, her one messy misstep. She's not interested in chasing further pain.

"Loving a child is the same as loving heartache," she's said more than once. She claims she wouldn't survive the devastation if tragedy were to befall Jonah, and I believe this feels true for her. I believe that she's never consciously wanted biological children of her own. I am, however, a man of science, and so it's difficult for me to believe that a primitive part of her brain hasn't issued the urge to procreate. She is a woman, after all.

And so I take her up on the offer. I let her get her maternal fix by picking up sandwiches and Cokes and playing bad cop to my lazy son while I head over to the Yacht Club with Nick.

4.

The marina is crowded with chipper families and their friends — friends who feel special because they were chosen as guests. They made the cut on a beautiful day. I walk Nick down Long Wharf, pointing out behemoth yachts and their puffed-out owners, pausing to admire the sleek speedboat I plan to buy when I retire. We circle back to the bait shop, and while waiting on line, I try to pick the boy's brain, but he seems to abide by the old adage to not speak until spoken to, which is a shame, because I'm running out of questions. Does he know how to tie a slipknot? A clinch? Has he ever been crabbing? Surfing? Mets or Yankees? Jets or Giants? Does he have a five-year plan? Two-year, then? What about school? Does he like it?

"School is okay," he says. "Fifty-fifty, and each half extreme."

What in the world does that mean? "What

63

does that mean?"

"You know, the good parts are great: classes, campus, freedom, so much happening. The weird parts are rough, though."

"Rough how?"

"The social scene can be dark. My advisor gives zero support. Everything is so damn expensive. A lot of obnoxious rich kids."

Was that a jab? A slip? "What about Jonah? Does he feel the same way?"

Nick shrugs. "I guess. Speaking of . . ." He is suddenly preoccupied with time and the parking lot. "Do you think we should call him again? It's almost eleven." He shades his eyes with one hand and searches in all directions. "Maybe he thinks we're meeting someplace else."

"He knows where to find us."

"Hey, didn't we see those guys at the thing last night?"

I jerk my head toward Nick's point of view, hunting for familiar faces. "Which guys?"

"Those." He points toward a forty-foot Belzona two slips away.

Frankie McAlister notices us staring and pointing. "Bobby!" he shouts. The rest of his party waves and calls my name.

"Yeah," I tell Nick. "They certainly were."

I'm not in the mood to be polite to the McAlisters and their boatload of friends, but it's too late for anonymity now, so I wave and make my way to them. "Frank," I say.

He gestures for me to meet him at the end of the slip, turning and shimmying past his wife, stopping at the stern to say, "Check this out," as he strokes the chrome details on a gleaming Mercury outboard. "What do you think of this baby?" he asks, oozing pride.

"A fourth engine," I acknowledge.

"Fourteen hundred horsepower." He rattles off specs better suited for a cruise ship, and Nick hangs back, introducing himself to Bonnie and the McAlisters' guests: Lars and Monique Clyborne; some lady named Lisa; Lisa's husband, Jack; and Luna Parks, who greets Nick like they're old friends. The ladies throw their heads back and laugh.

When Frank finally takes a breath, I say, "Luna, you look rested. I'm trusting no one disturbed you before ten?" When she stares blankly, I remind her of the red line she instated last night: "No calls before ten?"

"Oh, honey. I wouldn't dream of calling anyone before ten on a weekend."

I let it go and say only, "Good rule of

thumb."

"But goodness gracious, aren't you the lucky ones getting to host this dreamboat." She winks at Nick. "Wouldn't I just love to keep you in my pocket."

Monique says, "Last night was so much fun, Robert."

"Yeah," says Lars. "It was a two-aspirin kind of morning."

I open my mouth to give credit to the Children's Hospital Fund, but Luna asks, "Is Elizabeth here?"

"No, just the guys today. Jonah's on his way."

"Well, isn't that sweet," Luna says. "Every man needs guy time sometimes, don't you think? And we ladies need our girl time. Will you please tell Elizabeth to give us a call? I don't know why we never see each other. It's such a shame."

"She ought to come to one of our Garden Club luncheons," says Bonnie. "Elizabeth would fit right in."

"Oh God, not Garden Club," says Luna. "What she really needs to do is help us reboot our ancient book club. Literature is her thing. Tell her we *need* her, won't you, Robert?"

"Sure," I say.

"Promise?"

66

"Absolutely. She'll appreciate the invitation."

"Do you think so? I never can tell with her."

"She'll love it," I lie. "All right. We need to intercept Jonah before he steals the boat for himself."

"Now there's an idea," Frank says as they push off. "Hand her over and treat yourself to an upgrade."

"Never," I vow.

"Have you been out on his boat, son?" Frank asks Nick.

"Not yet," Nick replies.

"Crying shame what Bobby does to the damn thing. Steal her if you get the chance."

"Okay, that's enough," I say, and everyone laughs, although it wasn't a joke. "Nice seeing you all. Great motors, Frank."

Luna and Monique wave good-bye, but the rest of their party is already busy cracking coolers and smearing sunscreen on shoulders and noses. Enough of us.

Enough of them. "What a piece of work," I say to myself, and I'm glad Nick doesn't ask who or why, because they all are sometimes. Frank, Mo, Luna, the whole lot.

Jonah is still missing in action, so I drag Nick to our slip and put him to work unsnapping one side of the Bimini. We roll back the cover, and *My Lucia* dazzles in the sunlight. I ask, "Ever been in one of these?"

"No," he says. "But it sure is beautiful."

"Lapstrake construction. If it's good enough for the Vikings . . ."

"Wow."

"Nineteen-sixty-one Lyman," I tell him. "Twenty feet. It's the first thing my dad bought when he came into some money. He was just twenty years old. Can you imagine? Must have been nice, right? Bought her brand-new."

Nick admires the glossy teak and mahogany woodwork, the shiny fixtures and sleek trolling motor. "Unbelievable she still looks so good."

"She's had plenty of work done. Believe that."

"Yeah," he says. "Well, it shows."

I thank him and genuinely appreciate the admiration, because respect isn't always the reaction *My Lucia* gets. Nobody around here can stand it that I use my boat for its intended purpose — that I actually bring bait on board and let saltwater in — despite my attention to detail. Every year she is treated, sealed, varnished, and stored in ideal conditions, and every few years she gets some heavy-duty rework that wasn't in my budget but can't wait: a new engine or fuel valve, better bumpers or an upgraded GPS system or horn. Every bit of hardware, every windowpane, all of it gets the once-over and over again.

If I bought her at auction, it's quite possible that I'd take a different approach. If I'd hunted her down as an antique and entered her in shows and won blue ribbons, I'm sure I'd ban fish blood and guts, too. We have history, though, me and *My Lucia*. I spent my childhood fishing over her side on the opposite shore with my father, and although I mostly take her out for joyrides these days, I won't apologize for my utilitarian relationship with her. Father would either be proud or appalled at the love and maintenance I give his prized possession, but not the guys at this marina. They think I'm nuts. It may actually pain them to watch me load my rods and nets — which, truth be told, might be part of why I find it so satisfying. I do everything else a man is expected to do around here. Blue ribbons or casual judgments won't change this one thing.

Nick is finding places to stash my tackle box, cooler, fishing rods, and sundry crap: towels, sunscreen, hats, extra bottles of water that wouldn't fit in the cooler, extra snacks. I'm just about to ask what he's majoring in when he speaks first.

"So, your dad. He doesn't use the boat anymore, then?" A passive way of asking whether or not my father is still alive.

"No," I say. "My father died twenty years ago."

"Oh. I'm sorry." He doesn't know what to do with the bags of potato chips and pretzels in his hands until I point to the hutch up front. "My dad died when I was fourteen," he offers.

"Is that right?"

"Yeah."

"I'm sorry to hear that. Too young."

Over our shoulders, Jonah shouts, "Too young for what?" He looks rested, of course, and not at all bothered by his selfishness.

"Nice of you to join us," I say.

"You bet."

He wasn't raised this way — not by me, anyway — but I'm afraid this might be the real him. Maybe the thing that presented as depression for so long was actually his indifference to the rest of the world. On the upside, he's more confident and seems happy, which is better than walking around in a fog, I suppose, and boys will be boys.

I start the engine. Jonah unhitches the cleats and climbs aboard just as we pull away from the dock. Nick gets up to help, but his leg is asleep, and he nearly falls down, and I'm pretty sure I've wrangled the most useless crew in the bay.

"What prompted this family outing?" Jonah asks.

I adjust my sunglasses and steer out of our slip. "We thought it was a nice day for it. Isn't that right, Nick?" Nick agrees, I think, as we drift past other boats and other boaters, and everyone waves. Happy families. Lucky friends. Assholes who shit-talk my boat behind my back. Friendly strangers I'll never see again. They wave as we pass, and I nod or wave back. Once we clear the marina, I hit the gas and relax.

If my old man could see me now.

When we arrive at my most reliable cove, I distribute gear and fix my line and prepare to cast — but the boys are holding their rods like a couple of children playing with sticks, so I say to Jonah, "Don't tell me you've forgotten how to tie a lure."

He shrugs. "Had to make room in my brain for all of that valuable college crap, Dad."

"Give it to me." I hold out my hand, resigned and reluctant, and dig through my tackle box for another bucktail. "We should be able to catch some bluefish. Snapper aren't biting yet."

71

Jonah's doing something on his phone. Nick is shaking a rock from his shoe.

"You know, when I was a kid, I went fishing with my father every Sunday."

"Here we go again," Jonah moans.

"Oh, you've heard this before, have you?" I ask and toss him a Coke. His generation finds it cute to tease their fathers. I'd have gotten the belt for smarting off like that to mine.

"A million versions," he says. "We're not that weird, Dad. I don't know too many people our age who are big into fishing." He snickers.

I say, a bit too eagerly, "Nick fishes."

Jonah laughs. "No he doesn't."

We both look to Nick, who shrugs. "I mean, I've fished."

I force a grin. "Well, you sure did fool me. That pike story was convincing."

"Oh, I caught it. I did. That was when I was in Canada on this wilderness camp thing."

"Wilderness camp, huh?" I laugh.

Jonah glares at me.

"What?" I ask, still smiling. "I'm just saying, it's kind of nerdy. You seem a little old for camp in that photo, Nick."

"Jesus, Dad."

"It's okay," Nick says. "It's this, like,

72

outdoor program for grieving teens. My school did a fundraiser and sent me there when I was sixteen. I've gone back a couple of times to volunteer. Pass it on, you know? That photo was from last year's trip: my year of the fish." He laughs and gives up on his lure. "I hate to be a moron, but I think I may need some help with this, Dr. Hart."

He's sitting on his foot like a goddamn yogi again, and when he tries to stand and finds it numb, I lose patience and fetch his rod myself. Jonah is staring at me like I'm the one who killed Nick's parents. I busy myself tying ball bearings to monofilament.

"Well, that must have been something," I say. "Good for you." Having threaded the hook and tied a clinch knot, I dig in the cooler and crack a beer. "Your military school did that? Sent you there?"

Nick nods. "Mm-hm."

I return to my knots. When the lines are all prepped, we cast and wait. The water is calm and clear. Once or twice I think I feel a bite, but it's only the current. Only wishful thinking. Simply sitting here, though, watching my line pierce the water's surface and fade to black, I'm calmed. Connected. This is in my blood. I didn't come from a family of fishermen or oyster farmers like a lot of my friends did growing up. My father

73

worked the assembly line at Grumman building bomber planes, and then he got lucky with a freak promotion when his manager was crushed by heavy machinery. My father became a supervisor overnight. He became somebody, and he demanded I do the same. He'd take me out on his boat every Sunday and talk to me about work ethic and the value of a dollar. He made me tie my own lines. He made me a man. For this, I'm forever indebted to him.

Before he died, I did my best to return the favor. I flew him up to Alaska to go salmon fishing on the Kenai River. Vanessa was about halfway through her pregnancy with Jonah at the time. Bonding with my own father seemed appropriate. Everyone warned me that life would turn upside down once the baby arrived, so yes, it was a vacation, but it was also a way to honor my old man for all the fish that came before.

We caught nothing, not a single salmon — and not for lack of trying. Not for lack of salmon, either. They were running, all right, directly by our boat: hundreds, probably thousands of them. Most had turned from silver to red. Some pink, some burgundy, their bodies covered in white patches. We could have reached down and picked them up with our bare hands. Instead, we dangled our lines in turquoise water and watched the shoals swim past our impotent, sparkling lures, oblivious or disinterested or both. As it turned out, they weren't biting because they weren't hungry. They were too close to their spawning grounds and too close to death.

Those very fish, our guide explained, had been born in that very river. They'd hatched, then fled out to estuaries, then eased out to sea, where they'd eaten like kings. At last, they were returning home to complete the cycle, but this time, they could not pause to ease into the river, so they could not digest freshwater food. They'd eaten their last meal before starting the journey. Now their bodies were eating themselves.

This is why our spawning salmon had changed color. They were absorbing their own light-reflecting scales for spare nutrients, in turn stripping away their skin's protective film, in turn exposing them to fungal infections and exposing their flesh. "You see," said our guide, "they aren't turning that color. They're *revealing* that color." We were just seeing what had been there all along.

I guess I'd known a little about how salmon found their original spawning ground, how that was some kind of mystery or something. It's their sense of smell, I think. Maybe their own magnetic brains, I can't remember. I knew they swam upriver. I knew at least that much. I'd seen the inspirational posters and the *National Geographic* photos of hungry bears, but those photographers edit out the decay and demise. They do not show the luster caving in on itself, the flesh rotting on bone. Males will change shape. They'll grow humpbacks and fangs. Their bodies are preparing to fight to the death for their little zygotes, if that's what it takes.

Learning this made me sick to my stomach. I remember reeling in my line, wanting nothing to do with the hunt. My father — he responded differently. He cackled until he coughed up a mouthful of phlegm, which he spit into a handkerchief, which he then tucked back into his pocket. He looked me in the eye, and — I'll never forget it — he said, "That's fatherhood for you, Son. Turns the best of us into monsters."

Our guide backpedaled by explaining how most fish actually eat their young, which didn't exactly lighten the tone, but it did give me an excuse to look away from my father, who had succumbed to another coughing fit. He'd be dead from advanced chronic obstructive pulmonary disease in six months.

I'm not a monster.

I'm a good man and an excellent father, but I'm no sadomasochist, and I can call a spade a spade. Jonah is bored. Nick is uninterested. I'm tired of waiting. After a couple of hours, when it becomes clear that fish aren't willing to help the three of us bond, I give up and say, "Reel 'em in."

The boys don't hesitate. At least I tried. I raise my arm and wave back to the McAlister party waving at me from across the bay.

LUNA

Just when I think nothing will ever end this dreadfully boring story Lars Clyborne is telling and telling, Frank says, "There's Hart again," and lifts his arm in a mariner's greeting.

"Robert's son joined them after all," I say. "Handsome boys, aren't they?"

The women nod.

"Watch it, ladies," Frank says, and everyone laughs great big fake belly laughs, as if our wrinkled bodies are in terrible danger of being ravaged by young men. Bonnie is using her hand as a visor even though she's already wearing one. Monique is waving like she's just been crowned homecoming queen and this cruiser is her float in the parade.

"He's a weird guy," says Frank.

"You're a weird guy," I tell Frank. "We're all weirdos, and for your information, that boat is a collector's item. In some circles, it's a prize."

"Yeah," he says. "I know."

Bull. Frank McAlister is a numbskull who always has to *know* things, even when he doesn't. Nouveau-riche and full of shit. It's only a matter of time before Frank becomes the expert on boats like Robert's and tries to capitalize on his newfound wisdom.

Frank asks Lars, "Think we'd get a finder's fee if we hooked him up with a buyer for that boat? I might know a guy who would be interested —"

Well, what do you know? That didn't take long.

Bonnie starts in on her annoying habit of trying to protect the sanctity of her husband's precious *guy talk* with the *boys,* which means distracting chatty women, which today means complimenting my hair color, even though I bet she hates it — which is precisely why it's so fun to captivate her with banal details about highlights and lowlights and balayage, making her sorry for patronizing me so she won't do it again. I'm describing, in great detail, the way Alfonse massages my scalp during shampoo time, when Frank says, "How about a little something to eat?" At which point Bonnie jumps up and says to me, "Excuse me, sweetie. Duty calls."

I roll my eyes and volunteer to slice sau-

cisson and soppressata while Bonnie unwraps the brie. Monique devotes an obscene
level of care to arranging water crackers on
a tray like she's fanning a deck of tarot cards
— carbon copies of the same bland, beige
fortune — and I'm thinking *I'd kill* for a little
more wild in my life. Boredom's so bad for
the complexion.

A million hours later, we return to the marina to hug and kiss good-bye and make
empty promises to grab lunch next week so
we can laugh at each other's cute comments
about the weather. At last we part ways, and
I'm flooded with relief — but just as quickly,
my peace is surpassed by an oppressive fear
of being alone. These gaps between distractions are getting harder to bear every day. I
fill my ten-minute drive with NPR cranked
to max volume.

At home, I shout, "Darlings!" into an
empty foyer. My voice bounces off slate tile
and returns to me. "I'm back."

"We're on the patio!" Birgitta yells.

I kick off my shoes and slide my feet into
a pair of Ferragamo slippers by the door.
Our house smells like cardamom and sugar,
and I'm absolutely certain Birgitta will be
the death of me, but I grab a warm roll from
the kitchen anyway and head outside to

where my husband is lounging in a chaise beneath the wisteria. I say to his nurse, "Birgitta, you little cunt. You baked again."

She laughs. "I can't help myself, Luna."

"You'd better help yourself to half those cinnamon rolls or you'll make me fat and I'll end up with hip dysplasia, and I'm too damn young for a replacement, okay?"

She laughs again. I rest my hand on her shoulder, and we look at Graham, who laughs at the both of us, filling my heart just so he can wring it dry. "How was everything today?" I ask. "Did you two engage in acrobatic acts of sexual deviance while I was away?"

Graham smiles. My heart.

"Yes," Birgitta says. "Pulled a hamstring, broke a chandelier. I hope you don't mind."

"Not a problem." I wink.

Birgitta packs up books and tools that don't seem to be doing any good, and she pats Graham's hand and says, "Until tomorrow, sir." Then she's gone.

I tuck my sadness away and tell Graham, "I missed you today," kissing him lightly on the mouth, then the nose. "Frank McAlister was fanning his peacock feathers something terrible. He's too clumsy to even do vulgarity right. There was no one to make funny faces with but myself." I tear the roll in half

81

and hand the smaller piece to Graham. "This wisteria is going bonkers, isn't it?"

He grunts.

"Yes, I know it's poisonous, but our children are out of the house, so lighten up." I feed myself warm bread that feels like a warm hug from Birgitta, Graham's helper, my godsend. "Make room for me, would you?" I climb onto the chaise where Graham rests after he's exhausted himself practicing words. My husband, the genius who commanded a courtroom like no other — renowned as one of the most elegant and eloquent litigators in the whole state — is still struggling to master fricatives. How about that? He tries to wrap his fingers around my hand, but his grip is weak and uneven, so I squeeze back to distract us both from his loss of strength.

"We saw Robert Hart on his salty old boat. He'd taken out one of his son's friends, the most adorable boy. I'd say he's about twenty, twenty-one? He's just a doll, but good Lord if he didn't remind me of our Julian. He has that liquid quality to him. Do you know what I mean?"

Graham makes a sound. Birds chatter above us.

I look up and say, "They won't stop crapping on the patio furniture, but I can't bring myself to bother their nests. Russell thinks they're robins, but Birgitta swears she saw blue jays. Did you?"

He shakes his head.

"Me neither. I do miss the orioles." I can't remember when I stopped leaving quartered oranges in the window boxes — if it was before or after the orioles went away. "Russell says the rhododendron need to be cut all the way back to the quick. I hate to do it, but he's probably right."

Graham stares at our leggy shrubs, but he's not thinking about landscaping. He's thinking about his loss of authority. He has so much time now to think about everything he's lost. So do I, of course, but at least I get to run around hunting for hobbies and managing our lives. Graham just sits here ruminating on how he chose to live when he had choices. Not that he ever *chose* to prune the hedges, even then.

I measure my next words carefully. "J.R. Voss was out on the water, too."

Graham doesn't grunt or moan this time. Good. He's listening.

"Missy was with him," I say. "The kids, too. Monique went on and on about how brave Missy has been and how much stronger the Vosses are now. She said it's a blessing they're getting on with their lives." I

83

listen for Graham's heartbeat to hear if it's quickened, but the birds are too damn loud. "Do you know what Frank said? He said, 'All thanks to Graham.' Isn't that something? J.R.'s legacy is part of *your* legacy now, darling." I let that sink into Graham's damaged head before asking, "Aren't you proud of yourself?"

If Graham could speak, this is when he'd accuse me of being a smart-ass — but then, if he could speak, I wouldn't give two shits about the fate of J.R. Voss.

Voss versus That Girl.

Voss versus The Cops.

Victories on both counts, all thanks to my dear husband.

No, if Graham hadn't lost his verbal and fine motor skills last winter, those successes would be mere mile markers on our road toward retirement. Every lawsuit, whether nasty or righteous, was a means to our golden years, which should've been spent traveling the world, relaxing, dancing, eating oysters for breakfast and bonbons for dinner. Instead, stress and billable hours earned my husband an aneurism and me this. Lucky us. Now we have nothing *but* time to think about all of the shit we avoided before. Take, for example, J.R. Voss. Did we know he was an absolute squid who should've had his slimy tentacles chopped off and fed to sharks? Yes, sure. She was seventeen years old, that girl. *Seventeen.* She'd only just reached the age of consent. J.R. Voss is worse than chum, but where the law is concerned, chum is neutral. Chum has the right to an attorney, too, just as Graham and his firm have the right to be extraordinary.

The girl should have exercised her right to choose the same. This is what pisses me off. Her family hired that hack from heaven-knows-where, when what they *needed* was a firm like Graham's — not that my husband's loyalty was up for grabs. Graham doesn't even like J.R., but he favors him as an honorary member of some implied Brotherhood of Important People, so Graham took the case, drafted a nondisclosure, calculated the price of that girl's silence — a mere morality tax for J.R. that must've seemed like a fortune to her — and made a deal. She deserved a lawyer with enough confidence to refuse the offer and enough experience to warn her of how it would feel to stand in front of cameras and recite lines scripted by one of Graham's minions: "I misrepresented the relationship between myself and Mr. Voss. He never touched me inappropriately. I lied, and I am embarrassed and deeply sorry to Mr. Voss and his family for the damage that I've caused."

I watched the press conference in real time that day and told myself, *This is part of the job.* And, *Graham represents the law, not the person.* And, *Two words: early retirement.* People scoop actual shit at the zoo. People clean shit from airplane bathrooms and hospital bedpans. Those are *real* jobs people do so they can make a buck and get on with their lives.

At least we never scooped shit.

It's not our fault the girl hired a nimrod attorney, and I am not sorry that Graham is excellent at his job.

Was excellent.

Was a lot of things. Not anymore.

Thanks to my husband, people didn't just forgive J.R., they groveled. Acquaintances scrambled to offer testimonials of unwavering faith, even though they were the very same gossips who'd said, *You know, I always thought there was something off about that guy,* when they first read the headline: "PROMINENT LOCAL ACCUSED OF SEXUALLY ASSAULTING TEEN BABYSITTER." Oh, their faith had wavered all right.

J.R. surprised us all with his arrogance, though. Spectacular show. Went on a crusade against the police department, threatening to sue for defamation but winning in the all-important Court of Public Approval before filing the suit, which was only ever a bluff anyway. Such a claim would have been dismissed out of hand.

As for Mrs. Missy Voss — well, she's just enough of a dolt to tolerate him, but smart enough to make it work in her favor. She gets sympathy now and recently treated herself to a week in Rome, "just to get away." People called it self-care, but Missy Voss doesn't get my sympathy. She's getting my vacations, isn't that enough? I'm the one who should be gorging myself on antipasto in Trastevere with the love of my life. I did *everything* right. I married a good man who did *not* sexually assault our teenage baby-sitter, yet somehow I'm the one who's being punished. The universe is a cunning little bitch.

"These rolls smell like India, don't they?" I ask Graham, encouraging him to dwell on the past, too. We had so much power and freedom. We had *fun.* "They remind me of Sri Lanka as well, but Birgitta says the recipe is from family of hers in Norway. Isn't that something? They're heavenly, aren't they?" I stroke Graham's face, thinking, *Fuck you, darling.*

Ah, there it is, the pesky bastard: a recurring thought molded into a vice. My secret habit. I take another hit: *Fuck you, sweetheart,* for becoming a different person overnight, for smoking cigars and working too hard and eating too much red meat, for going to the doctor once a year instead of twice, for not keeping a cell phone in your pocket, for not considering how a disaster might affect me, your wife, the woman who tolerated your endless hours at the office because you promised me — you *promised* — it would all pay off right about now. I'll keep loving you, of course, but now you've forced me to hate you, too, so I'll keep loving you and hating you under my skin, forever and ever. Forgive me, my darling. I really am doing my best.

"Are you ready for a little supper?" I ask aloud.

He makes a sound.

"Good." I stand and help him rise to his feet. "Let's fire up the grill."

5.

Elizabeth is slicing lemons and adding fresh tarragon to homemade tartar sauce when we return. Four empty wineglasses are arranged neatly by the sink. Music I recognize but can't identify plays through speakers professionally hidden throughout our house.

"This sounds familiar," I say as Elizabeth kisses me on the cheek. She kisses the boys on their cheeks, too. "It's from a movie?"

"Dvořák," says Nick. "New World Symphony."

Jonah dumps his gear by the door and takes off his shoes. "I'm telling you. This guy is a walking Wikipedia."

Nick shakes his head. "Nah. I just know a little about a lot."

This guy.

"Well?" Elizabeth covers the bowl with plastic wrap and hands it to me. "How'd it go?"

"It was fun." I open the fridge and clear space.

"We caught nothing," Jonah tells her.

Elizabeth seems genuinely distraught. Charming and ridiculous. "Nothing at all?"

Jonah is all too happy to confirm: "Zilch."

"Were they biting?"

"Nope."

"Yes they were," I insist.

"Nuh-uh."

"Maybe not for you, but I had a few bites."

"Sure you did, Dad," Jonah says, and Elizabeth and Nick laugh, ruling his comment cute rather than disrespectful. I flick Jonah's ear — cute — and he claps a hand to the side of his face. "Ouch. Jesus, Dad."

"Robert," Elizabeth says, turning my name into a threat.

I wink at Nick, forcing him to take my side, forcing him to see that I'm not a punch line in this house. He smiles politely.

"Well," says Elizabeth, "I thought we could fry up whatever you caught and have fish tacos for dinner, but now we have an excuse to get pizza."

"Tacos sound good," I say.

"Let's get pizza," says Elizabeth, who never craves pizza.

Jonah's already casting his vote. "Cheese for me."

"Nick?" she asks.

"I'll eat whatever."

"Robert?"

I give in. What the hell. "Sausage and olive. I'll pick it up."

Elizabeth nods. "White with parsley for me." She seems to be suggesting I should place the order, too. She hands me a corkscrew. "Would you crack open a red?"

I choose to interpret her requests as deference, not demand. She trusts my taste. She ought to. It's hard to tell, though, if I'd have placed deference and demand on weighted scales if Nick weren't here watching. There seems to be something about the extra set of eyes — his particular set of extra eyes — that rattles our resting state, as though we are all engaged in performance art, knowingly or otherwise. Subtle and reckless performance: improvisation directed by our guest, who doubles as an audience of one. There are things we can say without reproach when Nick's in the room. Other things get cut from the scene. There's this tone Elizabeth is taking — not just of authority, but of ownership, so resolute — that feels enhanced, amped up for show. Jonah's reserve reads as swagger when Nick's around, and somehow, I fetch things. I become not the man of the house, but its manservant. How strange.

Last night, in this very kitchen, we were straightening bow ties and raising martini glasses, preparing to attend a gala honoring me and only me. People sang my praises to thunderous applause. Twelve hours ago, I was giving my wife the best orgasm of her life. I'd like to think my loved ones weren't just toasting me because the city deemed me special, that Elizabeth would want me even if she wasn't obligated by matrimony. I'd like to believe we don't need outside entities to validate our love or worth. We don't need an audience to be our best.

And yet.

I observe the small adjustments being made on account of our guest. Jonah is setting the table without being asked. He's setting it because Nick started it, and now Elizabeth is wiping down placemats we hardly ever use. I seem to be the only one immune to Nick's charms. *Charms,* like magic. Maybe dark arts, maybe not. Either way, it isn't cute, even though the table does look nice. Even though my wife and child are intoxicated and delighted. Even though. I feel like the only sober guy at the bar after midnight, watching people feel sexier and smarter and stronger than they are, right before the embarrassments begin.

Elizabeth waves her hand in front of my face and says, "Earth to Robert."

I blink away the blur.

"Wine, please?" she asks with a smile.

The line at Bella Torta is obscene. I guess no one cooks on Sundays anymore. It takes fifteen minutes just to place my order for one regular pie and one with half sausage and olive, half white with parsley.

"We can only divide white pizzas with other white pizzas," the cashier tells me.

"It doesn't have to be perfect." I lean toward her and say, "My wife can handle sauce."

"Sir," she drones on, "we can only divide white pizzas with other white pizzas."

"I'll pay extra. That's fine."

"I'm sorry, sir, but you're going to have to place an order for a pizza we make, or you'll need to step aside and let this gentleman go."

I turn around. The big guy invading my space says, "No worries, man. Take your time." He sounds sincere, but the line threads through the door and along the front window, so I study a menu hanging overhead and settle on one white pie with parsley and a regular pie, half cheese, half sausage and olive. I decline the girl's attempt to upsell me garlic knots and drinks.

Half an hour passes before the cook calls my name, so there's no escape when Ben Walters targets me for small talk. He seems to think I care about what went down at the last homeowners' association meeting, and about how he, as treasurer, proposed a revised landscaping budget that does not include Fraser firs.

When he finally takes a breath, I jump in. "Hey, quick heads-up. Jonah has a house-guest with volume control issues. If you guys get a noise complaint from our neighbors, just know that I'm already on it. Apologies in advance."

"You talking about Nick?" Ben asks.

I unclench my jaw to say, "Yeah. Am I too late?"

"Nah," he says. "Good kid. Met him at the market with Elizabeth the other day. He doesn't seem like trouble."

"It's always the quiet ones, isn't it?" I say.

"Quiet or noisy, which is it?" Ben belly laughs and smacks my arm. "Don't worry about it. Your stick-up-their-ass neighbors could use a little shake-up, frankly." With that, Ben returns to his favorite subject: arborist fees. Only when the kitchen calls my name do I excuse myself to ask for extra Parmesan and red pepper flakes, fleeing

94

with greasy boxes and insight into evergreen growth. By the time I pull into the driveway at home, a full hour has passed. Jonah's truck isn't on the street.

I enter the house unnoticed. The Beatles are blaring, so Elizabeth and Nick can't hear me over "Norwegian Wood." They don't know to jump or squeal or separate themselves. They're tangled up in each other, literally waltzing around the living room. She's holding eye contact with Nick, who's bobbing his head to the music's tempo, going, "*One*-two-three, *one*-two-three, *one*-two-*now-twirl*-two-three . . ."

They get jumbled, lose count, and laugh their heads off. I would slow clap if I wasn't hand-delivering their dinner. Instead, I clear my throat and make a joke. "Well, well. I run out for pizza and look what happens."

Nick, still laughing, offers to help me with the boxes.

"I've got it," I say.

"Elizabeth was just teaching me how to dance. I'm not very good."

"No," I agree. "Not very."

Elizabeth adjusts the stereo volume and catches her breath but doesn't look my way.

"I was so awkward on the dance floor the other night," Nick explains. "I thought I'd get some tips from a pro while I can."

I laugh. "Yeah, Elizabeth is some pro."

The front door opens and closes, and Jonah enters with a grocery bag full of fixings for banana splits: Reddi-wip, Magic Shell, crushed peanuts, M&Ms, bananas. He drops his bags and flips open the pizza boxes. "Really, Dad? Four pieces of cheese seemed like enough?"

"They couldn't split white with sauce," I try to explain — but Nick is quietly defending me by helping himself to Elizabeth's pie.

"The cheese is all yours," he tells Jonah. To me, he says, "My dad used to make white pizza. I love this stuff."

We avoid acknowledging Nick's dead dad, but Elizabeth does give Nick a tender smile.

We load up our plates and sit at the table to stuff our faces and talk with our mouths full. I try the white pizza just for kicks and hate to admit (to myself) that it's the best of the three. We talk and tell stories, and when we've made ourselves sick to our stomachs, we stretch and sigh, then gnaw on crust to ensure our misery.

Nick finds us charming, I guess, because he suddenly gets precious about the dinner and the day. "You guys are lucky to have what you have. I never got to go fishing with my dad. I don't even know if my mom ever fished."

I can't stand to ignore him again — to pretend like he's not desperate to talk about them — so I ask, "And how did they die, Nick?"

Jonah drops his fork. Elizabeth closes her eyes.

Nick doesn't do drama, though, which I respect. "My mom had ALS," he tells me, matter-of-fact. "It was long. It was awful. Wore my dad down. He killed himself two months after she died."

"Oh God," Elizabeth says, bringing her hand to her chest. "I'm so sorry, Nick."

"Thanks," he says. "In a way, it's almost romantic, I guess. Maybe I just tell myself that to cope. But they really loved each other. I think they couldn't live without each other."

Elizabeth clutches Nick's hand and keeps holding it on the table. When no one else takes the bait, I finally ask. "How did he do it?"

"*Jesus,* Dad."

"He put a gun in his mouth," Nick tells me. "Shot himself in the head."

"Oh, Nick. We don't have to talk about this," says Elizabeth. "I'm so sorry."

I understand that my wife and son find me brash — their dirty looks make this obvious — but Nick has mentioned his dead

97

parents so many times. He was practically begging to be asked. Plus, I'm trying to make an effort here. Isn't that what Jonah and Elizabeth want? They have a point, too. It's weird to have seen his face for so long without knowing him.

"Well, I'm sorry you had to go through that, Nick," I say. "I'm sorry you lost them so early."

"Me too," he says.

Elizabeth lets go of Nick's hands and clasps her own. She gets a bright idea and asks, "What are you doing for the rest of the summer?"

"I'm not sure," Nick tells her. "Bum around campus, I guess. Still need to find a job, but I bet Parks and Rec. will take me back."

Elizabeth shakes her head. "Why don't you stay here? Give yourself a break, hang with Jonah, *enjoy* yourself."

I chew harder.

"Yeah," Jonah echoes. "Why don't you?"

All eyes are on Nick, who shakes his head in a sheepish *I couldn't possibly* sort of way. He holds up a finger and swallows his food before saying, "Oh my God. Thank you, but I'm afraid you'd get sick of me so fast."

Elizabeth is on a tear. "No, we really wouldn't. You'd keep the guesthouse. We all

98

get our own space. It's ideal."

Nick wrinkles his face.

Jonah says, "Dude, do it."

After a moment of apprehension, Nick asks, "Really?"

"Of course," Elizabeth answers. She can't stop. "You'd be doing us a favor. Really. We need someone to keep the cobwebs away, don't we, Robert?"

I'm speechless, truly, because for starters, we already have someone to keep the cobwebs away, and she comes every Tuesday. Moreover, however, I am aghast at her gall. Didn't we just argue about the importance of running joint decisions by each other? Handing out alarm codes is one thing. Handing out long-term invitations is another altogether.

"Awesome, Dad," Jonah deadpans. "Thanks for the vote."

I find my voice. "I don't want you to feel pressured, Nick. These two drive a hard bargain."

Elizabeth glares through her wineglass as she throws back its last sip.

"I don't feel pressured at all," Nick says. "I'm overwhelmed in a good way, actually."

To this, Elizabeth lifts her brow and tilts her head as silent code for, *See, Bobby?*

"You've all been so generous," Nick says.

"Like, from the start, you've gone above and beyond. I hope you know how much I appreciate everything."

"Yeah, yeah," says Jonah. "But are you staying?"

"If you really, really mean it, I would love to stay."

Elizabeth grins. "We really do."

Jonah says, "Right on."

Nick looks to me now, waiting for my blessing, I guess. "Dr. Hart? You're sure I wouldn't be putting you out?"

My answer is coming, it really is, but Elizabeth gets there first. "Not another word, Nick," she says. "We're thrilled to have you. Aren't we, Robert?" She digs her foot into mine under the table.

"Thrilled," I say, wincing. "Just thrilled."

Elizabeth is already up and clearing plates. "Who wants dessert?"

The boys rise to help her make sundaes and plans.

After dinner, once again, I'm read the riot act behind a closed door. Elizabeth takes a hot shower to cool off, but she's still seething when she crawls into bed with a towel twisted around her head. I let her stir until she finally asks, "What the hell was that?"

"What are you talking about?"

100

"For Christ's sake, Bobby. You just behaved abominably to a guest in our home, and you want to know what I'm talking about?"

"Yeah," I demand, because there's no backtracking now. "I do."

"Everyone was uncomfortable — and I'd like to say, 'except for you,' or to believe you truly didn't notice, but only an asshole could be so oblivious, so either you're an asshole or you're a jerk. Neither possibility is particularly appealing. That's what I'm talking about."

"You can't turn my house into a hostel without including me in the decision, then expect me not to care."

Her chill redirects our storm, pointing now to my bigger error — a mistake already expanding, already overtaking any sound argument I might have made tonight. One singular possessive pronoun, one little word misfired, and I'm screwed. "*Your* house?" she asks.

"You know what I meant." But the damage is done.

"Well, I guess you meant *your* house, not ours."

"Lizzie," I say, "knock it off."

"Don't call me that." She holds up her hands and steps away when I reach for her.

"Don't touch me, Robert."

"It's our house. It's your house as much as mine, you know that."

"Great. Then you won't mind sharing *our* guesthouse with an orphan who happens to be your son's best friend. The place will be empty all summer. Nobody's using it. Did you not hear him say how much this means to him? Where is the problem?"

"Okay." I aim low. "Do you want to know my problem with him?"

"I'm sure you're going to —"

"I don't like him bringing drugs into this house."

Elizabeth laughs, dismissing me entirely. "What makes you think he brought drugs?"

"I saw them. I watched Jonah leave the guesthouse in a marijuana haze last night."

With an unnatural calm, she asks, "What do you mean, you watched him?"

"I was sitting by the pool. I watched him stumble out of a hot-box and sneak inside."

"You were spying on them?"

"No, Elizabeth. I wasn't spying on them."

"Did you say something to him? Did he know you were there?"

"No. I had nothing to say."

"So you just sat there quietly watching him?"

"Actually, I was doing my own thing when

he invaded *my* quiet —"

"You were spying on him."

"No. Does it not bother you that he brought drugs into our home?" My intentional use of the plural possessive only agitates Elizabeth more.

"As if you never brought grass into the house, give me a break."

"It's not his house, Elizabeth."

"What makes you so sure it wasn't Jonah's pot?"

"I can't believe this," I snap, and she shushes me, so I take a deep breath and lower my voice before asking, "Are you really protecting that boy, Elizabeth?"

"No. I'm just asking: How do you know?"

"Why are you so defensive of him?"

"Why are you so dismissive?"

"Because I don't like the way he looks at you," I say.

Elizabeth squints, tightens her lips and says, "Well I do," then turns off the light and rolls over without saying good night.

6.

I hear white water rapids before opening my eyes, before realizing it's only the shower, before realizing Elizabeth is in it. Her side of the bed is a knot of cold blankets. She never wakes up before I do. And didn't she shower last night? And when did she get out of bed, anyway?

She'd want me to say good-bye, to shout that I love her, even if she's shaving her legs or has shampoo in her eyes, but I'm not crazy about the way her vanishing acts outweigh mine these days, so I'll reclaim balance where I can get it. I brush my teeth downstairs with a spare Sonicare, waiting for her to call my name, to wonder where I am for a change, but her water is still running upstairs when I'm done, so I exit without saying good-bye, flipping the switch to open our garage door — but something stops me from leaving. It's an urge, and the urge is ridiculous, but my instincts are screaming, telling me no harm could come from putting distance between Nick and Elizabeth today. He ought to have the freedom to flirt with someone his own age, and she needs the space to snap out of it, whatever it is. I recall my offer to drop Nick at the beach before work. He'd said that sounded great.

So I close the garage door and backtrack through the house, following my own footsteps past the pool, across the yard, and out to the guesthouse, where the muffled sounds of string instruments float through. I say, "Nick?" and knock three times, then three again. I allow a few moments, expecting a shadow to appear behind the glass, but he does not answer, no shadows emerge, and so I twist the doorknob. The entrance to a house on my property is unlocked. That's permission enough. "Nick," I repeat, "I'm coming in."

Sunlight pours through sheer curtains, spinning a honey-colored womb around me. Violins trail off to silence. A public radio announcer details the anatomy of the next song — a fugue by some nineteenth-century German composer who never fully recovered from a childhood bout of scarlet fever, blah-blah-blah. I enter the room and assess the scene. Japanese picture books on his nightstand. Two empty water glasses.

Two glasses.

"Nick," I say quietly. "You in here?"

The bed is unmade. Pillows on the floor. On the coffee table across the room, his laptop is closed and charging. Next to it are empty beer bottles and a wrinkled *Outside* magazine. The dishes are clean, balanced vertically in a wire rack. There are no crumbs on the Formica, no bad habits in plain sight. I call out again for Nick as I move toward the hall closet, cracking it just enough to scan the empty shelves, bare hangers, the T-shirts and plaid shirts spilling from an open duffle bag. The door at the end of the hall is closed. When I open it, a night-light sets the tile aglow.

The bathroom smells of fresh mold. The source is apparent: six glass cubes filled with white flowers — six vases full of cloudy water that's already begun to stink — aligned along the countertop against the mirrored wall. Bruised and broken petals have started falling from sturdy stems. Elizabeth must have gifted him half of Luna's expired arrangements.

"Nick?" I say, but I say it softly and mindlessly. He isn't here. I shouldn't be here. But again, it's my house — the one place on this planet that belongs to me. The wastebasket is full of wadded Kleenex, magazine subscription cards, empty soap packaging. He's a Nivea fan, apparently. I don't even know what I'm doing here. I don't know what I hope to accomplish by opening the shower door and crouching low and inspecting the drain, looking for — what? What am I doing? Looking for Elizabeth's hair, I guess, like I'm some kind of Perry Mason. The German song commences its irritating first few measures, and I check myself. *Enough.*

Nick's voice echoes in this empty shower stall. "Dr. Hart?"

I don't react. For several long seconds, I continue to kneel without spinning around. He's been standing there how long? That sickly composer must have intercepted my radar. I rise and wipe my hands on my suit pants, as though they were Carhartt coveralls and I'm the handyman. "Nick," I say.

He's wearing gym clothes and standing in the doorway with his fingers laced behind his head. He's blocking my exit. Power move. "Is everything okay?"

"Oh, fine." I shimmy past him, past his sweat smell. "Where have you been?"

"Went for a run," he says, following me. "Like to knock it out before it gets too hot."

"You are a go-getter, aren't you?"

He snickers. So cocky, so cool, so transparent. I'm embarrassed for him and would just as soon leave and never acknowledge this whole run-in, but Nick asks, "Is there something wrong with the shower?"

"No," I say. "Thought there might be, but it turns out everything is fine."

"Oh." He shadows me into his messy room. "Well, that's good."

I step outside, but the power line connecting my brain to my feet misfires, bringing my whole self to a halt. I wasn't prepared to see Elizabeth tiptoeing toward us like she is. Her head is down. Her feet are bare. She's wearing short shorts with the elastic waistband rolled down and that sweatshirt that hangs off her shoulder, no bra. Again. She's too busy sidestepping twigs and anthills to have noticed me standing here yet, because when she looks up and sees me and not Nick in the doorframe, her body jerks. Her face falls, and yet, her face looks neat. Her hair is wet, water dripping down her neck. Her lips shine pink.

"Robert," she says. "I thought you'd left."

"Good morning," Nick says from over my shoulder.

Elizabeth shakes her confusion and smiles past me. "Morning, Nick."

"Are you wearing makeup?" I ask her.

"No, Robert," she lies.

"Really? Because it looks like you're wearing makeup." I'm as mortified for myself as for her, but if I resist holding her accountable for these shameless appeals for attention, she'll keep right on humiliating herself, and I value my respect for her too much to let it go.

"Oh my God. You're being such a weirdo."

"Well then," I say, biting back the rest, "I'm off to work." I smile at the both of them and leave my wife, barefoot and blushing, alone with sweaty Nick.

"I'm grilling branzino tonight," she shouts after me. "You'll be home early?"

"Barring catastrophe," I say without turning.

I trudge through the grass as though swimming in gelatin — trying to eavesdrop or make sense of what I saw — and still I'm haunted by a maxim that made the rounds back in medical school: *when you hear hoofbeats, think horses, not zebras.* The most obvious, reasonable diagnosis is the best place to start. I don't want to encourage my first instinct, but it would be irresponsible to deny it. The most obvious, reasonable conclusion I first drew is that Elizabeth got all prettied up and snuck over to visit Nick when she thought I was gone, because for whatever reason, Nick has an effect on her. She likes his attention. He likes hers. My stomach turns.

So that's my first impression, but there's a whole swarm of sensible alternatives. It's possible, more likely even, that Nick needed directions or advice or assistance with some domestic thing, and I should favor these possibilities, as I'd much prefer to see my wife for the woman I love and trust and value unequivocally than to see her as the other thing. We vowed to protect each other, to put each other first, to honor each other, and Elizabeth is principled and worthy of me, so why would I make her my enemy? She's getting attention from a boy who doesn't know better. Nick's foolishness is not my Lizzie's fault.

On my drive to work, I decide that my first instincts were zebras after all. I went to bed angry. I woke up late. By the time I get to the office, my anxiety has faded. There are no stampedes, just a bad night's sleep.

"Morning, Doctor," Simone says when I walk in the door. She stifles a knowing smile, the type born of poorly kept secrets.

"Morning."

"You see the paper yet? No? Never read your own press, huh?"

"Something like that." The last time I got

110

local press, it was for an architecture thing by that uppity historian who published images of our widow's walk on the front page, making our roof look like a charming gazebo aimed toward the sea — a proper pagoda — rather than a pile of rotting wood and peeling paint. I have a theory that all that hoopla in the press was orchestrated just to shame me into renovating. I'd been talking to the HOA about razing the roof. Now I'm stuck with an antique exterior. So no, I don't read my own press anymore.

Simone hands me my Americano and pops out of her swivel chair so she can follow me to the staff lounge.

"They say anything nice?" I ask.

"See for yourself." On the large round table in the middle of the room, a dramatic bouquet spills out like a fountain: tiger lilies, alstroemeria, eucalyptus, lisianthus.

"Strange arrangement," I say.

"I think it's beautiful."

"Big enough. Who's it from?"

Simone shrugs. "No card."

"When was it delivered?"

She shakes her head, unreasonably delighted. "I don't know any florists who deliver before seven in the morning — and I was on time today. Scout's honor." She holds up three fingers in the *okay* gesture, which I'm pretty sure is not the Girl Scout pledge. "They were sitting by the back entrance when I got in."

"Probably the foundation or something," I say. "Or the city. Who knows." I've already shifted focus to the local newspaper displayed beside the vase. I blow pollen from the front page.

"That's poisonous to cats, you know."

"Hm?" There I am above the fold, dancing to "Lady in Red" and being kissed on the mouth by my wife.

"Lilies," she's saying. "Lily pollen will kill a cat."

The headline: "CITY TOASTS CITIZEN OF THE YEAR: DR. ROBERT HART."

"So sad. Good thing we don't have cats in the office, huh?" She laughs and pats me on the shoulder. "Congratulations again."

"Thanks, Simone," I say without taking my eyes off the paper. At the bottom of the front page is a full-color picture of my family, which would be a point of pride had some idiot editor not chosen the shot with Nick as our surrogate son.

"Oh," Simone says, pivoting to face me. "Forgot to tell you: I think I found your diamonds."

"Hm?" I didn't know I'd lost any diamonds.

112

"The anniversary diamonds? There's a gorgeous pair of earrings at Jamison's Jewelers across town. You need to go look at them when you can. Wes is expecting you."

"Oh." I glance back and forth between Simone, so eager to please, and this photograph that feels threatening, somehow. On the front page of newspapers distributed all over town, my wife's fingers grip the shoulder of a boy who is not my son. That boy's arm cradles Elizabeth's waist. A terrible chill rises up the back of my neck, and I finally give Simone my full attention. "You know what? Maybe diamonds are too showy after all. She wanted tin. Let's give her tin."

Now it's Simone's turn for suspicion. "Are you serious?"

"Dead serious." I leave the newspaper on the table. It can wait. There's work to do now, patients to see, a reputation to live up to. "If anyone can track down an elegant piece of aluminum, it's you, Ms. Bristol."

She beams with the satisfaction of knowing her role is essential in my life, and it is. "Okay. I'll let Wes Jamison know you changed your mind. Aluminum it is."

I turn my back on poisonous lilies and the photograph actively etching itself in my mind.

Simone hands me a leather-bound iPad

with a clipboard on its case. "Jeremy Levy will be in soon for his seven thirty," she tells me. "Acid reflux and Botox."

7.

I swab my last throat culture of the day and hang my white coat on a hook. Simone is organizing the front desk.

"You almost out of here?" I ask.

She smiles and taps her pen on a stack of insurance forms. "Soon."

I shake my head slowly and smile: a proud father figure enjoying the glory of his influence. "Simone, you're too good."

"Oh, come on," she says.

"I'm serious. You're the best."

She spins in her desk chair, a sort of victory lap. "You're welcome."

I laugh. "Thank you. Don't stay too late, okay?"

She is smiling when she turns back to her pile of papers. "Good night, Dr. Hart."

"Night, sweetheart," I say, cringing before the word has fully left my mouth. *Sweetheart?* Really, Robert?

I bolt before Simone can give me shit.

Once outside, I return to myself. The sun is still bright and high in the sky. There's plenty of time between now and branzino. I call Elizabeth to ask if there's anything she needs from the store, and she requests onions, lemon thyme, and crusty bread. I select overpriced herbs in excessive packaging and nearly stop for rainbow cake displayed behind glass in the bakery, but it kills me to give second-rate cake a second glance. Tabloids and travel magazines line the checkout aisle. The local paper is not on display. Not that I need extra copies. I'd bet money our neighbors will bring theirs to the house, if they haven't already. Lizzie's friends, the few she has, might clip the front page and send it in the mail. That's what women do around here. With fine-point Sharpie pens, they draw arrows and write *Bravo!* or *Fabulous night!* on monogrammed sticky notes affixed next to people's photos. They'll draw a big black heart around our kissing picture, maybe, and obscure the article by writing, *King AND Queen of the night!* Or not.

The rage I managed to contain throughout my workday comes trickling back before flooding, full force. In my mind, I see Nick's hand on Elizabeth's waist. I hear her saying, *Don't you think it's cruel to make him*

116

watch us . . . ? How can someone so smart be so clueless?

She's expecting lemon thyme, but we won't be eating for another few hours. Thyme can wait. So can Elizabeth. My de-escalation is in everyone's best interest. There's not a soul in Sag Harbor I can call — not one good friend or mild acquaintance who could lend an ear without clanging the gossip chain — so I call my one good friend and mild acquaintance not in Sag.

Ray picks up on the first ring. "Hey, buddy," he says.

"Raymond."

"Sorry I pulled an Irish exit the other night. Couldn't get through the pack of groupies riding your dick."

"No groupies. Just a bunch of bums angling for free medical advice."

"Right, right."

I called for a very particular reason, but my concerns get stuck in my throat.

"So what's up, man?" he asks. "Did I run out on my bill or something?"

"Don't be a jerk. I called to say thanks for coming."

"Yeah, sure. You're welcome."

"Thought maybe you'd want to grab a drink after work. We hardly got a chance to catch up at that thing."

"Tonight?"

"If you're free."

"You in the neighborhood or something?"

"No, but I could be in" — I check my watch: four o'clock; traffic is a gamble, but I feel like gambling, so — "an hour fifteen."

"Real thirsty, aren't you?"

I don't reply.

"Yeah, sure," he says. "Bar None at five thirty?"

I do the math. We'd get half an hour, maybe an hour, to hang. Even if there's traffic, I'll still be back well before eight, just in time for fish and rosé. "That'll work."

"I can't stay long. Bianca's got some field hockey thing at six thirty, just a scrimmage, but I promised I'd go." He pauses before asking, "You okay, Bobby?"

"Yeah, of course."

"All right," he repeats. "See you then."

I exit the Citarella parking lot and head south, passing through Bridgehampton, driving into sun glare as I merge onto Sunrise Highway. Strange how time doesn't translate from city to space. In the city, I'd think nothing of budgeting an hour to hop from place to place. Manhattan is only thirteen miles long, two miles wide. The length of its hour is proportionate to its distance. This sixty-mile drive from Bridgehampton to West Babylon, while still only an hour, is a trip, not a night out.

The trip is worth taking this evening, and the drive is especially easy. No traffic, which is unusual. No construction. No complaints. When I get off on Livingston Avenue, I'm a little early, so because it's right here, right in front of me, I turn directly into North Babylon Cemetery and pull up to a spot alongside the service road. The perspective is achingly familiar, although I haven't visited in almost a decade. The shape of the shade below the trees has hardly changed. My mother's tombstone stands tall between a pair of dwarf spruce invaded by Virginia creeper. The granite shines. Nobody brings flowers to her grave.

I was nine years old when my mother died. Colorectal cancer. We were both too young for her passing. I didn't even know how to dress myself yet. I wanted to wear my blue sailor suit to her funeral. She'd loved those navy trousers and the matching jacket with white piping. I loved them, too, because when my mother dressed me for special occasions, she would squat low to the ground and tie a white silk ascot around my neck, and I would stare at her staring at the perfect knot between her fingers, and I could see up close how much she loved me.

She smelled like black licorice and a leathery fragrance I now know to have been Hermès Doblis, which was discontinued ages ago. I once paid two hundred dollars for the dredges in an ancient bottle, having caught a faint whiff of childhood coming from some lady in a Marriott elevator. I forked over the cash right then and there and gave her instructions on where to leave the bottle after she'd retrieved it from her room. A bellman delivered it to my suite that evening. With the door closed, the world locked out, I popped the cork on that tiny glass vessel with its gold stickers and purple velvet bow, and I breathed in those final drops, breathed them in and in again until nausea knocked me to my knees. I barely made it to the toilet before vomiting up my tuna-and-rye from the conference buffet. The Doblis went in the trash. I haven't smelled childhood since.

That sailor suit. It didn't fit. I guess it had been a while since my mother had played dress-up with me. Two days before the funeral, my father walked in on me struggling to button the double-breasted coat. With zero affect, he said, "Take it off. You're too big for that now."

I knew exactly what he meant by *that*. He meant the darling outfits my mother loved so much. He meant the little-boyness she treasured. I remember looking in the full-length mirror and seeing for the first time what my father must have seen all along, made even more cloying by a recent growth spurt. The gold buttons on my suit barely stretched to their buttonholes. The cuffs on my sleeves and pants rode high above my wrists and ankles. I looked like a boy wearing doll's clothes. I looked like a twit.

The next day, my father cut the tags off a brand-new Brooks Brothers suit that was slightly too big on my nine-year-old frame, and still it was nicer than any suit he would ever own in all his life. "You'll grow into it," he said upon inspection. With the rare nod of approval, he added, "Wear that to the service."

I did.

After the burial — after prayers and processions, quiet whimpers from strangers, booming wails from Nona — my father lit a cigarette and told me and only me, "Beautiful or faithful: You can never have both."

"Who?" I asked, or maybe, "What?"

"Women," he explained. "They can either be beautiful or faithful." He pointed at my face with two fingers and the cigarette clamped between them. Ash floated from his hand like sparks from a tiny gray firework. "Do you understand, Robert?"

I nodded.

Recognizing, perhaps, that I was still a child who might not grasp this key message without cementing it in the cornerstone of my psyche, he said, "Someday, God willing, you'll be sharp enough to pick a wife of your own. She will either be beautiful, or she will be faithful. Do you know what faithful means, Son?"

I nodded, thinking of churchgoers worshipping on Palm Sunday.

"Good. So that's your choice."

Strangers patted me on my shoulder as we walked toward a parade of cars with little orange flags clipped to antennae. When my father finished smoking, he let me stomp on his glowing Kent cigarette butt. I twisted my shoe into the gravel until he said, "That's enough."

We climbed into the limousine and the driver closed the door. Only then did I finally ask, "Which one was Mom?"

My father brushed a flake of ash from his lapel and cracked a smile that turned into a sneer. "Oh, she was beautiful all right." Staring through a tinted window toward the canopied burial plot, a tender grin lingered on his face. "She was one hell of a beautiful woman."

From this, I deduced that my mother must have been faithless, and so I reasoned — and for a long time believed — that Father was breaking the news that Mom would not be admitted to heaven after all. The preacher had been so cocky, so sure. But then, what do preachers know about women? Then again, what did I? My mother hadn't lived long enough to explain birds and bees and intercourse and the like. It would be three years before I found a cozy corner in my father's storage shed where I could masturbate to my stepmother's Victoria's Secret catalogs. It would be two years after that before I'd secure my first girlfriend. Infidelity, as a concept, didn't even exist for me yet.

While I may have missed the intended point of my father's lesson in the limo, his lesson wasn't futile, because I wasn't clueless. My mother did arm me with at least one valuable tool before leaving. She taught me how to recognize, understand, and appreciate beauty. On the day my father let strangers crank Mom's coffin into a giant hole, he confirmed as much by saying, *Oh, she was beautiful all right,* and I'd been glad to know we were in agreement. My mother was the most beautiful woman in the world. This was a fact.

I really didn't give much thought to the full extent of my father's theory until midway through medical school — which was, not coincidentally, when I first gave any serious thought to marriage at all. Vanessa wasn't beautiful. She was normal. She was loyal. *That's your choice,* my old man had foretold. I guess I never forgot that, even long before I got it.

A choice is a responsibility. Some things are pressed upon us: our names, for example, or our birthdays. We don't choose our innate talents. We don't get to pick out our demons. They are every bit as much our birthright as names and birthdays or genetic conditions. For the things we can choose, then, we have a responsibility to pick the option that will best serve us and cause the least suffering. Sometimes the best option still causes suffering, but that doesn't make it the wrong choice. What I'm saying is, I'm no victim. I married one hell of a beautiful woman.

For the first time in my life, I understand my father's bitterness and why he asked to be buried in Memorial Cemetery north of here. She'd destroyed him, hadn't she? She'd broken his heart, then she'd pulverized it by dying on us — and all I ever saw was the man who never loved me as much as she did. Too little, too late. Isn't that always the way? I start the engine and check the time. Ray will be getting off work soon, and so I go. I drive up Belmont and weave over to Bar None, where Ray has already grabbed stools and two bottles of PBR.

8.

"There he is," Ray says.

I untie my tie, undo my top buttons, take off my jacket, and roll up my sleeves. I should have left my suit coat in the car. My cuff links cost more than Ray makes in a month. I slide them into my pocket and take a swig of beer.

"Are you going to tell me what's going on," he asks, "or do I have to wait until you've had a few first?"

I raise my bottle in reply.

"Well then. Bottom's up, buddy."

We guzzle mediocre cold beer.

"How's Emily?" I ask.

"She's fine. Kids are good. Bianca is looking at schools. Leon just got a raise."

"And work is good?" I recognize my habit of posing declarations as questions, but tonight I need Ray to be stable and sound, so I stand by the prompt.

"I don't know if I'd call it *good,*" he

answers, "but it's not bad. Living the lineman dream, I guess."

This is Ray's running joke — thirty years running — because he was a lineman on the high school football team and now he's a lineman for the power company. He thinks it's pure comedy. We shoot the shit a while longer. We talk about the economy and the weather and our kids. When the next pause rolls around, Ray says, "Listen, Bianca's thing starts soon. I'm going to have to roll out of here before too long, so do you want to get to the point, or are you gonna keep pussyfooting around?"

"It's pretty fucking stupid," I tell him.

"I don't doubt that, Bobby."

"It feels crazy now, like I'm paranoid or something."

"Feels crazy to me already. Spit it out."

"I have a weird feeling about a friend of Jonah's, some kid who's staying with us."

"Tall guy from the party?"

"Yeah. His name's Nick."

"Grifter?"

"Not exactly."

"What, exactly?"

"Predator? He might be trying to seduce Elizabeth."

Raymond asks, "Trying how?"

"Crossing lines. He's got this subverted

alpha game going on, like sensitive but sneaky, but I'm the only one who sees it. So then Elizabeth invited him to stay all summer —"

"Why?"

"To be nice. He —"

Ray cuts me off. "You gotta shut that shit down, Bobby."

"What am I supposed to do? Kick him out?"

"I don't care." He shakes his head. "Do what you've got to do, man. Mark Wycott beat the shit out of Steve Dunn's car just because Steve winked at Shelly. Some guy I work with went over to another dude's house with a Louisville Slugger. Said, 'I'm going to ask you nicely once: never touch my wife again. Next time, I bash your brains in.' "

"Okay, well that's one approach."

"Two, actually, but you're not a fighter. Besides, that kid could kick your ass."

"He's skinny."

"He's young."

"We're young."

Raymond throws his head back and laughs.

"Look," I say, "it's just a feeling. Nothing's happened."

"Lucky you. Would you rather wait until

128

things happen? You want to collect evidence that'll haunt you the rest of your life? You've got your instincts. That's all the proof you need. I say shut it down now."

"How?"

"Beats me. All I know is that you cannot let this kid destroy your family."

"It's not like Elizabeth would ever do anything."

"Oh, it's not?" He twists his neck, his entire body. His stare is intense and invasive, making me sorry I ever brought it up.

"Shut up, Ray."

"No way, man."

"You're out of line."

"No," he says, "I'm not. Don't kid yourself, Bobby. Elizabeth did it before, and it worked out in your favor that time. As far as you know, she hasn't since — though, to be fair, that's just as far as you know."

"*Nothing* has happened, Raymond," I say, but my mind is under assault. All I can see is Elizabeth walking through the grass half-naked. Of course, I keep the image to myself. Maybe I want to save face, or maybe I just can't bear to put it into words, but maybe tough love is overrated in the first place. The trouble is, I can't kick this bad feeling in my bones.

"Excellent. You have an opportunity to

take precautions so nothin does happen."

I start to speak but Ray holds up a hand to shush me, and since I came all the way down here for his advice, I might as well take it.

Ray softens. "That shit that went down with Vanessa? You two almost destroyed your kid. You realize that, right? You fucked him up. It's taken Jonah years to get back on his feet, but he looked happy the other night. I haven't seen him that happy since his ninth birthday, man. Granted, I don't see him much, no thanks to you, but the effect of that trauma wasn't exactly subtle. He idolized you, Bobby. He worshipped you, and you broke his mother's heart and made them move into a shitty apartment so you could share your house with a woman who turned out to be a much better match for you than Vanessa ever was — I'll give you that — but do you think any of that mattered to Jonah when he was coming up and needed you? You weren't there."

"I —"

"I know. You wanted to be there. You got the shit end of the custody stick. That's the pitfall of a speedy divorce. Doesn't change the fact that you weren't there. Whatever. But he's finally come around. He's finally learned to like Elizabeth, maybe even love her. She's family to him now. You cannot let *this* family fall apart too."

I drop my head into my hands and massage my scalp, trying to offset pain with pleasure. Ray puts his arm around me and squeezes my shoulder too hard.

"I'm saying this because you're like my brother, and I love you, and I love that fucking kid of yours too."

"I know." I shake my head into my arms. My words are muffled by shirtsleeves and Fleetwood Mac.

"Listen. You've been married, what? Ten years? It's a hiccup. At ten years, most people would hate each other if they didn't have children to distract them and love them back, right?" He laughs. "You've lucked out with how good it's been. Now you've got to get through this shit together. You've got to address it before someone else does."

"Yeah," I say.

Ray's voice is balm to my open wound when he repeats, "Shut it down, Bobby."

I nod.

His insistence makes the whole thing real. If he weren't so adamant, I probably could've talked away my hunch — and it's still just a hunch. I could've tricked myself into believing I'm unreasonable or insecure,

131

but the gravity of Raymond's tone crushes all illusions. I'm Jonah's father. Protecting him is my job, even if he can't see the big picture — especially if the big picture means rescuing his closest friendship and his family from a collision course. Ray is right: there's too much at stake. Kids don't always recognize the motives driving their parents' interventions, but when kids become grown-ups, they look back with wisdom and respect, knowing we did it all for them. Someday, Jonah will thank me.

Besides, my son's serenity isn't the only peace at stake. People assume that the divorce was easy on me just because I was already in love with someone new. Vanessa got everyone's sympathy. So did Elizabeth's ex. No one knew how our partners had changed. Vanessa offered so much in the beginning, then flipped the script and began expecting too much. Her betrayal was passive and ghostly, the kind of trick that makes a man think he's lost his heart or soul. The thing I did, my betrayal toward Vanessa, it was out in the open. It happened publicly, and it happened quickly, and everyone dropped the gavel and called it bad. They didn't know the dark corners of our marriage. They didn't see that I'd done us both a favor by tearing the soiled Band-Aid off a gaping wound she inflicted in the first place.

"Bobby," Ray says, "I hate to do this, man, but I need to get moving."

"Of course. Thanks for —" I'm at a loss. Thanks for what? Thanks for meeting me, for straight shooting, for not making this weird, for not changing? Thanks for not giving a shit about Man of the Year and not hating me because I do? I care about seeing my picture in the paper. God, that picture in the paper. I feel queasy again, as for the first time it occurs to me to wonder if whatever happened this morning was already happening when Elizabeth wrapped her hand around Nick's shoulder. Does she have it in her to flaunt such a thing in front of my face? And —

Oh, Jesus. Was she thinking of him? When she closed her eyes and opened her legs, was she thinking of him when she came? Like a goddamn meteor shower, the what-ifs come crashing down. What if this isn't new? What if he loves her? What if she loves him? Who started it? Where are they this very minute? And —

"Bobby?"

I look up at my friend. Van Halen oozes from the jukebox like a corny soundtrack to our bromance moment. "Thanks for everything," I say.

133

He slaps me on the back, leaves me with the tab, and heads home to Emily and spaghetti pie. I nearly order another drink. I nearly throw a round of darts. Instead, I make the mistake of looking around this tired bar. These people come here every night to drink and play pool and bask in neon light, don't they? They tell the same stale jokes. They eat leftover spaghetti pie and salads that come out of bags. I don't belong here. I never did. I throw thirty bucks on the bar and leave. A herd of dudes bursts into laughter just before the door closes. I can't help but cringe. I can't help but hate them all.

EMILY

By the time Raymond shimmies down the bleachers — all, *Excuse me, pardon me,* slapping other kids' dads on the back — Bianca's side is up two points. It's just a clinic, not even a proper game for a proper league, but some of these parents are in it to win it, no joke.

"What did I miss?" Ray asks, kissing my cheek.

"Shirts and skins. White jerseys are skins. Gabby scored for shirts. Sarah, Leona, and Mikaela each scored for skins. Bianca's still on the bench. She's a skin."

Ray cups his hands around his mouth and screams, "Give 'em hell, B!" Our daughter glares at Raymond, then hangs her head and puts her hands over her ears. The lady in front of us spins around to judge Ray. He grins and says, "Hi," to her.

"So?" I ask. "How was it?"

Raymond closes his eyes and shakes his head.

"That bad."

An exasperated, *pfft.* "He's a mess, Em. Started crying at the bar, swear to God."

"Oh God. What's going on?"

"He thinks some friend of Jonah's wants to fuck Elizabeth." He says *fuck Elizabeth* right as the cheers fall off to silence.

"Jesus," I whisper. The lady in front of us twists to see who said *Jesus,* or maybe *fuck.* I whisper to Raymond, "So is he paranoid, or what?"

"I don't know. Boys that age are capable of some pretty deviant shit. I told him to shut it down regardless. Told him about how Mark Wycott bashed Steve Dunn's headlights in just for sweet-talking Shelly that one time."

The shirts score and the skins' parents boo. I tell Raymond, "Mark didn't do that."

"Huh?"

"Bash in Steve's headlights. That's not what happened. Mark didn't do it."

"Yeah he did," Ray tells me, then snaps to attention. "Wait, he didn't?"

"No. Steve cracked his headlight pulling into his garage after Mark's Fourth of July party last year."

"Really?"

"Yes. Really."

"Oh," Ray says. "Well, I told Bobby that Mark fired a warning shot and it worked."

"You'd better hope he doesn't try to impress you by one-upping Mark."

"Yeah, right," says Ray. "Like Bobby's got a violent bone in his body."

"Maybe not violent," I concede, "but desperate."

"Fair enough."

At least Raymond can see it. He's so good at overlooking his friends' flaws, but I guess that's the upside of devotion. My husband's loyalty is both the sexiest and most annoying thing about him, just as Bobby's reliance upon my husband is both his most endearing and most insufferable quality. I love Bobby like family — but more in the vein of brother-in-law than brother. My love for Bobby exists *through* Raymond. And anyway, his reaction is not our responsibility. Bobby may be impressionable, but he's a grown man, for crying out loud.

It's too easy to see him, still, as that kid we met when our paths merged in middle school. In that first week of the sixth grade, the three of us found ourselves aligned, our last names stacked alphabetically back-to-back, quickly triangulating our awkwardness into something remarkably strong. If

137

my maiden name had been Smith instead of Hawthorne, there's a pretty good chance I'd have never given Bobby a second thought. Of course, I'd like to think I would've still married Raymond, even if he wasn't a Harrison — that I wouldn't have ended up with a Smerda twin instead. I shudder to think it.

Bobby was a bit like Mowgli back then: scrawny, scrappy, out of place but not really aware of it. I guess he found his personal Bagheera in Ray. What would that have made me? Baloo? Fuck it. I'll be Baloo. We were a solid threesome, and later, a solid two-plus-one. Ray went out of his way to be sure Bobby never felt left out after we coupled up — sometimes to the point of overcompensation, in my opinion, but I couldn't be mad about that. Bobby was my date to every football game so we could act the fools as Raymond's personal fan club; and if one of us was sick, Bobby would get our assignments and help us finish them so we could rest. It was never a hassle to include him. It was always just love.

Such a decent kid. So fucking smart. So clueless, too. So powerless against his dad's obsession with pedigree. Bobby inherited it, like a disease. Mowgli deserved better.

The first time I saw it was junior year,

when Bobby spun the fuck out over that stupid American History final, like his entire future depended upon acing one exam — which was, I imagine, his father's prophecy. Bobby said if his GPA dropped, he'd never stand a chance of getting into his target schools. That was the first I'd heard of an Ivy League plan.

So he came up with that elaborate scheme to break into the classroom, steal the tests from the top drawer in Mr. Clifford's desk, then photocopy and distribute them to everyone else. This way he'd get an A while also ingratiating himself to the rest of the class. It was weird. I think the only reason Raymond agreed to help was because he hated seeing Bobby miserable. I stayed out of it, but Raymond loaned him the skeleton key that had been in the football team's possession for generations, and he drove and stood guard while Bobby snuck inside like it was Watergate or something. It was the end of the year, and Mr. Clifford was fed up with our shit, I guess, because when he realized what had happened, he went berserk. Refused to let us out of class until we each wrote the name of our top suspect on a piece of paper, folded it in quarters, and handed it in, anonymously. I wrote, *I DON'T KNOW.* Raymond wrote something similar, and Bobby claims he did too, but I couldn't help but wonder who *else* would have written Miles Dawson's name down, if not the guilty party.

Sweet, boring Miles Dawson. His seat was empty the next morning. He probably spent the day hating himself for being the perfect patsy, while Mr. Clifford bragged about catching and suspending a thief. Case closed. Mr. Clifford actually thanked the anonymous tipper who'd snitched. At lunch, Ray and I insisted Bobby come clean, but Bobby refused. He blamed Mr. Clifford for failing to investigate properly and said we shouldn't jeopardize our futures on account of other people's incompetence. That was the first time I thought, *Like father, like son.*

Cut to Ray telling Mr. Clifford that he would not be able to give any more information, but that he knew for a fact it hadn't been Miles. He wouldn't say *how* he knew, but he did swear it wasn't him, either. Technically, Ray was an accomplice, not a thief, so technically it wasn't a lie. I think Mr. Clifford was so spent at that point — and rightfully on edge about having suspended the wrong person once already — that he just lectured Raymond and sent him away. Miles returned to class and everything went back to normal, and that's how I learned that cheating is way more stressful than buckling down and doing the work.

I'd have filed that event under Dumb Shit Teenagers Do if not for the thing Bobby's dad said after graduation. He came up to me and Raymond so he could brag about Bobby heading to Yale. Then he offered it up without any segue: said he'd paid someone to write Bobby's college application essay. I swear he got off on how disappointed we were, like it had been his *intention* to tarnish his son's character. It worked, too — if only a little bit, but only because Bobby never told us himself. A while back, I brought it up to Raymond, but he'd revamped the memory entirely, claiming he always figured Mr. Hart was kidding. I saw the look on Raymond's face that day, though. There'd been no humor there. He'd been heartbroken to learn Bobby didn't trust himself enough to apply with his own work. Bobby was smart enough to get accepted on his own, but he went out of his way to ensure he'd always doubt his place there. He let his dad *pay* someone to invalidate his seat for the next four years — to delegitimize his relationship with an institution that would become his identity. What the fuck?

And still, in spite of the drama, we love

our Mowgli. On paper, he's a pain in the ass, but in real life, he's our brother. We have history, and we have fun, and if anyone needs proof of his character, they got it the day Vanessa chose him. She's as good as it gets. I'm sure Elizabeth is lovely. All I know is when Vanessa was by his side, Bobby stopped leaning on Ray to define him. Robert loved bitching and moaning about his stressful residency, never considering the rigors of Raymond's training — his four-year apprenticeship; his bruised body, shredded muscles, jacked joints; *his* stress. We really don't care if Bobby thinks he's a higher species because of the MD after his name. It's better he doesn't know what it took for Ray to earn journeyman after his, or how much money Ray makes, or how much we've put away while Bobby strains to hatch his own nest egg. His is on display. Ours is in the bank. Raymond doesn't brag because he doesn't have to. He doesn't complain about his hard work because that's what he signed up to do. As entertaining as it would be to watch Bobby strap on gaffs and scale a seventy-five-foot pole while holding back puke and vertigo, it's a good thing he lives in a separate world, tucked away in that old whaling port that doesn't look all so different from home. This way, things don't get competitive. And hell, if Bobby's most lovable quality is the fact that he's loved by Raymond, I'll keep loving the guy like a brother-in-law.

Ray cups his hands around his mouth and howls again, screaming our daughter's name as she finally leaves the bench and runs onto the field. I yell too, though not as loud as my husband. When the ball is in play, I say to Raymond, "Please don't get sucked into Bobby's problems."

He shrugs and says, "You know I can't help it."

Isn't that the truth. "You've got your own shit to deal with. You don't need his."

Ray puffs out his chest. "What shit do I have?"

"Well, for one thing: her tuition," I say, nodding toward Bianca, who is ducking from the ball instead of hitting it. "Something tells me a field hockey scholarship isn't in the cards."

Ray winces — out of empathy, not disapproval, since we honestly don't care what she does or how good she is, as long as she's getting something out of it. Ray folds his arms and says, "Don't you worry about that. There's a storm system rolling in."

"You better pray it's a hurricane."

"Hey, now. Let's not spoil the children."

143

He smirks like the adorable, cocky bastard he is.

"Are you kidding? Let's spoil them rotten."

Bianca intercepts a pass and the crowd goes wild — me and Ray in hysterics, obviously, but everyone else, too, even the tight-ass in front of us, who pumps her fists in the air — and Bianca is so surprised that she freezes, then looks up at us, not smiling exactly, but checking to make sure we're watching, which is just enough of a distraction for the other team to steal the ball away again, and everyone in the bleachers moans and sits back down — everyone except for Raymond, who keeps whooping at full voice, and maybe I'm imagining things, but it sure looks like Bianca's smiling now.

"Yeah!" Raymond screams one last time. He sits down and squeezes my knee. "Well, how about that?" Takes a minute for his energy to settle, but once it does, he says, "Don't worry. Bobby will be fine."

"I guess," I say, thinking to myself how it's not Bobby I'm worried about.

9.

Here's what's going to happen: I'll pull Nick aside tonight and tell him to pack it up and move on out. Whether or not I'm reading him or the situation correctly is irrelevant, because for all of Raymond's shortcomings — and he has plenty — the man made an excellent point: There's no sense in waiting for disaster. Run defense before the damage is done.

The drive home from Bar None serves up more traffic than I expected, but it gives me time to think about instincts and why I have them, and why it's foolish to ignore them. Ray's gut reaction confirmed my own. When I walk through the door four hours late, Elizabeth simply says, "Dinner's in ten," with a smile, and she accepts my wilted herbs, unexplained delay, and faint whiff of Bar None without comment. So I kiss her on the cheek, tell her how nice dinner looks, ask where the boys are, and try to act indifferent when she replies, "Out."

We eat, just the two of us, like normal, asking questions about work and what we've heard about the house next door that's up for sale, and what we've heard about our former neighbors. I clean my plate, clear the table, offer to do the dishes and do them. "When are they coming back?"

"Who, the boys? Beats me." Elizabeth falls into the couch and a book, so I settle into my leather chair to read the latest *Smithsonian* magazine, and everything's normal for a while. Normal and sterile and terribly quiet.

Eight thirty in the morning, I bang on the guesthouse door and Nick answers, rubbing his eyes, so I ask if I woke him, and he answers, "That's okay." When I insist on giving him a ride to a nice stretch of beach he hasn't seen, he resists until he doesn't. Takes him ten minutes to brush his teeth and put on flip-flops.

We hit green lights all the way. I ask, "So what's your deal, Nick Carpenter?"

"My deal?" He closes an air vent.

"You like jogging and pizza. You like fishing but don't fish. What else?"

He laughs. "What do you want to know?"

"Got big plans for the future?"

"Not really," he says. "I'm better at living life than planning it, you know what I mean?"

"No. What do you mean?"

He pauses, then answers, "I guess it feels important to do whatever is in front of me at any given time, to do it well and see where life goes. Sounds corny, probably."

I can't argue with that. "A little reckless, too."

"Yeah, maybe," he says, "but I don't want to wait until I'm old to do the shit I want to do. Like, maybe I won't get old. Or maybe it won't be fun anymore. I don't want to miss the fun."

"Interesting."

"Oh. There is one thing. I have an aunt, lived with her through high school. She's all the family I have left. I have this dream of helping her fix up the house. Maybe build her a screened-in porch. She worked hard to make that place my home. I'd love to do something for her in return. That's the extent of my future planning, though." He laughs.

I do not laugh. Nick Carpenter, the carpenter, waiting for his calling, dreaming of altruism, might enjoy one of those construction-for-charity gigs. Maybe I could hook him up, turn his departure into my

147

own act of charity. Better yet, I could send him to another one of his beloved wilderness camps for fucked-up men, where he'll spend the rest of the summer digging latrines or spotting belays — I don't give a shit what he does — and Elizabeth and Jonah will believe he wants to go, because once he's gone, I'll say, *Nick was too embarrassed to let it show, but seeing us as a happy family was too much for him. He begged me not to tell you, but you have a right to understand. Please, keep it between us. He'd never trust again, poor thing.*

Then I'll be the good guy again. I'll be at home in my home again, thank God.

But if Nick doesn't take the hint, or if he gives me shit, I'll call him out and say, *Did you think you could play me for a fool?*

And he'll say, *I underestimated you.*

And I'll say, *This is your only warning,* and he'll be gone.

Just imagining this scene opens a valve in me, relieving pressure I hadn't felt building until it's gone. This allows me to be courteous, even though I'd like to break his nose; and he is gracious, even though he wants to fuck my wife. Perhaps he's gracious not in spite of but because of his position — what he's been given: the opportunity to take what's mine.

I drive him to the farthest point on the beach and ditch him there. Leave the verbal threats and busted headlights to other men with other problems. I'll eliminate the symptom in good time.

Elizabeth's office door is closed when I get home from work, which means she's not to be disturbed: her top condition for working from home. Her handbag is draped open on the granite countertop. Through a gap between leather seams, the glass screen of her cell phone reflects overhead lights. If I were one of those desperate, insecure men, I'd probably sneak a look. Fortunately, I'm not one of those men, and my trance is disrupted by the click and creak of Elizabeth's office door opening, anyway. Next comes the high-pitched arc of her grand sigh, a ceremonial victory song marking the end of her day. I step away from temptation and fling open the refrigerator door so that I'm focused on condiments, not the contents of Lizzie's bag, when she enters the room.

"I know," she says. "We're out of limes. They are at the top of my list."

"You read my mind." I grab a plain Perrier, move to the table, take a seat, flip through today's stack of mail: business envelopes, pointless catalogs, fundraising materials that cost more to print and post than most donors are willing to give. Between bills, there's a pale blue envelope addressed to Elizabeth, torn open down one side. I flip it over to read the embossed return address.

"What did you get from the Parkses?" I ask.

"Oh, Luna sent us her copy of the paper, the one with our picture."

I open a piece of newsprint that's been folded carefully so as to avoid creasing our faces. In the margin, in broad, loopy letters, Luna has written, *Brava! Come see us soon, would you?* Painfully predictable.

Elizabeth rests a hand on my shoulder. "I should get in touch with that photographer to get those other pictures."

"Sure." Elizabeth traces a line from the nook of my neck down to the C7 vertebrae. My skin tingles. Without planning to, I say, "I've been a stress case lately. I shouldn't let it get to me. I should never take it out on you."

She draws maps on my shoulders for a few lazy moments before accepting my apology. "Already forgotten." Then she kisses the top of my head, and off she goes to the bar, commencing our evening ritual of cocktails and small talk before dinner and bed. Our routine wasn't always so steady. We used to go for long lazy walks, sometimes drives. We'd go out: cocktail parties, dinners, jaunts to the city for gallery openings or the odd performance. Pina Bausch for Elizabeth, Mamet plays for me. I've enabled predictability, equal parts boring and reliable: fertile ground for sneaking around.

So I say, "Want to take a walk? It's such a nice night."

She glances over her shoulder. "Now?"

"Why not?"

She examines the glass in which she's already poured two fingers of Scotch and drinks it down without ice or water, screws the cap back onto the bottle, and leaves her empty glass on the bar. "Let's go."

We follow the sidewalk through familiar territory, reporting gossip under our breath — *Did you hear Mary Ellen is thinking of selling the house?* And, *Martin's battling the HOA over that spruce,* which reminds me to schedule a tree-trim for the elm going rogue over our front yard. Gabriel would have complained, but his house has been on the market for six months while he sweats it out in his East Hampton upgrade, so he's not there to nitpick, and I kind of like a rogue elm. We cross over to the unfamiliar (*Who on earth drives a truck like that?*) and stumble upon a playground that never merited a second glance until now. Tonight, an empty swing set looks like a buffer. Juvenile, sure, but who can throw suspicious looks while facing forward? Who can get gridlocked while in motion, or be bitter adults when behaving like children? Elizabeth follows me across the grass, past a well-groomed sandbox, and watches me claim the highest-strung swing. Here's something I haven't done in at least fifteen years. Not since Jonah was a boy. Not since that nightmare jungle gym from Home Depot I assembled in our backyard.

Elizabeth laughs. "You sure are feeling at ease tonight, aren't you?"

I tuck my toes on the downswing. "Yes. Finally."

She wraps her hands around the chains, backs up until she's on her toes, and drops into the cracked rubber seat. "It's nice to see."

"How would you feel about getting out of town one of these weekends? Heading somewhere for a night?"

"Like where?"

"We could drive upstate or go to Nantucket. Or head into the city to see a show. Spa, room service. I don't know."

152

She floats with legs extended. For one weightless arc, we are synced. "Sure," she says, and we fall out of rhythm again. "That sounds nice."

She drags her toes in the dirt and comes to a stop, so I drag mine, too: a pair of adults dangling out of our element, unmoored and opened. In Elizabeth's pause, I feel her not saying something, and I know that the unsaid thing is what's driving distance between us, so I make a guess. "Do you miss the city?"

"No." With her heel, she draws spirals in the dirt. "Sometimes."

"All you have to do is speak up. We can go in more if you want."

"It's not the city, exactly," she says. "I mean, it's not anything, really. I'm fine. I couldn't live there again, I don't think, if that's what you're asking. I don't even know what I'm saying. Maybe I could. You asked, so I'm answering. I'm just saying, sometimes I miss the opportunities I passed up — not that they were mine for the taking. I miss the sense of opportunity."

"The sense of opportunity you felt in your twenties," I prompt.

"Sure."

"That might not be geography so much as time."

"Maybe." Elizabeth stands and releases the shiny chains. "Maybe this is just what getting older feels like."

I brush dust from the back of her jeans. "Well, if this is what getting old looks like, we're in good shape."

"I said 'older,' Robert." She puts her hands in her back pockets and returns to the street. This time she leads the way.

So she's restless. Not terribly surprising, and it wouldn't be the first time. Romanticizing her former life, though? Yes, this surprises me. I pulled her out of a quagmire she couldn't escape on her own, and she thanked me. She was miserable when we met, drowning in debt, unemployable, unemployed. What on earth had she planned to do with a PhD in Comparative Literature anyway? What did she expect her life to look like when she married a poet — a rookie professor of poetry, no less, as if being a poet wasn't bad enough?

He was faculty at Columbia at the time. She was a doctoral candidate in the same department. Realistically, she'd never have gotten a job in New York straight out of school, not at Columbia or anywhere, anyway. She'd have had to move someplace awful to find a vacancy, someplace dreary and Midwestern, and how would her marriage have fared then? Stuart wasn't going to leave his adjunct professorship, unstable and insignificant as it was. The Ivy League credential mattered to him, just as the Ivy League education mattered to her. Some people are like that, fine. But she was the one who attended a conference at the medical school just to escape the confines of her department, just to hear someone talk about facts and science for a change, and she was the one who approached me after my panel to say how much she appreciated my insight into the future of health care in America. She was the one who left her wedding ring at home that morning. Her eyes had been bloodshot and weary — the result of sleepless nights tackling her dissertation topic: Postmodern Applications of Classical Theory on the Feminine Sublime, or something, I soon learned — and her voice had been raspy and soft. I now know she'd only gone hoarse on account of fatigue and cigarettes, that she wouldn't always sound like Kathleen Turner, but something about her timbre threw me. She shook my hand and looked at me like a little girl trying to buy a ticket to my ferry heading far away from her island. *Anywhere but here,* her eyes seemed to say.

Falling in love, and so deeply this time —

so violently, actually, and disruptive and consuming — wasn't part of my plan. Once it happened, though, against my wishes, against my will, the cravings kicked in something awful. I tried forcing Elizabeth out of my system by overindulging, hoping to get sick of her so I could spare Vanessa all that pain, but indulgence only got me hooked.

Stuart kicked Elizabeth out as soon as he discovered that she'd been spending afternoons with me and not at the library, that she'd been napping in hotel rooms on my dime. She could have completed her program but couldn't bear the humiliation of facing her colleagues, who sided with Stuart. Besides, she'd have needed at least another year to finish writing her dissertation. In her revisionist memory, Elizabeth now measures that year as "so close," but I saw how desperate she was. Maybe she could've toughed it out if she'd had no choice, but she had me, and we were madly in love.

He obviously never got over her. A few years after Elizabeth chose me, Stuart started sending her birthday cards. He wrote a hokey message about forgiveness, and how he finally wished her "nothing but the best." Now he just signs his name, but he still sends them. His strategy for being remembered is so transparent, but I guess it works, insofar as making Elizabeth pity him enough to send birthday cards, too.

If she'd have stayed, she'd still be Stuart's literary accessory, and he'd be self-publishing chapbooks that no one reads, dedicating them to *my darling elizabeth* and expecting her to feel not just flattered, but honored. Meanwhile, she'd be holed up with a calico cat in a tiny apartment in Harlem, scribbling notes in a knock-off Moleskine and mass-mailing her CV to second-tier schools, facing rejection after silent rejection until someone in Indiana called for an interview from which she'd never return. I gave her a home with a pool and a garden, fresh air, a job, a respected husband with thick hair and a boat. She might miss the idea of that other life, but if she'd have stayed, right now she'd be wondering what might've happened if she'd said yes when that handsome doctor invited her for a drink after his panel discussion.

So the problem is boredom. Nick is only a symptom.

"Elizabeth."

She doesn't turn.

"What about giving their book group another try?"

"Their huh?"

"Luna's book group."

She moans and rolls her head. "Don't you remember how mortifying that was?"

"Of course I do, but it was so long ago. Maybe they've gotten better."

"Maybe. Not my job to investigate."

I pace myself. "Those women need someone like you."

"Yeah, right."

"Are you kidding? Don't act like you don't know this."

"Robert, those women don't want to discuss books with me."

"Oh, come on. They're not bad women."

"That wasn't a judgment call. It's a fact. They were talking about libidos and finances and other people's children. They drink white wine and discuss carbohydrates and heated tile."

"You went one time, Elizabeth. Once. Two years ago."

"Once was enough."

"I still think you might be generalizing, but if you're not, that's all the more reason to throw a wrench in their mediocrity."

"Why should I volunteer to throw wrenches?"

"Because you are brilliant, Elizabeth."

158

She tucks her chin and offers a crooked smile.

"You know I think you're a damn genius." It's true. I do.

She shrugs.

"Go to their stupid club, talk about their damn book, crack open their minds and show them who you are. Give them something new to talk about and maybe they'll surprise us with brainpower of their own."

"They aren't stupid women," Elizabeth says. "Luna is terribly sharp. She handles Graham's trust like she's the head of the IMF, for Christ's sake."

"So go show her there's nothing wrong with having conversations about more substantive matters than curtains and hormones."

"Hormones are substantive, Robert."

"Fair enough," I concede, knowing how close she is to saying yes, knowing she doesn't like being pushed. If Elizabeth could make more friends around here, she wouldn't need to search for Nicks to cure her boredom. Her midlife crisis.

"I'll think about it," she says.

"They should be so lucky."

The music box theme song of our neighborhood ice cream truck blasts from a bullhorn atop a refrigerated vehicle down the street. Children clutching fistfuls of dollar bills snatched from their parents' wallets answer the call of a lazy piper. The Entertainer.

"I wonder what they're reading," Elizabeth murmurs, and I smile.

This is a small step, and not a comprehensive solution, but I've successfully planted a distraction in her mind, and I've effectively boosted her softness toward me. All I want is for us to be happy, and so it gives me great pleasure to watch her mull over the possibilities of an idea she now thinks was her own.

10.

My heart-to-heart with Elizabeth brings a peace that lasts through the night, but first thing in the morning, Raymond squashes it by requesting a status report. He texts only a question mark, sufficiently cryptic for anyone who isn't us, but enough to make me resent him for acknowledging what he knows. I reply, *All good,* and erase our messages.

It's not all good, though. The symptoms and risks of Elizabeth's needs may be clearer, true, but addressing them without addressing Nick is like popping vitamins without removing the tumor. Healthy systems require both prevention and treatment.

Mark Wycott took a baseball bat to Steve Dunn's car. All I have to do is kick a kid out of my house. Confronting him would be a waste, given how this thing's being stopped before it starts. The most I could expect is an apology for dirty thoughts. Of course, the worst I could expect is a confession, which is out of the question, as the only thing more revolting than imagining this affair would be hearing Nick confirm its existence. That leaves me two choices: black mold or double-booking. The toxicity of mold is poetic, but I'd hate for fungus to be his parting association with our home.

Double-booking, then. An old friend, maybe a cousin, someone who reserved the guesthouse so long ago, it slipped my mind. Someone important — no, better yet, someone boring.

I knock, ready to tell Nick he's being replaced by a dullard, but he looks haggard as hell, so I have to ask, "Late night?"

"Yeah, right. Was up most of it with a fever, I think."

"What's the matter with you?"

He scratches his head. "Don't know. Achy all over. Took some Tylenol, so —"

I reach toward him without permission and place my hand just below his jaw, lightly gripping his neck, and pause here to imagine crushing his trachea with my forty-five-year-old hand, my hand that's punched walls and signed huge checks and touched Elizabeth in places he'll never reach. "Your glands feel fine," I say. "Why don't you let me drop you at the beach again. Fresh air will do you good."

He shakes his head. "I should rest. Don't want to get you sick."

My hands itch to grab him by the throat again, to assist in incapacitating him on this beautiful Friday, the very day Elizabeth happens to work from home, and so, not trusting myself to kick him out without kicking him in the face, I walk away dazed. His claims of sickness threw me, but by lunchtime I'm spinning, because either Nick was contagious and gave me his bug, or I've made myself ill imagining what might be happening at my house at this moment. Simone brings me Alka-Seltzer while I stretch out on the sofa in our lounge, and I tell her she's an angel, and "What would I do without you?" She smiles. Really, though. Everyone needs a Simone.

When I pull up to the house at five on the dot, my driveway is blocked by a black Expedition. Familiar, but not enough for me to place it. Familiar, maybe, because half my zip code drives a version of the same beast. I park behind it and trudge through the yard, opening the door to a mess of voices talking over bossa nova playing through my stereo system. "Hello?"

Elizabeth shouts from the den, "We're in here."

"Robert, you little worm," a voice calls — and yes, now I recall the black SUV I loaded and unloaded with flowers after my party.

"Hello, Luna," I reply, greeting Bonnie McAlister, as well — and two women on my couch who don't introduce themselves, which I appreciate, because I don't care to meet them, either — and Nick, too, perfectly healthy and terribly smug. He's sitting next to Elizabeth, his feet propped on my coffee table. I'm looking at him still when I tell Luna, "Three times in one week. Might be a record."

"Aren't you the luckiest?" she says.

"What's the occasion this time?" I ask.

But it's Elizabeth who answers with a semi-smile, and her cadence is peculiar — artificial but knowing, seductive almost — when she says, "We're planning our book club."

Luna points at me. "No thanks to you, naughty boy. I practically begged you to give Elizabeth the message."

Holding her gaze but harder, Elizabeth says, "Don't you love Luna's idea, Robert? She wants to revamp her book club to make use of my brain. Isn't that flattering?" Elizabeth is so proud of herself for discovering

164

what she thinks she knows, as if I'd derived pleasure from passing off Luna's suggestion as my own. Elizabeth doesn't understand that my moves are strategic, that my strategies are designed to protect her from humiliating herself. Liking Nick's attention is one thing. Needing it would be a disgrace.

"Feeling better?" I ask Nick.

"Much," he says. "Elizabeth talked me into an immune-booster tea from that café by the farmer's market. With all due respect for modern medicine, the tea might have worked miracles."

The ladies giggle, and Bonnie says, "You do have such nice color now."

One of the unidentified women says, "Yes. You're glowing."

"You did look peaked earlier," says Luna, reaching over Elizabeth to pat Nick's knee. "Poor thing."

Elizabeth says, "I drove Nick to the pharmacy for antihistamine and we swung by Java and Juice for a ginger tonic afterward. Bumped into these ladies, and here we are."

"Kismet," says Luna, "and not a moment too soon. Swear to God, the last book we read was a cookbook, for Christ's sake."

"It was bull-honkey," Bonnie tells me. "Movie stars don't eat like that."

Luna rolls her eyes. "We're desperate for

new blood. Elizabeth is going to *revive* us, and thanks to Nick, we're off and running. He mentioned Elizabeth's favorite book, and not a single one of us had read it. Aren't we pitiful?"

Favorite book? Elizabeth doesn't have a favorite, unless she does. I'd ask, but Luna and Company would draw conclusions and start rumors about Nick knowing my wife better than I do, so instead I nod. I'm trying to remember any book Elizabeth has ever mentioned, good or bad, when a voice behind me says, "It's out of print."

I spin around to find Jonah slumped in my leather chair. "Didn't see you."

"No kidding." He's staring at the phone in his hands.

"Did you have class today?"

"Yeah. Just got home."

"Are you joining their book club too?"

Jonah says, "If they'll have me."

"Oh, I *suppose* we can make room," says Luna, and everyone laughs. "Anyway, we were just paying our bill at coffee, so I suggested we come here for an impromptu planning session. But fine, *confession* time: I've been dying to see what you've done to the house."

"Well, I hope you approve," I say, trusting Luna to miss my sarcasm, which she does.

"Oh, it's fabulous. You never know whose hands these old houses will fall into, but clearly, yours are skilled." She winks at Elizabeth. "I'm just crazy about this mix of mod and classic. It kills me when new-money types destroy a home's character because its best features aren't *new*. Don't take that the wrong way. I'm not talking about you. Obviously, *you* get it — adding funky stairs and Japanese sliding doors while keeping the widow's walk intact, things like that. Isn't that the most glorious term? Widow's walk. Yours is lovely. I recognized it right away from that feature in the paper a while back."

"Well," I say, "good thing it's lovely, because it sure isn't functional."

"No," Luna gasps, and holds a hand to her chest. "Really?"

Jonah says, "Just try going up there and see what he does. Dad's threats scared me more as a kid than the roof ever did."

"Consider yourself loved," I tell Jonah. To our guests, I explain, "It's a death trap. The cupola, the balcony and railings: disaster. Suicide central at the moment, but we'll get around to it one of these days."

Luna purses her lips and flares her nostrils, as though she's smelled something sour but doesn't want to draw attention to the source. "Well, anyway, the interior is great. You should entertain more. Let me help you host a cocktail party. Will you, please?"

"We'll think about it," says Elizabeth.

Still looking at his phone, Jonah says, "There might be two copies at that antique spot by the harbor?"

Everyone except for me celebrates his discovery, and Bonnie says, "Have you read *Earthly Paradise,* Robert?"

I ask, "Steinbeck?"

Sympathy laughter from giddy women drinking beer in my den. And my wife. She laughs, too. So does Jonah. So does Nick.

Elizabeth explains, "It's Colette's memoir, more or less. Not the greatest work of literature of all time, but it's delicious and haunting, knowing what we now know. The way she rewrote herself is almost sorcery, and the imagery is to die for."

"In that case, proceed with caution," I say. When no one asks about me, I add, "If you'll excuse me, I need to regroup after a hectic day at work."

Luna waves good-bye without looking at me, and for a split second, it sounds like she might be asking me a question, but no, she's just soliciting opinions about Colette's braid. I might as well have vaporized as I trudge to my room with fire under my skin, calling on all the old tricks: counting backward, counting breaths, visualizing my heart staying calm, visualizing a gentle breeze on an empty beach. Behind me, a bottle cap hits our glass tabletop, sending ice picks through my skull, bombing my mental beach. I'm not mad about being excluded from their drivel. I'm mad that I care about being excluded. Those women are mistaking Nick's role in our lives. They think he's a connector. Nick probably agrees, and the longer he believes —

A digital bell chimes.

My head quiets, a Pavlovian tick. The digital bell chimes again.

Elizabeth has left her cell phone charging on her nightstand. Normally I'd ignore it, but nothing's normal these days, so — two new texts from her sister, Laurie. An inside joke, I presume. Nothing urgent or emergent, but now the phone's in my hand, so flicking my thumb feels natural, not treasonous. I scroll past texts from me and Jonah, some from colleagues, two billing notifications, an emoji from her father in Missouri. Nothing from Nick. Even the most innocent houseguest texts his hosts every so often, and vice versa — *need paper towels?* or *help yourself to leftovers,* or, *do you have a spare*

169

key? — but there's nothing here. Not a word.

Her photos: our house, a sunset, the overgrown elm in our yard. Happy family at Elizabeth's nephew's graduation last spring. Screenshots of book reviews, articles, and maps. Pictures Elizabeth took in dressing rooms, reflections of herself wearing gowns with tags still on them, tight jeans I've never seen, a skirt I recognize, or don't. They are intoxicating, these self-portraits in overhead light — proof that she would never buy a dress without knowing how it looks on her body from every angle, even when I'm not there to assure her.

Downstairs, someone breaks a glass, maybe a bottle. Something shatters. Our guests are occupied by an innocent accident, but so am I, because stumbling into Elizabeth's private world has made me greedy to know more, to know everything, completely — or, at the very least, better than those strangers downstairs.

Elizabeth calls my name. Her voice is too close. I darken her phone and hurry to meet her on the landing. She says, "We're all running to a bookshop, then dropping Bonnie at her car. We won't be long. You're blocking Luna so I'm taking the Audi." She skips back down to her fan club as I tell her to take her time.

More chatter, then less, then none. The front door opens, closes. Engines start, fade to silence. The house is mine.

Snooping doesn't come naturally, but I do my best, starting with our bathroom wastebasket (wads of innocuous tissue, strands of used dental floss) and moving on to Elizabeth's makeup drawers (cosmetics and earrings, medicine and junk, nail clippers, nail polish, files). No condoms hidden in the Band-Aid box. No love notes taped to the bottom of a jewelry box. Still, something feels out of place. Something's off.

Her closet and dresser: sock and underwear drawers, the toes of her shoes, the backs of her shelves. Check, check, check. Her pillow smells like my wife, not cologne or sweaty boy. No traces of someone who isn't me. Of course, there wouldn't be. Elizabeth isn't lazy. She wouldn't leave clues as cliché as lipstick on a collar, cologne on a pillow, used condoms in the garbage, dirty underthings where they shouldn't be. Elizabeth wouldn't save incriminating text messages or photos. She would never be so stupid, even if she were so bold, and her hair doesn't smell like cologne or get stuck in other people's drains because she's not dumb — or, better yet, because there's no smoking gun to find, which should be a relief, but it only sparks disgust, because now I see that it's come to this. Nick has turned me into a man who raids his wife's closet, rummages through dresser drawers, puts things back neatly where he found them, and even knowing as much, I can't stop.

Shoeboxes line the shelf high above Elizabeth's clothing racks. I have to use her stepstool to take them down, one by one, cracking the lids and inspecting their contents before putting them back. Sparkly high heels. Snakeskin sneakers. Thigh-high boots in white leather with fringe. The fourth box contains a pair of Frye boots I've never seen, but the soles are misshapen, the ankles scuffed and the leather worn thin at the toe. Instead of tissue paper, a folded piece of fabric lines the bottom of the box. It stays anchored when I try to lift it away, so I move the boots, and I remove the bundle beneath them: a thin white T-shirt wrapped around a notebook and a stack of greeting cards all tied up with a string. I recognize the top card right away. Shiny gold letters on recycled paper with rough edges. The card Stuart sent Elizabeth for her birthday last year.

My stomach lurches like I'm on the teacup

ride, and I have to sit down, propping this Frye box on my knees, untying the string, releasing all of those birthday wishes and a few auld lang synes. She saved them and hid them away, stacked atop a Moleskine notebook that already makes me want to vomit. I slide the elastic strap from its cover and open to a random page:

It is August, but
I have winterized our nest
for two larks, one Finch.

A haiku. Good Lord. That's so Stuart.

I turn the page to a handwritten sonnet. Another page, another sonnet. Shameless, this guy. Is he for real? Flipping from one dumb handwritten poem to the next, I'm starting to wonder if they're all odes to Elizabeth, every last one of them, when a pressed flower falls on the floor. Is a thistle even a flower?

I know better than to do this to myself — than to degrade Lizzie like this — but I'm already in too deep, so I find another sonnet and read —

North of Blue Eye, due south of Marvel
    Cave,
You came to be, a being forced to leave

— but, Jesus Christ, this fucking guy. *Of course* he would — of course he'd call it her "marvel cave." I shove the thistle back in the book and snap it shut, nauseated by the image of a vegan dweeb spelunking in my wife, disgusted with her for ever having found this shit appealing, furious with myself for knowing things I can't unknow. How bad Elizabeth's taste used to be. The extent of the secrets she still keeps.

I wrap everything in the ratty T-shirt and stuff the bundle back under her boots. What would she have done if I hadn't come along? Who the hell would she have become? I'd been so ready to write Raymond off when he made that crack about Elizabeth's past — about what she's capable of, her history of deception, but now — well, now this. Now I have to face reality. This is who I married. This is what she's capable of.

I return to the bathroom, splash cold water on my face, and soak my collar, but it doesn't matter. I should've changed into casual clothes by now, anyway. I turn off the tap and dry my neck, face, and hands, watching my reflection unbutton my shirt, watching my hands and head lose their grip. I stare into my own eyes and lift one arm, raise it overhead, poised to slap my face with my own open hand, but something stops me. My heartbeat pounds, dull but deafening: the rhythm of pulsatile tinnitus like a marching band in the distance, marching closer, closer still. Signs of trauma. Signs of shock. My gaze falls on a fixed point in the mirror.

Something felt wrong earlier. I couldn't name it, but my instinct was right. It was here all along. Elizabeth was still sleeping when I left for work, but she would have used it when she woke up, perhaps many times throughout the day, and at some point — before or after her shower, possibly before or after another barefoot visit to Nick, probably before their ride into town and their visit with friends, their cozy day, but definitely after I left this morning — someone visited my bathroom, so also my bedroom, and he left the seat up, that son of a bitch.

11.

Elizabeth and Nick are having an affair.

A complete thought at last. An internal explosion: mushroom cloud of fury.

I'll mold it into a mantra — *Elizabeth and Nick are having an affair* — repeated until the words are nothing but sounds, until their fallout settles in my system and goes dormant, inoculating me against emotional catastrophe. *Elizabeth and Nick are having an affair.* If I can undo it, I will. If it's too late, at least I'll be prepared.

I smooth my hair, regain composure, change into casual clothes. Leave the toilet seat up. Descend to my den, fix myself a drink, settle into my oversized leather chair. Count backward. Count breaths. Try to imagine my heart slowing to a peaceful pace.

I envision Elizabeth sitting here with me in this room with this late afternoon light, me asking if anyone else used our bathroom today, her playing dumb, her acting like everything is normal. Me questioning every measure of normal I've ever taken for granted.

Or: us sitting in this late afternoon light, me voicing my suspicions, me being right, her confessing, her confession ruining our lives.

Or: us sitting in our favorite chairs, knowing what we know, knowing each other well enough to spare the other details, loving each other well enough to wordlessly and mutually agree upon eliminating the problem, getting on with our lives, reclaiming *our lives.*

Everyone has trauma, everyone has loss, but sob stories don't grant impunity, and Nick messed with the wrong family man. I know all about how some men cure grief by attaching to the first woman who happens to smile or walk like the dead one did. Maybe the new woman laughs similarly, maybe her breath smells the same. One detail anchors a fantasy. The fantasy seals an open wound: infatuation fashioned as butterfly tape.

My father latched onto the shade of mauve my mother wore on her lips, the very same lipstick favored by Wife Number Two: Bette, who pronounced her name Betty, not

177

Bet; who had expensive taste and cheap style; who smoked Virginia Slims; who laughed louder than anyone in any room; who always ordered dessert and never inquired about the fate of her missing Victoria's Secret catalogs. She, too, left mauve stains on cigarette butts and kept ashtrays full of ghosts in every corner of our house. She left marks. I wasn't a fan of my father's second wife, but she had her moments. She had gall. My mother had hardly been gone a year when Bette came into our house bearing strong opinions and officious advice: morality clauses and gruff instructions that still hold real estate in my head. I'd return home from school bent out of shape over a classmate with sadistic tendencies, or my father would walk through the door oozing vitriol, blaming the cogs at his job, and Bette would say, "Don't give them the satisfaction of losing your cool. It's better to kill 'em with kindness." Her years as a Hart were brief, but her words are like eels in the coves of my mind. *Kill 'em with kindness,* they whisper. *Make them sorry they ever began.*

The garage door motor grinds twice: once to open, again to close. Silence fades into muffled laughter. A key in the lock. Chatter from all three cords in my knot of love and hate.

"You survived," I shout from my chair.

Elizabeth heads straight to the den. "Not only that, we had fun. Luna is a trip."

"See?" I grin. "She's not bad. You just needed to give her a chance."

"Oh, no," Elizabeth counters. "She's bad."

"She's the worst, Dad."

Nick nods. "She's kind of awful."

"But we figured something out." Elizabeth fixes herself a drink. "Nick did, anyway. Once you stop expecting her to be normal, she becomes wildly entertaining."

"The key is to watch her like she's a cartoon," Nick explains. He helps himself to two cans of LaCroix from my fridge, tossing one to Jonah, cracking open the other for himself.

"How insincere," I say.

Jonah throws himself over the arm of our couch. "I'd rather be insincere than intolerant."

"Nice to see you prioritizing, Son."

"Oh, relax," says Elizabeth. "We had a nice time." She nestles into her corner of the couch, and Nick returns to where he was sitting earlier, as though it is *his* place. Remembering something, Elizabeth asks, "Hey, is something wrong with the shower

179

in the guesthouse? Nick said you thought it was broken."

"False alarm," I tell her.

"What did you think happened?" she asks.

"Nothing. Just wanted to make sure it wasn't backed up."

She laughs. "Why would it be?"

"God, Elizabeth. It's not a big deal." Jonah snickers now, too, so I say, "The plumbing has given us problems in the past, so I was double-checking to make sure Nick is comfortable."

She smiles. "This is the first I've heard of our plumbing problems."

"That's because I always get to them first."

Jonah laughs. "Touché!"

"Touché, indeed," Elizabeth says, and they all raise a glass, or a can, to my wit.

Jonah heads to the kitchen and returns with four plates and a paper bag, distributing foil-wrapped burritos, plastic cutlery, paper napkins, hot sauce. Everyone's so chummy, so goddamn playful, that Jonah even suggests Scrabble at one point. Nick declines, saying Scrabble would keep them up all night, and Jonah asks Nick when he became a geriatric, so Nick explains that he doesn't want to push it and get sick again. For this, Jonah calls Nick a loser, and Elizabeth smacks Jonah in the face with a pillow, and Nick high-fives Elizabeth for defending his honor, and my head nearly explodes.

I seethe. Inside, I scream, but my rage is invisible. It's a talent. I mime boredom, stretching and forcing a yawn. Checking the time. Eventually saying, "Well, I guess we should call it." Wendy and her Lost Boys don't follow, though, so I drum my belly with open palms, and say, "Bedtime?" With this, their lively conversation halts, but only so all three of them can stare at me like I said, *Bath time?* Like what I said was wrong.

Elizabeth smiles at last, and her judgment vanishes. Another talent. "I'll be up in a bit." And she's Wendy again. So. Whatever. I'll sit and wait. Wait, watch, and listen.

They talk of feelings and aesthetics. Colette's goddamn braid. Flagrant sentimentality. It's such a shame, what we've done to our boys. We've taken away their power. These days, kids aren't allowed to develop strategy, because kids aren't allowed to be picked on or to pick upon. These days, assholes are called bullies, and sticks and stones are reported promptly to the principal for ignominious review. Children pass the buck without ever discovering how to defend themselves, how to attack, whether by baseball bat or random acts of kindness. I don't need a baseball bat. I don't need lawyers or restraining orders or ultimatums, either. I have brains.

Nick and Elizabeth are having an affair. The less I resist, the less power it wields. People have affairs. They're just another troublesome thing people have from time to time. People have heartburn and debt. They have nightmares and gallstones and doubts and regrets. I should know. I've built a career addressing ailments — which, come to think of it, uniquely qualifies me to inspect a person's body and mind just to point out flaws; or to provoke vulnerability, in a general way; or to grip a neck — and so it would seem I have access as well as brains.

Having finished his dinner, Nick cleans his share of the mess, says good night and takes his leave. Jonah and Elizabeth begin tidying the rest, but I say, "Shit. Forgot to test the pool water."

Elizabeth tells me not to bother, that she tested it this morning, but Nick is already halfway across the yard, so I mumble something about algaecide and slip outside to run after him. By the time I call his name, he is almost to the door of his borrowed bungalow. He turns and waits, and only when I'm close enough to speak barely above a whisper do I ask, "What are you doing in the morning?"

He frowns, shakes his head.

"Given how well you responded to that tea, a supplement system is going to change your life. We'll swing by the office, do an intake —"

"No, you really —"

"I insist. Obviously, you aren't expected to buy anything, but you'll have a metabolic profile for when you're ready. I'll hook you up with a free consultation before Jonah wakes up. Just don't tell those two." I nod toward the house, roll my eyes, shake my head. "They're always giving me shit about being too generous, you know? Good for the community, bad for the books." I laugh. He doesn't.

Nick says, "That's thoughtful, but seriously, I'm feeling better."

"You aren't going to believe how you feel when I'm through with you." I slap his shoulder. "Why don't you meet me downstairs at, say, seven. It's a plan."

Nick gives in, says, "Okay." Then he goes and surprises both of us by saying, "Thanks, Dr. Hart."

"Not another word."

12.

Saturday morning. Elizabeth is at yoga, Jonah is sleeping like the dead, and Nick is dressed and waiting for me in the kitchen when I meet him there at seven o'clock. He looks tired. I tell him this. He says he didn't get much sleep, but when pressed, insists that the problem is internal, not environmental. My house is incredibly comfortable, he assures me, and he apologizes for dragging me to work on a weekend, complains about how bad he feels. I tell him it's no trouble at all and that if he wants to feel guilty, he should pick another sin, to which he says nothing at all. The drive takes nine minutes. No radio, almost no small talk. Nine minutes of silence to accompany Nick's window-framed view of my beautiful world.

I park in my otherwise empty lot and enter through the back door, flip on fluorescent lights and lead Nick to Exam Room Four, where I line the table with sanitary paper and tell him to change into a cotton gown — atypical, but peak vulnerable — while I scavenge for a blank intake questionnaire, clipboard, and ballpoint pen. Mimicking my nurses' daily spiel, I say, "Answer as much as possible, but don't overthink it," and close the door, leaving him alone. In the staff lounge, I make and drink an espresso from a regularly descaled Keurig, take a seat, take a load off, debate whether a lab coat would heighten my authority or make me look like I'm trying too hard. Authority wins.

Five minutes. Ten. Enough time for Nick to grow antsy, but not so much that he'll come looking for me. To pass the time, I visit my in-office lab, where I load a stainless-steel tray with instruments from my nurses' wheelhouse — test tubes, syringes, swabs, quick tests: objects I rarely, if ever, handle, but Nick doesn't need to know how rusty I am with a needle.

In the exam room, Nick hands me his questionnaire, sparsely answered. His brevity is disappointing, but the cotton gown is delightful. Boxers would've been inappropriate for Jonah's friend, but street clothes are security blankets. The cotton smock with yellow dots democratizes.

185

Nick takes a seat on the table while I wash my hands with antibacterial soap, stepping on a hot water pedal, scalding my knuckles, suddenly aware that neither of us really knows why we're here. My good ideas flicker too rapidly these days. Logic fades, but not the urges, so these I can trace, at least, and I do — following my urge back to the desire to assess Nick on my terms, my turf. Following my desire to choke the daylights out of him.

Towering over a seated Nick, I check his glands: digital palpation of the submandibular, submental, and superficial cervical nodes. Nick averts his eyes, looking at my widow's peak rather than my left ear like most patients tend to do. I step behind him and wrap my hands around his neck — right above the bow where Nick secured his yellow smock — and press my finger pads along his thyroid, just inferior to the laryngotracheal framework. "Swallow," I command, and Nick does, allowing for elevation. He's uncomplicated from this angle. The back of a head is anonymous, apolitical. Choking a disembodied hairball would be emotionally uncomplicated.

Nick clears his throat.

"Your glands are slightly swollen," I say — and am immediately seized by regret. Well, damn. That's a first. Never before have I fibbed to a patient. There's still time to take it back, to say, *My bad.* Placing my fingertips behind his ears, I press my thumbs against his cheekbones. "Just checking your sinuses," I say, pressing harder. "Any pain here?" Although, to be fair, everyone's lymph nodes are different, so maybe his are slightly swollen, so maybe it isn't a lie. Pressing harder still: "What about here?" So maybe it's fine.

I tell Nick to say *ahhhh.* He obeys, and when I find his gag reflex with the tongue blade, causing him to wretch, I say, "Sorry about that," and turn quickly so he won't see me smile.

Pitch the stick. Dispose my gloves. Get a grip.

My job is remarkable. In what other work dynamic must one submit to inspection like this? No banker gets to squeeze another man's neck without resistance. Architects can't shove objects down throats without arrest. Doctors, however, are expected to do as much and more. Women let me record their weight. Men turn their heads and cough.

I hold my stethoscope to Nick's back for chest auscultation and tell him to breathe deeply. His exhale smells like coffee and

Wintermint gum. I pause to ask about his appetite (fine) and his insomnia (chronic). "Nighttime gets the better of me," he says.

I nod and move the chestpiece from one side of his back to the other. Lungs clear. Heart pumping from valve to valve, right in time. I ask, "And are you sexually active?" Through amplifying eartips, I listen for the acceleration of Nick's heartbeat while bracing for the reverberation of his voice.

"No."

"You don't have to be modest."

"It's true," he says. "I'm not at the moment."

I swap my stethoscope for an otoscope and stare into one ear canal, then the other, giving Nick time to wonder if and how my questions relate to his predation. With two fingers below his chin, I tilt his head back for anterior rhinoscopy. "I treat too many boys your age, I guess. So often, they're on the prowl."

He grunts — a laugh distorted by rigid posture, his posture rigid on account of the instrument up his nose. "Well. There's sort of someone, but it's complicated."

I step back to avoid ramming this otoscope through his skull. "Complicated how?"

Nick dares to look at me. "She's very

unavailable." He looks at the floor — and is he blushing? "Timing is a bitch."

I rush to sterilize objects that will need to be sterilized again later, just for the excuse to busy my hands, just to protect them from doing harm. "We'll run a standard STI panel, then."

"That's fine."

"Nothing to be embarrassed about."

"I'm not embarrassed."

My back still turned to Nick, I fiddle with the HIV quick-test in my hands, fairly certain (but not certain) that it's a run-of-the-mill cheek swab, nothing tricky, so I turn and say, "Open up," and hold Nick's jaw with one hand. With the other, I collect cells from the inside of Nick's mouth. "That's all there is to it," I say. "You wait here."

Grabbing my clipboard with Nick's questionnaire, I take my leave. On the other side of the door, heat blooms from my gut to my chest, from my chest to my neck to the top of my head, and so I return to my lab to seek a hit of busy work, opiate of the agnostics.

Small as it may be, to me, my lab is a labyrinth — organized by Simone, navigated by Nurses Lindsay and Clem. Such a gruesome investment, way back when. Such a risk: my own in-office lab, a burden be-holden to ever-shifting regulations, ever-expanding responsibilities, paperwork, fees, problems. My competition swore I'd regret it. Their doubts worked like double dares, and I doubled down. Big fat loan: approved. Construction. Applications. Drug rep court-ships: fancy dinners, cross promotion. Nurses with business brains, cutting-edge training. Television spots, magazine features, branded products, patents, profits. Vanessa believed the lab would either ruin me or be the beanstalk to my jackpot — *and* to my seat among giants, I joked, and she said sure — so she filled a prescription bottle with dried pinto beans and wrote *Magic Beans* on the lid, and we put it on top of my bookshelf by the door, directly in my line of sight from my desk chair, virtually invisible from elsewhere. Day in, day out, busting my ass, then one day: jackpot and giants. I astonished myself and outraged the compe-tition. Curmudgeons fought to stay in busi-ness. And here I am.

Childish of her, the magic beans. Sweet though, too. They stayed on the shelf long after our divorce was finalized. Don't know why. Maybe I was lazy, except I'm not. If Elizabeth noticed them, she never said a word. Not that she'd have cared. The bottle is in the back of a desk drawer somewhere, I'm pretty sure. Never could throw it away. Maybe I got sentimental, even though I'm not.

Now here I am, lost among the details that started it all: shelves and rows of cups and strips for urinalyses, throat cultures, glucose and lipid and pregnancy tests. I prep solution for Nick's swab, twist his cells into a vial, set a timer, and return to Exam Room Four to tie a rubber ribbon above the kid's elbow, to prep a needle like I do this all the time. Nick's veins are healthy and impossible to miss. "Just a little prick," I say. I haven't printed labels, because these vials will go in the trash. His serum levels don't matter to me. I just want to watch him squirm.

Then it's back to the nurses' station to dispose of sharps and check the timer. Ten minutes to go. He'll be antsy by then. Nobody — no matter how risk averse or sure the unlikelihood, no matter what — enjoys the moments leading up to HIV test results. People aren't thinking about weather or groceries or how nice a nurse was, how pleasant the wait is — including, or perhaps especially, those who pretend to have only been reading *Redbook* or *Sports Illustrated* or *Vanity Fair,* or those who act as though they'd forgotten why they were waiting in the first place. People hold their breath when I enter the room, and when I say "negative," they release a sip of air. Some confess their anxiety, while others laugh in such a way as to expose their delusions of immunity. Their righteousness was stupidity all along. Stupidity or trauma. The young ones aren't stuck in the eighties or nineties like their parents — a generation haunted by a plague that came by night; by outdated data and debunked myths, heartbreak and sleight of hand; by cellular betrayal — but the young ones hold their breath anyway. Genetic memory.

I entertain a wicked fantasy: Nick's face in that instant before *negative.* Or *positive,* in which case, he wouldn't sigh. He might hold his breath, and I'd have to remind him to inhale, and he might say, "How did this happen?" Then, God, the thoughts that would run through his head. He'd look at me, thinking, *Did I get it from this nice man's wife?* Then, *Did I give it to her?* Following that line of reasoning: *Have I put this nice man at risk?* Dr. Hart, his dear, sweet host who took him in and fed him and let him seduce Mrs. Hart on the sly. If he heard *positive,* he would tell Elizabeth, and she would tell me, and then, oh boy, the depth of disaster.

Or maybe he would try to sneak her to an anonymous clinic to get tested. By the time they both heard *negative,* the ordeal would have woken them up, spoiled their fun. Elizabeth would send Nick away, because she would see, at last, the potential consequences of her transgressions and how close they'd brought her to losing me. She'd salvage her devotion, and she'd grovel, and we'd thrive.

Or, bypassing scenarios one and two altogether, Nick might up and leave town without saying why. Somewhere very far from here — in, say, Alaska, at another camp for damaged boys — Nick would seek care, and he'd be so relieved to hear *negative* that he wouldn't blame me for a chemical quirk. *False positive results do happen,* the other doctor or nurse would say. They do happen. It's true.

The timer dings. Twenty minutes flew right by.

I lift the vial, hold it high, squint to read the strip: *Negative.*

I hear myself release a tiny breath.

Well then. A relief. I drop the swab in my pocket and skim the contents of Nick's questionnaire before throwing it away. He offered details on diet but not bowel movements. He gets the hiccups and has hay fever, but no food allergies or acid reflux. He trips and falls sometimes because, as he wrote in the blank, he is clumsy, not injured. Of course not. His joints are well-lubricated and young. Arthritis is years away. I fold the questionnaire and slip it into my lab coat pocket and head back to Exam Room Four, where I take a seat at the corner desk, crossing my legs, propping up my clipboard so Nick can't see the blank page. I glance at my patient — my violator: hazardous waste — whose vulnerability is almost worth my pity. I see him clearly: the object of my wife's desire. The sum total of her temptation: six foot, one-hundred-seventy pounds, BMI of twenty-one, no allergies, occasional hiccups, insomnia, regular exercise. Spoiled rotten with the passive riches of youth. The love of my life would betray me for this.

The anvil slams into my chest: the ache I've been avoiding, delayed by mantras and plans and an army of hypotheticals. Here he is, a terrorist in a cotton gown, holding his breath awaiting *negative,* secretly imagining *positive,* quietly burning. He is at my mercy. I could kill him or I could cry.

"Dr. Hart?"

The nerve. My God. The recklessness. My power simmers and shines, daring me to fight for this precious life I've built. *For Christ's sake, Bobby, take a stand.*

"Is everything okay?" he asks.

In the space between inhale and exhale, the blood below Nick's skin races to his brain, muscles, and heart, and he fades to pale, a side effect of a primitive reaction wasted on warriors who don't fight with swords, spears, or claws. Instead, we sit in sterile rooms carving bullets out of silence, playing chicken with subtext. Taking matters into our own hands.

We shouldn't be here. I shouldn't be in this room with this kid (with his unspoiled body and Wintermint breath) who is tempting me to toy with malpractice, tempting me to slay my own giant with one word: *positive.*

"Couldn't get a read," I say, fingering the blood vial in my pocket. "We'll send it to the main lab first thing tomorrow." I hear myself say, "Try not to worry, everything is probably fine," but the voice isn't mine.

Leaving Nick to change into his clothes, I escape, once again, to the other side of this door, where my hopes for relief are swiftly pummeled by the buzz of an electric motor grinding to life: my Keurig. Someone is making coffee in my staff kitchen. I follow the grind, walking the length of this hall like I'm walking the damn plank: defiant, unapologetic, ready to plunge. But it's just Simone hovering over the Keurig, holding the handle of a thermos, watching it fill. She doesn't hear me when I hang my lab coat on a hook. The machine quiets. She turns and sees me now but is not startled. She simply smiles and asks, "Coffee?"

I shake my head. "Already fueled. What are you doing here on a Saturday?"

"Digging out of a paperwork avalanche. What are *you* doing?"

Down the hall, the door to Exam Room Four opens and closes with a bang. It's too late to hide him, so I say, "Family favor," just as Nick steps through the doorway.

Simone adjusts her posture from familiar to professional, the effect instantaneous and subtle, and greets Nick, who approaches to shake her hand.

"Nick Carpenter," he says. "Jonah's friend from school."

"Simone Bristol."

I shake my keys, tolling the end of our rendezvous, and tell Simone to hurry up and finish digging so she can enjoy the rest of her weekend.

She smiles and nods. "Nice meeting you, Nick."

He says, "You as well," and follows me to

the parking lot. The clouds are gray, the asphalt littered with dark spots where raindrops have already fallen. Close at heel, Nick asks, "She your nurse?"

"Office manager."

"She seems nice."

"Sure," I say, thinking, *Really? Her, too?*

The sky opens before we reach the car. We're half-drenched when we buckle our seat belts. I say a prayer for my leather interior and pull onto the road, my windshield wipers squeaking like twin metronomes ordering me home, ordering me to drive faster, faster. A yellow light changes to red, igniting my rain-streaked windows with fits of fire as we pass through it. No thunder, no lightning, no drama — just rainwater evacuating our beaches, sending city snobs back to their overpriced timeshares, where they'll mix mojitos and play board games and track muddy sand onto other people's floors. To think, there was a time I wanted to grow up and be one of those barefoot visitors. The teenage Me would drive to East Hampton in the summer just to sit on benches or blankets to watch the city kids, to study the differences between Them and Us, observing urbanites as though they were alien specimens in a living lab — like in that *Twilight Zone* when a marooned astronaut winds up caged in a zoo on a distant planet, his natural habitat re-created by extraterrestrials ogling the creature kept behind four walls, a pretty yard, a picket fence. Joke's on him. The punch line: *people are alike everywhere.*

Hard to believe I ever aspired to work like mad in Manhattan just so I could escape to a beach house on the weekend. Now I know better. I live better, having bypassed the need for escape by shooting straight to the good life. I'm my own boss, playing Trivial Pursuit in my own fancy house, making my own mark. Upgrading everything. I was naive and tenacious enough to start a private practice before the system went berserk. Young doctors today aren't so lucky, but those are the breaks. The American Dream has always been a changeling.

I press my foot on the gas, rocketing toward a new mental picture: young people flocking to my world in pursuit of role models and model lives. They draft dreams around us, then they grow up to push us out. *Don't be Nick's interactive education,* I tell myself, and something flashes. For a moment, it seems like my brain is the thing flickering — lit up by a thought, sparks thrown from the thought — but the flashes are blue and white lights in my rearview mirror, activated half a second before the siren begins. "Goddamn it," I say, tapping the brake, flipping my turn signal. I hang a right and find a discreet place to park behind the bank. "Jesus, I pulled over already. You think he could turn those lights off?"

Nick doesn't answer. He just says, "Man."

For the very first time in my life, I find myself wondering if the rumors are true about the free-pass power of that classic line: *Do you know who I am?*

SAG STYLE ON DISPLAY
AT CITIZENS' BALL
by Diane Klein

On Saturday night, Dr. Robert Silvano Hart was named Citizen of the Year at the 36th Annual Sag Harbor Citizens' Ball. The event was held under a twinkle-lit tent near the water's edge at Marine Park.

The black-tie gala, billed as "A Celebration of Style," was open to area residents and their guests. Proceeds from ticket sales and the silent auction support The Citizens' Fund, which distributes donations to a selection of local charities. This year's beneficiaries include Memorial Children's Hospital, the Seashore Restoration Project, and the Laura Day Fund supporting independent arts education.

Dr. Hart — pictured here with son Jonah, wife Elizabeth, and family friend Nick Carpenter — said that being acknowledged for civic engagement is "a humbling reminder of [his] responsibility to continue serving our exceptional zip code."

In his speech, Dr. Hart said, "While I'm proud to assume the mantle of Citizen of the Year for the next twelve months, my commitment to this community is not a fixed term. Sag neighbors and friends, your health and the health of this great township are the reasons I love what I do." He drew laughter by adding, "And just ask my wife: I don't do anything I don't love to do."

Dr. Hart, who practices internal medicine, pioneered the local popularity of innovative, noninvasive treatments for whole-body wellness ever since opening his private practice in Sag Harbor nearly twenty years ago. Specialties include platelet-rich plasma injection, hormone replacement therapy, customized supplement regimens, and personalized weight management programs.

Previous Citizens of the Year include Vance Barrington, Milos Lee, and J.R. Voss. Last year's title went to Malcolm Potter, who, along with wife Margaret Kearny Potter, manages the esteemed Kearny Foundation. Donations from last year's event raised a whopping four million dollars to support Kearny Award grants. Mr. Potter says he is happy to see Dr. Hart accept the award, calling our new Citizen of the Year "salt of the earth."

Guests at Saturday's party danced to live music performed by Seaside Symphony and posed for pictures in a customized photo booth. Attendee Marsha Villenueva praised event planners for thoughtful touches. "The props are a hoot," she said, referencing the assortment of dress-up items available for guests enjoying the photo booth. Wigs, oversized glasses, costume jewelry, and light-up signs were among items on loan — but not, as Ms. Villenueva lamented, for keeps.

Gloria Pryce and Vonda Webber co-chaired this year's event. Luna Parks spearheaded decorations. Master of Ceremonies was Theo Carter, 2012 Citizen of the Year.

The Citizens' Fund invites all Sag Harbor residents to submit nominees for next year's award by visiting SagCitizens.org. From the finalists, new honorees are elected by a voting body comprised of previous Citizens of the Year. You may sign up for event planning committees online. See calendar page for details. Tax-deductible donations welcome all year. Visit SagCitizens.org/donate to make your gift.

13.

Rain falls in heavy sheets during my entire mind-numbing visit with Officer Diaz, who needs a hobby. She requests license and registration, asks banal questions, stoops to look through my open window, peeks at my center console, studies Nick, and finally leaves to prepare my ticket — all while managing, but barely, not to scratch my Audi with the metal tips of her government-issued umbrella.

"I could have gotten off with a warning," I tell Nick, "but figured, oh well, she's just doing her job."

He nods.

We wait. Me and Nick. Windshield wiper pendulums swing left to right, tick to tock. Rubber against safety glass. Minutes pass.

I drum my fingers on the steering wheel. "You think she'd have something better to do."

Nick shakes his head.

"Poor girl must hate her life."

Nick stares out of his window and says flatly, "Maybe she likes living someplace where a cop doesn't have anything better to do."

I dig my fingernails into my steering wheel's Nappa leather.

"On account of there being so little crime here, I mean."

"Yes, Nick. I understood what you meant."

After twenty dreary minutes, Officer Diaz gives me my ticket and I give her my business card, inviting her to call me any time she needs a tune-up. The rain hasn't let up when I merge back into traffic. Diaz follows too closely, distracting my eyes from the road, so I turn onto the first residential street, while she stays on the main drag in pursuit of her next offender. As she disappears from my rearview mirror, I mumble, "Twelve miles over the limit. Give me a break."

Nick watches the blurry picture of my world, not his, and says, "You aren't concerned about my health for any reason, are you? You'd tell me if I needed to be worried, right?"

Like music in a dream, a voice bubbles up inside of me. It says: *Well, well.*

"You never suggested supplements, so I was just wondering —"

Different versions of *positive* bubble, too. They surface, but then, *Bobby, think of your wife and child*. And so, *Not now. Later. Soon.* I tell Nick, "I'm sure everything will be just fine."

Day into night without a word from my wife and son about Nick's health or my pro bono gig. Nick either told them, or he didn't. Jonah and Elizabeth care, or they don't. Only one time do I worry about having to explain myself, and that's at the very end of the day, when I head up to find Elizabeth already in bed, wearing a white silk nightgown, leaning against a pillow propped against the wall, reading. She lowers her book, makes a show of hesitating, so I say, "What?"

"You got a call from that luxury dealership in Roslyn. Perry was checking in about the Aston Martin. He wants to know what you're thinking." To my relief, Nick's glands have nothing to do with it.

I undress. "Oh yeah?" Hang my belt on a hook. "What'd you say?"

"Not much, considering you never mentioned the test-drive."

"No? Yeah, well, I took it out a couple of

205

weeks ago for fun."

Her pause is an invitation I decline, so she says, "Okay. For fun. So then, you're not considering buying a car."

"Not tomorrow or anything."

"Right. Or the next day."

"Sure," I say, "not Monday."

"Very funny."

"How about: *no time soon.*"

"That's great."

"Why are you asking like that? Do we have financial concerns I should know about?"

"No." She laughs. "We're fine. We just — we can't get crazy. We can't start living like the McAlisters, you know?" She reaches for me, grasping at the air as an invitation to take her hand. "Even though they are *very* sexy cars."

I don't hold her hand yet, but I do see an opportunity to try out one of those conversations that makes couples stronger: an opportunity to strengthen our marriage's immune system. She makes room for me when I sit on the bed to tickle her wrist and say, "If you want to know when that test-drive happened and why, I'm happy to talk about it."

She closes her book and places it on the nightstand. "Please."

"It was the day I had my picture taken for

the award. The whole thing sort of sunk in. I was so happy, which was embarrassing, but I wanted to share my happiness with you. I called, but you were too busy to talk."

"I don't remember."

I nod.

"Do you not feel like I've been supportive enough?"

"You've been amazing." I squeeze her hand. "Really. It just would've been nice if you'd been excited, too — if you'd wanted to take me out for dinner to celebrate or something — but you were busy. I understand. It's not a big deal, but that's why."

"That's why you secretly test-drove a sports car."

"I wanted to treat myself, Elizabeth. To acknowledge the moment, in a way."

"Oh," she says. "Yeah, I —"

"You've been incredible."

"No, I know." She twists her mouth into a question mark. "Now I'm confused, though."

"Because?"

"Because it seems to me that the award was the treat. Right? And it didn't come cheap. Cost us far more than an Aston Martin."

Stay sweet. "Excuse me?"

"Well, they gave you that trophy because

of how generous you'd been with the Children's Hospital Fund all year, right?"

A zap at my throat. "No."

"It's not?"

"Are you suggesting we bought the honor?"

"God, no." She rubs my back: a pat on the head for a silly boy. "But philanthropy is a significant measure of character for this particular award. Right? Charitable contributions? You know this, Robert."

I should get into bed, sleep and start over, but that electric sadness zaps my throat and neck, zaps me under my skin from head to toe, and if I sit down I will feel it all, all too much.

Elizabeth holds out her hand again. "I didn't mean to upset you. Come here."

"Maybe I should sleep downstairs tonight."

Her hand falls back to her lap. She sighs, shakes her head and says, "If that's what you want."

It's not. What I want is for her to insist I sleep beside her, but she's called my bluff, so now I'm stuck. Backtracking shows weakness, and weak is worse than lonely, so I gather my pillows and blankets and leave Elizabeth, inviting her heart to grow fonder.

14.

It's four thirty in the morning when nature calls. Takes me a minute to figure out where I am. This isn't my nightstand. That isn't my wall. But of course it's my house (our house), after all. The boxer shorts I dropped on the floor last night are nowhere to be found, and I'm too tired to turn on a light or be bothered with decency, since nobody's down here anyway, so I head for the hall stark naked, half inclined to use my own bathroom in my own bedroom and crawl into my bed where I belong, but if I'm too tired for lamps, I'm not fit for confrontation. It'll be time to get up soon enough. An extra hour of solitude won't break me.

I'm halfway to the john when light passes through the banister overhead, casting long shadows on the living room floor. Directly under the landing like this, I can't see my bedroom door opening. Elizabeth can't see me here as she sneaks away to tap me on the shoulder to say, "It's almost morning," so that nothing looks out of place once the sun comes up. I should hurry back to the office, contort myself, and pretend to be sleeping so she'll feel sorrier when she retrieves me from exile, but I can't resist the opportunity to let her find me like this: nude, still, waiting in the dark, arms crossed, planted like a Praetorian Guard. I almost laugh out loud at the absurdity of delighting in a childish game of hide-and-seek.

But she whispers, "Good night," and the strips of light at my feet narrow, and with the slow click of a doorknob gently turned back into place, her light vanishes altogether.

Footsteps, but the feet descending our custom-built floating staircase aren't Elizabeth's. *Jonah?* Maybe he's hungry. Maybe he's looking for me.

There's no time to hide, and so I freeze, calling upon an instinct too readily eclipsed by its overhyped counterparts, fight and flight. Freezing deserves more respect. Possums play dead. Deer vanish under the camouflage of stillness. I ease into this shadow-draped wall and quiet my breath, stunned by this opportunity for insight into my son's world.

Through gaps between cedar slats, I watch

210

his bare feet touch down. This is all I see: the wide hem of dark pants falling around my son's heels, step by silent step.

Upon reaching the living room floor, however, the figure turns just enough for me to see that everything is wrong, because it isn't my son's body. That messy dark hair doesn't belong to my boy. Wearing nothing but drawstring pants hanging low, Nick Carpenter moves with the ease of someone who knows his way through my house in the dark: heading to the sliding glass door on the other side of the room, letting himself out, closing it behind him. He passes the pool and his naked back glows watery blue, and me, I vanish under the camouflage of stillness. Look at us: a couple of invisible boys. Like the possum that mimics death to save its life, my pulse slows. My fingers and toes grow cold. Only my pupils betray signs of life, and even then, only when Nick flips on the light in my guesthouse and makes himself at home.

Oh, Lizzie. Why did you have to go and do a thing like that?

My blood resumes circulation. My pulse quickens. Warmth returns to my hands and feet. I've lost touch with the rest of my bodily functions, but I go to the bathroom anyway just to look in the mirror to see for myself that I'm not having a stroke — that a brain hemorrhage isn't triggering hallucinations. Gripping the sink, I lean into my reflection and stare myself down, flexing and stretching features, hunting for signs of palsy, but it's just my face staring back. It's just my naked body and salt-and-pepper chest hair, my ashen skin, so I guess I woke up on the wrong side of the looking glass after all. I count back from fifty and get all the way to twelve before the anxiety lifts. Settling into my body, I piss and leave the seat up and make the decision to say, "Like a baby," when Elizabeth asks how I slept last night.

15.

My head is a hurricane. I sit in my office chair until the sun comes up, trying to reverse engineer a misunderstanding — a chance encounter on the way to the linen closet, an urgent message that couldn't wait until morning — but I hear a stampede and can't fool myself, and it doesn't matter if the hoofbeats belong to horses or zebras or barefoot liars, or whether the violation was born of insecurity or attraction or boredom or spite. Reasons mean little to the creature being trampled underfoot.

This time, I submit to fury. It envelops but does not overpower me; on the contrary, it empowers me. I see red, yes, but I see so clearly now. Elizabeth's betrayal is not born of lust, or a mockery of love, but of anger. It is an act of aggression directed toward *me*. Nick's body is her weapon in the flesh.

Vanessa called this sort of thing self-sabotage: the methodical orchestration of an illusion of control. Tactical self-destruction eliminates the risk of being destroyed by outside forces, and the self-saboteur walks away believing she chose the wreckage. If a wife, for example, were to feel overshadowed by her husband, such that she resents him, but fears losing him, too, she might engage in behaviors that let her believe she broke the marriage, not the other way around. Her desperation might be a challenge to the husband's honor, a test of his allegiance to his vows.

Elizabeth is daring me to fight for her — *handing me* her dirty blade with two sharp edges — to prove that my heart is not a pacifist. An irrational man might beat Nick with a titanium driver, break his limbs, throw him in the pool and watch him drown — which is to say, this man might seek acute relief by inflicting acute pain. I am a rational man, capable of seeking sustained relief by inflicting prolonged pain.

Nick watched his mother's body decay, her mind and emotions held hostage by a broken machine. He watched her slow demise, her agony, her dehumanization and demoralization and disgrace, and Nick watched his father carry that shame — internalized and mutated into its own disease: the bullet hole in a widower's head

— and buckle beneath its weight, violently abandoning his only son, to whom he bequeathed this spectacular shame, thus compounded. Nick inherited secrets and sickness, self-loathing and lies, fears of breaking and being broken, fears of loving someone enough to pass his inheritance along. Surely, in this legacy, there is potential for my sustained relief.

I fold the bed into a couch, place its cushions in their proper places. I dress in yesterday's clothes, piled on the floor, and sit at my desk, opening my computer to weed through the internet to build my case: statistics pulled from limited research, testimonials, conspiracy theories, drug trials. I mentally flag words and phrases and obtuse data. The goal: to radiate dizzying authority, too fluent to allow for doubt. For good measure, I read up on New Age quacks who claim to have the cure. Nick might like the clinic in Tijuana. Maybe he'd stay in Tijuana. To assist in Nick's wallowing, I print a few self-help articles. Psychobabble about coping with bad news. "Managing Emotional Shock." "The Science of Acceptance." Good grief.

The early morning sun is hiding behind a thick fur coat of gray sky. Storm clouds without rain. Soft gray waves. I step outside and hear the wind thrashing trees, and it sounds like the sea, and enveloped by sea sounds and rippling clouds overhead, it feels as though I could be treading on the bottom of the ocean when I cross the yard to visit Nick Carpenter one last time.

He answers after the first knock. The smell of fresh coffee greets me when Nick does. He's wearing a sweatshirt and baggy gym shorts. Unlaced sneakers. Wild hair.

"I need to talk to you."

"Okay." He gestures for me to enter, but I shake my head. This will be quick.

"It's about yesterday," I tell him. "It's serious."

He steps outside. Behind him, the bed is neatly made, the nightstand clear. No water glasses, no picture books. He asks, "What do you mean?"

"I wouldn't have put it together if you hadn't come in for a full exam — your foot falling asleep on the boat, or your occasional trips and falls. If I hadn't read your questionnaire or noticed your muscle spasms yesterday, I wouldn't have thought of it in a million years."

"What are you talking about?"

"I'm talking about early indications of ALS. I'm sure you are all too aware of the very slight risk of genetic transfer." I pause

216

to let the implication settle, but not long enough for him to process the questions flooding his mind. Muscle spasms would be meaningless even if I'd noticed them, which I didn't, and deep down he knows that, but I don't let him dig deep, because I'm already on to facts and statistics gleaned from my very recent research, adding, "I'm so sorry, Nick."

He shakes his head. "What indications? I don't even —"

"You need to find specialized care. Have these conversations with doctors who see it every day."

"This is —" He shakes his head again. "This can't be happening."

"I know this is shocking. There must be a reason it's happening now. Things like this force people to use their precious time wisely. I want you to go out and spend the summer doing things you've always wanted to do. When autumn comes, you'll make a plan."

Nick's eyes dampen. His act of feeling is too intimate, maybe even manipulative, and I steel myself as warmth flows up my spine, my neck, my brow, branches out inside my forehead — certain that sympathy would distract me, guilt would overshadow my goal — but this warmth on the rise isn't compassion. It's *victory.*

I hand Nick the articles I printed, saying, "Here. These might help."

He folds the papers in half, then fourths. Without glancing at the headlines — without making time for hope — he places them on the small table by the door. "Well," he finally says. "I guess that's that."

"Actually," I say, "there is something else." Despite rehearsing this part in my head, it doesn't come naturally, as I'd imagined. "It's tough, but it has to be said."

"Jesus," Nick whispers.

"The thing is — this conversation needs to stay between us."

"What do you mean?"

"It needs to stay between us," I repeat.

"You want me to keep this a secret?"

I nod toward the house and say, "For their sakes."

"You've got to be kidding me."

"No. I'm dead serious. If you share this with them before having a treatment plan, they will make things very complicated and dramatic."

"Jonah wouldn't do that," he says.

I should have rehearsed this out loud, but I've already committed, so I say, "Jonah would be devastated. He would add to your stress. He'd shoot the messenger, too."

"For doing your job?"

"Well, you're not my patient, really. I'm telling you all of this as a courtesy, as a family friend. I'm doing you a solid, but my diagnosis is off-the-record. Worrying everyone and pitting them against me won't change a thing for you. Bring it up when you have more information."

"Fine," he says, cutting me off, mercifully. "I'm good at secrets."

"I imagine so."

I'm good at secrets, he dares to say, mocking me on my ground, but I can play with subtext too, and yes, now that I'm all the way off-book, my next move feels inspired: a whisper from a muse. Excessive, but delicious. "There's another reason to keep quiet," I say, almost high from how perfect it is. "It concerns Elizabeth."

His eyes meet mine. "Elizabeth?"

"Yes." My skin tingles, and I've come this far, so: "She's pregnant."

He twitches, then fixates on me, and only by engaging so suddenly, with such intensity, do I see how disengaged he's been until now — as though he'd been a figure in a dream letting news pass through him. A ghost, but now he's real. "Pregnant?"

"Yes," I say, and then the kicker: "Two months along." Two months ago, Nick was far away from my wife. Two months ago, he was cramming for exams and wondering how to cause trouble. Two months means Nick couldn't be responsible for this new development. He doesn't need to know about my vasectomy or the likelihood of Elizabeth conceiving naturally. He only needs to believe that Elizabeth is carrying the wedge that will come between them. "It's a very high-risk pregnancy, and she's been warned, gravely, to avoid stress. Do you understand? She'd never forgive you if something happened as a result of distress. Over this."

Nick shudders, and he's a ghost again.

"Jonah doesn't even know yet. Do you see why this is so sensitive? He'll tell you when he sees you in the fall. If he doesn't, that means something went wrong. In which case: all the more reason to keep your mouth shut."

"I won't tell them," the ghost says.

My body feels lighter. "Let me know if you need a ride to the train station later today. Tomorrow at the latest would be best. I'd love to offer advice, but it wouldn't be responsible."

"I understand." His face is ashen. His eyes are dry. A husk of a man.

"Now, off the record? You didn't hear it

from me, but there are clinics down in Mexico trying things the FDA won't approve."

"Really?"

"Yes. Unconventional methods, but rumored to show promise. I guess people figure: 'What do I have to lose?' And really, who can blame them?"

He musses his hair, straightens his spine, flicks a nod. "I'll look into it." This time, he's the one who says, "You won't tell them, right?"

"Of course not, Nick," I promise. "I'm good at secrets too."

"Really?"

16.

So it's that simple, and I don't know if the sky really clears on cue, but beams of sunlight I hadn't noticed earlier now drop anchor in ground that feels more solid under newly firm feet — and me, I'm light as air. My heart is my friend again, pumping blood to every striation of every muscle in every limb, and I could run a million miles. I ran a marathon once, when I was twenty.

There's a folded pile of clean clothes on top of the washing machine, so I change into shorts and a T-shirt and my favorite merino wool socks — workout clothes I've been wasting on lazy Sundays, these days — and lace up bright white sneakers, unconcerned about whether or not my gym membership is current, because the gatekeepers at my gym require a handwritten note from God to break a contract. More important, the boy behind me is crackling and dissolving. The space in me that overflowed with rage is now hollow, with mere traces of residual rage. I could save them for Elizabeth, or I could leave them in the backyard to crackle and dissolve. I could hang hate on the scaffolding caging my marriage, or I could build us back up with love.

From the bottom of the stairs, I call up to Elizabeth to say, "Heading to the gym. Think about where you want to eat tonight. We're going out." I grab my keys and wallet and yell, "Just us," and I'm gone.

The sun peels off the last cloud in its solar striptease, and the landscape sizzles. On the radio, Johnny Cash and June Carter are singing Bob Dylan's song, and I turn up the volume and sing along, full voice. Windows down, I laugh out loud, liberated at last from the back-and-forth in my brain, the what-ifs and hauntings. My life is mine again.

The gym is crowded. A gal name-tagged *Claudia* checks me in at the front desk. There must be a note in my account indicating my hiatus, because she says, "It's been a while. So glad to see you back, Dr. Hart." She hands over clean towels. "Hey. You look really familiar."

"A young Daniel Day-Lewis?" I joke. "Afraid not, but I get it all the time."

She giggles: a perfectly girly little thing. "Come on."

"No? Well, I'm not Harry Connick Jr., either."

"I'm being serious. Were you in the paper recently?"

I shrug, playing bashful.

"That's it."

"It's no Oscar, no Grammy, but ... ."

"You're doing work with the Children's Hospital, right?"

I grin and take my towels. "Today I'm just a regular guy at the gym."

Claudia apologizes, believing she's crossed a boundary, so I say, "No big deal," and leave her to wonder about my big deal while I find a treadmill and run and run and run.

There's a trio of texts from Elizabeth waiting for me after I shower. She wants me to pick up a prescription on my way home, and did I get her text, and, *Let me know you got this.*

I reply: *Got the texts. Picking up now.* But when I finally make it to the front of the line at CVS, they can't find her order, and I have to check with Elizabeth to make sure the script got called in, at which point she tells me I'm at the wrong store. I was supposed to go to Rite Aid down in Bridgehampton. Half an hour later, Rite Aid hasn't filled it either, so I give up and head home empty-handed.

"There you are," Elizabeth says, like a goose chase for Ativan had been my idea. Again, the choice: love or anger. Elizabeth is vibrant. Buzzing. I'm disoriented by how glad I am to see her this glad to see me. She's done the cruelest thing, but hate feels too easy, too provincial, because yes, the worst has happened, but somehow we're here, standing in the kitchen, alive and awake and blinking like a pair of plague victims after the fever breaks. To my astonishment, rage falls back. Relief takes the lead.

She asks, "Did you run?"

I nod. "Rowing machine, too. A few weights."

"Tomorrow's going to hurt."

Maybe. Maybe not. Tomorrow is a foreign land. Today I have a choice: love or hate. Tonight offers a ritual reset, the opportunity to role-play forgiveness. "I want to take you out. Just the two of us." Love.

She glances over her shoulder, instinctively considering the boys' feelings and deciding they aren't hers to manage anymore. "Sure," she says. "That sounds nice."

"You pick the place." I crack open a Pellegrino. "Have you seen Nick this morning?"

"Hm?"

I drink from the bottle, carbonation like sandpaper on my throat, and wipe the back of my hand across my mouth before repeating, "Have you seen Nick?"

"No. Today, you mean? No, not yet." She pulls her hair up, but finding no rubber band on her wrist, her fists full of hair remain stacked atop her head. "I don't want to," she says.

I move closer, putting her in range of my sweated-out pheromones, my heat, and I slide my body up to sit on the counter. "What don't you want?"

"I don't want — to see Nick. I don't want to think about him." She lets her hair and arms fall, lets it all go. "I just want to go back to how things were before."

White-hot splinters pierce the corners of my eyes. "Things have been off-kilter around here," I say, suddenly certain I couldn't bear to hear her put it into words.

"Yes," she says. "They have." She scratches her collarbone. "It's been strange to have people around all the time."

I say, "It's been distracting."

She looks into me. Telepathy. She's asking, *What exactly do you know?* Maybe even,

226

How much do you know?

"All of it," I answer, and she closes her eyes. "It's all been too much."

One flight above us, Jonah yells, "Yo." We look up to find him leaning over the banister, listening to our private conversation about him invading our privacy. "I wasn't eavesdropping."

"Oh God," says Elizabeth. "We didn't mean —"

"Wait," he interrupts. "Hold on." His head disappears. Moments later, he reappears in full coming down the stairs. "My door was open, that's all. You guys are right, though. You're used to your privacy. This is a lot for you."

"Jonah," I begin, but Elizabeth interrupts.

"We love having you here," she says. "This is heaven for us, believe me." She must feel me wanting to acknowledge the gaseous way Nick permeates every corner of our world, because she flexes one hand — the hand closest to me — and in this tiny gesture, a mere extension of fingers, I recognize her scaled-down reaction, subtle enough for only me to see. In her way, she is lifting an arm, cutting me off, saying, *I'll take it from here.* "But you're right in that it's totally new for us. New is great, we just weren't prepared. We're adjusting." Her outstretched hand says, *I got this,* and I like it.

Jonah nods. "I understand. Which is why I'm thinking of going to Mom's for a couple of days. It'll make her happy and will give you guys a break."

"You shouldn't feel unwelcome here," I say.

Elizabeth quiets me again, saying, "He probably needs a break from us, too."

Jonah shrugs. "Nah. Mom's on my case, anyway. She'll never let me hear the end of it if I don't visit soon."

"Do what works for you," I say.

"I've got to get some crap together, but I'll probably roll out in about half an hour."

"Like I said, whatever you want."

He seems oddly touched by my flexibility. "Thanks, Dad." Then, in pure break from form, says, "Love you, man."

We both squirm — his words as surprising for him to say as they are for me to hear — but Elizabeth elbows my abs as soon as Jonah walks away, so I say, "Yeah, you too." Then, for good measure, "Love you too, Son," because God knows I do.

Elizabeth nuzzles against me — moved by a touching moment between father and son, made possible by Jonah's imminent departure. He'll only be an hour away, but an hour is plenty. Elizabeth presses her ribs against mine, wraps her arms around my neck and latches onto me. With hot breath against my face, she tells me that she loves me.

"I know," I say, meaning, *I'll forgive you as soon as I can.*

17.

Elizabeth picks Lemongrass. Wouldn't have been my first choice, not even my second, but I'm a man of my word, so Thai it is.

Our server seats us on the patio and tells us we've chosen the perfect evening to dine al fresco, because tonight is a full moon, but tomorrow it's supposed to rain again, so we'd better enjoy it while it lasts. We came here to eat, not to study lunar cycles, but he is correct. The night is lovely, and the food is very good, some of it great, even. Their tom yum is perfect, their pad kee mao spectacular, and these basil martinis are downright dangerous. Somewhere between cocktails one- and two-too-many, Elizabeth catches a feeling.

"I do love you," she tells me, lazy-like.

"Me too."

"You do?"

"Of course," I say. "Don't be strange."

"But you're a good man, Robert."

"Thank you, Elizabeth." I wave to a server. "Can we get some waters over here, please?"

"You don't think I'm a bad person?" Elizabeth asks me.

"No."

"I'm afraid I might be."

"That's ridiculous. Of course I don't think you're a bad person. I think you're a wonderful person. You're my wife."

"Plenty of people marry terrible people."

"Well, you're not terrible. You've made mistakes. I'm sure you've done bad things." I pick up my fork, put it back down, say, "Maybe even terrible things. Elizabeth, those things don't have to define you. Do you know what I mean?"

She shrugs. Her glassy eyes reflect candlelight.

"All that matters is what you do next," I say. "We have to put the bad things behind us so we can move on and be better. Right? That's the best we can hope for once the damage is done."

Elizabeth seemed to be listening intently, but now I'm unclear as to whether she was listening at all, or whether she's sleeping with her eyes open, or if she's just very interested in the planters crammed next to our table, because she hasn't taken her eyes

231

off them for a minute at least. Turns out it was the latter, after all, because when a busboy comes by with two waters, Elizabeth asks him, "Are those begonias?"

He scans the red flowers, leafy vines, ornamental glass balls, and concrete urns, trying to decide which of these is most likely to be a begonia. "You know," he bluffs, "I do believe so. Let me check with a manager, just to be sure." He returns minutes later to confirm that yes, they are begonias, and a stoic Elizabeth nods and thanks him.

"Sometimes I think we made a mistake," she tells me, and although I'd like to think she's talking about restaurant choices or season tickets, I know she means us, and it kills me. "Do you think that?"

"Never."

"Well," she says. "That's good."

"Do you really, Elizabeth?"

"No. Kind of. Not about being together. About how we hurt people, though. How I hurt them." She picks up the tiny spoon from a tiny jar of chili sauce, twirls it in front of her face, and smiles. "Did I ever tell you about how I used to spend my Saturday nights when I first moved to New York?"

"Maybe?"

"Bed, Bath and Beyond."

"No. This is new."

"I used to take the train down to Bed, Bath and Beyond and just look."

"For bedding?"

"No, Robert. At people."

I laugh.

"I'd go there to look at people."

"Oh. You're serious."

"Yeah, I'm serious. I'd go down there to watch grown men buying colanders. Women shopping for vacuum filters. HEPA filters for thousand-dollar vacuum cleaners. Can you imagine? I mean, I'm still not sure what to do with a vacuum filter — and not because I'm spoiled. Yeah, I know we have a cleaning lady, I know that, but it's not like we'd be living in squalor without one. It's not like I'd have us shuffling around on dirty floors. It's just that I grew up with mops and brooms. Didn't you?"

"Sure," I allow. "But we also had a vacuum. I'm certain your family did too, Lizzie."

"Fine. But it wasn't fancy. It wasn't *Our Man in Havana,* okay? Maybe we had a plain old vacuum, but it would have been a Dust-Buster. A Dirt Devil. I mean, you know my parents."

"I do."

"They aren't exactly the Dyson type. The

233

Miele type." She mouths the word Miele — *meel*-eh — to herself. "They'd never go out and buy a bread maker, right? A salad spinner? They're more into microwave dinners."

I smile. She said it, not me. "That sounds accurate."

"Not that I'm complaining. I mean, no one bakes a meaner Stouffer's French bread pizza than my mom. All I know is that twenty years ago, there were a whole lot of clean floors in Manhattan. There were a whole lot of couples eating off placemats."

"You watched people shop."

"Sometimes I'd push a cart around and fill it with curtain rods and those cookie press things that look like caulking guns. Sometimes I'd buy high-end Tupperware, whatever. For the most part, I just wandered around with my hands in my pockets. I didn't want what those people had. Believe me, I did not want their Cuisinarts and table runners. I just liked how weird it felt to watch them."

"Of all the places to people-watch in New York City, you went straight for the big-box chain. What'd you have against Grand Central? Penn Station?"

"But that's just it, isn't it? We're in this spectacular city where you can eat whatever you want whenever you want without ever having to cook or wash a dish, and we don't have to worry about fixing disposals or washers and driers in our apartments, because they aren't there to fix, and I'm loving my life there for a very particular set of freedoms. Then one day I find out there's a whole subset of individuals who actually want to stuff their cabinets with appliances. So I'm thinking either they have a whole lot of counter space, or they exist on a totally different plane. Obviously, it's both: counter space and different plane. And it's absurd and embarrassing to admit how eye-opening this was to me, because of course we were all on different planes, but for some reason, I could actually see the break whenever I walked down a housewares aisle. New York became prismatic."

"I can only imagine what those security guards made of you."

"Never mind."

"No, I get it."

"It was just weird, okay? Still is, a little. None of that comes naturally to me."

"But you're good at it."

"But I hate it." She licks her fingers and pinches the flaming wick of a tea candle in a votive between us. A ribbon of black smoke rises from her thumb and forefinger. She lets go of the wick, rubs her finger and thumb together and opens her hand, admiring the black smudges. "Do you know who was really good at it, though?"

"No," I say, and I almost guess, because Elizabeth's use of the past tense makes me think she must be talking about Stuart, who absolutely would have collected tea cozies and napkin rings — *North of Blue Eye, deep inside your marvel cave,* Jesus Christ — although his kitchen crap would have to have been handcrafted gifts from artsy friends. Never mass retail, not for Stuart. Before I can guess, though, and before Elizabeth can tell me, our server returns to sell us dessert.

"Sure," Elizabeth says without pause. "Coconut crème brûlée, please."

I decline but ask for two coffees, two spoons, and the check. "Who was good at it?"

"Shae."

"Oh?" All things being equal, I'd rather hear about the tragic figure from her youth than about her ex-husband, if only by a small margin, so I say, "Was she?"

"Yeah. It came naturally to her. Even in high school, she'd save all her money for trivets instead of movie tickets. In college, she had, like, a tea set and a cheese board with little cheese knives, and she *used* them.

I mean, we were eighteen years old, and she put out a cheese tray when people came over. 'Company,' she'd say. 'We're having company tonight.' I've always wondered if she did things like that when she was alone, too." Elizabeth's focus drifts, fades, realigns. "I never did ask her. Wouldn't surprise me, though, if she set out a hunk of Maytag Blue, a wedge of brie, and a block of sharp cheddar every night, just for her. Crackers and little knives."

"Crackers and knives."

"Want to know what I saw at the moment of impact?"

"Oh, hey. Come on." I say it sweetly, but it's an order. "Let's not."

"We were listening to *From the Mars Hotel,* trying to memorize lyrics so we wouldn't be pariahs among Deadheads, and that song was on and we were singing along. And that truck driver wasn't paying attention. Maybe he didn't fall asleep at the wheel. Fine. But he wasn't watching the road. He just wasn't. I know, because I saw the deer in perfect silhouette against his headlights, and those lights held steady for a good two seconds at least before they swerved."

"Elizabeth." I lay my hand on the table, palm up, but she doesn't take it.

"A deer in the headlights. Isn't that some-

237

thing? That's not the last thing I saw, though. It's like, I knew we were about to get slammed by an eighteen-wheeler, and somehow I had the presence of mind to think, *Keep your knees down,* so I wouldn't break my legs. Is that even a thing? I feel like I saw it in some awful Driver's Ed video, where a dummy's legs get smashed because its plastic feet were on the dash. I bet somebody's mom wrote in that part to scare kids into keeping filthy shoes off the glove compartment, right? Well, it worked, because I thought, *Keep your knees down, Elizabeth,* and I wanted to have a whole conversation with Shae, but there wasn't enough time to say even a single word, and I don't know what I would have said anyway. So I turned my head and tried to tell her everything with my eyes — and I don't know if this is even possible, like scientifically, but I swear, Robert, I swear I kept my eyes open the whole time. I was staring at Shae and I remember thinking, *Don't take your eyes off her, Elizabeth.* As if me bearing witness would empower her to activate some magical survival skills or something. Just, *Don't you dare look away.* And I didn't, not through the whole thing. She closed her eyes, though. At the moment of impact, she closed her eyes."

I'd never heard that part of the story, and I'm thoroughly horrified, but I'm also pre-occupied, because how am I to know which would be more inappropriate: asking Elizabeth to keep her voice down, or letting her carry on like this in public?

"That always gave me a little comfort, to be honest with you. I'm glad the last thing she saw was the inside of her eyelids rather than an airbag or shrapnel in her thigh."

I reach across the table and grab her hand and squeeze it very hard, hoping to pinch her back to the moment.

"You want to know the dumbest part?" she asks. Her speech has started to slur.

"I think we should talk about this later," I say.

But she's in her own world in her head, so my answer doesn't matter, and she goes and tells me the dumbest part anyway. "I didn't even like the Dead. Neither did Shae. We'd never been fans and wouldn't have even considered going to that show if Tonya hadn't been out of town."

I mimic the tone used by crisis counselors in movies, characters who successfully talk maniacs down from a ledge, when I ask, "Who's Tonya again?"

"Shae's sister. It was her Camaro, you know. Tonya had been flown out to some fancy interview in Memphis. Didn't get the job, but she let us borrow her car while she was gone. So we did. We were eighteen. What did we know at eighteen? We thought we knew what we wanted, what was best for us. We didn't care about the show. We just wanted to drive that car."

Her laughter explodes. People at nearby tables turn to see what the fuss is about, but Elizabeth has no volume control or self-awareness at the moment, so when she throws her hands up to shout, "We just wanted to drive," her napkin goes flying, cascading to the table, then her chair, then the floor. A quiet game of Plinko. Elizabeth picks it up, folds it in a square and puts it on her lap before resting her elbows on the table and leaning toward me.

She finds her inside voice. "I swore I'd never get over it, but people told me that I'd make other friends, that I'd move on. They acted like I couldn't feel for myself because I was only eighteen, like I needed them to feel for me and report back so I could be a person. But guess what? They were wrong. I was right, and they were wrong. To this day, I've never made a better friend, and I've never gotten over it. Never. And you know what else? We really did just want to drive. So it's like, fuck the Dead, you know? Fuck 'Scarlet Begonias.' "

We eat our crème brûlée because it's in front of us, but as soon as the bill comes, I sign and we're gone. I've had too much to drink, too, but I'm our best bet to drive, because Elizabeth is in rare, rare form — possibly in as bad a shape as I've ever seen her. I guess breaking ties with a twenty-year-old boy-toy might prompt flashbacks to being twenty years old and dumb, too, and all the stupid decisions people make, and all the senseless twists of fate that leave us sad and lost despite having zero perspective. Even so, her revelation was particularly disturbing, because I should have known it. I should already know all of the most traumatic moments branded in her brain, so I do wonder what else she's been holding back all this time. Compassion overrides the wondering, of course, and I ask, "How are you doing?"

With a mile to go, Elizabeth rolls down her window and leans against the door, eyes closed and mumbling to herself. She goes on and on for some time before saying, "I think I'm going to be sick."

"Should I pull over?"

She moans.

"Can you make it five minutes?"

She moans in the affirmative, so I accelerate and zip through neighborhoods until we reach ours, and maybe I did take those corners too hard, because Elizabeth really does look like she's about to vomit all over my leather interior. She stumbles out of the car, exits the garage, and heads directly to the hosta leading to our side yard. She leans over it in full yack position, but the sensation must have passed quickly, because she swats at my ankles when I try to hold her hair. By the time she stands again, she is reasonably composed.

"After you." She gestures hard toward the house.

I take her hand and lead her through the garage, up the steps, and into the kitchen. Once inside, she keeps on walking — through the kitchen and den, unlocking the sliding glass door and leaving it all the way open. I follow. She kicks off her shoes and drops her shawl thing on the ground, but she's still wearing her dress when she steps onto the diving board and walks out to the end.

"Elizabeth?"

She looks at me — a slow, seductive meeting of the eyes, a coy invitation to a secret we haven't yet shared — and she hooks me, and she knows it, so she leaves me to my longing and sends her gaze back down to her feet, forehead aimed toward gold-polished toes hanging over the edge of our board. Underwater lights project auroras on her legs. A full moon christens her head with drops of silver. I sit in a lawn chair, slip off my shoes, peel off my socks, and Elizabeth dives.

18.

Hungover doesn't cut it. *Lobotomized and beat the hell up* is more like it. Every muscle aches from that goddamn rowing machine. Every brain cell throbs from overindulgence. My mind is mush, my senses dull, and I wasn't half as drunk as Elizabeth last night, so I don't know how she's functioning. To be fair, she's barely functioning. I feed her acetaminophen and go outside to fish her underwear from the pool filter. She doesn't know how it got there. She doesn't remember what we did out there, so I remind her that we did everything. Elizabeth probably doesn't remember telling candlelit stories at Lemongrass, either, and maybe that's for the best. All of that talk of Shae and vacuum filters was a little unhinged, and I'd just as soon forget it, so we shampoo our heads and face Monday, even though I happen to like Mondays. They're instilled with the power to reset. There are days like that, specific times like that. Midnight on New Year's Eve. September of a school year. Every single Monday morning. Some people dread them. I relish the clean slate, the scrubbed record, the fresh start — although, to be fair, this start is brutal.

Simone shows me an aluminum sculpture she found at a local gallery: an origami-style swan in brushed metal. All angles.

"Interesting," I say.

She deflates an inch or two. "You don't like it."

"It's not quite Elizabeth."

"Too pointy?"

"Too cold." I pat her arm and take my clipboard from her hands. "Keep looking. You'll find it."

Elizabeth may not need diamonds, but she does deserve better than a tin swan for having weathered these clichés with me, coming out on the other side, by my side. We've maintained a delicate degree of tension — courtesy of the things we don't know, the things we hope the other doesn't know, the things do we know — and I'll be damned if we aren't better for it.

"Doc?"

"Yes?"

"Just a heads-up: I overheard Nurse Lindsay this morning saying something about a butterfly needle being caught in the flap of the sharps receptacle. She unjammed it, but then she said something about how she never uses butterfly needles, and Nurse Clem said the same, that he always uses straight needles too, so they were like, 'Well then, who the hell used this butterfly needle and didn't even dispose of it properly?' But don't worry." One corner of Simone's mouth turns up in a half smile. "I covered for you."

"Covered? I didn't — wait, why would you say that?"

"You know." She wobbles her head and smiles with both sides. "Because of," and she whispers, "when Nick was here."

"You didn't need to do that. You don't even draw blood."

"Neither do you."

"True. But more important, there is nothing to hide with Nick coming here. It was just a normal visit."

"So I should tell them?"

"No," I say. "No, let's not. Nick had some private concerns. That's all. You did the right thing." She beams, and I ask, "What did you tell them, exactly?"

"I said I was stocking inventory and a butterfly needle fell out and landed on the floor, and that I figured it was contaminated, so I unwrapped it to dispose of its parts properly. They believed me and taught me how to keep the flap from jamming."

"That was nice of them," I say, although I'm not exactly grateful for nosy nurses. I could have handled it, but Simone is so proud of herself — I've never met a gal who loves feeling useful as much as this one — so I humor her. "And it was *very* nice of you. Thank you."

"My pleasure," she says, and she winks. "No one has to know."

Maybe I contort my face, but I don't say anything — I'm too baffled by her goofy grin when she pivots and hurries off. This full moon sure is getting to people. Whatever that means.

It's nearly dinnertime when Jonah returns from his mother's after all of one night away. His duffle bag is slung over his shoulder. He's carrying an empty pickle jar full of herbs and a few zinnias from Vanessa's garden.

"These are for you," he says to me, or maybe Elizabeth. "From Mom."

"That was nice of her," Elizabeth says.

Generic pickles. Kosher dills.

I ask, "Where's your sidekick?"

Elizabeth washes sage, mint, and fennel;

finds a small crystal vase and fills it with water; then goes about rearranging Vanessa's zinnias into something presentable.

"I don't know," Jonah finally answers. "I was going to ask you the same question."

Elizabeth pretends not to care, but not me. I go out of my way to show I don't care, asking, "How would we know what Nick's up to?"

Jonah shrugs. "You saw him last." He turns toward the stairs, duffle bag in tow.

"Wait," I command. "He's not with you?"

"I came straight from Mom's, remember?"

Elizabeth moves next to me with her arms crossed against her chest.

"Yeah," I say. "So? What, did you leave Nick there?" It would be funny — maybe even too perfect — if Nick started in on Vanessa now that his run with Elizabeth is over. Wouldn't it just be too sweet if Vanessa's meathead husband gave Nick his comeuppance?

Halfway up the stairs, Jonah finally gives us his full attention. "What are you talking about? Nick didn't come to Mom's house."

Well, I'll be damned.

Elizabeth blanches, and I know what she's thinking. She's thinking, *He saw us.* I'm thinking the same, to a different effect. We're both imagining how we looked — our bodies in and out of water, glowing in the light of a snow-blinding full moon — but Elizabeth will be worrying about Nick's feelings, and whether he believes she only dove to get his attention, to trick him into looking through a window, to force him to watch. Such worries, however, miss the point entirely, because the beauty of our show was its spontaneity and purity. We salted Nick's wounds without meaning to. Our behavior was human nature, plain and simple, and by reclaiming my wife in front of Nick's eyes, we reset the animal order around here. We did it together, Elizabeth and me. She's paralyzed, though, so I'm the one who has to ask, "Where was Nick, then?"

Jonah rolls his eyes, lifts his shoulders, so annoyed with his father's stupid questions. "Here, right?"

I can't help myself. It's a riot. "Here all weekend?"

"I assume so." He gives Elizabeth a dirty look. "You guys didn't know that?"

Elizabeth says, "Relax, Jonah," but I can't hold back. I laugh out loud and throw my arm around her shoulder and kiss the top of her head as she whispers, "It isn't funny."

But it is, and I say, "He is one stealth son of a gun."

Jonah winces — embarrassed of me or for me, out of ignorance either way — and shakes his head all the way up the stairs, mumbling, "Unbelievable," or something like it.

"Glad you're back, Son," I call after him.

Though he still thinks he's too cool for most things around here, Jonah allows, "Me too," before slamming his bedroom door.

"Me three," Elizabeth mutters. She brings one hand to her mouth, as if silencing herself.

"Hey." I give her body a playful shake, and she wobbles in my arms, then falls against me. "It's okay," I assure her. "If he saw us, he saw us. It's our pool, our house. He should have made his presence known." I give her shoulders one last squeeze and leave her to recover. "He'll get over it." I snap a mint leaf from the wad of drooping stems and dirty flowers in this pristine cut glass, and I crush the leaf between thumb and forefinger, electrocuting the air with a bright, biting scent that brings to mind lamb chops on Easter Sunday and that neon-green jelly my father kept in the back of our fridge. "There are ants in these."

Elizabeth snaps at me, "Well, shake them out."

"Your grandmother's crystal is too nice

for this mess."

Elizabeth grabs the entire bouquet with one hand and transfers it back to the pickle jar. The empty vase casts rainbows on our granite countertop. "I'm sorry," she says, kneading her eye sockets with the heels of her hands. "I feel like I still haven't recovered from last night, and that's the only small vase I have."

"Hey, we have those square ones from the party. The centerpieces?"

"Yeah. You're right. Shit, I need to return those to Luna. I've emptied out most of them. They're in the garage. I put a few in the guesthouse, too. Help yourself." Walking away, she tells me, "I'm getting my book."

Her avoidance of Nick is an olive branch in itself — an honored term of our unspoken covenant: a silent pact to erase him from our lives. She's given me an in, though, so I say, "I'll get one from out back. I can check on Nick while I'm at it."

Elizabeth nods but doesn't look at me.

And so, once again, I cross my lawn, but this time it's just a lawn — not the bottom of the ocean, not a bad dream — and this time, Nick is just annoying, not haunting. I bang on the door, but he doesn't answer, and I couldn't care less what he's up to today, so I let myself in, once again.

The room is as bright and clean as it was a few days ago, and atop the tiny table by the door, the printouts about emotional distress are still folded in quarters, unread. There's coffee in the pot, socks at the end of the bed, and there's a trace of something putrid that grows stronger as I move down the hall toward the bathroom, stronger still when I open the door.

Half a dozen glass cubes filled with soggy stems are lined up along the backsplash, just below the mirror, their milky, moldy water smelling of shit. I grab one and leave the rest for him to manage, and when I tell Elizabeth how gross Nick is, she makes a sour face and goes back to her book. Without looking at me, she says, "It's supposed to storm later."

"Is that right?" I dump the rotten bouquet, pour the funky water down our drain. Nick might have walked straight to the bus station after our talk. Maybe he's at Mayo already, getting a valid opinion, putting an end to my fun.

Elizabeth holds a hand to her face. "Oh God, that does smell awful. Would you lower the umbrella before it starts?"

I squeeze organic dish soap into the glass cube, flushing it with hot water and suds scented with peppermint and eucalyptus.

Nick left his computer here, but kids travel light these days. Ultralight. "The umbrella," I say. "Yeah, sure."

Upstairs, Jonah's bedroom door opens and closes. He comes clunking down with his keys in his hands, and when I ask about Nick's whereabouts, he blows me off, and when I ask where he's going, Jonah blows me off again.

Elizabeth says to him, "Please tell us so we don't worry."

"For a drive," he answers, and she nods, and they leave me out of it, then Jonah's gone.

I fill the clean glass cube with cool water and add Vanessa's flowers, then place the arrangement in the center of our dining room table, where we ought to eat more often, setting places with placemats and cloth napkins. I don't even realize that I'm staring through the sliding glass door, out to the backyard, until Elizabeth says, "He'll turn up."

19.

It rains all night and well into the morning. Forecast says showers all week.

My deltoids and pecs are twice as sore as they were yesterday, and something's wrong with my hamstring, and it's monsoon season, apparently, but if Elizabeth mentions the weather again, I'm going to scream. Weather chatter is good for humoring cashiers or old men or acquaintances at mandatory networking events. Elizabeth and I should be digging deeper, discussing topics like *What to Do When Your Houseguest Goes Missing,* despite the fact that, days ago, I never wanted to hear our houseguest's name again. Even now — even in his absence, his vanishing — he's manipulating my time, staking space in my mind, so screw him. And anyway, I've got nothing to hide. I did him a favor. He *thanked* me. Maybe he's on his way back from visiting that clinic in Tijuana, and he'll say, "Dr.

Hart, great news! False alarm." So maybe I should go ahead and pack his things and change the locks before he has a chance to reboot his shenanigans, except that I'm supposed to be moving on already. I have work to do, a life to maintain, weather patterns to monitor.

The rain finally lets up on my drive home from work, but it's only a tease of a reprieve from this Chicken Little feeling I can't quite kick, because even when the sky clears and brightens the world, as soon as I pull my car into the garage, my internal world dulls all over again. More damage, more hassles: a dark streak of water staining the floor draws a line to the northeast corner of the ceiling, where a leak has sprung.

"You've got to be kidding me," I mumble, launching damage control, clearing the storage crates away from the mildew trail in-the-making, hoping the crates aren't filled with electronics, documents, photographs.

Elizabeth panics when I knock on her office door to tell her there's an emergency, but she's almost relieved when I say it's a leak, so I call it a flood to make it sound serious so she'll take me seriously. She starts hounding me with questions — *How deep is it? Do we need a pump? What about outlets? Should we kill the breaker?* — and I tell her to settle down. "There's no standing water," I say, "but it's a mess. Do you have that contractor's number? It's probably the damn gutters."

She's opening drawers to search for the phone number on old bills, when she says, "I told you we needed to have them cleaned," without looking up.

"You were free to arrange the cleaners yourself."

"You said you'd deal with it, remember?"

"Let me know when you find that phone number," I tell her, and head to my own office to crack open my ancient Rolodex — so old it's almost new again, probably hipster heaven, who knows — and flip business cards alphabetized by vocation. Somewhere between Electrician and Exterminator, my father's voice creeps into my head. It says, *You're paying other men to do a man's job now?*

I twitch and bypass Groundskeeper. Irrigation. Mechanic. Painters. Plumber. *Too much heavy lifting? Too messy for you?* Roofer. *What kind of man can't fix his own house?* Windows. *No son of mine.*

"Forget it," I shout to Elizabeth.

She steps out of her office and asks,

"Forget what?"

"That phone number," I say. "I don't need it."

"You found it?"

"No. I'm going to clean the gutters. I'll fix the damn leak myself."

She hardly reacts — probably because it's high time I offered. I exit through the garage, acting put out, like being needed is a burden, when in a carbon-dense place inside of me, I'm thrilled to say, *I'll do it myself,* for a change.

I move our cars out of the garage to clear space for the mess I'm about to make. Elizabeth stays in the house and doesn't complain when ladders bang walls as I unhook them from ceiling mounts. She doesn't check on me when I drop an open box of golf balls on the ground while searching for the PVC extension to my backpack leaf blower, which needs fuel, so I fill it and get a little high from the fumes. The attachment is nowhere to be found, though, and now I seem to remember loaning it to Gabriel next door before he moved. Thanks a lot, Gabe. Whatever. I'm young and agile and perfectly capable of leafblowing from a ladder.

I slip on leather work gloves I've only ever worn once, back when I pruned a Japanese maple to death, and I strap the blower to my back, testing my center of gravity before lifting a sixteen-foot Werner ladder with one hand and a plastic bucket with the other, taking great care not to bash our cars when exiting the garage, pivoting and making a sharp left at the hosta, at which point I get a good view of the gutter at last. The problem is obvious: a wad of leaves and debris, a whole nest of funk blocking drainage at the point aligned with my leak. That PVC extension probably wouldn't have cut it, anyway. I'll get a better angle from the top rung. I tighten my grip and walk toward a revolting stench, deciding that if a squirrel died in my gutter, I'll be man enough to handle it like a boss — which is to say, to call animal control. God, this smell. Jesus, it's vile. Can gasoline fumes trip olfactory nerves? Or trigger flashbacks, or summon sensory apparitions of flowers rotting in cubes of moldy water?

A branch cracks. So what if a shrub gets wacked by the back of my ladder? So what if my deltoids still hurt? Pulling my shirt collar up over my mouth and nose, standing under the gutter pileup, dreading what's up there, I realize I need a garbage bag, so I turn the ladder upright and go to plant its rubber feet in front of our best blue hydrangeas, which are all cracked and beaten and smashed, I now see, only to find my path obstructed, *obstructed,* obliterated, annihilated, and all I can do is question reality and hope this isn't it.

Am I dreaming? Am I flashing back to that summer of hallucinogens a lifetime ago?

Is this an event that's now happened?

("What did you do when you saw it, Robert?" someone will ask. "Dr. Hart, what did you do?")

Stepping back and back again, putting a couple of yards between me and the bushes, laying my ladder in the grass, perfectly parallel to the side of my house, keeping my gloves on, taking this contraption off my back. Leaving everything else as it is. Time untwists and stops being a thing, and it's as though the entire planet is only as big as me, a battered shrub, and the body rotting below my broken roof.

Making choices: to panic or not to panic.

("How on earth did you stay so calm?" someone will ask.)

I should yell for help or attempt to find a pulse — first, do no harm — but even with my shirt pulled over my face like this, even with gloves smothering my mouth and nose, I can smell the decomposition. I can taste it.

Not panicking, not yelling for help yet,

not attempting to find a pulse. I can't bring myself to touch skin that may have already blistered and loosened, blisters that may have already burst, flies that may have already laid hundreds of eggs apiece in open sores, and if the eggs have hatched, thousands of maggots already feeding.

Is this something that's mapped on my time line now? An irrevocable, unwanted No?

His legs are bare. The side of his neck is exposed too. It's all gray. Violet gray. His neck is contorted. All wrong. The contortion and the color and the smell assure me there's no point in attempting revival. Contortion and stench: more than enough. His arms and face are obscured by fat leaves and broken branches, by soil acidic enough to turn hydrangeas baby blue. Violet petals hover above and beside Nick's remains. Perfect blooms, having peaked, are already dying. Soon, they will be decay too.

("How did you know it was him, Bobby?")

I recognize that gray sweatshirt, those shorts. Ankle socks stretched tight by bloat and stained by putrid fluids. One sneaker knotted to one foot. I glance up, knowing what to look for now, and I see the reflector strip, the loose lace: the shoe stuck in my gutter.

("I stood there for two seconds that felt like

260

ten minutes. Time stood still.")

What happened here? Everyone will want to know. *How did this happen?* they'll ask about my house, my yard, my watch. This isn't my fault. I didn't even want him here, as a matter of fact. I wanted him out of my life forever.

"Shit," I hear myself say out loud. *Shit.*

Believing he was facing his mother's fate, he chose his father's fate instead.

He jumped.

This doesn't have a thing to do with me, nothing to do with me. He was depressed. He was a train wreck, this kid. *("Lost cause. Hole in his soul.")* We did our best, and really, I tried to help him. Whatever conversations we may have had only confirmed what he already knew — that he's genetically predisposed to a malady, that's all — and anyway, the conversation was between us, so it's irrelevant. If he told someone, if he made me sound bad somehow, I'll lie. His word against mine. There's no paper trail.

Shit.

Leather gloves still pressed to my face — *("two seconds, maybe three")* — I leave Nick, what's left of him, and walk directly to the guesthouse. My phone is in my pocket, and I'll call. I'll dial the number in less than a minute, but dead is dead, so a minute won't make a difference. One minute won't help the paramedics, or the authorities, who'll spend too much time as it is going through Nick's things. Those printouts about bad news and trauma might mislead them or create drama where there isn't any, an investigation where there needn't be one. He's dead. He's over. He isn't a person anymore. He's a bundle of meat and marrow shrouded in gym shorts and faded gray cotton, doing its best to become dust-to-dust.

I let myself into the guesthouse and am met with the rich, fecal stink of rotting flowers. I grab the pages I printed, still neatly folded on the small table by the door, and get the hell out of there just as Elizabeth opens the sliding glass door across the yard.

"Hey," she calls out, "I found that number. Robert?" She steps outside, walks toward me. "Robert, what is it?"

"Get in the house," I command, pointing to the door. She obeys, and I take off my gloves so I can hide these folded papers in my back pocket. I'll shred them. I'll destroy them after dialing 911. I'll dial 911.

"What's going on?" Elizabeth asks, barely a whisper. She grips her neck, pressing the insides of her wrists together just under her chin. I grab her arm and I lead her upstairs to our bedroom — as far from Nick's dead body as we can be without fleeing the premises — and I tell her what I found, who I found, what I saw, where. *("Why?" No one knows.)*

Her eyes glaze and she falls to her knees, technically conscious but sufficiently incapacitated to signal that I'm the one obligated to hold it together, maintain composure, offer assurance, to pretend I believe everything's under control, everything's going to be just fine.

Elizabeth whispers, "Get Jonah. Tell him to stay inside."

20.

No one lets you sleep after a thing like this. They're not quick to say, "So sorry for your trauma, Doctor. Go rest, we'll clean up this mess."

Instead, a troupe of experts makes and leaves new messes. They expect me to be sharp and willing and accessible, but nobody ever says, "One last thing, then we'll let you sleep." The deputy medical examiner separates me from Elizabeth from Jonah from me, and they take turns squeezing minutiae from our memories before first releasing me, then Elizabeth, who offers to make tea for our unwelcome guests. I meet her in the pantry under the guise of helping her find Earl Grey.

"How much longer can this take?" she asks me. "Haven't they harassed Jonah enough? He hasn't even had a chance to process this yet. It's so ugly. They make everything so clinical and technical and

264

unemotional. He's lost his best friend in the entire world. He doesn't need this shit. He needs you, Robert."

I rub her back. "I'm here for him. These guys will leave soon."

"When?"

"I don't know. I don't know anything right now."

"I may fall apart."

"Please don't," I beg. "We can lose our shit once they're gone, or not. We'll deal with this together. Do we even have Earl Grey?"

"No idea." She scans shelves, flicking labels with her fingers, turning cans, rearranging bags of rice and beans. "I don't even know what I'm looking for. I can't read right now."

I shush her and say, "Relax. Let me." After a good turn inspecting dry goods, I call it. "There's only English Breakfast and Matcha Green."

"Do the English Breakfast. I feel so fucked up, Robert."

"I do too."

"So fucked up." Her fingertips have gone pale from how hard she's gripping her own arms. "I can't go back out there."

"Stop that. You're going to hurt yourself." I take her hands and gently guide them to her sides. "We need to keep it together just a little bit longer. Try. Please." Before she can argue, I coax her out of the pantry and into the kitchen, where she hides her hysteria and puts a kettle on to boil. She appears to be sad and weary, but not fragile, not cracked, as she spoons loose tea into a ball and chain.

People in uniform track mud from the roof through the house. Our living room rug will need a steam clean after this. Some of our neighbors call or stop by to snoop. Acquaintances telephone, having heard through the grapevine that there are squad cars in our driveway. They pretend to be concerned rather than nosy. They're nosy.

I jot notes in the kitchen — a time line, officers' names — and eavesdrop as Jonah tells the medical examiner about Nick's next of kin, an aunt upstate who will, no doubt, be calling us to run through these same questions before long. *("What happened? What did you do when you saw him, Dr. Hart?")* The aunt will ask if there were warning signs. *("Why did this happen?")* She'll want me to paint Nick's last day for her, brushstroke by brick by breath by little bit. I'll repeat, *No, we never imagined.* I'll use the word "troubled" and I'll use the word "normal," and I'll balance them with artistry.

The last of the uniforms finally leaves at nine o'clock. The head cop, Officer Michael Buchanan, and the investigator from the office of the medical examiner — a physician's assistant named Zebadiah Walsh, although everyone here calls him Walsh — give us business cards and ask us to keep our phones handy for follow-up calls. Elizabeth laments the simplicity of leaving telephones off the hook.

"I can't believe we gave up our land line just so we can be more enslaved to these things," she says, and she opens the door and throws her cell phone across the patio, into the yard but barely — she has a terrible arm — and off she goes to her office. I rescue her phone from the grass. Not a scratch.

We take melatonin that doesn't work. Come morning, Elizabeth's in no condition to leave the house, so I offer to stay home with her for support. I even call Simone to tell her what happened, and for once she doesn't give me shit about taking the day off. Doesn't matter, though, because Elizabeth insists on heading to her office, so I guess there's no point in me staying home alone. Jonah begs to return to his mother's house. He's a grown man and shouldn't beg, but since he's given me right of first refusal to his life, I deny his request. "We need your support," I tell him, which isn't entirely true. What we need is his margin of neutrality: a rubber bumper between my sharp edges and Elizabeth's soft spot.

Were it not for all the muddy boot prints, one might never believe the degree of chaos we hosted last night, the rotting corpse we hosted for who-knows-how-long. There is quiet today. Calm. Empty mug in the sink. Folded newspaper atop the recycle bin. Quick kiss good-bye from my wife. Radio silence from my son. That goes here, this goes there. Order from chaos. Such is the way of the universe.

But there's a blank strip of plaster on my garage wall, reminding me that the stepladder is still laying by our broken hydrangeas. And there's a stain in the northeast corner, daring me to finish cleaning the gutter. Nick's shoe is long gone, sealed in a plastic bag, labeled and in custody at the morgue, probably. My own work should be a distraction, at least. A relief. It is not. When I go to grab my lab coat from my staff lounge, the smell of rot makes me wretch. My guts flash back to the stench of death, and I decide

PTSD is real after all.

"Jesus Christ." I cover my face with one hand, but my eyes sting and my innards twist anyway.

Simone comes running, ready to rescue. "What is it? Oh God. Are you okay?"

"That fucking smell." I point to the ridiculous bouquet that's been canopying our Keurig for over a week. "Get rid of that, will you please? It's making me sick."

Her lip quivers. Her feet don't move. My ever-faithful Simone, usually so reliable, fails me now in my moment of need.

"Hey," I say. "Please don't go catatonic. Don't you fall apart on me too."

I open my arms, which immediately feels idiotic, but Simone doesn't flinch at my gesture, as uncharacteristic and dumb as that may be. Instead, she leans against my chest and grips my shoulder blades, so I give her a halfhearted, fatherly hug in return — patting her back in cut time: *there, there* — but the way she falls into me is so help-less and committed that I relent and give her what she needs, which is to be comforted, and she transfers her need onto me so that when she finally peels away, I nearly ask her not to. I nearly beg her to keep hold-ing me like I didn't know I needed to be held, to keep her perfumed hair close to my

269

nose, to continue comforting me.

"God," she says, wiping her cheeks. "I'm so embarrassed. I'm so sorry."

"Don't be silly. This has been a very difficult time for everyone," I say, gagging once again. "I'm just having problems with that smell right now."

She hiccups back another round of tears, smiles, slouches and stares up at me, trying to say something.

"I'm fine, Simone. I'll be fine."

"I know," she says. "It's just — oh God, this is so embarrassing."

"What is?"

"I sent them."

"You sent what?" Of course, it clicks. "The flowers?"

She nods.

"Why on earth didn't you tell me? They're beautiful, Simone."

"You called them strange."

"They're beautiful. I love the flowers. It's the rotten water smell that's giving me trouble. Can we — ?" I jerk my head toward the hallway. She nods and follows to an open exam room, closing the door behind us. "Listen," I say, "I'm so sorry to have hurt your feelings. The flowers are lovely. Seriously."

She laughs, thank God. "Sorry I'm so

270

emotional."

"Don't be sorry. You did something very nice and I've been too stressed out to notice, and now, well, this nightmare is turning my head upside down."

"I can't imagine."

"Don't try." I check the clock. "Feeling better?"

She nods.

"Ready to get back out there?"

She shrugs.

"Is something else going on?"

She shrugs again and this time adds a funny look: dropping her chin while maintaining eye contact. She's pursing her lips, now biting the lower one, now fluttering her lashes. "I gave the flowers to you because I wanted to make you happy."

No bearings. No clue. "Okay."

"Because nothing makes me happier than making you happy, Dr. Hart." She steps toward me and lifts her hands. By the time I realize she intends to touch my face, it's too late to play cool. I jerk my head, my whole body, reacting as though her fingers are fire.

"Jeez." She draws her hands to her chest in prayer position. "I thought —"

"Oh God. You thought wrong." There's bite in my words, but there needs to be, for clarity. I can't manage anyone else's drama and can't afford to watch one more person go to pieces right in front of me. "I gave you the wrong impression somehow, and I'm so sorry. You are so important to me. It's true. I value you immeasurably — as my assistant. Here. At work. Of course, you're much more than that. You are the glue that holds things together here. Simone, look at me. Look."

She lifts her eyes, but her affection has gone undercover. "I'm your office manager," she says, "not your assistant."

"I'm married."

"I know. I thought —"

"Happily married."

"Okay. Fine. Call me stupid. I thought you and Elizabeth were having problems — you know, because of the tin."

"Because I'm not buying her diamonds?"

"Yeah. Because of that. And because you roll your eyes when she calls, and —"

"I do not."

She laughs. "You do too. You roll your eyes when she calls, and you wink at me when I take a message without asking."

"That's because I'm amazed at how well you read my mind, Simone. I wink because you are *great* at your job. It's like a thumbs-up."

"It's a wink."

"It's appreciation, but fine. I understand. You're doing the right thing."

"Yes, I know. I always do the right thing, all the time. I follow the rules. Maybe I'm late sometimes, but other than that, I do follow the rules."

"I mean, I don't have *that* many rules."

"No, I mean *the rules.*" She shakes her head and puts her hands on her hips, and she's stern when she says, "With everyone. I spend my whole life being a nice girl, thinking one of these days I'll finish first, but where has it gotten me, huh? I'm almost thirty, I'm still single, still at the same job, still being nice. I'm so tired of being good all the time. I thought maybe you —"

"Simone."

"Maybe I could be bad with you."

"Okay," I say, way past ready to wrap it up. "So now we know where we stand. This is good. Healthy communication. And I'm telling you, Simone, you just keep being yourself and you're going to be fine. You'll finish first, believe me."

She nods without looking at me and lets this soak in, but then she says, "Yeah," and her posture changes. She leans against the door again, crossing her arms this time. "So tell me something. How would you suggest

273

I channel my integrity if someone were to ask me about those blood vials?"

"What are you talking about?"

"The vials of blood you drew from Nick over the weekend. If anyone were to ask if I ever saw the two of you together, for example, or whether he was here for an appointment, or whether or not you drew a whole lot of blood that never got sent to the lab — or if you let me lie about it to cover your tracks. For example. If someone comes asking those sorts of things, puts me in that position, how would you suggest I continue being true to myself? A nice girl who finishes first."

"Come on, Simone."

"The medical examiner's office called this morning. Did you know that?"

"No." I step toward her. She doesn't cower. She doesn't move away from the door like she ought to. "What did they want?"

"I don't know. Haven't called back yet. Guy named Walsh wants to talk to me though."

"I'm sure he wanted to talk to me."

"He asked for me by name."

"Fine. Call him."

"I will."

I'd like to scream, *What is it you want from*

me? while shaking her hard against the wall, but I'm not sure what's happening here. "Well," I manage, "maybe you don't have to be so by-the-book if they ask those things."

"No?"

"You can just keep that stuff between us, because even though there is nothing to hide, I'd forgotten about that appointment completely. Forgot to mention it to the first responders. It's an irrelevant detail that would only complicate a simple tragedy. Nick needed a checkup, so I did him a favor. That's all. If we give people a reason to overthink it, they will."

"Oh yes. I imagine they will."

"So you'll keep that to yourself?"

"Sure." With that, she stands tall, smiles, uncrosses her arms and becomes herself again. "I just wanted to be sure I understood what you meant when you assured me I'll finish first. Whose integrity I'm protecting if I stay in the race. It's much clearer now." She smiles. "Don't worry about a thing. Have I ever let you down?"

"Never," I say.

"Then let's keep this entire conversation between us."

"That sounds great."

"Excellent." She glances at her watch. "Oh man. It's almost eight. Better get to it." She

opens the door, and with the perkiest smile
— the old Simone I know and love — says,
"Why don't you take care of that flower
situation yourself."

Six physicals in one day. One mononucleosis
follow-up, one viral conjunctivitis, one set
of stitches. One Munchausen by proxy. One
epileptic not tolerating his meds. One
migraine. *One livewire running reception.*
Simone wouldn't. Would she? My schedule
is too full to allow for obsession, but even
as I say, *What hurts?* or *How's your quality of
life?* and even as I tell myself I'm fine, a
choir congregates in the back of my head,
warming up discordant layers of unintel-
ligible phrases: little voices rehearsing a
fugue in my mind. And I'm not fine.
  When you hear hoofbeats . . .
  Kill 'em with kindness . . .
  Shut it down . . .
  Finish first . . .
  [Laughter. Applause.]
  Do you know who I am?
  "Salt of the earth . . ."
  "Dr. Hart, what did you do?"
"Investigator Walsh, please," I tell the
operator who answers the number on Zeba-
diah Walsh's business card. "Dr. Robert
Hart calling in regard to Nick Carpenter's

276

death. Yes, I'll hold."

If I'd handled things before they got bad, like Ray suggested, I wouldn't have had to resort to psychological torture, and Nick wouldn't have fulfilled his own prophecy, so I wouldn't be in this mess. Fool me once and all that. It won't happen again. This time, I'll engage the preemptive strike. I won't wait for Simone to defame me or worse.

"Walsh," the guy says.

"Robert Hart here. Returning your call."

"I didn't call you," he tells me.

"You didn't? But —" Strategic pause. "Oh God. This is so Simone."

"Excuse me?"

"My secretary, Simone. She told me you called for me, which didn't make sense, and now I know why. She's easily confused. Happens all the time. Too many names and faces, day in and day out, I guess. So sorry to bother you."

"No bother."

Walsh doesn't mention the fact that he called Simone this morning. Ah, so he's the type of guy who gets people to talk by saying nothing. I'm not falling for that, but I ask, "While I have you on the line, maybe you can tell me if you've heard about funeral arrangements?"

"Services won't be until the end of the week," Walsh says. "Up in Bovina."

"Catskills, huh?"

"That's right. Your boy can fill you in. Investigation should wrap up before too long."

"Investigation?" I ask. "What's to investigate?"

"Cause of death."

Dumbed down by death and its dealings, I say, "Oh. We figured it was obvious he jumped off the roof."

"Jumped or fell. Those are modes of death, though, not methods. As a doctor, you can appreciate the distinction. We need to determine specificity: whether he was under the influence of drugs or alcohol, whether he had any medical conditions that might have caused him to lose consciousness, whether he could have slipped and fallen — and then what actually did it. Head injury, cardiac arrest. You know, specifically."

"I hadn't thought of those things. Seemed cut-and-dry."

"Probably is. Occam's razor. Investigations are standard for all unnatural deaths. Can I do anything else for you, Mr. Hart?"

"Doctor, actually. Dr. Hart."

"Anything else?"

"No," I say. "That's all for now." I hang up and open the door to find Simone standing in front of me with her fist raised, poised to knock. "Had to take a call," I tell her. "Medical examiner's office."

"Zeb Walsh?" she asks. "Nice guy, right?" She doesn't tell me how she knows this, when she spoke to him, what she said or didn't, what her game is, just, "Your four o'clock is getting impatient."

I check my watch. 4:26. "Send her in."

ALEXIS

4:27.

Off the clock at five and still a mountain of paperwork to file.

"You coming out tonight, Diaz?" Lincoln asks me. Such a twinkle-in-the-eye kind of guy.

"Not tonight," I say.

He laughs. "Maybe tomorrow."

It's a joke at this point. People want me to share their social lives, because they like their social lives and can't imagine people not liking what they like. My personal life might as well be string theory — a way of thinking about existence that doesn't jive with their concept of reality. Brains break around here when I say I'm happy on my own.

If these guys weren't so annoying, I might be impressed by how hard they work to interpret my independence as low self-esteem. Randos like to tell me, unsolicited, that I'm a catch. They say it like I need convincing, which breaks *my* brain, because yeah, no shit, I'm a catch. Doesn't mean I want to be caught. Definitely not by a colleague's sister's coworker's friend's tutor's ex, who's "really nice," just not the tutor's type.

"Maybe tomorrow, maybe not," I tell Lincoln — and fine, I admit it feels good to be invited, despite the odds.

"Suspense." He rolls his eyes. "See you tomorrow, Alexis."

Four thirty. Half an hour to knock this out.

Top of the pile: traffic citation from the weekend. Tedium.

Robert Hart. The rainy day guy. Kind of an ass. Where do I know that name? I log into our system and track down his file. Clean record, but his name comes up in conjunction with a recent incident report. Very recent. Fatal accident. Well, shit. So that's where I know his name.

This morning's paper is still in my wastebasket. I shake off the dirty Kleenex and rice cake dust, open to the local page and find the death announcement under the "pending" section of the obits. There's no funeral scheduled yet, no details or picture, but I google the dead kid and find his photo online in seconds.

"Whoa," I say out loud. Chicken skin on my arms and legs. Creepy for no other reason than just knowing I laid eyes on a kid in his last days or hours. I should have looked harder. Poor kid seemed bored. Tired. Depression looks like that: boredom, fatigue.

I revisit the accident report. Responding officer: Michael Buchanan. Not a close friend, but friendly enough for me to feel comfortable visiting the Investigations Unit and interrupting his game of sudoku. "Hey," I say. "Just saw your report about the fatality response yesterday."

"Oh man." He shakes his head. "Gruesome."

"Mind if I ask what happened?"

"Waiting for the autopsy."

"Accident?"

"Might be an accident. Probably suicide. Strange deal, the way he threw himself against the banister, but I've seen stranger."

"Strange how?"

He crinkles his face and says, "Why are you so interested?"

"Not sure yet if I am interested. Strange how?"

He smiles, like I said something cute. Cute, like a little kid. "Well, okay. There's no good reason for him to have been up there teetering at the steepest point if not to tempt fate and gravity. The homeowner says he called the roof a 'death trap' and 'suicide central' in front of the kid days earlier. Gave me a list of four witnesses, plus the man's wife and son, who were all there and heard it. Jumping from thirty feet isn't exactly a sure thing, but finding the key and sneaking up are deliberate moves, right? Sad either way you cut it. Walsh at the ME is the lead investigator. We'll see what he comes up with."

I nod. And then, I don't know why, but I get curious. "Does the kid have family here?"

"Funny you should ask. Hardly any family at all. His life was one tragedy after another."

Depression. Suicide. Serial tragedies. He was just a kid, too young for this shit. "Any chance I can take a peek at the report?"

"What's up with you? Do you know the guy or something?"

"No, but I detained the homeowner the other day for a traffic stop and that kid was with him."

Buchanan squints and tilts his head and says, "You should have led with that." But I guess he's curious, too, because he rotates his laptop so I can read the incident report, so he can watch me read it. "Doubt it was him," he says. "Homeowner hadn't seen the Carpenter kid since Friday."

"That's not true, actually. I saw them together on Saturday."

"You ID the kid?"

"No. But it was him."

"You should have asked for identification."

"Well, I identified him with my eyeballs. Also, there's probably dashcam footage."

"Probably, but the son is the same age and build. Video from the rear of the vehicle won't help much."

"I mean, we could check."

"Nah."

I widen my eyes and thrust my head like a goddamn pigeon. "Hello? I'm standing here telling you that I saw the dead kid in that car on Saturday morning, and the homeowner was driving. What part of that isn't registering?"

Buchanan gets righteous with how composed he is. So cool and calm, with a little smile, when he reclaims his laptop, turns it back around, nods and says nothing but, "I'll look into it."

"You will?"

"Of course. If there's a discrepancy, we always look into it."

Yeah. I've heard this before. "Listen —"

"Diaz. I said I'll look into it." He stares at the door. "Thank you."

Interesting. Interesting because this feels awfully familiar. Too many blow-offs these days. Way too many to be coincidental. "Can I ask you something?"

"Hm."

"Is this about the Voss case?"

"Is what about the Voss case?"

"This," I say. "This way people keep shutting me out, then acting like they don't know why I'm irked."

"Come on, Diaz."

"Is it?"

As if I'm putting him out — like I'm the one acting shitty, when he's the one behaving as though he wants a place at the cool kids' table and the only way to get there is to adopt the cool kids' grudges — he says, "If you need it spelled out, then fine. Yes. It's about the Voss situation."

I manage not to scream or spit. I mimic Buchanan's composure when I say, "That's not fair."

"Listen, Diaz. I get it. You're passionate —"

"Don't patronize me."

"Don't get emotional."

"I'm not emotional." Well, that was the

wrong thing to say. And the wrong way to say it. My delivery wasn't flat enough. Not robot enough. Robot is what I have to be, constantly, between now and when I retire in twenty or thirty years. That's all. I have to be that and I have to rock my scarlet letter: E for Emotional. Just that. I've got to encrypt myself because I showed a feeling once and earned a spot on some invisible internal watch list.

"It's great you care," Buchanan tells me, like I need his validation. "You should care. But you cannot let this job become your whole life. You can't get wrapped up in other people's problems, or you'll go crazy."

"I'm not crazy."

"I didn't call you crazy." His tone, though: *Not yet.* "I'm just saying, be careful."

"Heard. Loud and clear."

So that's it. The Voss case is officially my poltergeist. *Emotional,* like it's dangerous. *Passionate:* euphemism for sinful. My whole life, I'm taught that the only way to be taken seriously is to do my job and do it well. So I do that, and I get here, and the rules change. People like Buchanan change them. Surprise! Dedication is a detriment now. I'm supposed to detach, loosen up, lay back, back off. I'm supposed to posture for a living on top of doing work I love that I'm only allowed to love a certain way.

It's not like I invented the whole work-ethic thing. It was taught to me, explicitly. *Find something you love to do,* Mom said, *and do it. Then it's not work.*

Bust your ass, Dad told me. *Your work will speak for itself.*

I was at the station the day that girl's parents brought her in. Chief put me in the room when she made her statement, said I'd make Kayla feel safe. I thought we wanted her to feel safe because a victim's emotional security matters. (*Emotional:* a handicap.) Turns out we wanted her to feel safe so she'd talk. She was miserable, mortified, didn't want to be here. Her parents forced her, nudged her, wept. They were pissed. Justifiably. They wanted J.R. Voss to be punished, and they wanted vengeance, damn it, on their daughter's behalf. Meanwhile, Kayla Scott died inside every time I asked, *And was that consensual? What about that? And that?* She hated me, then herself, more and more with every detail pried.

Charges were filed. Noise happened. Got louder. Seemed for a while that justice might happen too. That justice might make noise too. Then, *poof,* out of the blue, the Scott family withdrew charges. Problem solved in private arbitration. Translation:

287

Graham Parks and his cronies found her breaking point. Maybe it was something as simple as money. Might have been more. Might have been a splinter from the Scott family tree — something humiliating the mom or dad did in college, or some dumb thing Kayla said once, or any bit of gossip that could jeopardize or distract from their credibility. Proverbial dirty laundry to tip the proverbial scales. Whatever it was, it worked, case closed, and J.R. became a poster boy for the "wrongly" accused. Wrong is right.

Word traveled fast when Kayla recited that fucked-up statement on the courthouse steps. We all watched at the station, hovering around a live-stream on Peterson's computer, then watching the highlight reel from the news. Everyone was horrified. I was naive enough to assume we were horrified for the same reasons. "This is sick," someone said, and I nodded. Sure was. Someone else said, "She needs help," and I agreed, thinking trauma counseling, but apparently they were thinking Bedlam, because when Peterson said, "Kids these days will do anything to get on television," the other guys nodded again.

Not me. I didn't nod. I asked calmly, "What the hell are you talking about?"

When Peterson turned the question back on me, emphasizing *you,* I said, "This is bullshit."

When they asked if I was deaf or didn't watch the video clip, I said no, I'm not deaf or blind, and fortunately, I'm not dumb, either, because, "I know how this shit works."

They said, "Enlighten us."

I said, "Guys like J.R. Voss do what they do knowing nobody wants to be in that girl's shoes. This performance he cornered her into is a public threat to every other Kayla out there who might consider ratting out pervy old men."

"Voss isn't old," was Peterson's rebuttal.

Lincoln asked a fair question about how I pick and choose what to believe, but before I could answer, Dennis said, "Oh, give it up. That girl wants money and ten minutes of fame."

And I said, maybe loudly, "No one wants to be famous for this shit."

And Dennis had to add, "She's a fame whore," emphasis on *whore,* and people laughed.

So I said, maybe yelled, maybe shouted in his face, "*You* are exactly why most of us keep our mouths shut."

Boom, splat, screech to a halt. Everyone

289

stuck on my word-choice. *You,* meaning "guys like you." *Us,* meaning "I've got skin in the game." Translation: *Alexis Diaz has trouble separating the personal from the professional.* Translation: *Keep an eye on her mood.*

Mood, like the symptom of a deadly disease.

Then it was quiet and awkward.

Chief called me into his office the next day. Said I needed to check myself. Also said the Voss case was complicated, he understood that, but I had to let it go. "J.R. Voss has done a lot for this department," he told me, but it meant something else. It meant, *J.R. Voss buys a shit-ton of pancakes at our annual pancake breakfast, so back off.*

The modus operandi around here seems to be *optics first,* but they don't care about how bad it looks tiptoeing around fancy people's feelings. So I guess Robert Hart is somebody around here — Citizen of the Year, whatever that's worth or isn't — so I guess we're expected to bow down, back off, play it safe.

If it's optics they're worried about, maybe someone should consider how dumb we look when we worry about fancy people's egos more than our work.

Fancy people. Guys like Robert Hart, MD.

Fine, Buchanan. I'll look into it too.

21.

The casseroling begins. That was quick. Sticky notes on our freezer door inform me that a neighbor brought Mexican chicken, packed with Hatch green chilies and soggy tortilla chips, to be baked at three-fifty at our leisure. McAlister's wife brought some kind of shepherd's pie thing, and one of Elizabeth's colleagues dropped off frozen lasagna from Costco, God bless her. A sealed tin of Earl Grey is sitting on the countertop next to bread and cocktail onions. I hear Elizabeth laugh, and I follow her sniffles into the entry hall, where she's sitting on the floor, knees up, back against the wall. She's smiling even as she rubs mascara into her face.

"Guess who just walked in?" she says to someone on the line. "Yes. Yes, he's right here."

I shake my head *no*.

"Oh, Emily, I can't tell you how nice this

has been," she's saying. "I'm just so glad you happened to be there. I know. I know, we will." She hands me the phone, saying, "It's Raymond."

I shake my head harder and walk away. "I'll have to call him back."

"Robert. Wait, Robert." I hear her tell Emily or Ray or both, "Damn. He just raced to his office. I think he might have a work call. Exactly, exactly. Well, shoot. Of course. I'll have him call Raymond when he's done. Oh, believe me, I will." She laughs about something, offers an effusive good-bye, and comes to find me when she's off the phone. "What on earth?"

"I cannot deal with him right now, Elizabeth."

"He said he's been trying to reach you for days. Thinks his texts aren't going through?"

I nod and say, "I'll try him in a bit," as I turn on my laptop and pretend to be doing very important things. "What were you doing talking to Emily? Why were you crying?"

Elizabeth tucks her chin. "Seriously?"

"But why were you crying to her?"

"Ray called looking for you. He said you gave him my number ages ago, in case of emergency. I told him you've been overwhelmed these past few days, and then I told him why. He was shocked, obviously.

Then he asked how I am, and I don't know what came over me, but that question made me want to bawl my eyes out. I don't think Raymond was prepared for that, though, so he handed the phone to Emily, and — Jesus. I can't believe I've never really gotten to know her. She's kind of awesome, huh?"

"Why are you so soft on the Harrisons all of a sudden? You hate Ray."

"I don't hate him. I've never hated him. I just thought he was a pig."

"He is."

"Well, now I think he must have a good side I haven't met yet, since Emily chose him."

"You don't have to sell me on them. I've known them for ages, remember?"

"I liked talking to her. I told her we'd try to go to their Memorial Day thing this year. Why haven't we ever gone?"

"You're romanticizing them because you're emotional. They're fine. They're not all that great, and we always have Memorial Day plans, so don't worry about it."

She winces. "Well, it felt nice to talk to someone."

"Well, talk to me, then." I open a document, pretend to care about its contents. "Let me finish this and I'll be right in."

Elizabeth shakes her head and closes the

door behind her. I probably should offer to sit with her now, but the choir in my head is still singing. The moment the door clicks shut, I open one of those incognito tabs on my browser — knowing that incognito has its limits, making a mental note to scrub my search history after my obsession wanes — and look up the term that's been haunting me ever since hanging up the phone with Walsh. Behind every polite greeting with every patient who passed through my office today, the only thing on my mind was *coroner's investigation.*

I hit enter and dive deep: coroner's inquest, autopsies, cause of death, proximate cause, worst-case scenarios I've avoided entertaining until now. If Nick told anyone about how I fucked with his head — and he could have called or visited or emailed someone the minute I walked away — then his reason for climbing to a "death trap" and leaning his weight against a rotten banister could fall to me. The district attorney could bring action, in theory. In reality. Press charges. Wrongful death. What the fuck.

I scrub my browser, clear my cache, dump my electronic trash. Double-check my downloads for stray materials concerning amyotrophic lateral sclerosis, or stem cell regeneration treatments south of the border, or message boards about fidelity and infidelity — cybercesspools of whining men with addictions to negative feedback.

I return to my family with positive feedback, a positive outlook: a shining example of life going on. The casseroles keep coming. The questions, too, but no information. Wednesday into Thursday into an argument with my son about Nick's funeral upstate.

"It's going to be tough to clear the whole day with work," I tell Jonah.

"Unbelievable," he says. "You do realize that Nick was my best friend. He was my roommate, and he died in our backyard — *your yard* — just days ago. This isn't optional for me and Elizabeth. We're leaving at seven tomorrow morning, with or without you."

Elizabeth speaks for me, saying, "Your dad will be there, Jonah."

I breathe through it. "Of course, Son. Whatever I can do to support you."

So now I'll have to ask Simone to cancel my appointments and reschedule two dozen patients, a burden she'll add to her growing list of complaints. She'll be even bitchier about delaying our meeting.

Jonah heads upstairs, and I tell Elizabeth, "We'll need to book a room in the Catskills. Last minute. Won't be cheap."

"I'll do it," she snaps, but she'll regret it. We're going to be the spectacle. Nick was staying with us. People know this. They'll ask questions. Who's to say Nick kept his tryst with Elizabeth a secret? Who's to say he didn't tell someone about the diagnosis. I say softly to Elizabeth, "People are going to want to know about our relationships with Nick. Some of them will have heard about us already."

She doesn't flinch. She just says, "It's not about us, Robert."

"Maybe not, but it affects us, and I hate funerals, Elizabeth. I hate going when they're for people I love, let alone someone I hardly knew. I'll be there. It's settled, but it's stressful."

"How inconvenient for you," she says.

"We're going, aren't we?"

"Yes," she says. "We are."

22.

The drive to Bovina takes five hours, but we leave a little late, so we're only a little early for the one o'clock funeral, pulling up to the area Interfaith Center at twelve forty exactly. Jonah slept in the back the whole time, and Elizabeth read, and I drove. In the trunk is a duffle bag filled with Nick's things. How Jonah plans to deliver it to Nick's aunt without making a scene is beyond me, but he insisted, and I relented, so here we are.

In the sanctuary beyond the foyer, an organist plays "Take My Hand, Precious Lord." My mother got that one, too, by request. Mounted on either end of the room are signs with arrows pointing toward curved corridors. The arrow pointing left reads, *Chapels. Prayer Rooms. Classrooms. Men's Room.* The one pointing right: *Library. Altars. Exit to Meditation Garden. Ladies' Room.* And in the middle, the tributes.

There was no visitation, and an open casket was never in the cards, not with a body as badly decomposed as Nick's had been, so in lieu of a formaldehyde-soaked cadaver covered in grease paint, we are forced to acknowledge phantoms tacked to cork-board: a portrait, a diploma, a handwritten letter to God. Beside the guest book are scrapbooks stuffed with blue ribbons, news-paper clippings, notes and Polaroids, class pictures, photo booth strips, report cards. Garish flower wreaths and headshots hang from easels by the door.

"I didn't know Nick swam competitively," I say to Jonah.

"In high school, yeah. Turned down a couple scholarships, I think."

"Why did he quit?"

"Wanted to, I guess."

I shake my head, thinking of lost potential, and Jonah walks away to make small talk with an usher. Someone taps me on the shoulder, and I step aside to let the person pass, but when the person says, "Hey," I feel my worlds collide even before turning to match the voice and face.

"Jesus, Raymond. What the hell are you doing here?"

He's wearing a suit, and Emily is next to him, wearing a black dress. She takes my

299

hand, squeezes it gently, then hugs me around my waist. "We're so sorry, Bobby."

Over Emily's shoulder, I ask Raymond again, "Seriously, what are you doing here?"

"We heard about what happened. I've been trying to reach you."

"Yeah, but why are you here?"

Emily releases me and returns to Raymond's side. "We came to support you," she says, earnest but maybe defensive, too.

I shake my head. "You shouldn't have come."

"We wanted to," Raymond says, just as Jonah rejoins our party. He hugs Emily as Ray says, "This is what friends do."

Instead of correcting him in public, I ask, "Can I talk to you in private, please?"

Jonah, whose arm is still wrapped around Emily's shoulder, whispers, "Dad."

So I whisper back, "Stay out of this, Son."

Ray follows me down the left-arrow hallway, saying, "Bobby, we didn't mean to upset you," and he follows through the first open door, too, into this private chapel. "You're going through some real shit, man, and you don't know these people. We didn't want you to feel isolated and, well, frankly, I've been worried."

"You should have called first."

He shakes his head. "I've called you half a

dozen times. I've texted."

"You shouldn't be here."

Ray stuffs his hands into his pockets. "What the hell is going on?"

"What do you mean? I found a dead body in my bushes and now I've got to convince a bunch of strangers that there's no place else I'd rather be. That's what is going on."

Ray shushes me. "Dude." He whispers, "Know your company."

No one else is in the chapel, but he's right. This isn't the place. "I wasn't expecting to see you here, okay? It feels aggressive."

He laughs. "Aggressive?"

"Inappropriate."

Raymond raises his voice. "Who are you right now? Don't tell me you've turned into a guy who uses words like 'inappropriate' to talk about loyalty."

"Ray—"

"I always show up for you, Bobby."

"That's true," I say, desperate to de-escalate.

"So? Do you need me to say it?"

"Say what?" From the belly of this building, the organist begins to play "Take My Hand, Precious Lord," yet again. Nausea I've been suppressing all week starts to creep. My belly feels like a snake nest hatching, and all the snakes are crawling up my innards and esophagus, trying to escape through my mouth. I gag, clear my throat, try to cough the snakes away.

Ray says, "One minute this kid is living with you and possibly sleeping with your wife. The next he's smashed in your yard. And all I know is that somewhere between A and B, you vowed to get rid of him."

I say, "Stop," but the word sounds strange. My words sound strange. The snakes.

"If you'd have picked up the phone, we wouldn't be here, but Emily said you wouldn't talk to me."

This air is too thick, the light milky. Behind Raymond, a ceramic dead Jesus shines on the wall. "What did you tell Emily?"

"Emily loves you, Bobby."

"Nick killed himself. He was depressed. He had problems, but he didn't — he wasn't doing that other thing. Forget it, please. I picked up on something, but I interpreted it all wrong."

"I understand." A stained-glass skylight spits primary colors on Ray's face. "Like, a lot. That's why I'm here. Because I picked up on something too, and I sure as hell don't want to interpret it wrong."

"What are you saying?"

"That I'm your friend. You can talk to me."

Raymond isn't just my friend. He's my brother, and I love him, but he isn't listening to orders or silent treatments. He's forcing me to resort to the cruelest sting. "You don't know me," I say, burning my throat on the words, choking on snakes and words. "You think you know what's good for me, but this is proof that you don't have a clue. To be honest, it's freaking me out, Ray. I feel like you're obsessed with me, like you're stalking me, and it worries me." I cough. "I'm uncomfortable. Maybe that's what you're picking up on."

My oldest friend shakes his head, but as a show of disappointment, not a response.

"Nick was Jonah's friend," I remind him. "That's the end of the story."

Raymond turns away, taunts me, turns back to say, "I've always defended you. When people talk shit, I tell them, 'You don't know the real Bobby.' When they say you've changed, I stand up for you, but maybe they're right. Maybe you are just a prick nowadays."

"I'm not a prick."

"Give Jonah my condolences." Then, "Elizabeth, too. Oh, and just so you know, you can't trick me into fulfilling an abandonment fantasy. You're a prick, but we're stuck together, so don't pity yourself over this. Call me when you can be decent," he says, and leaves the chapel.

The ceramic dead Jesus sinks back into the wall, color-dull. Taking a seat in the closest pew, I drop my head into my hands and try to breathe. Breathe. Daydream of stretching out and sleeping on this dark wood, so tired and sick of fielding questions, of shaking hands and being civil — of being civilized, for that matter — when I'd rather break furniture or nap on it. My head won't quiet. If only it would quiet.

I smell Elizabeth's skin before feeling her hand on my shoulder. She thinks I'm bored, or crying, or verging on a breakdown, or breaking down, so I sit upright and smooth my sport coat, saying, "It's okay, Lizzie," and I smile to keep from doing those other things. "Everything's going to be okay."

She takes mercy on me. Or maybe she just wants to avoid a scene. Either way, she sits beside me and withholds words, questions, judgments, advice. For this, I'm beholden to her. Just as I coaxed her out of the pantry, she's building me up for Round Two. She kneads my shoulder in the affirmative, Mickey to my Rocky, and I don't mind, because she believes in me and deserves a strong man, so I lace my insides tightly inside. Even in the grit — perhaps especially here in the grittiest, ugliest, most tragic and wretched For Worse — we are Better. *'Til death do us part.*

23.

Naomi Miller is a sweet lady and broken one. Through chatty friends and neighbors, I learn about her sister, who was Nick's mother, who really did die of ALS, and about how Naomi carried Nick's family after that. Before Nick's dad took his own life, he named Naomi as Nick's legal guardian. She was the one who helped Nick move into the dorm room he and Jonah shared. Naomi was the one who cosigned Nick's loans, managed his debt, and so, I'm told by friends and family, she wasn't just next of kin. She was practically a second mother. Aunt, mother, executor of his estate. Gracious hostess, gone to pieces.

We follow a caravan of cars from the funeral parlor to her house for the reception. It's a nice house. Nice yard. On her walls and mantel, photos of Nick illustrate a happier, brighter boy than the one I met. Laughter, team photos, candid shots. Uncomfortably plain.

I say to Elizabeth, "I don't get it. Didn't he grow up in the system?"

"The system?"

"Yeah. Like, foster care. Juvy."

Elizabeth rolls her eyes. "What?"

"He made it sound like that."

"No he didn't."

But he did. He talked about fundraisers for special camps serving unfortunate teens. He sold himself as a literal charity case, dark and brooding, but all along, his home base had windows in every room and calico curtains on every window and flowering crabs behind every curtain. His history was dreadful, but he lived it in a sunlit box that smells like butter and brown sugar and mountain air, with an aunt who displays photos of him in silver frames. He was on the swim team. He had friends. I say, "He told us he was homeless this summer."

"He said he hadn't made plans," Elizabeth reminds me. "He didn't say there was no home on the planet where he could go. Besides, this was only home for a few years. He moved here from Ohio, and now his bedroom is Naomi's craft room. I can't blame him for wanting to hang out with Jonah rather than sleep next to pipe cleaners and mosaic tiles."

"How did you know that, about his bedroom?"

"Nick told me. Come on. Let's get the mingling over with."

I cringe at her acknowledgment of pillow talk with Nick, but stuff it away as we wait in single file for our turn to fill porcelain cups with bitter coffee from an industrial-sized carafe, probably borrowed from a church or rec center or Rent-A-Center. We link ourselves to a chain of people who apologize too much, who say, "I'm sorry, you first," every time they reach for the same thing as someone on the opposite side of this narrow buffet. We load our plastic dessert plates with cheese cubes, finger sandwiches, sugar cookies, and peanut butter balls. We fall in line.

"It doesn't make sense," someone says, because that's all anyone can say, as though being alive is easier to understand than life ceasing to exist.

He was doing so well.

He must have been suffering so quietly.

Was he seeing anyone? Was he sick?

A man's booming voice rises from the crowd to say, "That guy would know."

I should walk directly to the porch where all those old, deaf people wouldn't bother me, but curiosity gets the better of me, and

308

I look, and yes, the big man in the corner — big like Navy SEAL, not Santa Claus — is pointing to me. I saw him earlier, mingling with a few boys around Jonah's age. Not quite old enough to be their father, not young enough to be one of them.

"You're a doctor, right?" the man asks. "Wasn't Nick staying with you?"

Balancing a plate full of finger food with one hand, I raise the coffee cup in my other hand as salutation. "That's correct," I say. "Nick was our guest. I'm so sorry for your loss."

"What's your name again?"

"Robert Hart." The living room shines attention on me, and I abandon hope of a quiet exit. "We're heartbroken. It just doesn't make sense."

A sixty-something lady with a salt-and-pepper crew cut says, "Saddest thing ever."

The big man says, "Sad and very, very weird, to tell you the truth."

The salt-and-pepper lady introduces him. "This is Hank Skillman. He runs a summer program Nick just loved."

"Oh, right," I say. "Outward Bound?"

"Onward and Upward," Hank corrects. "We were a huge part of Nick's life."

"Yes," I say. "We've heard about you. Big fish."

Elizabeth jumps in. "Of course, we can't imagine how you're feeling, Hank." She looks around the room. "All of you knew him so well for so long."

A middle-aged guy seated on the piano bench talks about the sports his kids played with Nick, and a woman in a business suit adds, "He was a wonderful team captain."

"I used to babysit Nick," a girl announces. "My parents were close with his parents."

Elizabeth sits between the babysitter and suited lady, but my snake-in-the-throat shimmies, so I excuse myself to avoid vomiting on their round-robin eulogy. To the nearest stranger, I ask, "Bathroom?"

The stranger's mouth is full of food, but he nods and points to the foyer, so I carry my plate and cup into the entrance hall, where I bypass the narrow door to the powder room and walk up the stairs instead, desperate for a square inch of privacy, but the door at the top of the stairs is locked and someone says, "Just a minute," when I jiggle the doorknob. Moving along, roaming the hall, entering the first open doorway, setting my plate and cup on the nearest table, dropping my head between my knees, breathing deeply. The pit in my gut settles, and I realign, open my eyes.

Dowels are mounted on the wall, displaying rolls of kraft paper and colored foil. A sewing machine stands atop a fitted cabinet with unmarked drawers on either side. Acrylic cases stacked along the edge of the desk are labeled by bead type or sequin shape, wire gauge, and thread color. Wrinkled patterns cut from parchment paper are pinned to a strip of corkboard bolted to the wall. So this was Nick's room, once upon a time. Now Naomi Miller makes jewelry and Christmas tree skirts in here.

Someone knocks on the open door. "Robert?"

I turn to see the big man. "Hank, was it?"

"That's right."

This time, I shake his hand. "I am so sorry. For your loss."

"Yeah, well, I'm sorry if I snapped at you down there. Out of my head over this thing."

"I understand."

"I'm just confused," Hank says. "Something had to have happened."

"People do terrible, out-of-character things when they're depressed."

"Yeah, but Nick had it under control. Makes me think he stopped taking his meds or something, but that doesn't make sense, either. None of it does."

Meds. Interesting. I file this information away and say, "You couldn't have foreseen this. None of us could. He suffered silently."

"So what?" Hank snaps. "We had a pact. My kids pledge to reach out if they ever get the urge to hurt themselves or someone else. They've all been to hell and back, but they have tools. Nick didn't call anyone."

"Maybe reception was bad."

"Seventeen kids and three staff are on that list. None of us got messages. He didn't try hard enough." He steps closer. "Tell me something else. You ever hear of him using drugs?"

"What?"

"I probably shouldn't say anything." Hank sits down and starts playing with zigzag scissors. "Might just be for family."

"What might be for family?"

"Something in the autopsy." He flexes the pinking shears in his hand. "You didn't hear that from me."

I swallow. "The autopsy's back? I didn't know."

"Why would you? You hardly knew Nick."

"I mean, I knew him."

"Believe me, you hardly knew him."

"Of course."

"Those cops won't tell, anyway. They only talk to get information." Percussive *snip-snip.* "Hey. One more thing. Is it true you knew how dangerous your roof is?"

"Yes. That's why it was off-limits. Nick knew that."

"Yet somehow he was there." Hank puts the scissors back where he found them and stands. "You probably shouldn't worry, though. I keep telling Naomi to go ahead and file a suit, that it's the insurance company that takes the hit, not you. She gets all sensitive about it, but she's starting to come around, now that she knows she'd be suing you in name only, really. That's what insurance is for, right?" Without pause, he says, "Well, I should go," and doesn't bother looking at me, let alone saying good-bye, when he leaves me alone in a room full of glitter and brass tacks.

24.

Elizabeth is on the porch, listening to college kids tell stories about Nick: how they knew him, how he changed them, how much he'll be missed. At the edge of nearby brush, the fireflies flash mating calls. Before Elizabeth can ask where I've been, I mouth, "Later," and she nods, which is fine by her, it seems, since she's engrossed in the conversation, clicking beer bottles with strangers and calling them by name. I'm half asleep in my head, and still a bit punch-drunk from my run-in with Hank Skillman, so I'm relieved to notice the slight flare of Elizabeth's nostrils, the subtle pinch of her brow bone as she suppresses back-to-back yawns. I cover my mouth and yawn, too. Jonah smacks his neck and says something about the mosquitos, and just like that, Nick's buddies are gathering their empty bottles and bringing them inside to leave by the kitchen sink. Jonah's searching for the recycle bin, but Naomi tells him to leave it.

"For once in my life, I've hired help to deal with dishes tonight," she says, prompting a round of affirmations from the women. Men straighten their ties and search for their wives' handbags.

Naomi Miller holds one of my hands and one of Elizabeth's and makes us promise to call her if we're ever back in the area, and she hugs us hard but holds me back to say, "You have a wonderful son, Dr. Hart."

"Robert. Please."

"I hope you're very proud. Devoted, sensitive, so very smart. Majoring in English, yes?"

I nod, although this is the first I've heard of it.

"He was a wonderful friend to Nick. You know, I've been thinking about how much Nick must have been suffering" — she flutters one hand by her face, waving off emotion — "and how maybe he never would have beaten those demons, no matter what, but maybe he was able to hang on longer because of his friends. Maybe Jonah made it possible for me to have a little more time with my Nick. I'll forever be grateful for that."

I pat her hand. "It was far too soon."

She nods. "Treasure your child." Looks

me in the eye. "Do that, please." Her nose flushes. She blinks in triple-time. "I'm so sorry. How can a person even cry this much? Where does it come from?" She wheezes out a tiny laugh.

I say, "Your brain is producing leucine enkephalin. It's normal. It's what happens when we cry. Your body is making a natural painkiller to help you survive this, and it's washing stress hormones out of your tear ducts. Those tears are coming from the part of you that wants to heal."

She drops her hands away from her eyes, and she is smiling. "Thank you," she says, and she composes herself and encourages us to get some good sleep for a safe drive back in the morning but hopes we'll consider eating at her favorite diner, where the pie is outstanding. "Oh, and Robert? I think you might have an angel in my Nick. He'll be sitting on your shoulder, keeping an eye on you for the rest of your life."

I shiver. "Good night, Naomi."

We check into two rooms at a twee bed and breakfast, but Jonah joins me and Lizzie in our room for Toblerone and half of *Con Air* on TV before disappearing across the hall. We all need rest, to hit reset so we can extricate ourselves from a web of mourners

— so many people with quiet lives, picking our brains and sharing exclusive parts of themselves, deciding we qualify for inclusion simply by virtue of having known the permanently Excluded. They've left us drained to the bone, marrow-dry.

Sleep sweeps into the room, but before it can take me, I remember what I meant to ask Elizabeth. "Did you know Jonah is an English major?"

"Mm-hm," she moans, sleep-thick. "Good night."

I wrap my limbs around her curled-up body — the little spoon to my Big Dipper. Me: Ursa Major. The Great Bear. Elizabeth's hair smells like an ashtray, thanks to the smokers on Naomi Miller's porch, but this doesn't stop me from burying my face in her neck and breathing myself to sleep.

NAOMI

Sorry has begun to change. The shape of the word — the word itself — feels slippery and gross. There's nothing firm about *sorry*. It's oily or something. Soapy. People keep throwing it at me, but I feel nothing. Soap bubbles out of their mouths that pop in the air, and then there's nothing but air and soap film.

Are they giving me permission to blame them for having families while mine returns to the cosmic chopping block? Do they feel like they did something wrong? *Did* they do something wrong? Is my nightmare their fault?

No. They're not that powerful. If they were, they'd be gods, and everyone keeps telling me God has a plan, so is this my sorry friends' plan? Of course not. It's just a convenient time to get religion — to concede power to the mass of dark matter at the center of our universe. The Great

Unknown. The big black hole that keeps sucking up everyone I love, that keeps sucking and sucking all the love from my life without any reason or plan.

"Naomi," says my old friend Mia, "tell me what I can do to help." She's fluffing pillows so she can feel useful, so she can feel better about herself.

"Not a thing," I say. "Really."

She is relieved but doesn't show it and makes me promise to call her if I need anything, and I promise even though I won't call, which she knows. So she goes too, and now no one else is here but the hired help rinsing cake plates in the kitchen.

Hank Skillman shouldn't have harassed that poor doctor. People like to point fingers so they can place blame, because it's easier to hate someone than to contemplate mortality, but Dr. Hart has been through enough. He had to deal with the aftermath of life leaving a body. That's a terrible burden. I should know.

Hank shouldn't have planted all these questions in my head, either. About the phone calls, the pact. Now I'll always wonder. That's a terrible burden, too. But then tonight, before he left, the way he pulled me aside to tell me what Dr. Hart told him? That the accident had been

319

foreseeable? I preferred not knowing that. "I got him to admit it," Hank said, like he'd run some sting operation. Now I have to decide what to do with the information, which is a burden, too.

Up until now, every time Hank said, "You should sue," I could say, "Ah, but Palsgraf versus the Long Island Railroad," and he'd concede that the law was on Dr. Hart's side. A person cannot be held responsible for an unforeseeable accident that occurs on his property. I figured that out right away. If the accident was foreseeable, though — reasonably foreseeable — well, I guess that would change things. Everything. And like Hank keeps reminding me, the whole point of homeowner's insurance is to cover accidents, and I owe the Harts nothing, and I'm all alone now and need to take care of myself. He's not wrong.

I pay the lady in my kitchen and tell her to take all the cookies she wants. She slips the check into her apron pocket and begins filling a gallon ziplock with dessert. I say, "I'm going to bed now. Just lock the door behind you."

She doesn't mention the Universe's plan or the healing power of Time. She doesn't spit words like soap bubbles out of her mouth. She just says, "Good night, Naomi," and now I'm sure I undertipped her, and I feel terrible, but not bad enough to write another check.

On my way up the stairs, I pass a lineup of photographs on the wall. Becca and Marco and Nick, my parents, some aunts and uncles who've also died or fallen out of favor. Everyone gone. This is how it happens, I guess. People just live until they don't, and at some point someone's left to tell the story, but no one cares unless you're famous, and we're not famous. So then, we're gone.

Becca probably could have been famous if she'd had any talents. She had that thing about her that made people pay attention, but she never used it to her advantage. The most ambition she ever showed was with her hypochondria. Hard work, being so nervous. She was always asking doctors to run tests for deficiencies and syndromes, but things changed when she met Marco. She said he made her feel better in a general way. I called him Rasputin behind his back.

When she phoned and asked if I was sitting down and told me she had ALS, I was almost relieved, because it was too absurd to take seriously. She started in on a wacky set of symptoms, so I got out of my chair and started emptying the dishwasher. I was about to suggest she stay away from the internet when she said, so I went to see the doctor and he sent me to specialists and Naomi, I have ALS. Then I did drop the plate I'd just taken out of the bottom rack. It shattered into three big pieces and a thousand splinters, breaking apart like an iceberg I'd seen on a nature show. And still I didn't sit down. I just stood there in the middle of the mess and listened to my sister explain what was going to happen to her body and when.

I was very sorry then. Sorry like a boulder, not a bubble. I'd wasted so much time with resentments that worked like poison. My latent, passive, malignant hate didn't make my sister sick, and it didn't kill her husband or son — my beloved nephew, oh my God, *what have you done?* — but it did taint the decent years that could have been really good years, and now everyone is dead and all I have are memories of decent years tainted by hate followed by loving years tainted by death, which isn't a whole lot to live for.

Decent years tainted by hate, and for what? I should have been happy for Becca. Mother and Daddy were the ones who thought she was too good for anyone — which on the one hand speaks to how high their standards were for her. On the other hand, it shows why Marco never stood a chance. When Becca left for that seminar in Montreal and came home with a Canadian boyfriend, I was excited for her at first.

She said, "He's really different, Naomi."

And I said, "When do I get to meet this really different guy?"

She said, "Soon," but it was months before he came over for dinner, and by then, our parents had poisoned my opinion with their criticism. I thought it was in service of love, the way I tolerated and even indulged Mother and Daddy's disapproval. It felt noble, this skepticism I adopted, this loyalty to their judgment. I offered blind faith for no better reason than because they'd had sex and made me. Now I have no way of trusting whether the thing I call love isn't hate in disguise.

I've spent years trying to figure out why our parents' venom was so potent. My best guess is that Mother and Daddy weren't shielding Becca so much as themselves. If they'd accepted Marco as good enough for Becca, it would've meant Becca wasn't as special as they believed — or worse, that their assessment of Marco had been wrong, and they hated being wrong.

But I was shielding myself, too, because if

I'd accepted that my parents were wrong, I would've realized they didn't know what was best for us, and if they didn't know best, then no one had the answers. I wasn't ready to be that alone.

How unbearable the world must have been for Nick. Why didn't he come home? He didn't even call to say good-bye. How angry and alone he must have felt.

How selfish and stupid I must have been, believing he was doing so much better.

So now I'm wondering: Why *didn't* he call Hank or the boys on that list? It is peculiar. Hank is right about that.

But wondering can make a person crazy, and I can't afford to lose my mind on top of all these other losses. It would be a shame to go mad analyzing and overanalyzing Hank's questions, spinning them into theories, hunting for blame, feeding my hate, searching for clues that will be revealed in the coroner's report soon enough, anyway. *Let the experts do their jobs, Naomi.* They're authorities. They're the law.

Laws and rules and systems. Precautions, protections. Ever since we were little: be good girls, listen to Mother and Daddy, marry nice boys, obey the law. Trust the men in charge for no other reason than because they're in charge. Trust your parents because they made you. Trust that the Universe has a Plan. Trick yourself into believing that a plan makes things better, that these laws, rules, and systems serve the Plan, which we'll never understand, so don't bother asking questions. It's a mystery, isn't that marvelous? Don't spend much time wondering, or you might go mad.

My body is centered in the doorframe: heels in the hallway, toes in my craft room. The moon is waning but bright. Jars of glitter twinkle in its light. This had been Nick's room. When he went to college I indulged a stupid fantasy, believing that if I built a sanctuary for my creativity, I might actually finish the projects suggested in *Martha Stewart* magazine and *Redbook* and *Domino,* and then maybe I'd stumble upon a skill worth developing into a hobby. Then I'd have a hobby. In other words, then I'd have a reliable distraction from the ache, and it would live down the hall, just as Nick did when he distracted me, so gently, from my feral grief. The Ultimate Ache.

Nick said, *Go for it.* He swore he didn't mind, so I swapped out his bed for a Singer, never dreaming he'd think, *There's no place for me now.* Never dreaming he'd keep that thought to himself, or that maybe, to him, I was just a lady — another person in charge, expecting blind trust — and not a home, which is what Nick was to me.

Did he sense how terribly I'd treated his father? Did he always resent me, and I just never noticed? Maybe I'm an idiot for hoping he'd been too young to remember my cattiness, that he only knew me as an ally. After Becca got sick, I started visiting more often. Marco and I joined forces out of necessity, and I got to know him, then love him, and then I was so ashamed. Eventually, I rented out my house and moved in with them to help while Marco was at work. After Becca died, Marco thanked me for being his friend, which was horrible. I'd been so unkind to him and had called him Rasputin behind his back, and in the end he was a wonderful man who loved my sister more than life itself. So then he was gone, too.

After Marco was buried, Nick became my ward, my world. All of a sudden, a teenage boy was sleeping down the hall. It was very disorienting, but I thought I'd done okay. I didn't think I'd made things so unbearable that he'd throw himself from a random roof. But I guess I did make things that bad, because now he's dead and all I have is a craft room and a ton of acquaintances with God on their tongues. The only people who didn't treat me like an iceberg ready to break apart tonight were that lady in my kitchen and that doctor from the Hamptons. I bet it wouldn't have scared him if I'd referenced oblivion instead of angels. He's probably not afraid of the truth, so he probably didn't need my protection. A person can waste a lot of time and energy trying to protect people from imaginary danger. A person can invent a lot of problems that way.

If I wasn't so selfish — if I hadn't been so focused on preparing myself for temporary loneliness, never considering the permanent kind, never considering *this* Terrible Ache — then this would still be Nick's room, and it would be filled with priceless artifacts from the Era of Nick. I could've curled up in his bed and breathed into his pillow, and the smell of it would have reminded me of him, and I could have had a nice, cathartic cry like they do in the movies. Loud and snotty. That won't happen, though, because there's a Singer sewing machine where his bed should be, and here's the kicker: I still can't sew for shit.

Glitter, needles, brushes, glue. If I had a sledgehammer handy, I'd bash these knick-knacks to bits, but all I have is a cute little jewelry hammer and a mallet for leather-work, so instead I go to my own bed down the hall and grab a pillow and comforter to drag back to the fucking craft room, where I make a nest on the floor, swaddle myself, and lay my head down. I run my finger along a seam on the hardwood, and I try to remember what Nick smelled like, and I cry for Nick, for my sister, for my brother-in-law, for myself and my parents, who never knew what they were missing, but God, they missed so much — and for all the terrible choices I must have made to leave Nick with no will to live.

And for what?

All that time, trying to do the right thing, and in the end, I did the worst thing. I failed my family. I'd give anything to go back and do it better, to do it right. Barring that, I'd give anything to rewind and undo, or barring that, to disappear.

It makes sense, finally, why some people clock out early. How the fight stops being worth it. How faith and sorry stop being enough, and explanations start being mandatory. I'm sick of hearing about angels, when what I need to hear are answers. Hard to talk of heaven when the last flicker in my life has gone and died, and I don't know why.

25.

"She'll be okay," I assure my wife and son as we load the car in the morning.

Elizabeth says, "No she won't."

"Stop being a pessimist," I tell her. "That lady's a survivor. It'll just take time."

She shakes her head and lets it go. We're all tired. Bad beds. We don't wait in line for breakfast at Naomi Miller's favorite diner. We don't buy pie to-go. Before antique shops open, without taking in views or fresh air, we're on the road. Nick's duffle bag is no longer with us.

My son insists on driving. Says it'll relax him, and I'm here to support. Believing she'll get carsick otherwise, Elizabeth takes shotgun, leaving me to play carpooled kid in the back. I ask Jonah about his curriculum, trying and failing to make conversation. He says he's not in the mood to talk about school. I tell Elizabeth we should return upstate to see the foliage in the fall, and she nods and smiles but hides her teeth. No suggestions for better views, better trips. She reclines her seat and closes her eyes, leaving me to stretch out in the backseat, to consume as much room as possible, rejecting the smallness of my position. Sunlight catches Elizabeth's stray hairs, igniting a fiber-optic halo around her head, and all of the tension from recent weeks — anxieties snagged on parties and sins, remedies and consequence, task and duty and choices made or lost — all of it dissolves. There is only air between me and the people I love, and it feels uncharged, alpine-thin. There is only space and a shimmering halo.

I break our silence to offer my son quality time. "Why don't we head to the marina when we get back. Take the boat out for a bit."

He grunts. "I don't think I can manage today."

"Come on. The water will be good for you."

"Not today."

"You can drive." I hear myself bargaining, inching toward begging, and shut my mouth. I know better now, learned the hard way, back when Jonah took my love in concentrated doses only. Every other weekend, Vanessa would drop him off so I could flood him with evidence that I'm the cool guy he'll want to be when he grows up — or at least a guy he'll want to hang out with of his own accord, paternity notwithstanding. I stocked lures: Xboxes and season tickets, a bottomless supply of Entenmann's, all the movie channels, all the privacy and autonomy he could want. I swore openly as passive permission to do the same. I learned to grill steaks to perfection. I taught him the same. But boys don't respond to coddling, to being smothered, and we can't expect them to respect fathers so available as to deny their sons agency — an essential character vertebra passed down to me by my own father, who may not have been perfect, but who was brave enough to let me want things so I could grow the spine needed to acquire them.

So I say, "Another time, then," about the boat ride, but now I'm stuck making good on my bluff. Fine. Whatever. Top-tier problem. I'll head over to check the fuel and scrub algae while Jonah stays home to — what? To grieve? What does grief as a verb even look like, anyway? Inaction. Inactivity. The absorption of sadness compounded by expectation. Public displays of melancholy. Spontaneous meltdowns. Private countdowns. Heaven forbid we tempt the appearance of peace by coping constructively. Heaven forbid we make an effort to flood our brains with serotonin tapped by sunlight and connection. No, the world might find us vulgar and crass — unfeeling, when all we want is to sanitize ourselves from these relentless feelings — and so we reject our bodies' medicine and feed the nuisance instead. We actively mope, turning a terrible thing into its own organism so we'll have something to shape and tame and contain: a creature removed from the Terrible Thing. Grief becomes an adorable, shaggy mutt nipping at our heels in the street. We don't want it, and still it follows us against our will, endearing us to everyone who sees. Making sure everyone sees.

Jonah fiddles with the stereo occasionally, flipping mostly from NPR to silence and back. We're home before the rush of weekenders begins arriving from the city.

"What about you?" I ask Elizabeth. "Feel like heading out on the boat?"

"Me? No," she says. "I need a hot shower. Maybe a bath."

"Lizzie —" I start, but she interrupts me.

"Could you do something for me, please? Don't call me that. I know you're being sweet, but it grates on me. It's infantilizing. And Lizzie is not my name, anyway."

"Seriously?"

"Yes."

"How could you have never said this to me before?"

She shrugs. "I'm saying it now."

"Do you find it infantilizing when people call me Bobby?"

"No. You choose to be called that. That's fine. It's not the same thing, anyway."

"How is it different?" I ask.

"It's different," she says, "because we're not the same person." She touches my cheek with one hand and brings her mouth to mine for a quiet kiss. "And I'm glad for that." Her forehead falls against my chest, so I stroke her hair. I hold her shoulders as she sinks into my sternum and falls silent for some time. "I'm going to take that bath now."

I say, "Okay," and pat her back as a sign of release, but she stays pressed against me, so I wrap my arm around her again and wait for a clue to what she needs. Of course, I can't read her mind, so I do nothing. Finally, after nearly a whole minute lost, she peels herself away, touching my cheek one more time before trudging upstairs to bathe and grieve.

The marina is busy as usual. Happy families.

Happy friends. I'm holding a bucket filled with rags and bottles of cleaning solution when someone slaps me on the back and says, "Robert." Frank McAlister holds out his hand.

I shake it. "Frank."

"How you doing, buddy?"

"I'm all right."

"Are you? Because listen, I heard about what happened at your house. I mean, no one can believe it. That's just a nightmare. And you're the one who, you know — found him, right? Because, man, you can't unsee that, can you? Better you than Jonah or Elizabeth, though, right? You do what you have to do."

"Yes you do. How's everything at your house, Frank?"

"I mean, you know, relatively speaking, I can't complain. Headed to your boat? Great. I'll walk you. So hey, listen, if you don't mind me asking, how long had the kid been out there?"

I mind. "Almost three days, they think."

He winces. "Aw, man. I can't imagine the smell. That's just — was it as bad as they say?"

"Too much *CSI*," I tell him, but holy hell. Frank is into this, isn't he? It's been on his mind. He's been entertaining visions of

334

vultures pecking cold flesh, maybe the neighbor's bichon with Nick's femur in its mouth, screams and sirens, that sort of thing. Fantasies.

He finally takes the hint and starts blabbering about other shit — like how difficult his life's been ever since his front desk gal quit, so now his front office is a clusterfuck — and I'm itching to shut him up, but when we reach my slip, he says, "I'll never get over this boat, Robert. She sure is a beauty."

Well, I'll be damned. He loves my boat. His relentless criticism of *My Lucia* all this time has either been for show — or, like the boy on the playground who pulls pigtails for attention, he's been trying to flatter me. "She sure is."

"I can appreciate a bit of sentiment in a man, Robert."

"Hey, now."

"I mean it," he says. "This boat is your tell. There's honor in keeping ties to your past."

"How do you mean?"

"You know, like how this boat is a statement. Everyone respects that about you. You're proud of your roots. Everyone thinks that's great. Don't get me wrong. No one would hold it against you if you traded 'er in for that speedboat you've been eyeing."

I fake a laugh. "Is it that obvious?"

"Totally. But hey, when you're ready, I'll hook you up with a good buyer for this beauty, make sure she stays in good hands. I know a guy who might be looking soon, but like I said, when you're ready. Just keep it in mind."

"I will." Glancing around the marina, from boat to boat, boater to boater, I try to see what Frank and, apparently, everyone sees. Everyone but me.

"Sorry I asked about the smell," Frank says. "Of the — you know . . ."

"Don't worry about it. Hey, thanks for the food. Tell Bonnie we loved the shepherd's pie." At least I think the shepherd's pie was Bonnie's contribution to our freezer. "You guys didn't need to do anything, but we appreciate it."

"You bet. She wants to do more. Elizabeth should call her, seriously. Bonnie loves it when people lean on her for support, you know? That's what friends are for."

I assure him that Elizabeth'll be fine — that in fact, she hardly knew Nick, because he was Jonah's friend, not mine, and certainly not Elizabeth's. So yes, a terrible thing happened on our property, but our hearts ache for Jonah, mostly, and we'll be okay.

336

Frank cuts me off. "Hey now, I wasn't suggesting anything by saying Elizabeth needs support. Everyone knows your old lady is tough as nails. I mean, come on, she lets you keep a boat named after another woman. Bonnie would shit."

"Lucia was my mom's name," I tell him.

"Still."

"It's bad luck to rename a boat."

"Yeah, I know, but still. Bonnie would have painted over it, luck be damned. But hey, so it's Lu-*chee*-ah? I always thought it was Loo-sha. Like Saint Lucia in the Caribbean. Huh."

"That's French."

"Sure, sure. Then there's Lu-*see*-ah. What's that?"

"You feel like grabbing a beer?"

Frank looks at me as though he's just noticed me standing here. "Now?"

I shrug.

He checks his watch. "Quarter to eleven. How about a coffee?"

"That'll do."

Frank helps me cover my boat — my dead father's boat, named after my dead mother — and we head to the clubhouse for a coffee, then a Bloody Mary, then a pitcher of local brew and a basket of steamers. By two o'clock, two sheets to the wind, I cave to

337

Frank's insistence that the community do something nice for our family — to show support for what we've been through, he keeps saying.

"Everyone feels so bad, you know? The wives. Everyone." He leans toward me. "I'll let you in on a trade secret. The sooner you let 'em do something, the sooner they'll drop it." Well. This makes sense. The casseroles, the condolences. By forcing meatloaf and favors upon us, concerned friends have made themselves part of the story: a tragedy worthy of legend, a rumor that bears repeating. Frank misreads my smile, though, and says, "Am I right? Tell you what: We'll let the girls put together a memorial — maybe a benefit for suicide hotlines or something — to show support and pay respects. You won't have to do a thing," he insists. "Leave it to Bonnie and Elizabeth. They love that stuff."

"You don't know Elizabeth," I say.

"The hell I don't. I know women."

The hell he does. "So, listen," I say. "Just out of curiosity — I'm not selling today or anything — but just for kicks, tell me about that buyer."

26.

"That's really weird, Dad," Jonah tells me back at the house.

"It is so weird," Elizabeth echoes. "Why do they care? They didn't know him."

"No, but they know *us*," I explain. "They care about us. I thought you'd be touched." Truth be told, the party made more sense when Frank sold me on it. "It would be healthy to change up the mood around here. We'll celebrate Nick's life."

"The funeral was yesterday, Dad. You weren't so thrilled about celebrating him then. Some of us need more than twenty-four hours before we can fake a celebratory mood."

"Please," Elizabeth says. "We're all so tired. Robert, your idea is weird, and I don't get it, but if you and Jonah want to plan it, I won't try to stop you."

Jonah starts to explain why he's out, but when I tell him about the fundraiser part, and how we could make a big donation in Nick's name somewhere, he relents.

Elizabeth says, "Just know: I'm not cooking."

"Me neither," says Jonah, who has never been expected to cook in his whole life.

I say, "Good. Because the whole point of this thing is to let our friends do something nice for us — because they want to."

Elizabeth laughs. "In our house?" She shakes her head. "The real centerpiece of this party will be morbid curiosity, mark my word. But whatever. Oh, and I'm not arranging flowers."

"No flowers," I say. "Neither of you will have to do a thing. It'll be fun. Trust me."

I keep my word for nearly two days, but on Monday morning, as Elizabeth and I are scrambling to leave the house — for early appointments, escape, or both, jury's out — she hands me a sheet of paper without comment.

I glance at the list in my hands, names and phone numbers, and ask, "What is this?"

"This," she says sweetly, as she searches the kitchen for an unidentified something, "is the guest list Bonnie just emailed me. Please note the subject line: 'Backyard

Benefit.' She's so glad we're opening our home for a good cause. Apparently, we are hosting a fundraiser for the suicide prevention organization of our choice."

"Lifeline is good," I offer.

"I'm not calling all these people, Robert. I don't have time. We are charging cover for a potluck dinner here in less than a week, apparently, but I've got fifteen midterms to grade. Summer intensives, no less. It's too much."

"That's fine." I scan the names of couples, neighbors, friends of friends, and I read Bonnie's message. "It's not a cover charge, Elizabeth. She says, 'suggested donation.' "

"You need to invite Raymond."

"Elizabeth."

"I'm serious. Invite Ray and Emily. If you want to allow people to satisfy their need to support you, then you have to include him. Period."

"I'll think about it."

"No. You'll do it. I'm not covering for you anymore, and I'm not filtering their sympathy just because you can't handle it. Enough is enough."

"Fine. I'll invite them."

"Invite the kids, too." She spins around, still searching for something.

"It'll be done by the next time I see you,"

I tell her.

"That sounds great. Where on earth is my bag?" She throws her head back. "I can't breathe in this house."

I hand her the oversized satchel she'd hung on the doorknob already, a bag teeming with double-spaced essays. For a moment, her anxiety threatens to spill in the form of tears, confessions, or a proper panic attack, but she sucks it back in and says, "Thank you."

"You're welcome." Keys in hand, we leave through the kitchen door to the garage and head to our cars. I can't breathe in this house, either.

The guest list is a priority, but when Simone shows me my book — appointments back-to-back, open to close, all on account of rescheduling for that goddamn funeral — it becomes obvious I'll never get through the invitations today. Or tomorrow. And I promised.

Pressing my luck to the limit, I kick off the workday by saying, "Hey listen, would you mind knocking out these phone calls when you get any free time today? The numbers are right here, you don't have to look anything up. Just give them the details in that top paragraph: Sunday, six o'clock, address, et cetera. Tell them no flowers, please." I roll my eyes to remind her of our inside joke that's not funny. "Oh, one more." I grab her pen and scribble a name and phone number at the bottom of the page, perhaps the only number I know by heart outside of immediate family and my childhood homes. "Raymond Harrison. He's my oldest friend. You might have met him at a holiday party one time or another. Big guy? Just — I don't know. Make sure he knows I want him there."

Simone stares at the page, then up at me. "Doc?"

"Yeah."

"We need to talk."

"I know. How's tomorrow? This day —" I nod toward the appointment book.

"This can't wait."

I check the time. "Can you do it in five minutes so doors open on time?"

"I need a raise," she says. Well, that's unexpected. "I've been here a long time." She sounds nervous and rehearsed. "I do my job, and I do it very well, but I also do lots of things that aren't my job." She shakes the guest list. "This is personal assistant stuff, Dr. Hart. I should have set better boundaries in the beginning, but this isn't my responsibility. Neither is shopping for

343

gifts for your wife. Neither is covering your bases." She pauses, letting this last part settle. In a hard whisper, she says, "I lied to the cops for you. You realize that, right? I've practically perjured myself."

Fire in my veins. "Do you even know what perjure means? What are you suggesting?"

"I'm not suggesting anything. I'm asking for a raise."

"Or else?"

"Or else I quit, or else — well, what are *you* suggesting?"

I stiffen. "Are you trying to blackmail me?"

She plays innocent with, "Do you really think that's the kind of person I am?"

"I don't know what to think. I'm sorry. This is a very stressful time."

"Yes. Of course it is." She stares into space, her head bobbing gently, then she freezes and looks me in the eye. "And you know what? I hadn't thought of it before, but you bring up a very good point. This has been an exceptionally stressful time. If I were to lose my job or be forced to quit, it might be difficult to keep ignoring the things I ignore as part of my job. Is that what you were suggesting? Because if so, you understood what I was saying even before I did."

I've never done this before. "How much?"

"Forty percent."

"A forty percent raise? That's pitiful." She's sitting here with my kryptonite in her back pocket, and the best she can ask for is forty percent? If her dreams max out at a forty percent increase in quality of life, she has let me down. Disappointment makes a poor bargaining chip.

She points to Bonnie's stupid list and says, "Then don't ask me to do two jobs." There's a knock at the main entrance. It should've been unlocked by now. The nurses will already be in the staff room — hopefully not eavesdropping on Simone's negotiations — and I don't have a minute to think, let alone plan an idiotic party.

"Help me with this," I beg. "We'll sit down and talk about the raise in depth later. I value you and want to make it right." To ingratiate myself completely, I say, "You can add your name to the list. Elizabeth would love to have you."

"You've got to be kidding me."

I throw my hands in the air. "I'm doing my best. Please meet me halfway."

"I'm letting in your seven-thirty hypertension. This conversation is on hold, not over."

"Fine."

"Also, I said *practically* perjure. I know what perjury is."

I clear one landmine just in time to make way for another, because an hour later, Mr. Walsh from the medical examiner's office calls again. I check my voice mail over lunch, listen to his invitation to swing by the office at my earliest convenience, listen to him say, "We have a few questions concerning the death of Nick Carpenter."

It takes four days and two additional voice mails before I find time to pay Zeb Walsh a visit in a building I've driven by a thousand times without ever considering what transpires here. It's enormous. Modern. Expansive. And single-purposed. The Office of the Medical Examiner. All of this, all for death. Medical examiners, deputy medical examiners, forensic medical investigators, scholars in labs. Toxicology labs, crime scene labs, serology labs. Front desks.

A receptionist takes my name and sends me upstairs to another receptionist, who tells me to have a seat and doesn't call my name for another seventeen minutes, at which point she leads me to a windowless office crowded with a desk, two chairs, a file cabinet, a tiny couch.

"Mr. Hart." Walsh rises from his desk to shake my hand. "I was wondering when you'd finally get here. You got my messages?"

"Doctor, actually. And yes, I did. It's been a busy week. Took off time for the funeral."

"How was that?"

"Sad."

"I bet."

"What can I do for you?"

He sorts through some papers, stores them in a drawer, redirects his attention to a computer monitor, flips to a page in his notebook, then asks, "Remind me, when was the last time you saw Nick alive?"

"Let's see." I pause to be certain my story is straight. "I last saw him the Thursday — or was it Friday? — before he died."

"Mm-hm." Walsh checks his monitor once again. "You got a traffic citation last weekend."

"That's right," I say. "Speeding. I was speeding."

"Anyone in the car with you that day?"

"Yes." I swallow, or try to, anyway — try willing my pharynx to squeeze — but my throat feels paralyzed, or weaponized, as though my own body is choking me into silence.

Walsh is still staring at his monitor, one finger over his mouse, and he looks at me and asks, "Who?"

I smile. At least my facial muscles work. I clear my throat to be sure my vocal cords do, too, and when a sound happens, I say the first thing that comes to mind: "My son, Jonah."

Walsh looks at his monitor again and begins to type, hitting far more keys than necessary to spell my son's name. He asks, "Where were you going?"

"We were coming from my office," I say, and knowing better than to volunteer details, I still add, "He needed to use the printer."

Walsh leans back and gives me his full attention. "You don't have a printer at home?"

"We do. Sure. But he needed to print a large document. Book-length. Something to help him cram for an exam. He's in summer school. The inkjet at the office is better for that sort of thing. We didn't have much ink at home." Shutting up is harder than it should be.

Walsh asks, "Why didn't he drive himself?"

"Hm?"

"Does your son have a car?"

"Oh. Yes, he does."

"So why did you drive him?"

"To let him in and make sure the system was online."

"Was anyone else there?"

"No. Just us. The office is always empty on the weekends." As soon as I say it, I hear in my head the demonic grind of that goddamn Keurig, and Simone saying, *Nice to meet you,* to Nick.

"Well, that about does it," Walsh says. He flips his notebook over, obscuring his notes, and stands to see me out. At the door, he shakes my hand. "Thanks for coming down."

"Of course. Anything I can do."

His grip is too tight when he says, "One more thing," and he's still squeezing my hand when he asks, "How'd the exam go?"

"Hm?"

"How did he fare in his exam?"

What else is there to do but play dumb? "Exam?" *Play dumb.* Play dumb until the end.

"The big exam. Didn't you say your son was cramming for one? The document?"

"Oh, right." A smile slips through my cracks, and because I can, this time I tell the truth. "You know something? I have no idea."

It's taken this long for me to revisit the scene of Nick's death, but now that I've lied to the police when I had nothing to hide, my interest is piqued. Once home, I head upstairs to the skinny door between the upstairs bathroom and Jonah's bedroom, and I slide the key from its hiding place on the trim atop the doorframe, but a key wasn't necessary. The police must have left it unlocked.

I tug a chain hanging just inside the musty spiral staircase leading up, but the lightbulb is dead, so I climb the stairs and nearly head-butt the trapdoor, which lifts with ease, and I step up into the cupola, an antique bubble, taking note of the cloudy window panes and overgrowth obscuring an otherwise splendid panorama of my property, neighborhood, town.

So this is where Nick stood before he threw himself to his death. Did he take in the view, too? Did he even appreciate it?

On weathered benches framing the interior of this room, varnish peels in shiny strips. I could have painted it white, fixed the wiring, added pillows, a coffee table, stacks of magazines. That sort of thing might work for people who live in the past, but not for me. Frank McAlister has me all wrong. I'm no champion of bygone days. Overhead hangs the sole decoration: dulled prisms on a dated chandelier that can't catch light.

I wiggle the loose knob on a swollen,

splintered door opening to the roof walk. Until a couple of weeks ago, this place hardly ever crossed my mind. Twice a year, tops: first freeze, first thaw. I clean up leaves and check for leaks and contemplate tearing the whole thing down. Then I lock the door again and forget this place exists.

From a distance, our sculpted banisters suggest the Italian belvederes after which they were modeled, but up here, the effect is more Dr. Zhivago's winter palace crusted with seagull feces instead of icicles, salt crystals instead of frost. There's no warmth here. No reason to hang out, except to dive off.

A widow's walk: even the name portends doom. Some dumb romantic probably made it up, swooning at the thought of sailors' wives standing on platforms like these, waiting for long-lost mariner husbands, dead husbands. I suppose "chimney cleaner's walk" didn't summon the same architectural esteem (or need for prickly building codes). So maybe the romantic wasn't dumb, after all. Maybe he was a marketing genius.

I appraise the deck, built so far to the northeast corner of our house that most of my property isn't even visible from here. One can see the sky, the skyline, almost the sea, part of the swimming pool, all of the guesthouse. From below, looking up from the pool or guesthouse — or in a photograph, like those featured in our local paper last year: neighbors celebrating neighbors in photo essays validating our property values — we sell a strong illusion. People complimented those pictures of our home. They still do. But the elm is overgrown, and the linden is getting out of hand, too, so there's not even much of a view anymore.

I move toward the broken beams where Nick stood at the steepest angle of our roof. A thirty-foot drop to the ground after that. Centering my hips in the gap Nick's body made, I dare myself to look down the path worn by one-hundred-seventy pounds of young man on his way to his end.

"Dad?"

I spin around to see a figure blurred by the dirty windows between us. Jonah is standing square in the middle of the crow's nest, facing me. "Hey," I say, moving toward him. "What are you doing up here?"

"Door was cracked," he says, still motionless behind the glass.

"Let's go down. You don't need to see this."

"It's okay," Jonah says, but he doesn't move.

I pass through the doorway, stopping below the busted chandelier. The perfect thing to say escapes me, so I put my hands in my pockets and wait.

"What are you doing up here?" he asks.

"I went down to the medical examiner's office today. They're still working on that official report. Got me thinking about this place."

"What are they working on? It's so stupid. There's no mystery here."

"They're just doing their job."

"Waste of our taxes."

Of *our* taxes? The prospect of Jonah earning enough income to pay that guy's salary is hilarious, but I'm not in a laughing mood. "Total waste. Hey, listen, I need you to do something."

"What?"

"If anyone from the police or coroner's office calls you — anyone who wants to ask about Nick, anyone at all — don't answer. Let it to go to voice mail, then tell me right away and we'll go from there."

"Why?"

Why? Because if they know I lied about the kid in my passenger seat, I'm toast. "I have a hunch they might try to blame us, since it happened at our house."

"For real?"

"Maybe. Premises liability for an unsafe structure. I'm not sure, but I don't want to take any risks, especially with a wrongful death charge at stake."

"Jesus, Dad. She wouldn't do that."

"Who?"

"Nick's aunt. Naomi. She's not going to sue you."

"Grief makes people do crazy things. All I'm saying is if *anyone* reaches out to you about it, we need to handle communication as a family. This affects all of us."

"Fine," he mumbles.

"This is serious, Jonah."

"I said *fine.* Do you think I want to talk to them? I never want to talk about it again."

At least we have this in common. I eyeball the stairs Jonah is blocking, and as though guessing the password to a kids' game, I say, "I know. I'm so sorry, Son."

He nods and grants passage, leading us back down the spiral staircase. I close the trapdoor behind me without looking back. The place held no power for so long. Now it hovers over us. Its dome compresses our space, invades our days and nights, hosts bad choices decaying above us while we sleep. I suppose now I'm going to have to renovate or destroy. I lock the door, slip the key into my pocket, and slap my son on the back as we part ways.

28.

Sunday morning, a good nine hours before the party, and Elizabeth is stressing about clutter and supplies. She's dusting neglected corners of our house — gaps in bookshelves, backs of speakers — and pitching old candles burned down to the quick, replacing them with new ones, lighting wicks.

Jonah has risen to meet her frenzy. At ten in the morning, he laces his shoes and recites, "Fancy paper plates, fancy paper napkins, vegetable platter — what else?"

Elizabeth points to a list Scotch-taped to the door. "Get some cash from your father."

"You two are missing the point," I tell them. "This is supposed to *relieve* our stress. This is something people want to do for us. Besides, they won't be here until six. Relax."

Elizabeth shakes her head, but Jonah says, "Do you know how many times Bonnie McAlister has called this week? She's basically stalking Elizabeth with all these great ideas about catering and charity. It hasn't been relaxing, and we need toilet paper."

Elizabeth says, "For God's sake, Robert, that ladder is still out there." She points to the side yard, where I left the ladder at the police officers' request, and then I'd forgotten, and now it's probably killing the grass.

I say, "I'll put it away."

"You will," Elizabeth says. She tells Jonah to hurry back so he can clean the pool. He doesn't argue or give attitude. Their disdain for this party — a nice gesture they refuse to see clearly — has brought them together in some sort of trauma bond.

Frank and Bonnie arrive exactly half an hour early, bearing a platter of bruschetta and a bottle of cabernet. Jonah's still in the shower. The pool hasn't been cleaned.

"Bonnie." Elizabeth takes the tray. "Frank. You really didn't have to do this."

"Not another word," Bonnie says, as though Elizabeth had just thanked her. "We came early to help. Now what can we do?"

The rest of our guests trickle in around six, six fifteen, six thirty, and suddenly the house is full. There aren't so many people — maybe thirty, maybe more — but the activity is such a contrast to our lives of late that it feels amplified, magnified. Simone doesn't show, but Ray and Emily do. They bring Bianca, who has changed far too much since the last time I saw her.

"Leon couldn't make it," Ray tells me. "Band practice."

"Good for him," I say. We make small talk and I take drink orders, but when I leave, Ray follows me to the bar. He tells me he was glad to be invited, and how he hopes we can talk, and I look around the room and say, "Oh, shit. Hold that thought. I need to grab something. Be right back." I hurry off, pretending to launch an urgent search for olives, but Ray isn't dumb. He must know this isn't the time or place. I wait until he's locked into a focused conversation with Bonnie's pastor before I slip back into the mix, joining a conversation already in progress.

Lamont Carver is saying, "Only at open-casket funerals."

His wife, Kelly, says, "I did when I was ten. My grandmother died at home, and I'll never forget my mother forcing me to go into her room to pay my respects. Oh, but there you are, Bobby. My God. To see a body like that? My heart just aches for you all."

I repeat my standard reply: "I'm just glad no one else had to witness it."

People agree. My son, who has been hovering throughout, adds, "Some silver lining."

Kelly grabs his hand and tells him he's in her prayers, and now it's someone else's turn to share war stories. Jonah is polite but transparent as he waits for the lull that doesn't come. Finally, he nudges me and mutters, "Dad, can you talk for a sec?"

I excuse us. "What is it?"

"I'm only saying this because I'd want to know if I were you — no judgment, just saying — but you should check in on Elizabeth."

"Check in?"

"She's really been drinking."

"So?"

"Like, a lot. She seems drunk."

"I'm sure she's fine."

"She's drunk, Dad."

"She's fine. I'll deal with it, okay?"

"If you say so."

I assess the scene and change course. "Nice party, isn't it?"

Jonah shakes his head and walks away. His signature move.

Across the room, a bell tolls: silver on crystal, spoon to goblet — the universal call for attention, a toast to be made. Guests convene in the living room, finding arms of

360

chairs on which to sit. Conversations fall to whispers, and all focus turns to Elizabeth, who is still tapping flatware against her wineglass. I stand tall in the back of the crowd, arms crossed at my chest, a lighthouse signaling reason, her sobering beacon.

"Hi," Elizabeth says. "Hi, everyone. I wanted to thank you all for coming. I know most of you didn't really know Nick, but it means a lot to us that you'd go out of your way to honor his memory and show up for Jonah — and for the cause. So thank you."

Some guests prematurely raise glasses. Others mutter kind words. Most of them, though, are bubbling with anticipation for the sentiment threatening to spill.

"So I've been thinking about something," she says, enunciating with pained focus. "There's this thing my dad likes to say. He says, 'You can measure people's privilege by how much shit they disturb for fun.' He says this whenever politicians or pro athletes recreationally throw their lives into turmoil, you know? His theory is that the people who get dealt crappy cards in life don't have the time or energy or inclination to make life more difficult than it already is. They're too busy working to make things better. But the lucky ones? The ones who were born into better, without any effort on our part —"

From a stiff crowd, a trace of forced laughter rises and falls.

"Well," Elizabeth continues, "my dad says we lay our own traps just so we can pull ourselves up by the bootstraps. He says we do that so we can feel equal, because if we are equal, we don't have to feel guilty about our good luck. We can tell ourselves we earned it."

Now there is a polite cough and a rustling pantsuit, but no laughter. No one likes a killjoy. *Oh, Elizabeth. Watch yourself.*

She closes her eyes and rubs her nose. "The reason I bring this up," she says, "is because Nick made me think about it a lot. Here was a kid who was born into what, by most standards, would appear to be a very fortunate upbringing. Loving parents. High-end education. Then life dealt him really crappy cards — like, hardcore crap. He didn't ask for that shit — and that is not the kind of self-serving drama my dad was talking about, trust me — but here's the other thing: Nick didn't martyr himself. He didn't. Most of us probably would have. I mean, I got some crappy cards too, at his age." She closes her eyes once again, and this time she holds up a hand, palm directed toward me in anticipation of my reaction. "Now, Robert. Let me finish. It's okay. I'm

362

fine." She blows me a kiss and addresses a room full of spellbound faces. "Whatever. I saw some shit, okay?"

How can I rescue her without making it worse?

"And anyway" — she laughs — "yeah. For twenty years, I've carried sadness around, letting it get in the way, like my pain is unique. I don't really know any other way to deal but to feel bad. See, this is what was so confusing and enlightening and irritating about Nick. He accepted his horrible, shitty, fucked-up life and went on to make good friends with good people."

Tears light up her eyes. She doesn't look at my son, but I do. He is stoic. He is strained.

Elizabeth continues, "And anyway, it's just dumb, really. It's dumb, the messes people make. This shouldn't have happened to Nick. His life shouldn't have ended like this. It's so stupid, you know? So fucking sad." The tears sink back into her face, and she pulls herself together. Miraculous. "So, anyway. Thanks for coming. Thanks for giving money to this cause, and — I don't know. Maybe thanks in advance for never mentioning this toast."

My guests laugh — clucks of anxious relief, a coop of hot air breathed back into the room.

I raise my glass to seal the frayed ends of my wife's sort-of toast. "To Nick," I say.

Everyone follows my lead, repeating "To Nick," as though we're embarking on some new journey together, forever changed by a young man who's no longer with us, when in fact we'll soon forget that he was with us, because he barely was.

We drink.

29.

I charge Elizabeth, post-toast. By the time I reach her, having dodged a few social obstacles on the way, she and Rick Lester's new girlfriend, Bess, have been targeted by Luna Parks, who seems to be claiming, at high volume, that she invented avocado toast.

"Sorry to interrupt," I say. I put my arm around Elizabeth, who squeezes my hand on her shoulder. I take it as an apology for her public speaking debacle. She is forgiven.

"Well, anyway," Luna says, "I'll bring you some, but you have to eat them right away or they'll go bad. You just let me know when works for you. I mean, really, this whole thing is like a horror movie." Addressing Elizabeth, she adds, "The only difference, of course, is if this was a movie, you'd have died first."

Elizabeth scowls. "Gee, Luna. What a thing to say."

Bess adds, "And in this setting, no less."

"On account of you being the beauty queen, sweetheart. Oh my God. You know what I'm saying." She shakes Elizabeth by the shoulders. "The pretty one is always the first to go." To me and Bess, she asks, "Isn't that the thing? Beauty queen first? I can't remember. Oh, lighten up. I'm sure the eccentric one dies next." She nudges Elizabeth, as though they share a secret: two dead gals walking in the movie in Luna's mind. My wife manages a smile.

"Remind me again, Luna," Bess says. "When does the bitch die?"

I've heard this woman speak all of two sentences, and already, she's won me over. Nearby friends gasp and turn to watch — not eavesdropping, but flat-out observing in delight. I'm tempted to step in and rescue Bess, but something tells me she doesn't need backup. After a few terrifying moments during which Luna's humiliation teases chaos, Bess smiles. She goes so far as to laugh. Luna, caught off guard, laughs too. What else can she do? She points at Bess. "You — are a wild one, aren't you, buttercup? I'll be damned." She shouts across the room to Rick. "You've got yourself a firecracker here, Mr. Lester!"

He nods and raises his glass, and to my

astonishment, Bess picks up the conversation as though nothing happened. "How long have you two lived here?" she asks Elizabeth.

Assured that Elizabeth is in good hands, I say, "Will you all excuse me? I think we're running low on club soda."

Jonah leeches onto me not two steps away. "Well?"

"What?"

"Do you see what I'm talking about now?"

"She's fine, Jonah."

"Dad."

"She's fine."

He follows to the garage. "I really need to talk to you."

"Damn." A blank strip on the wall reminds me that the ladder is still laying out in our yard. The gutter still needs cleaning.

"What is it?"

"Nothing." I shimmy over to the shelves where we stock surplus crap from Costco.

"Can you listen for a minute, please?"

The club soda should be here. Tonic water, too. "Do you know where all those bottles went? The Schweppes?"

"I think Elizabeth brought them inside already. But Dad —"

"Not right now, son."

"This can't wait."

367

"Fine," I say. "What is it?"

"So I was just talking to Matthew, and he said his mom ate at Lemongrass last week. He said she saw you and Elizabeth there."

"That was rude of her to not say hello."

"Whatever. Matthew said his mom thought Elizabeth had a lot to drink that night, too."

"Are you serious? Which one is Matthew's mom again?"

"Super long hair, flower dress."

"You've got to be kidding me."

"She wasn't shit-talking or anything. She just mentioned it, I guess, and I wouldn't have repeated it except —"

"What? Spit it out."

"This is really awkward. I don't even know how to say it."

"Say it."

"All right. Fine. Fuck it. Fine." He shakes his head. "I was just wondering if it's okay for Elizabeth to be drinking like this."

My stomach twists. "She's not an alcoholic, Jonah. I don't even think her sister is a real alcoholic, if you want to know the truth. Laurie just likes going to those meetings. Don't put Elizabeth under a microscope because her sister is a fuckup." I pretend to care about the contents of this shelf. "Not that it's up for discussion, but if you care so much, she actually took an Ativan before dinner that night, unbeknownst to me, which was clearly a mistake but also none of Matthew's mom's business." I slap his arm. "Let's go back in and face these idiots."

Jonah doesn't follow. "Wait," he says. "I'm not talking about that."

I give up and ask, "What do you mean?"

"I don't think she's an alcoholic." He closes his eyes, shakes his head. "This is so awkward."

"Spit it out, Jonah."

He breathes through his teeth. "Fucking fuck. Okay. Fine. Is Elizabeth pregnant?"

Stay cool. "Are you kidding?"

"What? No, I'm not kidding."

"Elizabeth is not pregnant. Jesus Christ, Jonah."

"Really?"

"Yes, really. What made you think that?"

"You have to promise not to tell anyone. I'm serious, Dad."

"Jonah, tell me now."

"Promise."

"Jonah," I snap.

"Okay. So remember how I told the cops I hadn't seen Nick the day before he —"

"Yes."

"Well, I was so panicked I forgot that I'd

talked to him the night before. By the time it clicked, I couldn't backtrack or I'd look like a liar, so I stuck to my story. It's not relevant anyway. It wouldn't have made a difference if they'd known. The thing is, though, when we talked — the night before, you know — Nick told me he thought Elizabeth was — you know."

"Pregnant."

"Yeah."

"Why did he think that?"

Jonah rolls his head. He wants to leave this conversation, garage, house. Escape this scene. Evacuate. But he's stuck now, so, "He said, because you told him so."

This must be how military commanders feel, or quarterbacks, or team captains. Be quick, resolute, always on the offense. Never be surprised by an attack, never fail to anticipate a play. I wonder if self-preservation is more strategy than strength. Summoning my army of wits, I say, "He shouldn't have told you that."

A strange current charges my son: flickers of feelings that don't suit him. Outrage. Craze. "Why would you have talked to him about it and not me? I know it's none of my business, either — but how was it any of his?" Without any warning or windup — without a history of violence, as far as I know — Jonah throws a right hook smack into the drywall. Pitiful form.

"Jonah," I snap. "What's wrong with you?"

He kicks the wall and follows up by slapping both hands against his head. Knuckles red, he grunts like an animal.

"Jesus Christ. What the hell is your problem?"

He drops to a squat, head between knees, palms smacking the sides of his temples.

"Look at me."

He obeys, and when he does, he's changed. A bull in the bullring, ready to charge.

"Listen to me," I command. "You need to chill out. Do you hear me? There is a house full of people on the other side of that wall. Now is not the time for a tantrum. Be a man. Get it together. Do you hear? This is nobody's business but mine and Elizabeth's. Not yours. Not Nick's. No one's."

"But —"

"But nothing," I snap. The back of my brain scrambles for an excuse. "If you must know, Nick overheard me talking to Elizabeth. He asked me point-blank. He caught me off guard, so I confirmed it — but I also made him swear he wouldn't talk about it, because first of all, I didn't want you finding out like this. Secondly, though, there was always a high risk of spontaneous abortion simply because of Elizabeth's age. She didn't want anyone to know until we were in the clear."

"Okay?"

"And this is exactly why we didn't talk about it." I pause, weigh my options, and proceed with the best one. "She lost the baby."

"Oh God." He rocks on the back of his heels, and for a minute I think he might fall down, but he steadies. "Shit."

"Yeah."

Head in hands, he manages to say, "I'm sorry."

"Yeah. Me too."

The steam recedes. He inspects his knuckles and kneads a sore hand.

"Now can you see why we wanted to keep it to ourselves? It's been very upsetting for Elizabeth. She does not want to talk about it. Nobody knew she was pregnant, and nobody knows she's not now, and that's the way she wants to keep it. We have to respect that."

"But weren't you — ?" He mimes scissor snips with his good hand.

"Yes," I say, taken aback at his knowledge of my anatomy. "I was, yes. But even though it's none of your business, I had it reversed a few years ago. We thought maybe we'd try, but we changed our minds, and by then, we decided not to redo the procedure. Elizabeth is forty-two, you know. We figured that ship had sailed. But we figured wrong."

"Oh." Humbled by his ignorance, he rises, adjusting his posture and inspecting the fresh dent in my wall. Powdered plaster collects on the concrete.

"Now, I've got to tell you, you are freaking me out a little bit," I say.

"I know. I'm so fucked up, Dad. I seriously can't take any more. Everything's so fucked up around here. I'm freaking myself out too, okay?"

"I'm not talking about the wall."

He looks at me and asks, "About what, then? What else? What part of this shit pile freaks you out?"

"About just now learning that you talked to Nick the night before he died. Am I hearing you right? You talked to him the night before he died?"

"Yeah."

"And yet you told me and the police and everyone that you didn't have any contact with him for days."

What had been fury moments ago becomes reckless panic before my eyes. "I didn't mean to lie. I swear. I was all bent out of shape, and it doesn't actually make a difference. I mean, I realize that's not the point, but it doesn't matter whether I talked to him that night or not. He killed himself. He was going to kill himself regardless. I just have to keep telling myself that or I'll go insane, Dad."

We both jump when the door to the house opens and Kelly Carver nearly tumbles down the steps in our garage. "Oops," she says, giving us a once-over, glancing at Jonah's plaster-dusted pants. "I was looking for the bathroom."

I direct her to the correct door, and she leaves, and it's just us again, but we can't do this here. So I say, "Jonah, when you hold things back, you risk all of us getting in a bind with the people investigating Nick's death. If there's anything else you're hiding, you need to tell me. It won't bring Nick back. I'll grant you that. It makes a difference to us, though."

"Okay," he says, too calm, too sure. He should be scuffing his sneaker against the concrete floor like a kid who's been put in his place, but he stands tall like a man, holding eye contact. "I just forgot."

"Okay, then. Stay here. I'm going to bring you a cold pack. You're going to ice that hand for fifteen minutes and get ahold of yourself before coming inside. But first, you're going to bring in that ladder from the side yard. Hang it on these hooks by the time I get back."

He nods.

Before leaving him, I ask once more, "Anything else you want to tell me?"

He shakes his head.

I leave my son to lick his wounds, and I wonder if he knows I know he's lying.

30.

Why in the world would Jonah lie to me?

He claims to have heard that pregnancy bullshit the night before Nick died — but I didn't feed Nick that lie until morning. Maybe the forensic pathologists and medical examiner got it all wrong. Maybe Nick was only two days dead when I found him. But no, the consensus was three days. Everyone at the funeral seemed to have accepted that as fact.

I do not press for details when I deliver the cold pack, because there's a damn party at my house. I should be enjoying it. Just when that starts to feel attainable, though, I run into Ray, who pulls me aside.

"Can we bury the hatchet later?" I ask him. "This crowd, you know. These people."

"No, man. I think we should talk."

"I can't do this now."

"You can't *not* do this, Bobby. It's serious." He leans close and whispers, "It's about Simone."

The name almost doesn't register, so foreign does it sound coming out of Ray's mouth. "My office manager Simone?"

"Yeah. Her."

"Okay, fine." I lead Ray outside. We take a seat on a pair of woven pool chairs. From this angle, looking through a wall of glass at the cocktail hour unfolding in my own house, it's as though I'm watching animals in a cage, or live theater on mute. "What about Simone?"

"She's a problem, Bobby."

"What are you talking about?"

"She's trouble. I straightened her out, but you need to keep an eye on her, man. I'm serious."

"What do you mean, you straightened her out?"

"She called me," he whispers, "about the party. She invited me and then got weird, saying she knew we were old friends."

"Yeah, I told her that."

"Fine, but she made it sound like she had some inside info. Whatever. And I said, yeah, we go back to the beginning, and I don't know — I guess that made her trust me or something. She sounded weird, I'm not going to lie."

"And then?"

"That was the end of it. I said, yeah, we'll try to be here. I was still pissed at you and, dude, you should have called me yourself. What the fuck?"

"Come on, Ray."

"It was rude. So anyway, that night she called me again."

"At home?"

"On my cell, but I was home, yeah. It was late."

"What did she want?"

"Well, that's what I wanted to know, right? What did she forget? Am I supposed to ask Emily to bring something or whatever?"

"And?"

"And, buddy" — he leans closer — "she asked if I had a minute to talk about you."

"What did she say?"

"She started out acting timid, saying she was worried about you, saying she was worried about herself. She told me about how she'd covered your ass as a favor, but how she's doubting herself now. Swear to God, Bobby."

"I believe you. What else did she say?"

"Well, let's see. She said that kid came into your office a few days before he died. She said none of it was on the books, and that you drew blood that never got tested, and that the whole thing was shady, but that she covered for you when the cops called. She said she had to tell someone the truth or she was going to lose her mind. You ask me, she already has. You ask me, she's the one you should have gotten rid of."

I flinch.

"Sorry. I don't mean it. Sorry about that. But you know what I mean, right? Because Bobby, she wanted to talk about this shit, so it's like, you better count your lucky stars she chose me, right? And you haven't even told me everything yet. You're going to have to one of these days, you know. And you'd better hope that girl hasn't told anyone else. She swore she hadn't. And trust me, she definitely hasn't now."

"Why?" I ask. "What happened?"

He smiles, takes a long drink and sucks his teeth, followed by a disgusting, self-satisfied exhale — an audible, *Ahhhh.*

"What did you do, Raymond?"

He is smug and proud. "I shut her up."

"What did you do?"

"Relax, dude. Relax." He gestures, palm-to-concrete, for me to lower my voice. "I let her know that not only would I tell the cops that she lied and tampered with evidence — making her an accessory and in violation of whatever health shit she thinks she broke — but I reminded her that she'd lose her job because of it. Who would want to hire her then?"

"Ray."

"And I said I'd tell the cops she's a psycho."

"Raymond," I nearly shout. "Tell me you're fucking with me."

He grins. "I got your back, buddy."

"This is having my back?"

"I told her I'd be first in line to testify that she's a bunny-boiler."

"What are you saying?"

He laughs out loud. "Glenn Close with the dead rabbit."

"Yeah, I got that, dickhead. But what exactly did you tell her?"

"I said if she fucked with you, I'd be right there ready to blame her for malpractice and sexual harassment and some other stuff. I said she should watch her back. She started crying at that last part. I won't lie, that felt pretty bad. Tried to soften it a little, but that only made it worse. God. This was pretty fucked up of me, wasn't it?"

"Jesus, Ray. What is wrong with you? Sexual harassment?"

"Somewhere at some point she's bound to have stepped out of line, right? Everyone does."

"Malpractice doesn't apply to receptionists, Ray."

He smiles and makes some clicking sound, as though I'd guessed a secret, and I do not react, ever mindful that the panes of glass dividing me and my guests could quickly flip, turning my guests into the audience and me into the show.

"Here's the deal," I say, edging as close to the truth as possible without touching the line. "I had that irrational freak-out about the kid, but I was wrong. It was midlife crisis shit. I still wanted to get rid of him, like you said I should, just to keep this house from going crazy — just to keep me from going crazy in this house. So I said yes when he asked if I'd take a look at his swollen glands. Figured I'd size him up, get his weak spot. Had him into the office, drew some blood, and changed my mind. He was fine. Nothing came from it anyway, because he went and offed himself before I had a chance to interfere. He was fucked up. That's what I was picking up on, okay? He wasn't sleeping with Elizabeth. He was desperate for a mother figure, and he was lost and crazy. Hand to God, Ray, I didn't have anything to do with this shit. You've got to believe me, man."

He is earnest and childlike when he says without moving his lips, "I do."

"You believe me."

"I do. You should have told me all this earlier. You had me going out of my mind over there, Bobby. I thought you'd snapped, and then that nurse said that shit."

"Office manager."

"Whatever, dickwad. She made me think maybe you'd gone off the deep end over this kid. What was I supposed to do?"

"It's fine, Ray." My objective: de-escalation. My sole purpose in this, my final exchange with Ray, is to convince him that his distance and silence will demonstrate loyalty, which is his most valued virtue of all. I can't have him turning on me. He knows too much. Until that report comes back from the coroner, Ray is dangerous to me and my family. "You did right, man, okay? It's just — you weren't all off when you called her crazy. Simone."

"I knew it." He snaps his fingers. "I could sense it, Bobby, the way she spilled her guts."

"Well, I know her. I know how to handle her, and right now, it's a delicate situation."

He whispers, "With her?"

"God, no. Not delicate like that. I mean, with the cops. They're asking questions, making something out of nothing, but I lied to them about that appointment."

382

"Why?"

"I panicked."

"So tell them. Get them off your case."

"I would, but it's too late now. Do you realize how bad that would look? How bad that would make me look?"

He thinks on it and nods.

"So here's what we have to do." *We,* I say, intentionally grouping us together, making sure he believes we're still a team. "We have to lay low. Ride this out until those assholes stop nosing around. They'll get bored eventually. And I'm saying this for your own sake, man: you need to go dark for a while."

He laughs. "Get out of here, man."

"I'm serious, Ray. I'm looking out for you. You don't want to get involved, and you sure as hell don't want to piss off a — what did you call her?"

"Bunny-boiler."

"Right. Leave her be. Let her calls go to voice mail and keep your side of the street clean. They'll close the case eventually and we can all get on with our lives, but in the meantime, we have to ride this out without making something out of nothing."

"Nothing," he says, looking up at the roof, but he takes it all in and caves. "All right. If that's how you want to play this."

"It is."

"You have to call me if shit gets out of hand again, though."

"I will. In the meantime, don't worry about me. I'll be fine. I can take care of it."

Unconvinced, he nods.

"All right," I say. "I have to get back in there."

He nods again.

"Take home some of those cake things for Leon. Some sandwiches, too. Have a good time in there, buddy."

"Sure thing," he says. Somber. Resigned.

I slap him on the shoulder and walk away, knowing that this was the end of us. I wonder if he knows it too, and if he feels the pinch of grief, sensing this might have been our last meaningful conversation, the end of an era. One more witness down.

I go inside and say polite words to people without hearing their responses. The cloud in my ears is too loud. I have nothing to hide or defend, so I don't need Ray's assistance, and anyway, he's the one who demanded I trust my instincts. My instincts say he could be my family's undoing. He should have dropped it. I did nothing wrong. When I step away to refill my drink, Ray and his family are already gone.

SIMONE

I check the time on the sly. Eight fifteen.
Time to come to grips with missing Dr.
Hart's party altogether. Probably. Unless it
runs late and this dinner ends soon. Gina's
the one who told me to book a table early
so I could try to make both, and it's her
birthday, so I didn't feel guilty. The others
don't know that's why our reservation was
for six thirty — in Southampton. Kind of a
haul, but this place gets amazing reviews,
and reservations are hard to land, so no one
questioned the drive or the time. Best available for a party of six. And, I mean, dinner
was amazing. But, I mean, it's been almost
two hours.

Then again, these are my best friends in
the world, plus Rosie, so why the hell should
I be eager to race off to some other party —
one where I might bump into Raymond
What's-His-Name, who thinks I'm crazy
and threatened to ruin my life. I'm such an

idiot. I'd die of shame the minute I saw Dr. Hart's wife, anyway.

Aisha nudges me under the table. "How you doing?" she whispers.

"Fine," I say automatically, before even realizing what she's really asking, which is how I'm feeling about meeting Gina's new girlfriend. "Honestly, I'm fine. I like her."

"Yeah, but still," says Aisha.

"Gina and I were friends for a long time before we were more-than-friends. This part is easy. Seriously. And I do like Rosie."

Aisha smiles. "Okay. Just checking."

I thank her and mean it, because she got me out of my head and back into my body, in this chair, at this table, celebrating one of my oldest and best friends — who, miraculously, is still my best friend after how complicated things got for a while there: friend to girlfriend to ex-girlfriend and back again, with minimal scarring. I'm surprised, actually, by how little this stings. How glad I am to see Gina so happy with someone else.

Violet is telling stories about nannying for two kids with more hobbies than brain cells, a fancy house that smells like candles that smell like salad, a mom who doesn't believe in luck. " 'You make your own luck,' is her motto," Violet tells us. "She thinks anything is possible with hard work and a spit-shine."

Gina hangs her head. "Oh God. The worst."

"Luck is just another word for endurance," Rosie offers.

"Fuck that," says Michelle. "Luck is being born a white guy with money. Period."

We all have to agree with that, even Rosie.

"Speaking of . . ." says Michelle, turning to me. "How's your White Guy With Money, Simone?" To Rosie, she says, "Simone's in love with her boss. He's a fox and plays it up so she'll go above and beyond her job description."

I make a sour face and say, "You're so stupid." Everyone laughs, and I add, "The boss I'm *not* in love with is fine, thanks." Maybe I'd have laughed too, a couple of months ago, when it was all fun and games and fantasy, but ever since I spoiled the fantasy with games, the fun is MIA. Gina's the only one who knows the whole story: the flowers, the failed attempt at a kiss, the hard bargain and blood. The rest of them would die of embarrassment if they knew what a fool I made of myself.

One thing I can laugh at, though: job description. What job description? It's not like this was my dream job. I wanted to be an interior designer. I wanted to go to

Parsons, but the BFA would have cost me close to two hundred grand in tuition alone, never mind books and housing, never mind dinners with friends. So I thought: Well then, I'll get my MFA instead. But by junior year at SUNY Old Westbury, I knew that a hundred-thousand-dollar master's was nuts, too. So I thought: I'll intern, get my foot in the door. On-the-job training is more practical anyway. Practical, my ass. Couldn't even get a temp job, let alone a dream job. I was applying for half a dozen restaurant gigs a day when I got my interview with Dr. Hart. He offered to pay me twice as much as I'd have made temping, plus benefits, and I could move close to the beach, to the Hamptons. What was I supposed to do? Decline and wait for a wish to come true? Whoever heard of a dream job, anyway? Rich people. People who have the resources to buy fantasy careers. The rest of us fantasize about retirement. We dream about how we'd spend our vacation days if we had enough money to take a dream vacation in the first place.

But I have this: a seat at a round table adorned with faces of friends I've known my whole life — plus Rosie — who won't let me lose myself. We've nursed one another through countless heartaches and family catastrophes and always vote for the wildest choice, with consequences ranging from spectacular to spectacularly bad.

Still, they don't need to know about the flowers, favors, miscommunications, or bottom line — or about how that kid jumped off Dr. Hart's roof and how the timing couldn't be worse but also couldn't be better, since it overshadowed my stupidity, so maybe Dr. Hart will forget the whole thing. Or maybe his friend will ruin my life, and I should just go ahead and die. But the server arrives with a cake full of candles, and by the time Gina makes her wish, I've nearly forgotten all about the other party.

When the bill has been paid and our stomachs stuffed to where it feels like they might rupture, we wander to the parking lot for extended good-byes. It's still light out. Ten years ago, we wouldn't even be dressed to go out yet.

I compliment Rosie on handling us so well. She says, "Are you kidding? I'm so happy to finally meet you," and lets me hug her like we're old friends, which I can tell we might be someday.

When Gina tells Rosie, "I'm stealing her for a second," and pulls me aside, I give her the thumb drive with a bow on it that's been in my pocket this whole time. "Seven play-lists. One for each day of the week. Happy birthday, boo."

She hugs me hard and asks, "Can you still make it to that thing?"

"I doubt it, but whatever. The whole thing is weird and morbid, anyway. I didn't even know the kid. Nobody did."

"Super weird."

"I know."

She glances at the others, then turns back and drops her voice. "You doing okay?"

I shake my head. "How did I get myself into this mess?" The flowers, the kiss, the hard bargain and blood. The threats from that guy who could ruin my life.

"Because you fell in love with the douche," she says. "Stop beating yourself up."

I let my hair fall in my face to make sure our friends can't see or hear me say, "His friend scared the shit out of me, Gina. I thought I was doing the right thing. I'm seriously worried about Dr. Hart. I didn't know what to do and really believed his friend would be able to help. I'm so stupid."

"Stop it. Stop being so hard on yourself. It's time you take care of your own damn future. You don't have to protect those guys. I still think you should up and quit."

I shake my head. "That place would fall

apart. He'd be helpless."

"Listen to me. Guys like that? They're already protected. He'll be fine. The system is designed to make sure he'll be fine. You want to get yours? Work outside of the system. Just do me a favor and don't feel bad. Please? He has no problem watching his own ass, right? You've got to watch yours."

I twist to look at my own ass because it's easier to crack a joke than to acknowledge that maybe Gina's right: maybe he doesn't need me. She hugs me long and hard, and with her lips near my ear, whispers, "Use that blood if you have to." As she walks away, she calls out, full voice, "Believe me. He'll be fine."

The drive from Southampton to Dr. Hart's house takes half an hour. Eagerness turns to nervousness on the way. I haven't visited this neighborhood since — shit, since Jonah Hart's high school graduation a few years back, probably. There was a double rainbow that day. I wore my yellow sundress with blue flowers on the hem.

I wonder if he wonders why I wasn't there tonight.

I wonder if he thinks I had a date, or if he even knows that I have friends. He'd probably be surprised to learn I used to date one of them, that I've had sex with other women and that I have sex with men, too. He probably doesn't see me as a sexual creature at all, or as anything other than the lady who operates the beautiful French carousel that is his life. He needs me, sure. But he doesn't need to know me. Why would he?

I wonder if he even noticed I didn't show.

On his block, I kill my headlights and roll to a stop across the street from his house. The lights are on in almost every room, but there aren't extra cars in his driveway or on the curb, and the only people floating back and forth in that bay window are Dr. Hart and his wife. He's a different animal when he's not wearing that white coat at work. I wish he were an uglier animal.

And her. She's untouchable. Makes it look so easy. The weird thing, though, is that nothing about her is all that special. It's not like she has the perfect face or the perfect body or even the perfect clothes. If it wasn't *her* in that skin, people might not even pay attention. If she lived in, like, Kansas or Dubuque, or any place where it's hard to get sushi and Botox — the kinds of places where no one knows how to cut hair and the only jeans you can try on before buying are regular blue jeans that do nothing remarkable for the butt — she might even pass for plain. But the way she carries herself makes it impossible to look away. And it's not even, "Oh, how pretty." It's more like, "Whoa, what is that?"

Could be she's not all that interesting under the highlights and lip gloss. Who knows if she believes in luck. She's never been rude to me, but she's not particularly warm, either. Could be she's just a Mrs. Potatohead: fully accessorized, hollow inside. One thing's for certain. Somewhere along the line, someone told her she was special. Someone drove it home and made her believe it, so now she feels obligated to wear diamonds and those jeans that make her ass look amazing. Someone told her she was the only person who could fill an Elizabeth-shaped hole in the world. Said it until she believed it.

The kicker is, that person made it true. Even if I do spend more hours of the day with Mrs. Hart's husband than she does, and even if I am the one who keeps his life on track, she's the one who helps him tidy their beautiful home after a party, and I'm the one who probably only got invited so I'd stay on his good side. I'll go home to an overdone one-bedroom apartment all alone, still thinking of him and what he thinks of me. That's not the kind of woman I am. Usually am. This shouldn't be me.

I stare at my glove box. Inside is the blood vial I found in Dr. Hart's coat pocket last week when I took it to be laundered. The questionnaire, dated and signed by Nick Carpenter, is in there too. I wasn't being nosy. I always empty the pockets before I drop off his lab coats, dumping out Tic Tacs or pen caps or paper scraps, whatever. Never found a blood sample before, though. Not before this. Grossed me out to keep it in the cup holder, so I threw it in the glove box. I didn't exactly forget about it, but I didn't have a plan for it either. Lately, though, it's been on my mind. Gina is good at reminding me. I have no clue what that kid was doing there, what his blood was doing in Dr. Hart's pocket and what it's doing in my car now. All I know is that the blood was from that dead kid's body, and Dr. Hart intended to hide it, so it feels like a powerful thing to have on hand. Just in case. And powerful feels good.

31.

All in all, the party wasn't bad. It had its moments. I smiled and even laughed when nonverbal cues indicated the appropriate times to smile or laugh, and tried to make eye contact when people spoke, and made the most of elastic good-byes, but my mind was on Raymond and whether he'd back off, and also on Elizabeth, what she was saying and to whom. She traded wine for water shortly after giving her toast, but her unpredictability was distracting nonetheless. So many unpredictable people. I kept an eye on Jonah, too, as he gave polite answers to the same questions asked over and over, and I drew comfort from his capacity to resist doing further structural damage to his hand or my house. Most of our guests left at a reasonable hour. A few stragglers forced aggressive kindness upon us, insisting upon filling our fridge with Tupperware and throwing away every last crumpled cocktail

395

napkin. Having bonded — perhaps over their shared fascination with Luna's social ineptitude disguised as social savvy — Elizabeth and Bess exchanged phone numbers and made tentative plans to catch an upcoming opening at Guild Hall. The whole evening was what one might consider a success, as these sorts of things go. We raised a few thousand bucks for a suicide prevention program serving our community, someplace Elizabeth tracked down, or Bonnie maybe.

All in all, it was pleasant, and at times, I felt the shackles loosen. After our generous friends left, I slept hard and woke up believing my secret might press itself into the past, smoothing out my bold decision — my brave decision — to fight like hell for my family. I woke up loving people and trusting my secret to blend into what's behind me.

But my peace hinges on so many conditions: if the detective just takes me at my word; if he resists fact-checking with Jonah; if Jonah forgets all about that pregnancy lie; if Elizabeth reins in her appetite for self-destruction; if my computer hasn't hoarded an invisible archive of searches so hackers can't poke holes in my story; if Ray backs off long enough to let me slip out of his life, and if he stays out of mine for a very long time, which will break my heart but serve the greater good; if Simone fears Ray enough to keep her mouth shut, but not so much that she risks tattling; if my nurses forget about the butterfly needles so there's no trace of Nick at work; and if Nick told no one, absolutely no one, about the diagnosis, then it never happened. I can close this chapter of my life. If Elizabeth only did what she did out of boredom or spite and not out of love, or worse yet, falling out of love, then we can fix this. We can be the couple who survived this episode. We'll be our own heroes.

For an hour or two last night, for a minute or ten this morning, these circumstances felt possible. I was unburdened, but it was fleeting. The first disruption came from Jonah, who left a message while I was with a patient. "The medical examiner's office called," he told me in a voice mail. "He wants me to swing by the office at my earliest convenience. What should I do?"

He called again an hour later, saying, "Call me, Dad," and nothing else.

He is leaning on me because I asked him to, so now I'm stuck having to advise. Do I ask my son to lie for me? Do I dare tell him the truth?

The third call came shortly thereafter. This time, it was Buchanan for me. In his voice mail, he omits the little detail about contacting my son. I'm to swing by the department at my earliest convenience to answer a few questions. Again. Seams in my carefully compartmentalized system begin to blur, and I'll be damned if my hands aren't shaking when I ask my first patient of the day, "What hurts?"

I'm shoving food into my mouth between appointments — a meal replacement bar that tastes like candied rubber *(we sell these things?)* — when I get a call from an unknown number. Local. I ignore it, but a minute later, the same number calls again. Ben Walters from our homeowners' association wants to extend his sympathies, which, of course, means wanting to gossip.

He says, "You know, I got a tip that kid had troubles. Right when he got here, actually. Some neighbors — won't say which, but you can guess — weren't feeling his wake-and-bake vibe. Got complaints about the smell of pot. I told them I'd issue a warning, but after you pointed it out at Bella Torta, it seemed excessive. You said you were on the ball, so . . ."

He'd been fond of Nick back when everyone thought he was perfect. Now that everyone thinks Nick was troubled, however — and now that Nick's dead, moreover — Ben is quick to take credit for seeing the signs first.

When I attempt to get off the phone, Ben gets to the real reason he called. Acknowledging the sensitive timing and that it's not an explicit area of HOA oversight, he needs to discuss my plans for the roof walk.

"This story has caused a lot of conversation," he says. "I've been thinking, there might be something positive that can come out of it. If you went ahead and secured the structure now, it would demonstrate commitment to the security of this community, you know? We have to stay up to code, but it's good optics when people set examples, too. If you lead, people will follow, and hopefully we can avoid accidents like these in the future."

Accidents like these, he says, as though this is a common variety of accident that should stop happening all the time. He probably prepared and rehearsed that pitch with his wife. One minute he's a fan. The next, he's a critic. One year, my roof is getting front-page press. Now it's earning warnings and hosting horror and facilitating gossip. I tell Ben what he wants to hear, which is that I'll absolutely start looking into it. When he presses for hows or whys and time lines, I tell him my waiting room is starting to pile up, but that I'll get on it as soon as possible, and "thank you so much for being proactive and supportive during this difficult time."

Ending the call brings small relief, since Ben Walters has thrown me off schedule. My waiting room is gridlocked, and although my patients have granted me a grace period because they've all heard the chatter, relayed the chatter, (gotten high off the chatter), their good graces won't last forever.

The proper order of things has collapsed. I can't even escape the building at the end of the day — fresh air ten steps away — without being sucked back toward sick breath, hot germs, and antiseptic. Simone's the parasite this time, saying, "Dr. Hart, wait. We need to talk."

Ten steps from freedom, I spin around and say too loudly, "What do you want?"

She is unfazed. "To finish the conversation we started."

"We didn't start it. You started it. You blindsided me."

She lets my desperation fade before saying, "I want a raise."

I tell her the truth: that life is volcanic at the moment, but when things settle, we'll talk.

"That won't work for me." She hands me

a pair of documents printed on bond paper. The first is a spreadsheet listing her responsibilities, and in corresponding columns, the distribution of time per task in a given week, the dollar values for each per hour, skill sets required, continuing education courses she wants me to fund. The other sheet is her resume. Up to date, well designed. She says, "I had a hunch you might be too busy to talk, so I made it easy for you. That's what I do. Everything is there. Go home, read it over, let me know if you have questions. I'll expect an answer by next Monday."

"Come on, Simone. A week from today? You know how difficult things are right now. Life's been —"

"Crazy," she interrupts. "I know." Off she goes, saying, "It's always crazy."

She walks like a drum majorette back to the desk where she manages my life. All of these years, so steady. She sure picked a shitty time to have a growth spurt.

I escape through the back door, but the outside is no better. Damp air and petrichor zap my nerves: a hotwire of nausea, crushed hydrangeas, decay, denial, soggy mulch. Even in death, Nick is still spoiling things.

Locked in my car, I flip the visor mirror to check — and, yes, my jawbone is flushed, my neck covered in welts. I broke out in hives in college, had panic attacks, too. Couldn't get it under control, even in medical school, where Step exams were so excruciating that I categorically eliminated considering a career in academic medicine, or any specialization requiring a fellowship, for that matter. I built a life around quality of life. Hives weren't part of the plan.

Green light after green light all the way home. I'm trying hard to remember what my next move is supposed to be, but I'm so tired. We're all tired. We need sound, dreamless sleep. I inhale this ozone-bright rain smell and get hung up on memories of bliss in those days after Nick's death, when none of us knew he was dead. I just thought I was free. Silly me.

Maybe the air is to blame, but when I grab these papers on my way out of the car, holding this document Simone forced upon me — her sales pitch, her overwrought effort to frame extortion as business — I'm overcome by sensory recall, remembering how it felt to snatch articles and ads from the guesthouse after finding Nick's body. I'd folded them and tucked them into my back pocket with every intention of destroying them, and even though I can visualize myself visualizing myself going through with my intent, I can't for the life of me remember if I really did it. This isn't like me — or maybe it is. Maybe this is my new normal.

My hand is shaking when I open the door to my house. I try willing my heart back to tempo, willing those printouts destroyed. Surely I shredded them, and even if I didn't, there's still hope those jeans are at the bottom of my hamper, untouched. I should hurry. I should run to my closet to whack-a-mole my next risk, but my body protests. I'm just so damn tired.

No one is home. I stand alone in a giant room, listening as, one by one, the *If*s detonate inside my head. Jonah is being questioned. I am being challenged. Simone is growing bolder. Down come the pillars of my sanctuary. My job is suffering. My reputation is suffering. I'm supposed to set an example through the structural integrity of my house. *My house.* I'm supposed to set an example by giving away money, by giving nice speeches, by giving all my strength and support to the woman and child in my care, and I failed at this most basic level.

Down comes my sanctuary. This is the house I strengthened and molded to be good enough for Jonah, to let me be the father who makes him proud. I trudge up the stairs and turn left instead of right, and

I knock on Jonah's door, just in case he beat me home, and I fake a willingness to face our respective voice mails from the county medical examiner's office. It's come to this. When Jonah doesn't answer, I let myself into his room, a bedroom once decorated with Transformers posters and Star Wars sheets. Now the walls are blank. One family photo in a silver frame is propped atop his dresser: me and Vanessa and Jonah, age three. This was back at the old place, the starter house Jonah can't possibly remember. In the photo, he's holding tight to his mother's back, and she's holding tight to mine, and I'm bending down in a field of fallen leaves. We are stacked like a cairn marking Long Island autumn, and we are happy.

I did not kill anyone. All I did was make a choice, a choice to have a conversation — and at the time, it was the best choice, the right one given the situation. Circumstances have changed, though. Drastically. A government employee is going to ask my son whether or not he rode with me down to my office a few weeks back to print papers for some made-up exam. If Jonah tells the truth, I will be deemed a person of interest. Maybe it'll be announced on the news. If Jonah lies, he'll do it for me, and consequently, his image of me will shatter. Down will come his father, the hero figure, and he still needs me. So the question becomes: What's the new right choice if protecting my family is still the bottom line?

I lie down on Jonah's bed atop a predictable Ralph Lauren comforter: faded plaid in primary colors. This is where my son lays his head at night. This is his view at the end of the day. It is dim and stark and lonely here. What does it feel like to fall asleep in this room, knowing that life split long ago into two separate tracks, both of which are true, neither of which is pure? This is my great unknown: the distance between his life here and his life there. How does it feel to be him? He was a child here, and then he was gone, and then he came back to me as a stranger. Can I ask him to lie for me now?

Every choice I've ever made was to shield him from the losses prepared for me as a child. I rose up so he wouldn't have to. Could it be that everything I've ever done — the hard work and the love, the steps forward, the backlash, all of the bitter ends and bright ideas — has been wasted? I fell for the fallacy that serenity is a meritocracy, but there is no credit earned or redeemed. I strained for this. I bent my trajectory and changed my tongue for this, and traded up for this, but nothing rolls over. Every day begins anew underwater. Every day I work my way to the surface, and every night I sink all over again. I've turned amphibian. I'm the Leviathan caught between Scylla and Charybdis.

That's fatherhood for you, he said. *Turns the best of us into monsters.*

The answer is no. No, I cannot ask him to lie for me. I cannot ask him to soil his respect for me. I will fall on the sword for him, and I will tell the investigator everything. I'll come clean, the ink will dry on Nick's death certificate, and we'll find a way to get on with our lives.

I roll onto my side, slipping my hands beneath a pillow, tucking into the fetal position — the shared pose of each raw human, bound and protected by our mothers' fluid and flesh, oblivious to more: we were all this, once — but I'm ripped from the moment by the unremarkable discovery of evidence that my kid is a slob. He's the sort of slob who leaves trash in his bed. My fingers guess before my mind does: a candy wrapper, an Alka-Seltzer package.

But no. It's a condom wrapper. My son left an empty condom wrapper under the pillow on which he sleeps. He hasn't changed his sheets in weeks.

I blink. I blink to change the channel in my head and blink again, progressing pictures in a carousel slide show rotating in my mind. Images and possibilities exchange for the next and the next and the next as I scan back through the progression of their friendship. The desire to please. The need to include Nick in our lives. I think of the silent messages they exchanged on the boat, threading hooks. They sensed each other the way only lovers can and do, and all this time, I missed the signs because I was fixated on a red herring.

Elizabeth wasn't sleeping with Nick. Jonah was.

Downstairs, the garage door motor grinds open, bangs closed. There's plenty of time for me to flee, but I'm so damn tired. Eyes fixed on the landing at the top of the stairs, I lay here clutching an empty Trojan wrapper in one hand and a worn pillowcase in the other. Footsteps approach and ascend slowly, falling into the same rhythm that brought me here. I'm resting like a child in my own child's bed, fully clothed in the dark, counting the beats of a weary march as it grows closer.

32.

Jonah doesn't see me stretched out in his bed until he is standing a few feet away. "Shit." He stumbles backward. "Jesus, Dad. You scared the shit out of me."

Sensation returns to my arms and legs. Still gripping Jonah's trash in my fist, I lift my head, then my body, to sit on the edge of his bed.

"What are you doing here?" he asks.

Leaning my elbows against my knees, unsure of my position or plan, I take in the person before me, a boy I've misread all this time. He silenced himself. He felt the need to disappear.

"Dad?"

He suffered and hid. *He hid from his own father.* I find my voice. "Got your message."

"Oh yeah? Well, do you want to hear the update?" He's frantic, fried at the ends.

I nod.

"That investigator called again a little bit ago."

"Did you answer?"

"No. I told you I wouldn't. I did what you asked, but he's freaking me out." Jonah wraps and unwraps his headphone cords around his wrist. "Can he keep calling like this? It's harassment, isn't it?"

Now is the time to ask about his relationship with Nick. *Now.* I open my mouth to extend support, but no sounds come. The details still won't compute.

"I'm losing my mind, Dad. I'm seriously going crazy. Do you have any idea what he wants to talk to me about?"

In my head: visions of their late nights in the guesthouse, their inside jokes — their book club, for crying out loud.

"Dad. Are you even listening to me?"

I look at my boy, who is wild in the eyes. "Yes. You're not going crazy."

He laughs. "You have no idea."

"Jonah." I harness my calm. "Is there something you want to talk to me about?" This is the introduction to Parenting 101, is it not?

He squints, sticks his neck out, throws his arms in the air. "What's wrong with you? Yeah, obviously I need to talk to you. That's what I'm trying to do, Dad. Hello?"

I nod, desperate to reverse this unraveling. "Why don't you tell me about something else — something that has nothing to do with the detectives."

He huffs and shudders as he shrugs his shoulders, flaunting every marker of disdain he's mastered in his years of angst.

"Let's talk about what you really want to get off your chest."

He laughs again and fidgets, pacing the room, then taking off his socks and shoes, presumably just to stay busy.

"Something more personal."

"What do you want from me?" He walks from one wall to another and back, no longer faking purpose. Just pacing. "I don't know what else you want me to say."

"I think you do." I'm the dad with open ears, an open heart, an open mind.

Jonah kicks his dresser. His face is flushed when he screeches, "What are you asking?"

I wait.

"What do you want me to tell you? That I was up there when he died?"

My heart quickens. My skin tingles and head spins, but I stay composed when I say, "Yes. I want you to tell me about that."

He closes the door and this room shrinks. "I watched him die, and I lied about it, and now I'm fucked. Royally. Because if this investigator finds out, he's going to think I have something to hide. What do you think will happen then, huh?" The cool drains out of him. Hopelessness fills the cracks. "Could he try to frame me for murder?"

What the hell were they doing on the roof? Did a lover's quarrel end in suicide? Blind rage? I ask, "What happened up there?"

Jonah slams his back against the door and slides down like some silly girl in a corny music video. I look away, noticing nicks in his furniture, stains on his curtains.

"Jonah?" I keep my tone velvet-soft. "What were the two of you doing up there?"

He takes a deep breath, lets it out over several seconds. Finally, he says, "I go up there sometimes. That key just sits there on the doorframe. No one noticed if I took it, or if I left it unlocked. Used to go up in junior high and pretend I was a sniper. In high school, I'd hang out up there sometimes just to break a rule. Stupid stuff." He holds his face with both hands, hiding from me like a kid playing games with a baby who believes that what he can't see can't see him. "And Nick was curious, so I showed him. He lost his balance and fell, smashed into the balcony and went over the edge. It wasn't my fault."

"Of course it wasn't." Of course not. Still,

411

the picture blurs. "Why were you up there?"

He lifts his shoulders. "Privacy."

The crow's nest was their love nest, then. Mildew, hornets' nests, splinters, lead paint, but yes, privacy, too. I'm assembling time lines in my mind, aware that young men keep secrets, aware that Jonah's sexuality is his business, his private acts are none of mine. And yet, this is my house, he is my son, and something isn't making sense. "Tell me what happened."

Jonah jerks his head, snapping the neck of invisible prey in his mouth. "I promised I wouldn't," he says.

"Promised who?"

"Nick," he says.

I fill in the blanks: "Because you loved him."

Jonah stares at the ceiling, shrugs, shakes his head. "You don't understand."

"Jonah. I already know," I bluff.

His face falls. His eyes widen but he does not say a word.

"I know everything," I lie.

Just like that, my boy is unburdened, he slumps low and asks, "You do?"

I nod.

He breathes a sigh that turns into a wail. "Thank you for finally being real with me." He hugs his legs and hangs his head, saying through a muffling net of limbs, "How long have you known?"

Play it safe. "Not long."

Jonah convulses, or something. "Why didn't you tell me?"

"It seemed best to let the two of you handle it."

"But didn't you feel like — like it was your place to get involved?" His desperation breaks my heart. His obfuscation tests my temper.

"It wasn't my business." I want to comfort my son, not coddle him. So what? He's gay. Own it, don't be wimpy about it. "Whatever special relationship you and Nick had, there's nothing to be ashamed of."

"Wait," he says, with a lightness to the word that reminds me of how he spoke as a child. Less worry, more confusion. "Wait, what are you talking about?"

I cock my head. "What are *you* talking about?"

"The thing you knew — the big secret — was that me and Nick were *together*?"

I grit my teeth. I've said too much.

"That's *everything*?" he asks.

My cool cracks. "Well, what then, Jonah? If that's not it, what the hell are you crying about?" Scraps of memories. Details. The events flip and shift in a watery time line —

my early consultation with Nick, Jonah leaving for his mother's, and before all this, footsteps on the stairs — and yes, something else: my bedroom door. It opened and closed late that night. Early in the morning, rather. My son is smiling. The walls of his room shimmer and throb. "Tell me now," I demand. My equilibrium tips. "Tell me, Jonah."

"I'm afraid you got it all wrong." He is cold and steady when he says, "Please don't be mad at her, Dad. It's not her fault."

I blink. That's all. I blink and hear, *her, her, her.*

"I don't know how this happened."

Her. My skull creaks. "How what happened?"

"It wasn't on purpose."

"Say it." From behind my eyes, a sharp cold radiates to every groove in my brain, every crack in every bone. Ice and marrow. I want to light my own son on fire for relief, but first I repeat, "Say it, Jonah." My teeth rattle.

"It was an accident," he allows. "It just happened. Somehow it happened."

"What happened?"

"We happened," he says.

And just like that, my world shatters.

"Me and Elizabeth."

Get out, I hear in my head. *Get the fuck out of my house.*

I hear myself say, *You're lying.*

I hear, *Fuck you,* too.

I can almost feel my fantasy: the sensation of my heel connecting with his face, the sound of my foot cracking his jaw — teeth knocked down his throat as I force-feed him my DNA, code passed down to him by me, life given by me. But he'll need his jaw to tell this story, and he's not getting off that easy, so instead I say, "I'm listening."

33.

He begins in the worst way: "The first time was an accident."

This can't be happening.

"We didn't plan it," he reiterates. "I never even really knew her until recently. I used to hate her, actually. She'd been the thing that came between you and Mom, and I was the one who had to watch Mom fall apart every day. I didn't live here. I was a kid. All I knew was that Elizabeth was the reason Mom was a wreck, and kids aren't supposed to clean up messes like that. I stuck by her since you didn't. What the hell else was I supposed to do?

"For so long, it's like she didn't even exist to me. She wasn't even a person, more like an evil force. But after I went to college and you made me come back here, I didn't have a choice but to get to know her. I didn't want to. You understand that, right? She wasn't the one who'd been missing from

416

my life. You were. All those times you tried to get me to bond with Elizabeth, all I really wanted was to bond with you, Dad.

"So here I am, back in this house, you trying to force me and Elizabeth into quality time, and me with a head full of stuff I'm learning and liking in school — and maybe I'm not great at it, maybe I'm embarrassed about not being great, even — but here I come to find out Elizabeth teaches this stuff. For the very first time, we had common ground. You got your wish. She was willing to help me. I remember what started it. It was Bulgakov, remember? Remember when I brought him up last Thanksgiving?"

I shake my head.

"Well, I did. I wanted to talk with you about it, but you'd never read it, so you told me to talk to Elizabeth instead, and I hated you, Dad, for not being willing to fake it for once. Just, like, pretend to give a shit about what your own son is all about. Try to know me."

"Don't you dare blame me for your depravity."

"I'm not." Jonah drops his head between his knees and says, "I'm just explaining that I didn't know her as a kid, and she didn't know me then, either. She never saw me that way." He rubs his hands against his face. "She only got to know me as I am now. As a man."

I exhale a bitter sigh of mock amusement. "When you bonded over *Lolita*?"

He lifts his head slowly, locking eyes, calm and cool. "I said Bulgakov, not Nabokov."

I ought to cut out my boy's tongue.

"We just talked at first." He sounds sorry but not contrite, almost like he feels sorry for *me*. "We had a connection."

She laughed at his jokes and brought him ice cream. These aren't acts of lovers. But she also went out of her way to embrace his world. She befriended and pampered his best friend. This sort of thing, I'll concede, is symptomatic of romantic love.

"She freaked out after the first time and made me promise to forget about it. I tried hard. We couldn't help it, though. We really care about each other, and what we had was different from what you two have. I'm not saying it's better. It's just different. We tried to be sensitive about keeping things separate, too. That's why we chose the roof, designated it just for that. But Nick's death ruined everything. Now she won't even look at me."

He gnaws a fingernail, takes a breather and continues: "The night before Nick died, Elizabeth heard him trying to sneak up there in the middle of the night. She said she couldn't sleep because you two had a fight. You slept downstairs that night, right? Whatever. The point is, she heard someone trying to get to the roof and assumed it was me. She texted me in the middle of the night and told me what happened, said we needed to talk. She was worried we were getting too close to getting caught, but Nick was oblivious at that point. Believe me. He was too much in his head about something."

"About what?" I ask.

"Doesn't matter. But the next morning, after you shouted up about going to the gym, I texted Elizabeth and told her to meet me on the roof when she woke up, and I went up there and waited. That's why the door was unlocked. And I guess Nick was outside already for some reason, and so he saw me appear up there, which is why he knew it was unlocked. The next thing I know, he's up there with me, and I'm freaking out, worried that Elizabeth will come up and everything will go to shit.

"I asked Nick about the night before, and he said yes, he'd tried going up there. He'd been upset about something and wanted to get away, and he remembered me saying that's where I'd go to escape in high school, so he tried, but the door was locked. But he was still spazzing, still hard-up for privacy. And I thought his timing was really weird. Like, what in the world was he doing outside at that hour? For him to see me go up, I mean?

"I told him the roof was too dangerous, and tried to convince him to turn around, but he went crazy. He begged me to either leave him alone or be a friend. I couldn't warn Elizabeth to stay back, because I'd left my phone downstairs, but I figured if she heard Nick talking she'd turn around, so I said, 'I'm listening.' "

I'm listening, too, piecing the time line together and remembering how free I was that morning when I started my engine and drove off to the gym, away from the drama. That memory collapses, felled by a detail I thought I'd dodged. "What was worrying him?" I ask Jonah.

"I didn't know yet. And I was freaking, so I suggested we get Elizabeth. She's better at crisis than we are, you know? But he was adamant we not upset her. When I insisted, he snapped. That's when he told me Elizabeth was pregnant." Jonah looks at me with the limp hope that I'll correct him. "As you can imagine, this was pretty shocking for me. I'm not ready to be a dad, you know? I asked Nick to give me a minute, just a minute to think, but that was a bad move, because sitting there silently meant we weren't making noises to warn Elizabeth, and suddenly, there she is. Things got really weird really fast."

Rage courses through my body and into my head, compressing into a bullet.

"Nick was so clear, you know? Hyperalert. Hard to explain. Afterward, I kept trying to convince myself that maybe he was like that because he was fucked up or something, but I know in my soul he was stone-cold sober. We were the thing that made him run. It was us. It was our fault, Dad."

Jonah tells the ceiling, "Elizabeth is the one who looked guilty right away, and she said something to the effect of, 'It's not what you think,' which might as well have been a confession. That's when Nick checked out our setup and realized there was something to hide. From that point on, it was chaos. I tried to get him to relax, asked if he wanted to take a walk or a Vicodin."

"Why would you have Vicodin?"

He sounds bored when he says, "You can buy anything at school, Dad. RAs sell them."

"Great."

"It's not a big deal. We only took them if

we were super stressed, or like, on special occasions or whatever. That's not even the point, anyway, because Nick said no." He rubs his forehead. "I don't know how long we were up there. Might have been minutes or seconds. I can't make myself forget it but can't seem to remember, either. Nick started apologizing, and Elizabeth almost started to cry, but she was still blocking the stairs, so Nick ran outside to the deck. All I did was grab him. I was trying to contain things, so I ran after him and grabbed his clothes to hold him back. His shoe wasn't tied, and it was slick up there, you know? I was trying to stop him. I grabbed his shirt but lost my grip and he went flying right into the banister. It smashed clean through. He went over. That was it."

Jonah bangs the heel of one hand against his head. "He just wanted some privacy, Dad. You were always hovering, riding his jock. Maybe if you'd given him some space."

"That's ludicrous. I hardly *knew* the kid."

"Yeah, but you were always doing shit for him, taking him fishing or whatever. What the hell? When's the last time you offered to take me fishing?"

"I asked you after the funeral, didn't I?"

"Yeah, but before. Before Nick came around, you didn't want to do anything together. Suddenly you're obsessed with my friend and we're all buddy-buddy or whatever."

"Enough about the fishing. That has nothing to do with this."

"Doesn't it?"

I picture them on the boat, swapping coded looks, and this leads me back to the thread that pulled me into this rabbit hole in the first place. These two: the boys. "Jonah, you can tell me: Where was Nick in this love triangle?" I ask.

"You've got to be kidding me."

"Well?"

"Even now. Even in this, it just has to be about someone else, doesn't it? Nick wasn't the third in our triangle, Dad. You were."

My eyelid twitches, my jaw clenches and tension surges — but this time, it's not a homicidal urge. This time, it's the absolute denial of linear time, the desire to reverse the present and choose another face-to-face, another outcome, a different moral to my story, because this isn't how my story goes. I ask, "Why didn't you call the cops?"

"I wanted to, I swear, but Elizabeth made me promise not to — *and* she made me promise not to tell you. She went a little crazy, Dad. Something snapped. She started shaking me and asking what I saw, asking if

I'd made eye contact with Nick, wanting to know if Nick's eyes were open or closed. She was insane about making sure I didn't see the body, and she kept forcing me back to my room, like I was some little kid. 'Go to your room,' she kept saying, so eventually I did. I came here and waited for her to bring everything down: the sleeping bags and pillows and stuff."

My stomach turns.

"That's when Elizabeth sent you out for prescriptions that didn't exist. She was trying to buy time to clean it all up, and it worked, because by the time you got home, I'd zipped everything into a duffle bag to bring to Mom's house, remember? I threw most of that stuff in a dumpster across town. I threw the rest in different dumpsters, which made me feel like a criminal, but it was an accident. He was in the wrong place at the wrong time. Big-time."

Jonah had been carrying an enormous duffle bag. Laundry, I'd figured. Looking back: so much laundry. Also, looking back, he and Elizabeth were both acting odd. I thought he'd been nervous to talk about giving me and Elizabeth space. And Elizabeth — I thought she was licking her wounds from a childish affair that had met its end. I guess it did. Different co-conspirator, different end. I guess that means, too, that when she hugged my neck, Nick was already in the bushes, and she knew it, and he wasn't her lover. He wasn't the one.

Did she see him when she bent over the hosta that night? When she refused to let me hold her hair? She changed after that moment, but then, I suppose, a corpse jutting out from under the hydrangeas would be a sobering sight. When she stood on the diving board and gazed at me, was that an apology rather than seduction? When she dove, was it an invitation, or was it an effort to wash it all away? Baptism by swimming pool. And here I thought I was all she wanted.

My own son turned on me so severely, so terminally. My own flesh and blood — but then, no. His flesh. His blood. My seed. He carries proteins encoded by my body, true, but he is not me in mind or form, and Elizabeth is impermeable. She and I are not halves of a whole. We are the color made by overlapping circles in our Venn diagram, a color that exists only through each other. I can connect to her, put myself inside her — I can enter her and still not crawl around inside her head. She is separate from me, divided by skin, thought, fantasy, history — a whole her-before-me I'll never know. We tell stories. We learn each other through anecdotes and confessions, but as with her precious books, I visualize the scene in the theater of my mind without ever knowing if my vision matches hers. I see the truck, the sister, the school, the long-dead best friend, the ex-husband, the thesis, and what I see is little more than a police sketch of her memory — which is, itself, once removed from an objective reality, if one exists. The only things I know about her, the only things I know for sure, are the things we share: a dance, a dinner, a kiss. But even these are watered-down wishes, because is she even thinking of me when we kiss?

I look hard at my son, trying to see what Elizabeth could possibly see — and only now, yes, in this terrible lighting, maybe he could remind me of me, after all. I've always distrusted people who say he takes after his father, the same ones who called him my spitting image when he was a newborn. They say those things to be polite, but Jonah doesn't think like me or see this world like I do, and these differences are by design. I raised him to have different architecture than mine. I raised him in a loving household, and when the love was lost, Vanessa and I aimed for two loving households. Jonah doesn't have a clue what it feels like to lose a mother, or to have a father whose demands were impossible to satisfy. This ignorance is my gift to him.

Now, though, as I study his face, I spot the resemblance I never noticed before. He does have my features: my dark brow, my strong chin, my hairline, no question. I say, "You and Elizabeth watched Nick fall to his death, and you let him rot out there for three days."

Jonah rocks the back of his head against the door. "This wasn't easy for us, Dad. I kept saying we should do something, but she said we had to remove ourselves and let it unfold how it would've unfolded if we'd never been there. It's like she thought if she ignored it, somehow the whole thing would never have happened."

I think back to that day. Jonah returning home with his duffle bag and a pickle jar and the news that Nick hadn't been with him. Elizabeth suggested I get vases from the guesthouse. She asked me to go outside and lower the umbrella. And the next day, when I noticed the leak in the garage, she went rigid when I told her there was an emergency, but she relaxed when I told her it was a flood, like she'd been expecting worse. And when I finally did make the damn discovery, and she came outside, I shouted at her to get back into the house, and she obeyed without question or hesitation. "You wanted me to find him."

"I need your help, Dad."

"How dare you."

He whispers, "They're about to find out."

"Who?"

"That guy who keeps calling," he tells me. "Mr. Walsh at the medical examiner's office. If I go in there and spill my guts, what's going to happen to our family?" He's asking the right questions, even as he continues to manipulate by reminding me that if his story were to surface, we'd all be ruined. The police would know that my child lied about witnessing Nick's death, that he lived for three days with that lie, never bothering to tell anyone, never bothered at all. They'd ask Jonah about whether he was alone, and eventually he'd say no. He'd say why. How long until the scandal leaks? Would they charge my son with some kind of involvement in Nick's death? *Was he involved in Nick's death?* Why should I believe my son didn't throw his best friend off the roof? Because my son is a colossal disappointment, not a murderer. He's a grown man crying baby tears over his disastrous attempt to swing his dick around my house.

I'd come out looking a fool, too: a failed

father who couldn't control his own kid, an impotent husband incapable of satisfying his own wife, a clown for letting this happen right on and under my roof — the scene of two crimes. First the police station would laugh me out of town, then my whole community. I'd lose business and friends, and Elizabeth would be crucified. She'd be right back where she started when she left Stuart, which would confuse her into thinking I'm no better than him, which would be fine if I was ready to lose her.

Jonah wants me to consider my fate — lost business, lost stature, an exiled son, and another ex-wife, leaving me alone in the place where the worst happened — but he hasn't given enough thought to his own fate. I can cut him off, shut him out, make him lose his father. Hell, if I wanted to flex, the state might lock him up, shun him, institutionalize him for sociopathic sexual deviance. Maybe. And yet — his machinations, poorly executed though they may be, are not useless, because if Nick wasn't right in the head, he alone would be to blame. The battalion in my prefrontal cortex aims to fire.

"I need your help," Jonah says.

"If I help you," I tell Jonah, "then you will do two things for me."

He nods.

"Leave this house and don't come back until you are invited, explicitly, by me and me alone. That day may never come, but if it does, I'll make the call. Not you. In the meantime, don't contact me, don't show up at work, don't trespass on my property, and don't look at my wife."

He nods.

"Number two: You will never tell a soul. Not one. Not a future best friend or spouse, not a therapist, and never, ever your mother. You'll let Elizabeth live out the rest of her days without knowing we had this conversation. You won't send her letters or emails or texts, and you won't look at her funny, because you won't look at her at all."

He says, "I swear."

"On your life," I insist.

"On my life."

"I can help."

"I don't want to go to jail."

"Shut your mouth." Still sitting on this bed, still gripping an empty foil wrapper in my sweaty fist, I say, "Listen to me. Here's what we're going to do."

34.

I'm here alone, sitting in my favorite chair with my feet up, drinking bourbon and staring at the sunlight dimming on my wall, when Elizabeth finally makes it home. It takes a minute for her to notice me watching her. When she does, she jumps. "Hey. I didn't see you there. How are you feeling?" She hovers, combing her fingers through my hair.

"Better," I say. "Much better."

"I tried calling you. So did the pharmacist. We tried a few times. Did you get our messages?"

I look up at her.

"She couldn't find your prescription in the system."

"No? Hm. Isn't that strange? I wonder what happened."

"Got you some over-the-counter stuff. Acetaminophen with caffeine, I think. Not sure how that's supposed to help a migraine, but it was the best I could find. Do you want to call and I'll run back out?"

"No," I say. "That won't be necessary."

There was no migraine, no prescription to fill. Borrowing a page from Elizabeth's playbook proved useful nonetheless. It bought me time.

"Okay." She hesitates. Perhaps she recognizes the play. Perhaps she senses me gripped by something more disruptive than a headache. "I'm sorry you aren't feeling well. How was your day otherwise?"

I pause, even though I've already prepared this answer. "It was enlightening."

"Really? Sounds far more interesting than mine. What happened?"

"Oh, let's not talk about me. How are you?"

She finds her place on the couch and says, "Okay." But she leaves it at that. "Are you sure you're all right?"

"Why?"

"I don't know. You're acting funny."

"Am I?"

"Yes."

"Must be my head."

She waits for me to elaborate. I don't. The sun won't set for another hour, but its white light has shifted to rose gold. Cast in the glow, Elizabeth looks like a porcelain doll as she becomes aware of the quiet — aware of our isolation from every other living creature in the world.

She asks, "Where's Jonah?"

There it is. Does she always look for him right away? Have I only now noticed? "He's gone."

"Where did he go?"

"I don't know. I just decided it was time for him to go."

She tucks her chin into her neck. "You asked him to leave?"

"Yes."

I observe every faint violation of her controlled stillness when she asks, "Is everything okay?" There is fear in her voice. There is uncertainty.

"You know, Elizabeth, I think it will be."

There is desperation in her eyes. There is regret.

I say, "We have been dealing with some pretty unusual circumstances around here."

She nods.

"I think we all wish none of this had ever happened."

Fear, uncertainty, desperation, and regret. "Robert —"

"And I think Jonah will feel better if he gets away from the place where something so bad has happened. A thing like that can do long-term damage, you know. It can traumatize a person."

She shivers.

"I think he'll cope better if he isn't sleeping below the site of that trauma, don't you?"

She nods slowly, assessing before offering, "It's traumatic for us, too."

"Yes. Yes it is." I take a sip of my drink. "You look very pretty in this light."

She blinks and blinks again so slowly I wonder if perhaps she's fallen asleep, and maybe that wouldn't be so bad. Maybe we could both close our eyes and start again tomorrow, letting this all be a bad dream. So I wait, but she is awake and alert when she says, "Sometimes I think I'm made for this life. Sometimes there's no place else I'd rather be. And then sometimes I don't know what I'm doing here."

My knee-jerk defense is to ask, What is *here*? What is *this life*? But I know where here is. I know this life. My reflex subsides, and I'm left with the strangest sensation, both foreign and familiar, not unlike déjà vu, but much clearer. It washes over me, bringing with it the calm that comes from staring into a mirror and seeing my own face reflected back: visibility as proof of existence. I hear myself in her words, and in

434

hearing them, I am heard. Through her, I am realized and made real, because I too understand what it feels like to work so hard with the singular purpose of getting some-place — to this life, this beautiful life — that upon arrival, having rendered the need for such work obsolete, having put down the struggle — a self-imposed struggle — I come to find myself hardly recognizable in my resting state.

These things flicker through my head, and then, as with déjà vu, they are gone. What a tiresome trail we break. I say, "Me too."

The wall shifts from rose gold to some-thing redder. Our house is silent.

"Elizabeth."

"Hm?"

I don't know what. "We are a team."

She nods.

"This life. It will change again."

She sits in this. We both do, until finally she says, "I think you're right about it being time for Jonah to move on."

I nod.

We absorb the space between us. "I'm ready to move on too."

I nod again. "So am I."

We sit here like this, soaking up our divide, as the sun goes down and the wall fades to ever darkening shades of dusk.

35.

I pull up to the Suffolk County Medical Examiner's complex at quarter of nine in the morning to find Jonah already parked in the lot where we've planned to meet. Well, look at that. For once in his life, he is early — early even with an hour drive from his mother's house. I park next to him, and he moves from his driver's seat to my passenger seat. No bouquets of flowering weeds from Vanessa this time. I wonder where Jonah told his mother he was going all cleaned up at this hour. He missed a spot shaving.

When I called Simone to say I was running late, she asked why, and I said family emergency, which was honest, but still promised her we'd talk today. She said she sure hoped so. Then she threatened to call in sick tomorrow and every day from now until the talk happened. My first thought was to let her, so I could fire her with cause, but then I thought it through and realized how right she is about how screwed I'd be without her. She backed me into this corner, so she'll get her way, and this whole day will be one of talks and negotiations. Beginning now.

I take two ibuprofen from the bottle in my center console, shake two more into Jonah's hand, and say, "It'll all be over soon."

We rehearse our story one last time. Jonah doesn't need to know that his meltdown was timed perfectly with mine. He only needs to think that I'm rescuing him despite everything he's done to hurt me. In turn, he's agreed to one proviso. If Walsh asks about the young man who was in my passenger seat when Officer Diaz pulled me over to complicate life with a speeding ticket, Jonah is to say that it was him. My son wanted context. I told him he has no right to ask questions, but if he must know, I'd given Nick a ride to the store that morning — Jonah had been sleeping — and forgot all about it. Changing the time line now would complicate everyone's lives. When Jonah hesitated, I made it clear that my participation in his colossal cover-up was contingent upon his assistance in my white lie.

Of course, my help is a crapshoot, and our plan won't gild my image, but we picked the softest available sin. Yesterday, after Jonah spilled his guts, but before he packed his things for Vanessa's, we brainstormed options and decided to blame the guy who's not here to defend himself. Jonah researched the relevant details on his computer, not mine. We talked through a loose script, leaving enough truth in our fiction for it to feel real. Even having covered our bases, and even with the true parts anchoring my ethics, I still sweat on our way past the front desk once we enter the building. I hope to hell I won't break out in hives on our way up the elevator, down the hall to Walsh's office, and all the way to the receptionist who takes us to her boss like we're very important people.

Walsh greets us but does not comment on the weather. He doesn't waste our time with idle drivel, either. He gestures for us to sit in the two folding chairs on the other side of his desk, and we do, and he waits. When the silence gets weird, he tells Jonah, "I am sorry for your loss."

Jonah thanks him, and looking down at his hands, says, "When you asked if I knew any reasons Nick might want to take his own life, I said no, and I meant that. It wasn't a lie. There still aren't any reasons good enough to do what he did. It still doesn't make sense."

"What Jonah is trying to say," I explain, "is that he can't comprehend *any* excuse for Nick's decision, which is why it didn't occur to him to share with you the things he told me last night."

Walsh leans forward, rests his elbows on his desk, looks at my son, waits, listens, and so we tell our story.

A work of pure fiction, our story goes like this: Nick had a drug problem. Sophomore year, he'd gotten hooked on pills acquired illegally on campus — benzos, stimulants, but mostly opioids — and Jonah, having grown wise, feared for his friend's life and intervened. Jonah helped Nick kick, but in the end, no one could save Nick from his demons.

My fabricated detail: that I'd assumed Elizabeth had been looking for envelopes or stamps or tax returns when I opened the desk drawers in my home office last week to find that their contents had been shuffled. Never in a million years did it dawn on me to suspect Nick of ransacking my desk, searching for my NPI and DEA numbers — which I don't keep at home, obviously, for the record.

Jonah roots my lie in yet another: just last week, Nick had been asking Jonah about

439

my home office, and where I'd keep my prescriber numbers, or maybe samples of meds — which, again, for the record: not a chance — and Jonah, because he's responsible, told Nick he'd crossed a red line, that he needed professional help, at which point Nick laughed and insisted he'd only been joking. How could we have known that Nick's dark humor was malignant this time?

Jonah adds false finishing touches: that he was used to hearing about Nick's temptations and impulses, that this was part of the process — a process that worked, until it didn't, because Nick had stayed clean that whole time, or so Jonah had thought. Upon sharing this information with me last night, I tell Walsh, I made the connection with the desk drawer and Nick's covert search for contraband. He hadn't been joking after all. And one more thing: there'd been a complaint filed with our HOA about Nick's use of marijuana in our guesthouse. If Ben Walters had consulted me immediately, there might have been time to intervene, but alas, the gateway drug strikes again. I hang my head.

And scene.

Zebadiah Walsh scrapes his pen against a pad of paper. He's thinking about the autopsy, whatever it revealed, knowing that if traces of opiates had been found in Nick's blood — say, the lingering effects of Vicodin popped like vitamins in college dorms — it would have registered as an unspecified opioid, no different from heroin or morphine. The same would apply to a hair sample, if toxicology ran one, which isn't likely.

Noting two smiling children in a frame on his shelf, I ask Walsh, "Do you have kids?"

Without looking up to confirm that I'm referencing the photo behind him, he says, "Niece and nephew."

Even better. "We build our whole lives around our children's happiness. Nick's aunt, Naomi? She was like a mother to Nick, and now she's lost everything, which is why, if possible, we hope to keep her memories of Nick pure."

Walsh turns his notebook over, places the pen on top. He opens his computer, types, clicks his mouse, clicks again. Finally says, "Jonah, did you know your dad got a speeding ticket recently?"

One second. Two. Everything I've done for him. I look at my son. He's looking at Walsh, but my son is not afraid. He smiles and says, "I was in the car with him when he got pulled over. First and only time I've ever seen him make such a careless mistake." To me, he says, "Never going to let you live it down." My boy.

After an hour of interview questions and crocodile tears, we make it out of the office, down the elevator, through the lobby, and to the parking lot before drawing an honest breath. Jonah opens his mouth to talk, and I say, "Later." We'll discuss it later.

He ignores me and speaks anyway, though, saying, "Thank you."

He can't know the extent to which his little lie covered my ass, too, but he lied so well that I say, "You're welcome," to this person, this human being who came from me and carries bits of me, but who hated me enough to fight dirty. My son and my wife conspired to hurt me with their bodies. Hate like that doesn't grow from indifference. I say, "You did great in there."

He nods. In this moment of softness, I'm tempted to ask my only question. Jonah could tell me who Nick was referencing when he mentioned a crush on an unavailable woman. But tying my loose ends might untie Jonah's, and anyway, none of it matters anymore.

We stand here on fresh blacktop on a pleasant day in June, parting ways, with the opportunity to choose our parting words wisely. My son and I are dangers to each other. Maintaining our balance matters. It especially matters now. But we're also partners. My son and I just created something together. We told a lie together. We vowed to hold our secret sacred, and our secret is the first thing we've shared since he was a child. Is this healthy? Surely not. But maybe it is a starting point. We might systematically hate each other until something changes our minds, but if a change is in the cards, we will have reserved a foundation in our present balance. Like the trump card I'm withholding from Elizabeth — my knowledge of her darkest act, her most scathing betrayal, *the* most wretched wrong — this day could be the token we save, me and my son, to be redeemed as a starting point should we ever start again.

I choose to keep the token pure. I bite my tongue and do not break the spell. Instead I say, "I love you, Son."

He is part child, part man — part alien, part me — when he says, "Thanks. I love you too."

■ ■ ■ ■

ONE MONTH LATER

■ ■ ■ ■

36.

"Is that it?" I yell.

Simone pops her head around the corner. "That's it," she confirms. "Last one."

"All right. I'm making a run for it."

"Come up here before you leave, okay?"

I change out of my lab coat and walk back down the hall to Simone's desk, meticulously organized and freshly adorned with a fishbowl full of glass flowers. She has been a gem ever since I decided to give her a raise. Fifty percent and an extra week's vacation. Keep your friends close and your enemies closer, they say — and while Simone is hardly an enemy, she could've become one if I'd allowed it. I won't allow it. Instead I'll keep her in-the-know, an accessory to anything she could ever criticize, and I'll make sure she's happy.

"Now don't be weird about it," she tells me, guarding her laptop screen. "Have an open mind. I swear there's no subtext. This artist is hot. A good investment. I think it's perfect."

She rotates her computer to reveal a thoughtfully photographed piece of Mexican folk art from a gallery in the city. On a frame of intricately tooled sheets of tin, two panels are opened like church doors on tiny hinges, revealing a mirror inside. Above it all floats a sculpted tin heart crowned in flames. On either side stands a painted tin figure: a pair of skeletons — one wearing a tuxedo, one in a wedding dress — flashing full sets of teeth etched into a smile without flesh.

"They're the *Día de los Muertos* bride and groom," Simone points out. "Sugar skulls. You can use it as a mirror, or close the doors and it's a standalone sculpture. It's functional. It's beautiful, timeless, playful, romantic, and — it's aluminum." Her cockiness is well earned.

I pull my wallet from my pocket. "Simone, it's perfect." She takes my credit card. By Monday morning, the wrapped gift and a lovely note will be waiting for me on my desk. All I'll need to do is sign my name. "Buy yourself a nice lunch on that while you're at it," I say. "Have them call me if they give you any trouble."

She smiles and says, "Will do."

Elizabeth is painting her face when I get home. She's leaning over the bathroom counter, wearing only a strapless bra and a slip that starts at her waist. In front of her is a crystal tumbler marked with bright pink lipstick kisses.

"Has it been thirty days already?" I ask.

She nods.

"And?"

"Eh." She dusts her cheekbones with gold powder. "Same old vodka."

I smile. "Well, you did it. I'm impressed."

"I feel better mentally. Emotionally. It's empowering to know for sure I'm not dependent on it. Laurie's still the anomaly."

"Well," I say, "congratulations. I'm glad that's over."

The first week had not been pretty. Without alcohol to anesthetize her, Elizabeth shuffled around weepy and out of sorts, but then it got better. Then we started talking. Not about Jonah, of course. Not about the Unspeakable Thing, but about Nick and loss and grief and about what the two of us have lost — simply by virtue of staying together long enough to lose eras of infatuation, to witness change in each other, to be changed — and about what we hope to discover yet. In solidarity, I teetotaled too, at first, but she let me off the hook after a few days, and I obliged.

Then came the call from Zebadiah Walsh. Cause of death: blunt cardiac injury as the result of a self-inflicted fall from height. End of story. So my need for a drink declined naturally.

There wasn't any mention of drug use, as far as I know. Maybe Naomi Miller got the full report, but I'd like to think Walsh spared her. I made the request. That's all I could've done.

Elizabeth buckles her feet into formal combat boots that are somehow also sandals. Half-naked in high heels, she asks, "Can you be ready in fifteen minutes?"

"Yes," I say, marveling at how, after everything, the messes and worse, this woman still drives me crazy sometimes. I run my fingers along the curve of her waist, slipping my hand under the elastic of her skirt. "Are you sure we only have fifteen minutes?"

She is unamused. "Yes. Hands off. I spent half an hour on this face and hair." She slaps my wrist, and I release her to disappear into her closet.

"Fine. Later."

"Yeah," she says, "later." She returns wear-

450

ing a steel-gray dress held up by a chain around her neck. She turns so I can zip her, and I do. "We have to be on time. I told Bess we'd pick her up at six."

"How is Bess?"

Elizabeth smooths the creases on her dress and digs through her jewelry box. "All right. She and Rick are on the rocks."

She stops there, daring me to ask for details just so she can say, "Don't worry about it." She's been getting some kind of kick out of hiding the inner workings of a friend-crush on Rick's almost-ex-girlfriend, Bess. Elizabeth explained, one time, how Bess satisfies something unique for her — something I can't provide, in other words — and when I reminded Elizabeth of how capable I am of meeting all her needs, she only rolled her eyes, so now I play along. In truth, I think she's hoping to make me jealous, so it's sort of cute.

She chooses a pair of aquamarine earrings and carries them with her, patting my cheek as she leaves the room. "Twelve minutes."

I dress in a suit and tie. From the hollows of my walk-in closet, I ask Elizabeth if she'd like to join me in checking out speedboats this weekend.

She asks, "You're really doing this, huh?"

"Deal's almost done. *My Lucia* will be

captained by a retired mogul in Fort Lauderdale come Monday. No regrets."

She sings, "If you say so," then appears before me, jewelry in hand. "You about ready?"

I tell her I am and follow her downstairs. It is a good house, our house. I briefly considered satisfying the HOA with a rooftop remodel, but that would nearly eat up my whole speedboat budget, determined by the sale of *My Lucia,* so instead, I changed the lock, sealed the door. Good enough.

In the kitchen, Elizabeth transfers her wallet and makeup from one bag to another. I eyeball a stack of mail. Flipping over a large open envelope, I ask, "What's this?"

"Oh." Elizabeth moves close to me, leaning in as she fastens an earring. Her skin smells warm. "Those are the proofs from those portraits that photographer took at your banquet. I asked her to send them before everything went to shit, obviously. Thought they'd make good Christmas cards, but that's probably a little morose now."

I shake the contents from the envelope and scan a glossy sheet of thumbnails, honing in on two images circled in red crayon. Elizabeth stays by my side, staring at the pictures too.

"Those were her favorites, I guess," she says.

In the first, Nick Carpenter, alive and reasonably well, grips Elizabeth's arm. It is the very same photo published in the newspaper two months ago, when all I saw was Nick's hand on my wife. I'd been blinded by a diversion. The second picture is of just the three of us: me in the middle, my wife on one side, my child on the other. We are close and we are laughing, digitally captured in a state of joy and intimacy.

I try not to imagine what they were thinking that night, just as I so often try to un-imagine the entire nightmare. Of course, sometimes I can't help wondering where Elizabeth goes in that pretty head of hers. I watch her leave the house early for work, or draw a bath right away when she comes home. I pay attention to whether her eyes are open or closed, and how she moves with me, and how she toys with me, and I've determined that the worst is behind us. I'm the one with the secret now, and she feels it, and the undeniable weight of her curiosity — sensing, as she does, that I know something damning, and that the thing is too dangerous to speak out loud — lets me know that she's wondering, too. We're latched together by our twin secrets, by our twin curiosities, and the little bits of not-knowing fortify the thing that binds us. In our love, the gaps aren't losses, but endless pools of possibility.

And yes, I wonder too about Jonah, who is lost to me, but still very much alive to me. He's my son. I've asked myself if it's possible that everything he told me was a lie, a story meant to hurt, but what kind of person goes that far? That's not the child I raised. That's not the story I can live with. Besides, Elizabeth's silence on the matter has all but confirmed its validity in my mind. She does not ask about Jonah or reference him in passing. These are not the omissions of an innocent woman. So then, it is almost impossible to hope that Jonah's story was a lie. What is possible is that I could forgive him. Not yet or now and maybe not ever. But unlike with Raymond, who may as well be dead to me, there is still possibility with Jonah. There is hope. We are family, after all. In the messes we make, the awakenings, the messes we fix, the lives we choose and the ones we inherit, in the better or worse, the ambiguity and ambivalence, in the things we can never undo and the things undone in effort, and the parts we maintain — in our bodies, in our molecular composition, in our lust and our ambition, and our best attempts at right and wrong — we are family: part of a pack, a school, a pride. It is cruel and it is vital, and at the end of it all, I will know that I did my best for him, my son, my seed. This is my life and my legacy. Heaven knows I wouldn't trade it for the world.

ELIZABETH

My train leaves the station just before noon.
This wasn't how I'd planned to spend the
day, but now that I'm en route, it feels so
right. Flexing the soles of these old boots
feels so right, too. I tap my heels together:
stacked leather against worn leather.
Through double-paned safety glass, the
world whirls pink and green.

To think: a crucifix did this.

At coffee this morning, when Bess noticed
me noticing the turquoise-and-silver cross
around her neck and answered, "No, I'm
not Catholic," before I could ask, she
explained, with a straight face, how the
pendant is her superhero talisman. It had
belonged to her late mother, who'd charged
it with love and strength. Now Bess wears it
to prep for things like job interviews — or,
even though she's sick of talking about him,
her impending breakup with Rick, who is
too boring to see Bess as more than an

object of his desire or proof of his desirability. We agreed that a crucifix-as-armor is doubly fitting when confronting an emotional vampire.

Bess said, "I know it's silly, but . . ." so I told her the truth: to me, it isn't silly at all. Then, before old superstitions *(if I talk about it, I'll ruin it)* could intervene, I confessed that I used to do something similar with a pair of boots — the Frye shit-kickers I wore all through high school and into college, the ones I was wearing when Shae went through the windshield of her sister's Camaro while I thought, *Keep your knees down, Elizabeth. Keep your feet on the floor,* and, *Don't you dare look away,* and, *Oh my God, don't you dare go away.*

Bess didn't call me morbid or self-centered for turning her story into mine. She called me a wonderful friend. Then, zero judgment, she let me change the subject. We talked about her job prospects and how I plan to spend my days before school starts again, and everything was normal — so normal, in fact, that I rode the feeling all the way home, straight into the house, straight up to my closet, where I took the shoebox down from the highest shelf like it was the most unremarkable thing to do. Despite the late-summer heat, despite not having done this in a decade, I stuffed my feet into socks and slipped my socked feet into harness boots supercharged with Shae's love and strength. I didn't rationalize or reflect — even as I removed a cotton-wrapped bundle from the bottom of the box, put the lid back on the box, put the box back on the shelf, carried the bundle downstairs, pulled a faded paperback from my office shelf, marched to the kitchen, and left Robert a note: *Heading into the city for the day. Will catch the 5:51 back. There's spaghetti pie in the freezer. xo E.* Without overthinking my feet or their direction, I just walked, feeling Shae stir with every step: love and strength holding me against the world. Now I'm halfway to a ritual I thought I'd put to rest — armed with a pair of time machines, no less.

I reach into my bag and choose the faded paperback first, flipping it open to a dog-eared page, skimming highlighted passages and trying to remember why they once moved me, but my eyes drift to the backs of my hands marked with sunspots I call freckles. I should be more diligent about SPF. I should be more disciplined about cleaning my diamond. Once upon a time, I cleaned a ring routinely. Now I rarely take one off.

I really did leave my first ring in that worthless ultrasonic cleaner on the day I wandered into Robert's seminar at Columbia. I truly forgot to put it back on my hand — an honest mistake, with a case to be made for selective memory — but Robert had no excuse. He left his wedding band behind on purpose. All it took was me introducing myself after his lecture for Robert to suggest we continue our conversation over drinks. I knew he would seduce me with his body language, with his other world, with a life I recognized from magazines and soap operas and Victorian novels, and I was ready to seduce him in turn. I fancied myself Colette bypassing her vagabond years, flying straight into the arms of high-brow Husband Number Two. How tired I was then, having learned as all spoiled bohemians do that Bohemia is only fit for Prague and fiction, when along came Robert Hart, MD, booking suites at The Lucerne twice a week, insisting I order whatever I desired from a room service menu that never changed. And so I ate duck à l'orange and steak au poivre and escargot and pot de crème, and I took bubble baths in an actual bathtub, and for two months, I was in heaven. This was before the menu grew tiresome, before Stuart grew suspicious, then wise — long before Robert would start expecting me to be the one to prepare the pot de crème, the duck à l'orange, the steak tartare. The tartar sauce.

I fan my fingers, letting my diamond catch light, throwing rainbow confetti on the ceiling of this train car. A little girl pops her head over the back of the seat in front of me, raises her eyebrows and puckers her mouth in the shape of *ooh* with no sound. I smile and rock my hand back and forth, demonstrating cause and effect for the towhead with a sateen bow in her hair, and we *ooh* silently together until her mother asks her to please sit on her bottom.

Rolling past Babylon, I swap one book of poems for another, running my hand over the cover of a Moleskine I haven't touched in ages and hesitate to crack, even now. My body warms just holding it. If I break the seal, I'll have to negotiate whether the warmth is warranted — whether its pages deserve their place in my heart — jeopardizing the reasons I hold them dear. There was never a reason to have hidden the book all these years, except for the vague comfort drawn from knowing relics of my former life exist, carefully preserved just so I can keep a secret with myself. A book of poems. A ratty T-shirt stolen on my way out, plucked from the bottom of Stuart's hamper, just-in-case. I was afraid of wanting both worlds, of craving his smell, but I chose Robert and never looked back.

This book, however, slightly more than just-in-case, is one of those things — pralines, David Lynch films, Stuart's poems: the things I can't resist that make me sick — and so I turn to the inside cover, where one of us Scotch-taped a cyanotype of dandelion tufts and our cat's whiskers. White lines on Prussian blue twist a thorn in my heart. I flip the page, confronting haikus and triolets. An elegy. Stuart's crusade: a return to poetic form.

I admire designs made by words on paper without yet reading the words themselves. Unlined pages tattooed with ink and tea stains, tear stains, lipstick stains like passport stamps where I'd kissed Stuart's verse — kissed his portraits of my body, my psyche, my effect on him. His perception of my effect on the world. I stop at a page marked by a stem of pressed sea holly and feel a pang of guilt for not remembering why I marked it, not recalling any particular fondness for this sonnet at all. It must have meant something to me, though, and so I

461

read — *North of Blue Eye, due south of Marvel Cave* — and hold a hand to my mouth, tracing the line of my rebel smile. For a moment, I'm twenty-eight all over again.

Stuart was an absolute nerd about my roots, fetishizing Missouri like it's the other side of the planet, but he was from Oregon, not Osaka, and the Ozarks aren't all that different from Myrtle Creek. Thanksgiving in Joplin with my family was cultural tourism for him — and consequently, often revelatory for me too. My parents adored Stuart. If he tended bar with a heavy hand, he could get them talking something fierce, telling stories about me, stories I'd never even heard — not that I needed to hear them all, like the one about how I was likely conceived in a Best Western in Branson while my parents were in town for a family reunion at Silver Dollar City. I could have lived without that visual.

Stuart found it romantic, though, and wanted to go there, to Silver Dollar City — "to see where the magic happened," he joked, and I gagged — and I refused, but we did take a tour of Marvel Cave. It was as corny and beautiful as I remembered. More beautiful than corny through Stuart's eyes. He delighted in place names: how Marble

Cave was rechristened after miners failed to strike marble; how the tiny town of Blue Eye, Missouri, mirrors Blue Eye, Arkansas, across the state line. A pair of Blue Eyes hiding in the heartland. He viewed my history like it was a classic film about an average upbringing, rather than just an average upbringing, which is what it was. I liked how that felt, seeing my life his way. It was exciting. At first.

Way back when, a year or so before our marriage fell apart — before I suicide-bombed what was left of it, that is — I found a therapist on campus and spilled my guts, desperate for a practical solution to an emotional quagmire. How could I possibly find fault in a husband who worshipped me, who wrote notebooks full of poetry about me? Why was I so unhappy? When the therapist asked what I valued most in my life with Stuart, I pretended to be joking when I answered, *Our cat, Finch.* The therapist didn't laugh, though. He was so earnest when he said, "The beautiful things that grow from decay can make it awfully hard to leave the garden."

After I stopped judging his platitude, I was gobsmacked to find it rang true. And so I understood that I hadn't been seeking marital advice so much as permission to leave. My therapist offered the practical solution I thought I wanted: sit down with Stuart — the only other person in my marriage, the only person in the whole world entitled to an opinion on the fate of my marriage — with a willingness to ask and answer the uncomfortable questions I'd been avoiding. Have the difficult conversations, this man advised. He made it sound so simple. Instead, I blew the whole thing up. My terrorism was absolute — designating a victim, a villain, an event — while sparing Stuart from having to ask the only question that mattered, from having to hear me answer, *No, I don't love you anymore.*

To punish myself, I denied myself that which I valued most: Finch, my career, the respect of my peers. I let Stuart keep the cat, the friends, the apartment, restaurants and cafés. These sacrifices felt so generous — signing over the rights, erasing myself for his convenience — that I hardly considered how it must've felt to coexist with all that evidence of what we shared: the furniture, the plants, the holes in a wall where I hammered nails before thinking to check for studs. The calico cat named after a bird. Meanwhile, I kept nothing but a ratty undershirt and a journal full of handwritten poems that could almost get me high. Rolling the stem of sea holly between two fingers, I read on —

North of Blue Eye, due south of Marvel
  Cave,
You came to be, a being forced to leave
Your single-cell utopia to save
Yourself, you see, for you'd begun to
  cleave.
Bereft, so severed by your Great Divide,
You built a world beneath your mother's
  skin.
Like this, you split apart and multiplied,
Then nine months on, were pushed away
  again.
Mother to Dickinson to sisterfriend:
Each life you fused to refused to make
  fast.
Yet every failed attachment's bitter end
Prepared the open wound to better graft

My pneuma, form and vital heat to yours:
A heart made whole by Love's return to
  Source.

— and am reminded of why his poems could make me queasy, too.

I was Stuart's muse. He loved to remind me of this fact, frequently, ostensibly to flatter me, but I'm not sure he knew much

465

about muses, those goddess-nymphs, violently talented daughters of a Titaness who
never forgets. Maybe if Stuart had consulted
me before picking me apart on a cellular
level — dramatizing my embryonic angst in
iambic pentameter, as if he knew, as if he'd
been there, *as if* — I'd have appreciated his
intentions a little more. But no, he'd never
risk *not* seeing me as a love-starved parasite,
incomplete from conception to grad school,
only made whole, at last, through him. And
he wondered why I held myself back. He
accused me of trying to be mysterious, but
I was never posturing. I was just protecting
what he refused to see: that I was secretly
whole the whole time.

Stuart didn't know why I went up to the
Cloisters to circle the quince trees and sit
on cold stone, that I'd pass those hours talking to Shae, telling her everything I couldn't
or wouldn't talk about at home. Expanding.
Sometimes I'd commune with her at River-
side Park, or the Botanical Gardens, or
when I was feeling particularly compressed
and in dire need of space, down in Battery
Park. Or, later, the High Line. Stuart didn't
know the things I told Shae in my head. He
never saw how complete I was, or how
straight my thoughts were. After he found
out about Robert, he kept saying, *You aren't*

thinking straight, and, *This isn't the Elizabeth I know,* and I'd reply, *That's just the trouble, isn't it?*

Our train doors open at Jamaica, and the girl in front of me waves good-bye with one hand while her mother drags her away by the other. My feet lead me to my connecting train, and I settle in, and the world is blacked out as we shoot through the tunnel to emerge in Penn Station, like it's the most ordinary place in the world for me to be. So I walk, letting these boots propel me into a flow of bodies passing through corridors, up stairs, down streets. I am but a single part of a greater system, people pumping like molecules of blood through arteries and capillaries and one-way streets, the city's life force keeping tempo with our collective pulse: beats broken by oncoming traffic, a magnificent system radiating health. People at a crosswalk gather around teenage boys doing backflips on the corner as Salt-N-Pepa's "Push It" blasts from a boombox. I speed-walk to the beat, bob and weave, choose my route by choosing streets I can cross without having to pause. By the time I reach the High Line, I've reclaimed the clip of my former self, a rhythm useless in Sag Harbor but essential here. The city sets our pace, and we abide.

I take the stairs at Thirtieth Street, climbing to the park hovering over Tenth Avenue. It's grown so much since I left, yet the view remains the same. I'd come down here to sit beside Russian sage, trying to smudge the oppressive stink of home life: coffee and cigarette breath, ammonia-soaked litter, afternoon sex, bacon, peppermint and vetiver oils, that goddamned laundromat downstairs. Exhaust from the washing machines pumped a cloying mix of mildew and chemical perfume into the alley and our window at all hours. Stuart tried cover the smell by burning incense from the head shop down the block, and while it worked at first, my brain eventually merged the olfactory files. To this day, Nag Champa makes me gag.

I take a seat on an empty bench, wood slats crusted with pigeon crap and greasy bits of shawarma. A sumac casts lace shadows on raised beds. I gaze into shadow-leaves like they are tea leaves and picture my old apartment: the jute baskets holding plastic pots of philodendron, spider plants, and devil's ivy hanging above the kitchen sink; our living room full of beautiful books, peace lilies, succulents; light streaming through a far window, illuminating dust crystals of cat litter suspended in the air like so much glitter — and for half a breath, I'm twenty-five all over again, wondering what the future holds, wondering if I'll be somebody someday, wanting to be more than someone's something, but wanting to be a part of a pair anyway. Getting my wish. I'm twenty-six and full of love, stroking our kitten's Jackson Pollock face, marveling at her religious devotion to play and limitless capacity for forgiveness, delighting in her tiny meow that was more of a chirp, telling Stuart she sounded like the house finch that nested just outside my bedroom window in Missouri one summer and Stuart saying, *Finch it is.* In my mind, Stuart holds a match to a stick of incense mounted on a wooden sleigh on the kitchen counter. Sick to my stomach, I hold a hand to my mouth.

On the reclining lounge chair next to mine, a musk-soured man stretches out and pulls a half-empty sleeve of Saltines from a bulging pocket on his stained cargo pants. A mangy pigeon lands on his belt buckle, and I suddenly feel like crying. "Shae," I whisper, summoning two ghosts: Shae's and the long-gone side of myself who could sit for hours in parks around the city, almost (but not quite) believing in telepathy and afterlives.

I open my eyes. People pass in and out of

the scene sprawled before me, eating sandwiches and tossed salads, talking on cell
phones or talking to themselves. I close my
eyes again, and when I open them seconds
later, the scene has changed, if merely by
degrees. New players are eating, talking and
walking with the flow, drifting along with
the current of this place. A woman in
platform sneakers trips in front of me but
does not fall. She turns to stare at the pavement, blaming it for her misstep, but she
keeps her pace, and the scene changes once
again. I break a blade of zebra grass from
the potted prairie at my back, imagine Shae
by my side, whisper, "I miss you like crazy
today." *It isn't silly at all,* I told Bess just this
morning, and so I turn my whisper inward
and silently tell my best friend everything,
pulling every tiny tooth that's been gnawing
at my conscience all summer. The whole
truth and nothing else.

Life jumped the tracks again this summer.

You would have liked the boys, Shae. They
were sweet, both of them. Smart, too. They
reminded me of us, a little bit, in so far as
what a match they were and how tragic it
is. I suppose, to understand what happened
to them, it might help if I begin with how
we got here.

It all started when Nick came to live with us — except, well, wait. That's not true, is it? It would have started when Jonah came to live with us — only that's wrong, too, since technically, the whole mess started before Nick knew we existed — and, to some degree, before Jonah and I met. Forgive me. It's hard to know where to begin when it's hard to know how it began.

Jonah is twenty now. He was just a kid when I broke up his family and moved into his house. I don't blame him for hating me. He had every right, and he was too young to understand how messy his parents' marriage had been, and anyway, I wouldn't have wanted that for him. Vanessa was an incredible mother. Jonah lived with her through high school and barely stayed with us. He threw the daddy out with the bilge water, if you will. I think that for Jonah, his father's choice to leave felt like a punishment, like Robert was saying, *You're not good enough to earn my place in your life. You don't deserve this happy family,* and I was the witch who gave his father the power to disappear.

The thing is, Jonah and I didn't have a bad relationship because we didn't have a relationship at all. There was nothing. Then, this past year, something changed. He started opening up a bit, and everything got much better early this summer, when he moved in with us. Proust bridged the gap, if you'll believe it. I helped Jonah enroll in summer school at Stony Brook, gave him tips on which professors to avoid, that sort of thing. When he realized he'd signed up for a course in which his only text would be the madeleine passage — a whole six weeks of madeleines — he nearly strangled me for suggesting it, but he ended up loving the class and wanting to talk about it, obviously, which (big surprise) led to us facing our own recollections of how things unfolded for our family, which led to us telling our sides of the story, which led to — well, I guess it led to us seeing each other. We got to fix some of what could be fixed, just by broadening our peripheral hindsight. It was extraordinary. We became friends.

Robert didn't notice. I didn't point it out to him either. My connection with Jonah had been so vulnerable, our conversations so personal, that I couldn't bring myself to betray the boy's trust. Mostly, though, it was nice to have something that was just ours, mine and Jonah's. Robert's not exactly a Proust kind of guy. I wasn't keeping a secret, I just didn't want to brag about making a connection where Robert couldn't. I didn't want to rub it in. Besides, I figured Robert would notice, eventually. He would have, too, if Nick hadn't come along.

I'd give anything to rewind and do it differently. No, this part is my fault. I was the one who pushed for him to stay in our guesthouse all summer. He'd lost both of his parents — mother to Lou Gehrig's, father to suicide — and my heart broke for him. Plus, I liked him. Most important, though, he was Jonah's best and only friend. They were brothers-by-choice, and while I'm sure they'd have connected if Nick's parents had been alive and well, I truly believe Nick's particular history had a particularly profound effect on Jonah. After so many years of identifying as the victim of a broken home, Jonah started questioning his very understanding of victimhood and family. He stopped feeling sorry for himself. Nick healed Jonah in many ways, and in doing so, he cleared the way for Jonah to see me as an actual human being, flawed and complicated. Can you imagine the mercy it took for Jonah to offer me a second chance? The grace? He gave it to me — not forgiveness, exactly, but a fresh start: a tabula rasa — so I accepted it and never looked back. Starting over with him was my joy. I owed this joy to Nick.

So yes, I embraced the idea of Nick spending the summer with us. The truth is, our house was fun with those boys around. They wanted to read just so they could ask me questions. They thought I knew things. I know that sounds cocky, but you can handle it, right? I enjoyed being appreciated — admired, even. By straying from my tired syllabi, I realized how passionate I still can be. We tried to start a book club, the kids and I. It was sweet, you know?

Then it all came crashing down.

Goddamn it. There's another one. They're everywhere now, phrases I never noticed before that have become dangerous: crashing down, pushed over the edge, at the brink, tipping point, nosedive, rotten, smashed to smithereens. Broken. Busted. Falling for it.

The Terrible Thing happened early in the morning. Robert had been driving me nuts. Nothing serious. He'd just been a little neurotic after getting through an event he'd been stressing about. It was a banquet, a community fundraiser thing, but he was the honoree, and I think he didn't know what to do with himself when it was over. Anyway, we argued, and he slept in his office the night before, then he left for the gym very early in the morning. He didn't even come upstairs to change clothes, but he did shout up to me before leaving the house, told me he wanted to take me out to dinner, that I should choose a place. I suppose he wanted to make nice.

I was still in bed, drifting in and out of sleep, but he couldn't have been gone for more than a few minutes when I heard stomping on the other side of my bedroom door. I scrambled to the hallway, where the door to our widow's walk was wide open. A girl was standing right in front of me.

I recognized her right away. The only time I'd seen her in the flesh had been the night before, although I hadn't been sure, at the time, that it was her. But in daylight, it was obvious. Long red hair. Full cheeks. Full everything. Freckles. She'd been on TV tons last year. The paper, too. Right away, I recognized those eyes that said, *This can't be happening,* even though I didn't yet know what *this* was, this time.

Her name is Kayla. Kayla Scott. She's seventeen and has a pet iguana and likes house music and wants to be an architect, only she didn't apply to colleges because she was too busy being depressed and disgraced her senior year. Of course, I didn't learn those things from the news. To hear reporters tell it, she was an oversexed, overdeveloped teenager who must have been asking for it because she had good posture. I only learned those other things from Jonah after Kayla left our house on the day Nick died.

She used to babysit for a prominent family in town before the kids' dad started putting his hands on her. She told her parents, and they went to the police, and a big, messy scandal erupted. Then one day it all stopped. The girl held a press conference and told the cameras she'd made the whole thing up. It was obvious she was lying, that she'd traded dignity for closure. Her eyes had been full of tears that day, but also full of fury — just like they were when we stood face-to-face on the upstairs landing in my house. My brain had been sleep-fogged, but I recognized the tears and fury, so I asked what happened. She said, *Nothing happened. I swear,* so I tried calming her, even though I didn't understand, but she kept repeating, *Nothing happened. We just fell asleep.*

That's when we heard a terrible sound coming from the open door leading up to the roof. A crack and thud echoing down the spiral staircase, followed by Jonah's footsteps. And to think: I was worried about Jonah breaking his neck tumbling down the stairs like that. How quickly the kaleido-

476

scope twists. Jonah's features seemed to be melting into something unrecognizable when he ran into the hall and said, *It was an accident.*

I forced myself back into my body and asked, *What was an accident?*

He quietly unraveled; the noise and violence were trapped inside of him. Banging fists against his head and making faint animal sounds to accompany tears that wouldn't come, he whimpered, *It was an accident.*

That's when I kicked into management mode.

I told Kayla and Jonah to go to my room, sit on the bed and do nothing until I got back, then I ran up to the roof and moved through the crow's nest out to our widow's walk, where I noticed the broken banister at the opposite end of the deck. I can't remember how I got there, if I walked or ran, but the next thing I knew, I was peering over the edge of our house, staring at the shape of Nick's broken body splayed in the bushes — the terrible angle of his neck, his head twisted all wrong, eye open: cubism in the flesh — and at the derailment of so many lives at once. He was — it was beyond my wildest nightmares. If there was a chance of saving him, I'd have called 911 immediately,

477

but it was worse than bad. It was *irreparable.*

There I was, standing in bird shit, wearing nothing but a white silk nightgown, staring at the dead body of a boy who'd brought peace into my home, feeling myself crack — inches and seconds, at best, from losing my mind — when something dawned on me: I was the adult in this situation. Adults don't get the luxury of melting down. My job was to convince the kids everything was under control. And so I went back inside.

Jonah and Kayla were waiting as I'd instructed, sitting on the edge of my bed like a couple of schoolchildren in time-out. I crouched in front of them and asked what had happened. In turns, they told me about how all three of them had been at a party the night before, and how the party had been broken up, but how they didn't want the night to end, and so Nick said he wished they could camp on the beach, but Jonah said he could do one better. He snuck Kayla and Nick up to the crow's nest so they could pretend to be camping under the strangest summer sky.

They'd gone up long after I'd fallen asleep, and Robert had been sleeping in his office, so he wouldn't have heard them sneaking around. At some point very late that night, though — or early in the morning, rather — I did hear something. It had been an utterly unfamiliar sound, and I'd shot out of bed and turned on my light, trying to place the source — whether it was coming from the house, the ceiling, the sky — and stepped into the hallway, where the door to the roof was ajar. At first I'd been frightened, but then I heard laughter and relaxed. I closed my door behind me and tiptoed up the spiral stairs toward the crumbling cupola we only visit twice a year to check for leaks. Jonah, Nick, and the girl who turned out to be Kayla were burrowed in blankets and sleeping bags, sprawled on the benches below the windows in our crow's nest. I didn't want to embarrass Jonah in front of her, so I held a finger to my lips and whispered, *It's time to go to bed,* and all three of them started packing up without protest. Then I went back inside with Nick behind me. I said good night to him, and he went downstairs and presumably out to the guesthouse while I went back to bed. I assumed Jonah and Kayla were on their way down too. But they weren't.

In my room that next morning, Jonah and Kayla told me about how the two of them had talked a little more, then accidentally fallen asleep. They woke up to the sound of Robert's car leaving for the gym in the morning, at which point they stepped outside to stretch in the sun. Kayla told me she then thanked Jonah for being nice to her. She said her friends had turned on her that year and she never thought she'd trust again, but that Jonah and Nick had been so kind and respectful, so she told Jonah how much she appreciated it, and I guess Jonah replied, *Of course. We're friends,* and he'd opened his arms and Kayla had hugged him — as friends.

This is how both of them swore it went down.

This is when Jonah gazed over Kayla's shoulder, over the pool and the yard to the open door of the guesthouse. This is when Jonah made eye contact with Nick, who was standing just outside, staring up at his best friend hugging the girl he liked.

Yes, Jonah knew Nick had a crush on Kayla. In fact, he told me the only reason he didn't try something with her is because Nick had called dibs. Bro code, Jonah called it.

I know. Don't start.

Nick jumped to conclusions. He stormed inside and up the stairs, which is what woke me, surely, and he called Jonah a traitor and accused them of screwing around after he'd gone to bed, at which point Kayla stomped downstairs and defended herself to me. *Nothing happened,* she begged me to believe. *We didn't do anything, I swear.*

Jonah claims he and Nick exchanged insults on the roof. They exchanged secrets Jonah still won't tell me to this day. Nick was upset about something bigger than jealousy — something personal, and serious, and big enough to warrant hysterics — but Jonah insists on preserving his friend's dignity on this one point, at least, and so I've let it go.

Believe me, that was the least of my concessions.

The boys fought for the first time that day, and the last. Jonah was still trying to get inside to enlist my help, but Nick pushed him in the chest. Nothing like that had ever happened before. I'm sure both of them were stunned. Jonah was still blocking the exit, so Nick stormed out of the crow's nest and across the widow's walk. Jonah has never been a fighter. His instincts are for shit. But he was shocked and hurt, so he ran after Nick anyway and pushed him from behind, intending to shove him *against* the balcony, not through it, but the wood was rotten.

I didn't mean to, Jonah kept saying. He was hyperventilating, whimpering like a sick

481

animal. *I didn't even push hard.*

The woodwork was rotten to its core.

That morning, I stayed crouched on my bedroom floor, still barefoot in my nightgown, while Jonah and Kayla blurted out details piecemeal; and although I've considered it, I'm certain they couldn't have corroborated a fake story in the short time I'd left them alone. They weren't strategizing; they were confessing, spilling their guts in acts of spiritual survival. I believed them and believe them still, so I allowed myself a minute to pause and assess our options.

My brain knew to call the police before three minutes became four, then five, then suspicious, but I stretched each second to the limit, because right there in front of me were two kids whose lives are still fat spools of ribbon. They had what the rest of us long for and mourn: opportunities, chances. So much potential. So many possibilities.

Everything got really slow — like being on acid, you know? Remember how it seemed as if hours had gone by and we'd look at the clock and it had only been two minutes? That's how this was. Everything was bright like that, too. So crystal clear. It's like I was possessed by a sense of purpose, and that purpose was two-fold: to keep Jonah from becoming That Guy whose best friend shattered right in front of him, and to keep Kayla from becoming That Girl who bears the sins of reckless men, again and again. She'd been broken once and had managed to build herself back up. Was it fair to ask her to go from being seen as the slut who ruined a rich man's life to being known as the prude who caused a duel to the death? Would it have been fair to expect her to trust anyone, to love anyone, to make friends, to be forgiven or ever forgive herself if, once again, she was disregarded, discarded, forced to live with a truth no one believes?

Would it have been fair to deny her a say in what came next?

We had one minute, maybe two, to decide.

So I asked her. *Kayla, what do you want to do?*

Her chin twitched. She pouted like an infant overcome with a primal need for love and relief. Then, suddenly resolute, she said, *I want to leave here and have none of this be real. For none of it to have ever happened. I want it to all go away.*

I turned to Jonah, who answered without being asked, *Me too. I want it to go away, too.*

I told them that if I helped them, they could never talk about it. Ever. I warned them that it would be a lonely secret and a haunting one. Kayla said the truth would haunt her whether she kept it a secret or not, but that at least she could live with the truth. Another round of lies and accusations might kill her. The atrophied part of my heart began to twitch, and I could feel myself at twenty, living inside of an obsession with all the things I wanted to take back — the stupid concert, the stupid car, the stupid decisions that wrecked my life and ended yours. How many nights have I tried to dream a different route: exiting for food, leaving an hour earlier or later, taking a backroad, taking a bus? Me driving. Me dead. How many times have I woken up certain heartbreak had killed me already?

My twenty-year-old self flickered: a body on a journey, my parents urging me to fill my life with *my* life, my father telling me to never settle, my mother asking, *But are you happy?* Their lives crackled in my atoms, and I could feel how hard they worked to give me choices, and how I chose until the choosing frightened me by shedding light on me, and how bright I was then, but how late it is now, and how the rules weren't written for me, anyway.

Kayla was right: reality is painful enough.

I asked if she needed a ride. I don't think she understood the implications of my question when she answered, *No,* so I asked how far away she lived, and she said, *Six miles.* She said her parents would be at church. They let her sleep in on Sundays. They wouldn't notice she'd been gone. I told Kayla to leave through the back door, to circle the block if necessary, but to avoid our side yard, no matter what. I made her promise to never tell anyone she'd been to our house. Jonah's ass was on the line, I reminded her. Mine, too. She promised, thanked me and was gone.

Then it was just me and Jonah.

He slid from the bed onto the ground, struggling to steady himself on all fours. I rubbed his back and shushed him, knowing time wouldn't pause to comfort us — time couldn't support the weight of my adult stepson dry heaving on the floor, mucus swinging from his face like a blown-glass pendulum — and that police aren't big on excuses.

Jonah was begging, *Please help, Elizabeth, please.* I'd been the source of so much pain in this boy's formative years, and now he was in my arms, moaning, *Please.* He wailed, *They'll put me on trial for murder.* I accepted his fear as fact.

He was giving me a choice: to help or not. I'd been so eager to support Jonah on my

485

terms. Book club, Proust. But this was gravely different. This was my chance to do something big and daring and meaningful for him, a gesture wide enough to swallow all the ways I'd done him wrong, even if — no, *especially because* it gave me no pleasure. This was my test, my one true opportunity to heal the broken thing. It wasn't about favor. I could have let Jonah hate me, if he'd had anyone else to turn to, but he had no one. He'd lost his best friend. He was so alone in the world, and so I said, *Leave it to me.*

I started giving orders. Jonah helped me clean the house, the roof, the stairs. We checked and double-checked the warped flooring for sneaker scuffs. I couldn't bring myself to inspect Nick's body for signs of a struggle, and for days afterward, I agonized, thinking, *Maybe Jonah was wrong?* He swore up and down he hardly touched Nick, but, *What if I could have saved him?* And, *What if Jonah's fingerprints are bruised onto Nick's skin?*

The autopsy showed death on impact, by the way. There's nothing we could have done.

Yes, of course I wanted to call the police. Of course I wanted to call Robert, to tell him everything and ask for help, but in allowing for a pause, I'd let the whole thing turn watery. Jonah was begging me, *begging,* to let Robert hear the truth from him, his own son. Jonah wanted to handle it like a man, he said, which apparently meant facing Robert alone. Maybe this is simple, but I kept thinking, *Jonah knew him first.* I kept telling myself that I had to honor their relationship by letting Jonah choose how he would reveal this most wretched truth. In the end, I decided Jonah had the right to confess on his own terms, so I tricked Robert into running errands, which bought us time to hit reset — and while we reset, Jonah told me about Kayla, and all the things she used to want, and how Kayla's favorite person in the world was her grandmother, and how her grandmother had given Kayla an around-the-world ticket as a high school graduation present. She'd planned to leave for Bangkok the following week. I chose to focus on this: Kayla shopping for dragon fruit at a floating market or dropping coins in bronze bowls at Wat Pho. I pictured her dwarfed by the reclining Buddha's golden feet, wishing on pearl-tipped toes.

I had no clue what I was doing. Was I helping Jonah? Leading him astray? There was no time to predict. I only knew that once we made the decision to cover tracks, there was no reversing course. By the time I could see straight, it had been over an hour, at which point I panicked. What kind of psychopath waits hours to call the cops? Who cleans and disinfects in the meantime? Crazy people and criminals, right? I could've pretended to have just discovered Nick's body, but the thought of lying to the police sent me into a dissociative state. Like Kayla and Jonah, I wanted it all to go away. I just kept thinking: floating market, pearl-tipped toes.

Robert couldn't know that I'd deceived him. If he found out, he'd have every right to leave me, or commit me, or report me — yes, *report me,* because I'd made myself an accessory to something that might now be a crime — and so, quid pro quo, I agreed to let Jonah confess his own way if he agreed to erase me and Kayla from the story altogether.

Two hours after Robert had left for the gym, I helped Jonah pack a duffle bag with all of our cleaning supplies and every object that had come into contact with Nick that morning. Later on, Jonah threw some of it away and washed the rest at his mother's house. When Robert finally returned from the gym, he was so happy, insisting I choose

488

a dinner spot. He wanted to make me happy. We had a chance to reset, too. So I picked a Thai restaurant where I could eat noodles and drink broth and drink spirits in a secret ritual unfolding in my mind. Every time I swallowed, I thought, *floating market, pearl-tipped toes, tabula rasa.*

A week after the disaster, Kayla left the country as planned, and she's out there now, exploring and seeing and being herself as a person at the market, in a temple, in the world, and she hasn't been decided yet. She still gets to decide.

And Jonah was spared from something awful, whether something as abstract as gossip or as fixed as an involuntary manslaughter charge. A felony record. A lifetime of doubt. I've decided if there's a possibility Jonah will find the freedom to forgive himself — maybe even to believe, in time, that his worst day wasn't his fault — I'd probably make the same choices again.

As for Robert — a week or so later, I came home to find him nursing a migraine, staring at the wall. He told me Jonah had moved out, alluding to a difficult conversation they'd had. It became clear Jonah had kept his word. He'd told Robert about the argument, the shove, the accident, but left me and Kayla out of it. He'd taken the fall.

My heart broke for my husband, sitting in that chair wanting to tell me an enormous secret but believing that to do so would betray his own son. I wanted Robert to forgive his child, whose only offense, as far as he knew, had been self-preservation. Yes, I could have filled in the details Jonah omitted, but doing so would have disrupted the fragile balance of our truths, and so I swallowed the scraps and tried to move on.

The irony is, for as hard as Robert and Jonah work to protect how they're seen by the other, they actually would understand each other perfectly — better than anyone in the world, really — if they showed themselves fully. Jonah learned his coping skills from his father, after all. He inherited Robert's wiring. It's in their blood, their mannerisms, their ways of moving through the world, their pride — which is also their shame — and their defense mechanisms: image and privacy. What they present, what they hold back. What they believe people need to believe, when in fact, no one does except for them. They're cut from the same cloth, and they don't even know it.

But it's not my cloth, not my wiring. All I can do is try to get on with my life, with our lives, even if I can't stop reliving that day in my head. Again and again.

I've been reliving so many things.

Do you remember Belize? When our guide's lantern died halfway down the cave? How dark it was? And how the water was just deep enough that if I'd lain down and filled my lungs with air, I could have floated all the way into the belly of that mountain? It felt like the world had swallowed us whole. I tried to touch the person in front of me to get my bearings, but when I reached out, no one was there. I panicked but couldn't tell you so. It was like my body and voice had disappeared. Then you put your hands on my shoulders from behind and said, *I'm with you. I'm here.* The darkness only lasted a few seconds, I bet. Someone turned on a headlamp and everyone laughed. But I remember feeling as though you'd read my mind, and I could feel myself again, even in the abyss.

I've been thinking about that a lot. About how, if you were the one in a body, in a crisis, and I was your neglected spirit guide, I'd do my best to steer you through the abyss, too, whispering in your ear, *I'm here.*

I *am* here, aren't I? Still. I'm the one who has to live with me, still. Always. It gets lonely sometimes, even with love in my life. Shae, forgive me. I have something to tell you: I made a new friend. You'd like her, honestly. She's fiery. But believe me, she'll never replace you. She couldn't. We're all on the same current, I promise.

A stranger is shouting at me. I blink, stirred from my daze, and he shouts again. He's ordering me to smile. I hadn't even realized I'd been crying, but I don't stop crying, and I don't smile.

My Saltine neighbor tells the stranger to fuck off, and the stranger fucks off, so I give the Saltine man a tiny nod. He returns my greeting. Then he breaks his last cracker in half, feeds it to a rat-with-wings nesting on his chest, and resumes his repose.

With the backs of my freckled, sun-spotted hands, I drag tears across my wet cheeks. A cluster of angry drivers lay on their horns all at once, drawing my attention to the jarring chaos of Tenth Avenue. It's just an ordinary avenue. Just a few million ordinary people navigating the drama of their lives below a manmade garden of earthly delights. I lick tears from my lips, stand from this bench, hoist my bag high on my shoulder and head toward the stairs, toward the chaos of ordinary lives. One worn-leather step at a time.

Back on the street — brick and pavement, trash and spices, no trace of the bamboo or prairie and peace overhead — I buy a bar of chocolate-covered marzipan at the nearest bodega. My train leaves at ten to six, which ought to allow just enough time for me to return to myself. What a strange day this has been. So many strange days in my not-yet-long life.

The strangest of late runs through my head again, as it has all month, on a loop. It was the evening Robert told me I looked pretty in setting sunlight. Everything was half an inch out of place that night. He'd had a migraine. I've never known Robert to get migraines in his life, but he asked me to pick up a medicine I couldn't find, and when I came home empty-handed, he was sitting in the dark all alone. He wasn't himself. Somber. Still. I chalked it up to the migraine. I used to get them with my periods when I was a teenager, and I remember hiding from light and the whole nine, too. I felt sorry for him.

But the way he looked at me, the way he spoke — so clear-eyed, so sharp, cool and contained, not pained — gave me chills. The way he said, "Isn't that strange?" when I told him the pharmacist couldn't find his prescription. The way he said his day had been "enlightening."

I'd asked, "Where's Jonah?"

493

He'd said, "Jonah's gone."

Jonah erasing me and Kayla from the story was a relief but also a burden, because I could feel Robert hating his own child, and I remember feeling scared. Yes, I was afraid of what my husband knew, but I was also afraid of my husband. He was so bitter and covered in thorns. Fear tightened the line between us.

Robert said, "You look very pretty in this light," without warmth or love, grief or regret. He was stone and I was sand. "You look very pretty," he said, and I knew the rest was best left unsaid. So much of our lives: unsaid and unseen. So many versions of ourselves mutated by other people's minds. My own husband isn't imaginative like Stuart, but now I have a stepson who's hooked on Proust — a fact which, of course, makes me smile, because wasn't it Proust who said, "Love is a striking example of how little reality means to us"? So maybe Robert will never be the one to whom I can say, *Isn't that just too perfect?* But Jonah might be.

And then, of course, the laundry: finding confirmation of Robert's inner world, folded and hidden in the back pockets of his jeans. "Managing Emotional Shock." "The Science of Acceptance." Being reminded that he struggles and copes in his own way. Wanting so badly to soothe his pain. Recognizing that he, too, guards an inner world, just so he can keep secrets with himself. Understanding that it's not my job to storm his fortress.

At Penn Station, I take my place in the ticket queue. Once again, my mind returns to the night we sat in the den, watching each other watch the other. The sun was setting, and I was afraid, but then came that strange flash of clarity. It was as though two songs in different keys had landed on the exact same chord at the exact same time, and in that moment, I almost believed this was the point of it all. So much dissonance, so much noise, all in hot pursuit of alignment, and when we find it, for a fleeting moment we are one and the same. Is this why we cycle through ambivalence together, why we create and clean messes together, why we volley words and feelings back and forth, aiming for the places that best reflect us in each other — even as we shield these reflections from judgment and scorn out there in the world? Even as we distract ourselves from other people's struggles in the world — those with far higher stakes, those caused by challenges not self-imposed? From these, we shield ourselves, too. Maybe my father is right: we plant obstacles just to have something to overcome, and in witnessing our breakdowns and consequential triumphs, we become our own proof that we've earned this good fortune and love. This life.

I looked pretty to him. When he said it I believed him and wasn't surprised but wasn't flattered, either, because it hadn't been a compliment, exactly. He was simply making an observation. Telling me what he saw. But it startled me, because I realized something: I already knew it. I knew exactly how my skin would be glowing in that light, the way shadows were carving my bone structure at dusk, the way his strange mood was unsettling me, and how much it excited him to see me unsettled, and how powerful that made me, exciting him like that. My disquiet had been genuine, at first. Unaffected. And still, in that moment, I knew that Robert saw me as fragile, which made him feel powerful, which makes him happy; and happy is easier to live with, and I was exhausted and desperate to move on; and so I chose to sit there looking fragile, so he could recharge, so we could get back to normal.

Of course, normal was dissolving already. A spell was breaking in my bones. Sitting there in silence, looking pretty and fragile, I understood: there has *never* been a time when I haven't been aware of how my husband sees me. How I look. Looking pretty. Looking like Ingrid Bergman in *Stromboli.* Looking like Ingrid Bergman on Stromboli, for that matter — which is exactly how Luna and Monique see me too, for entirely different reasons. Like I'm the harlot on their island. Like my supply of what they want or need or loathe is limited, or depleting.

On a cellular level, with Stuart: always knowing he'd peel me into strips to weave onto a page. Recognizing I'd want to love the thing he weaves, the way I'm seen. Moving accordingly.

This isn't the Elizabeth I know, he'd say, and I'd reply, *That's just the trouble, isn't it?*

The Elizabeth he knew served the story of his life. She existed in his head as a pretty thing who opened his heart and broke it, who created space by leaving; and Robert exists beside me, as I exist beside him, all sparks and noise and alignment; but I am the one who has to live with myself. The Elizabeth in my head is relentless. She's made of memories, mismemories, thoughts sprouted from smarter people's thoughts and from misinformed people's thoughts, too, and of judgments by people who use me as props in their own sagas and judgments about people I use in mine, and of habits, instincts, and emotions, but mostly memories and the beliefs they build. Sometimes, the flashbacks are like flesh wounds, surface-breaking and raw. Sometimes they're closer to keloid scars, luminous and hard as mother-of-pearl under my skin. They are lodged in my body and mind, cobbled together to fill the shape of the person I believe myself to be. The Elizabeth I know serves the story of my life.

I hadn't even realized how clipped my story felt until the morning I found myself face-to-face with Kayla Scott, who had every reason to size me up as a resource but didn't. Instead, she looked at me like we were already connected. Like helping her and helping myself were the exact same thing. Like I was the channel, not the source. The current, not the charge. Like our supply was infinite already.

I'd almost forgotten what that felt like — to be seen as a channel and a current, to see that way, too. To communicate in an electric language that doesn't feel like betrayal, after all. It feels like relief: getting to practice seeing and being seen that way with Bess, a new friend with a fresh start. It's been so long since I've had a friend to practice with. To see what happens. To see.

Approaching the ticket window, I reach into my bag for my wallet and touch my paperback instead: an anthology of poetry written by dead women whose names have become clichés, whose poems once summoned in me an ecstasy and wonder so raw, so devastating that I considered this volume to be my personal Bible — *my holy book,* I liked to say. On the day we met, Stuart spotted me reading it at the Hungarian Pastry Shop on Amsterdam, and he'd approached me as a stranger, quoting verse, and I'd said to myself, *Why not?* And I'd said to him, "I'm Elizabeth." The rest became our history.

I couldn't have imagined then how things would unfold and implode, that I was choosing a partner who'd suffocate me and a grad program I'd come to loathe, or that my parents really wouldn't be upset if I quit — that they really meant it when they said they just wanted me to be happy, and that "being somebody" meant nothing to them — or that, one day, I'd fall in love again but better, and I'd trade my sticky cocoon of a life for the bright sting of sea salt in a literary Eden. I'd marry a man who lets me keep my own oxygen, and we'd nest in the coziest hamlet in the Hamptons, just like Steinbeck did, and E. L. Doctorow and James Fenimore Cooper did, too. So maybe someday I'll look back on this summer and say, *I didn't know if we'd ever heal from that horror, but look at us. We really did.*

I thumb the sueded edges of my holy book's pages, open the back cover, remove the postcard tucked inside: a photograph of a gilded temple, spires aimed toward the heavens, the neon-pink words *Bangkok, Thailand* printed over the image in fat cursive letters. On the other side, Kayla has written my work address and nothing else. There is no message, no signature, but I know what it means. In the blank space, she is telling me she's out there, opening, widening. She is thanking me. Reminding me that we're in this together.

I return the postcard to its hiding place and drop the book into my bag. "Bridgehampton," I tell the cashier, who doesn't look at me when she takes my debit card, swipes it, slides it back through a gap in bulletproof glass. The man who'd been behind me moves beside me and shouts at the window, "Great Neck!"

Back I go, walking the length of a line full of people going home to their families, their lovers, friends, dogs and cats, their couches, and framed photographs — images that have become the memories, galvanized just so — or heading to airports, jobs, parties, plans, or leaving secret meetings, leaving it all behind. Someone elbows me in the ribs, and I apologize, then take it back. Through damaged speakers, a muffled voice announces a track change, and an undercurrent of commuters reverses direction right on cue.

Below glowing screens where Solari boards should be, a crowd gathers to stare at backlit lists of departure times, tracks, and destinations. I join them and join their upward gaze, too, and it's like this — squinting alongside strangers, all of us searching for our homes — that I hear my own voice saying, "I'm with you," out loud. When no one seems to mind, or object, or notice at all, I say, "I'm with you," again. "I'm here."

JONAH

A man in jeans and a T-shirt steps into the hall and asks if I'm Jonah, and I say yeah and follow him into a room that basically looks the exact same as my advisor's office — except my advisor only knows how to schedule classes, not how to handle answers to questions like *How was your summer?* when the answer is, *Pretty fucking tragic.* For that, she only knows how to pick up her phone and schedule an appointment with this guy, Angus (who is way too chill to be a counselor or therapist or whatever, despite his meat name), but campus policy requires her to *blah-blah-blah,* so here we are. Me and Angus. He thanks me for coming and asks if I've done this before, and I say yeah, once or twice a long time ago, so he explains some stuff and I sign some stuff, then it's on to small talk, the worst. He asks, "How was your summer?"

"Pretty fucking tragic," I answer for the

second time today, which cracks me up, because this guy is probably the opposite of my advisor. Angus probably lives for this shit.

He only sort-of smiles, though, when he says, "I'm fucking sorry to hear that."

Even if I wanted to spill my guts, I never can. I made promises — to Dad, to Elizabeth, to Nick. With Kayla. Promises we made together: superpromises. "I don't even know why I'm here."

Angus shakes his head and says, all somber, "None of us do." Then again, but quieter, "None of us do," and I realize he means, like, in an existential way, and with pretty solid delivery, too, so we both laugh now. Hey, he's got a sense of humor at least. If I told him about the roof — about Nick and our fight, and how Nick swore me to secrecy about Dad diagnosing him — or Kayla and Elizabeth and the shit we did and didn't do, or Dad's lies, or the lies we told together (superlies?), Angus would probably assume I'm joking. He'd leave work today with stories about the hilarious client referred to him by a dud advisor. But, well, superpromises. Only, I've been wondering something. "What do you think of a person who goes back on a pact with himself? Like, let's say he promised himself he'd keep a secret, but then he tells?"

Angus mulls it over. "I think, as long as he asks for and grants himself permission to tell, then the contract is dissolved, so he's not going back on a promise at all."

Of course he'd say that. I change it up and ask, "Do you know who Colette is?"

"The French writer?" he asks, and I mean, okay, I wasn't expecting that, but I nod, and he says, "Sure."

"I read her memoir this summer. Did you know she had an affair with her stepson? Like, in real life."

"I did not."

"She did." I chew a thumbnail. "Her second husband's teenage kid. That's not in her memoir, though." It should've been. The true parts are the most interesting parts, no matter how she edits her story. Then — I don't know where it comes from — I blurt out, "I don't want to become my dad."

Unfazed, Angus shrugs. "Good news. That is scientifically impossible." He has a point.

"Well, so the reason I mentioned Colette is because when I learned that thing, about the stepson, it gave me an idea" — and it takes me a sec to say — "to do something." Deep breath. "Something bad." I'm over here hanging my head, trying to decide if I should let this cat out of the bag or whatever, when I look up to see Angus is super spooked, and I'm horrified to realize he's jumping to the *worst* wrong conclusion, so I intercept his thought, going, "Oh God. Gross. No, not *that.* Elizabeth and I are friends." I hold up my hands. "Swear." We laugh from relief. "We were friends, anyway." Buzzkill. "So, okay. The thing is, when I read that, about the stepson —"

Angus rotates his chair a few degrees so he's facing me completely, but not in an intimidating way.

"I was really mad at the time."

He nods, but not in a patronizing way.

"Mad at my dad."

He's just paying attention, like it's no big deal.

So I ask myself permission to say, "I told a terrible lie," and grant myself permission to be heard when he says, "I'm listening."

ACKNOWLEDGMENTS

Melissa and Pouya Shahbazian, thank you for seeing and throwing sparks from the start. You are truly extraordinary friends. Joanna Volpe, literary agent of my dreams: thank you for being the smartest, savviest, coolest, kindest force of nature imaginable. Jaida Temperly, Abigail Donoghue, Devin Ross, Meredith Barnes, everyone at New Leaf Literary & Media, Chris McEwen, and Jackie Lindert: *thank you.* Many thanks to Jackie Cantor, editor extraordinaire, for your literary sorcery, and to Jennifer Bergstrom, Jessica Roth, Sara Quaranta, Chelsea Cohen, and everyone at Gallery Books/ Simon & Schuster for bringing this book to life.

A world of gratitude to: Milan Popelka for loving great stories and adventures, too; Adam Wilson for launching this ship; Beth Miller for the Long Island field trips; Dee and Trevor McWilliams for being bad-asses;

507

Leslie and Joe DeLaRosa and Dr. Philip Siegert for your wisdom; the Kerouac Project, Jentel, Hambidge, the MacDowell Colony, and my MacDowell and Arctic families for your support and magic.

Big love to sweet Jim, Kimberly, Erica, Christina, Cari, Lisa, Amy, Sara, and Olin for your early reads and open doors, and to my family for everything. Charlotte, David, Alex, Montgomery, Ellie, Layla, my Finches, aunties, uncles, cousins, and our Queen B, Marthann Bennett: I love y'all like crazy.

Most of all, beyond measure: thank you, Mom and Dad, for being the best guides a human could wish for. I'm so proud to be your daughter, so lucky to learn from you and love you and be loved by you. Thank you for being brave and wild enough to never flinch as I've hacked my own path. To, instead, shine light on the path. Thank you for this life.

Despite the things these characters made me write, my respect for modern medicine knows no bounds. I could never have invented a shadow side without so many fine examples of the bright side. Dr. David Walker, thank you for being brilliant and for fielding weird questions and explaining best practices so I could build a character

508

who defies them. Dr. Alexander Langerman, Dr. Randall Starling, Dr. Mazen Hanna, Dr. Robert Lorenz, Dr. Mohamed Kanj, Dr. Edward Desai, Dr. Edward Soltesz, and Kay Kendall: thank you for being so good at your jobs.

To all registered organ donors and families of donors: thank you.

ABOUT THE AUTHOR

Caroline Louise Walker grew up in Rock Island, Illinois. For her fiction and nonfiction, she has received fellowships from The MacDowell Colony, The Kerouac Project, and Jentel Arts. She holds an MA from NYU. *Man of the Year* is her first novel.